Richard Steele

The Lover

and other Papers of Steele and Addison - Edited by Walter Lewin

Richard Steele

The Lover
and other Papers of Steele and Addison - Edited by Walter Lewin

ISBN/EAN: 9783337387136

Printed in Europe, USA, Canada, Australia, Japan

Cover: Foto ©Andreas Hilbeck / pixelio.de

More available books at **www.hansebooks.com**

The Lover, and Other Papers of Steele and Addison. Edited by Walter Lewin.

—◆—

WALTER SCOTT
LONDON: 24 WARWICK LANE
PATERNOSTER ROW
1887

CONTENTS.

	PAGE
THE LOVER	1
ADDISON'S PAPERS ON MILTON'S "PARADISE LOST"	203
MISCELLANEOUS PAPERS:—	
SIR ROGER DE COVERLEY'S HOUSEHOLD	313
WILL WIMBLE	316
	318
	321
	325
	327
	330
	333
	335
	339
SIR ROGER DE COVERLEY AT WESTMINSTER ABBEY	342
SIR ROGER DE COVERLEY AT THE PLAY	345
SIR ROGER DE COVERLEY'S VISIT TO SPRING GARDEN	348
DEATH OF SIR ROGER DE COVERLEY	350
ALEXANDER SELKIRK	353
A DOMESTIC PICTURE	356

☞ FOR FULL LIST of the Volumes in this series, see Catalogue at end of book.

CONTENTS.

	PAGE
THE LOVER	I
ADDISON'S PAPERS ON MILTON'S "PARADISE LOST"	203

MISCELLANEOUS PAPERS:—

SIR ROGER DE COVERLEY'S HOUSEHOLD	313
WILL WIMBLE	316
SIR ROGER DE COVERLEY IN HIS PORTRAIT GALLERY	318
APPARITIONS	321
WITCHCRAFT	325
SUNDAY AT SIR ROGER DE COVERLEY'S	327
SIR ROGER DE COVERLEY AT THE ASSIZES	330
GYPSIES	333
THE MERCHANT	335
SIR ROGER DE COVERLEY IN TOWN	339
SIR ROGER DE COVERLEY AT WESTMINSTER ABBEY	342
SIR ROGER DE COVERLEY AT THE PLAY	345
SIR ROGER DE COVERLEY'S VISIT TO SPRING GARDEN	348
DEATH OF SIR ROGER DE COVERLEY	350
ALEXANDER SELKIRK	353
A DOMESTIC PICTURE	356

INTRODUCTORY NOTICE.

HE first of Steele's numerous periodical publications was the *Tatler*, the initial number of which appeared on Tuesday, the 12th of April 1709. It professed to be written by " Isaac Bickerstaff, Esq." This name had been made popular by its use for a famous practical joke played by Swift on Partridge the Astrologer, and its adoption by Steele in connection with the *Tatler* served to bring the new enterprise into notice. In introducing the paper Isaac Bickerstaff remarks : " I shall from time to time report and consider all matters of what kind soever that shall occur to me, and publish such my advices and reflections every Tuesday, Thursday and Saturday in the week, for the convenience of the post. I resolve also to have something which may be of entertainment to the fair sex, in honour of whom I have invented the title of this paper." For some time each number was divided into several parts, dated from different localities, and under one or another of these heads appeared news, politics, and social gossip and criticism. Addison, who did not know beforehand that Steele was about to publish this paper, soon recognised the hand of his friend in the work, and promptly offered his aid. His first contribution appeared in No. 18. The *Tatler*, after Addison joined it, gradually changed its character. Politics received less attention, and essays on literary and social topics became ultimately the leading feature.

Steele and Addison had already long been friends. They met first as schoolboys at the Charterhouse when Addison went there in 1686. There is some obscurity about Steele's early life. He appears to have been the son of a Dublin attorney, and to have been born in that city on the 12th of March 1672. When he was scarcely five years old his father died ; at least so we may gather from a passage, seemingly autobiographical, in the *Tatler*, No. 181. His circumstances were poor, and he entered the Charterhouse in 1684 only as a foundation boy, on the nomination of the first Duke of Ormond.

Addison was born six weeks later than Steele. On both his father and mother's side his family was connected with the Church. His father was vicar of Milston, and afterwards dean of Lichfield ; his mother's brother was Dr. Gulstone, bishop of Bristol. Addison himself was intended by his father for the Church, but chiefly by the influence of Charles Montague (afterwards Lord Halifax) this purpose was changed, and he rose to be a Secretary of State instead of a bishop.

Addison and Steele both proceeded to Oxford from the Charterhouse—Addison in 1687 and Steele two years later. Steele left without a degree and entered the army, and Addison, with a pension of £300 a-year from King William, went on his travels abroad. Before the *Tatler* united them for almost the first time in a public work, Steele had risen to the rank of Captain. He had published several works, including *The Christian Hero* (1701), a moral essay directed against vices to which he was himself too much addicted, and several comedies. In 1707 he had received the post of Gazetteer, and had also been appointed a Gentleman Waiter to Prince George, the Queen's husband, but the death of the Prince deprived him of this in the following year. He had married twice. His first wife was Mrs. Margaret Stretch, a widow. They were married, probably, in 1705 or 1706, and she died in December of the latter year, leaving him considerable property in Barbadoes. In 1707 he was married to a friend of hers, Mary Scurlock—the famous " Prue " of his correspondence. She died on the 26th of December 1718.

Meanwhile, Addison, recalled from the Continent in 1702 by the death of the king, which stopped his pension, had written *The Campaign*, an ode in praise of the Duke of Marlborough, and had thereby won for himself, not only a certain reputation but also an Under-Secretaryship of State; and a few days before the *Tatler* appeared he had gone to Dublin as Irish Secretary under Lord Wharton.

The *Tatler* continued to be published twice every week until the 2nd of January 1711, when it suddenly ceased. "The printer having informed me," writes Steele, over his own name, in the last number, "that there are as many of these papers printed as will make four volumes, I am now come to the end of my ambition in this matter, and have nothing further to say to the world under the character of Isaac Bickerstaff." He adds that the work has been for some time disagreeable to him. The *Tatler* had won many friends, and was enjoying a large circulation, but it had also made some enemies, and probably Steele was not sorry to exchange it for a new enterprise, which should have its merits without its defects. That the discontinuance of the *Tatler* was such a sudden act as to seem almost like a freak, seems evident. Swift wrote to Stella on the 2nd of January 1711, "Steele's last *Tatler* comes out to-day. . . . He never told so much as Addison of it, who was surprised as much as I. . . . To my knowledge he had several good hints to go upon, but he was so lazy, and weary of the work, that he would not improve them."

The *Spectator* appeared two months later. Steele was still the editor, but the work was quite as much Addison's as his. Steele was a man of brilliant ideas. He could devise and project; but, had it not been for Addison, more than one of his fine plans would have been ineffectual. Steele conceived the *Tatler;* Addison improved, and, in the *Spectator*, perfected the idea. Sir Roger de Coverley was a thought of Steele's, but the Sir Roger that we know is Addison's work. The first sketch of the popular baronet, drawn by Steele in the *Spectator*, No. 2, is admirable, but, by comparison, crude :—

"The first of our Society is a Gentleman of *Worcestershire*, of antient Descent, a Baronet, his Name Sir ROGER DE COVERLY. His great Grandfather was Inventor of that famous Country-Dance which is call'd after him. All who know that Shire are very well acquainted with the Parts and Merits of Sir ROGER. He is a Gentleman that is very singular in his Behaviour, but his Singularities proceed from his good Sense, and are Contradictions to the Manners of the World, only as he thinks the World is in the wrong. However, this Humour creates him no Enemies, for he does nothing with Sourness or Obstinacy; and his being unconfined to Modes and Forms, makes him but the readier and more capable to please and oblige all who know him. When he is in town he lives in *Soho Square :* It is said, he keeps himself a Batchelour by reason he was crossed in Love by a perverse beautiful Widow of the next County to him. Before this Disappointment, Sir ROGER was what you call a fine Gentleman, had often supped with my Lord *Rochester* and Sir *George Etherege,* fought a Duel upon his first coming to Town, and kick'd Bully *Dawson* in a publick Coffee-house for calling him Youngster. But being ill-used by the above-mentioned Widow, he was very serious for a Year and a half; and tho' his Temper being naturally jovial, he at last got over it, he grew careless of himself and never dressed afterwards ; he continues to wear a Coat and Doublet of the same Cut that were in Fashion at the Time of his Repulse, which, in his merry Humours, he tells us, has been in and out twelve Times since he first wore it. 'Tis said Sir ROGER grew humble in his Desires after he had forgot this cruel Beauty, insomuch that it is reported he has frequently offended in Point of Chastity with Beggars and Gypsies : but this is look'd upon by his Friends rather as Matter of Raillery than Truth. He is now in his Fifty-sixth Year, cheerful, gay, and hearty, keeps a good House in both Town and Country ; a great Lover of Mankind, but there is such a mirthful Cast in his behaviour that he is rather beloved than esteemed. His Tenants grow rich, his Servants look satisfied, all the young Women profess Love to him, and the young Men are glad of his Company : When he comes into a house he calls the Servants by their Names, and talks all the way Up Stairs to a Visit. I must not omit that Sir ROGER is a Justice of the *Quorum ;* that he fills the Chair at a Quarter-Session with great Abilities, and three Months ago, gained universal Applause by explaining a Passage in the Game-Act."

The *Tatler* has a certain attraction which we miss in its more famous successor. It lacks the grace, the dignity of the *Spectator,* but the very negligence which it displays makes it more companionable. Its name is well given ; it chats with us in a home-like and comfortable fashion. It is not a mere

Spectator which stands aloof and pronounces judgments. Hazlett says he has always preferred the *Tatler* to the *Spectator*. "The *Tatler* contains only half the number of volumes, and, I will venture to say, nearly an equal quantity of sterling wit and sense. 'The first sprightly runnings' are there: it has more of the original spirit, more of the freshness and stamp of nature." The *Spectator* contained fewer personalities than the *Tatler*, and kept entirely away from party politics, which was a gain, but, in a certain way, a loss also. In short, the *Tatler* bore the impress of careless, light-hearted, jovial, blundering Dick Steele; the *Spectator* that of the cultured, dignified, pure-souled Addison.

The *Spectator* was published daily from Thursday, the 1st of March 1711, until Saturday, the 6th of December 1712, in all 555 numbers made up into seven volumes. Steele then announced that "All the members of the imaginary Society which were described in my first papers, having disappeared one after another, it is high time for the *Spectator* himself to go off the Stage." A year and a half later No. 556 appeared, "to be continued every Monday, Wednesday and Friday." This revival, forming the eighth and final volume, was the project and chiefly the work of Addison. Steele had no hand in it whatever. It lasted only six months.

Of Steele's periodical publications the *Tatler* and *Spectator* are by far the most famous; but he undertook a good many other works of a similar kind. No one—except perhaps Leigh Hunt—ever projected so many serials as Steele. Some of these ran only a few numbers; none of them had long lives, as the following list will show :—

The Guardian	from	12 March 1713	to	1 October 1713.
The Englishman	,,	6 October 1713	,,	15 February 1714.
The Lover ...	,,	25 February 1714	,,	27 May 1714.
The Reader ...	,,	22 April 1714	,,	10 May 1714.
Town Talk ...	,,	17 December 1715	,,	13 February 1716.
The Tea Table	,,	6 February 1716	,,	2 March 1716.
Chit Chat ...	,,	6 March 1716	,,	16 March 1716.
The Plebeian...	,,	14 March 1719	,,	6 April 1719.
The Theatre ...	,,	2 January 1720	,,	5 April 1720.

Of these, the *Englishman, Reader* and *Plebeian* were avowedly political papers ; the *Guardian* was commenced as a successor to the *Spectator*, and on similar lines ; but the editor's political zeal overcame him.   Dr. George Berkeley (afterwards bishop) wrote in its pages.   Addison contributed fifty-one papers ; Steele himself eighty-two.   Addison also assisted with the *Lover* and the *Reader*, but not to any considerable extent. Good specimens of his work are to be found in No. 10 and No. 39 of the *Lover*.   In this periodical Steele is at his best. The rôle of mentor to young men, and especially to young women, was especially to his liking.   He had a genuine respect for women.   In most of his essays on social topics he had something to say of or to them.   His attitude toward them is well stated in the *Spectator*, No. 4, where he says—

"I take it for a peculiar Happiness that I have always had an easy and familiar Admittance to the fair Sex.   If I never praised or flattered, I never belyed or contradicted them.   As these compose half the World, and are by the just Complaisance and Gallantry of our Nation the more powerful Part of our People, I shall dedicate a considerable Share of these my Speculations to their Service, and shall lead the young through all the becoming Duties of Virginity, Marriage, and Widowhood.   When it is a Woman's Day, in my Works, I shall endeavour at a Stile and Air suitable to their Understanding.   When I say this, I must be understood to mean, that I shall not lower but exalt the Subjects I treat upon.   Discourse for their Entertainment, is not to be debased but refined.   A Man may appear learned without talking Sentences ; as in his ordinary Gesture he discovers he can dance, tho' he does not cut Capers.   In a Word, I shall take it for the greatest Glory of my Work, if among reasonable Women this Paper may furnish *Tea-Table Talk*.   In order to it, I shall treat on Matters which relate to Females as they are concern'd to approach or fly from the other Sex, or as they are tyed to them by Blood, Interest, or Affection.   Upon this Occasion I think it but reasonable to declare, that whatever Skill I may have in Speculation, I shall never betray what the Eyes of Lovers say to each other in my Presence.   At the same Time I shall not think my self obliged by this Promise, to conceal any false Protestations which I observe made by Glances in publick Assemblies ; but endeavour to make both Sexes appear in their Conduct what they are in their Hearts.   By this Means Love, during the Time of my Speculations, shall be carried on with the same Sincerity as any other Affair of less Consideration. As this is the greatest Concern, Men shall be from henceforth liable to the greatest Reproach for Misbehaviour in it. Falsehood in Love shall hereafter bear a blacker Aspect than Infidelity in Friendship or Villany in Business. For this great and good End, all Breaches against that noble Passion, the Cement of Society, shall be severely examined. But this and all other Matters loosely hinted at now and in my former Papers, shall have their proper Place in my following Discourses : The present writing is only to admonish the World, that they shall not find me an idle but a very busy Spectator."

Frivolity among women troubled him, and he made an honest effort with his genial preaching to attract them to better ways. As Thackeray says—"All women especially are bound to be grateful to Steele, as he was the first of our writers who really seemed to admire and respect them. . . . It was Steele who first began to pay a manly homage to their goodness and understanding as well as to their tenderness and beauty." The *Lover* was first issued as a broad-sheet, and then, after completion, it was revised and reissued in an octavo volume together with the *Reader*. From this edition the present work has been printed.

Addison, as well as Steele, was an active politician ; yet, though his services to the Whigs, with whom he associated himself, were great, he would be incorrectly described as a party man. He derived, on his side, much benefit from the connection, and rose to a Secretaryship of State and a seat in the Cabinet. He was M.P. for Malmesbury from 1708 until his death, but he broke down in the only speech he ever tried to make in the House. He was more successful when he sat in the Irish Parliament. He was valuable to his party as a painstaking and conscientious administrator and as a writer. Of his political papers, those which compose the *Freeholder* are, probably, the most important. Addison was a man of letters more than a man of affairs, and he treated political subjects accordingly. These essays in the *Freeholder* are good reading still. The last political service that he undertook was in opposition to his life-long friend. In 1719 Steele was fiercely assailing the Whig Government in his *Plebeian.* Addison had then only lately withdrawn from office on account of ill-health, but he was called from his retirement to defend his former colleagues, with whom he was in hearty accord. He then produced the *Old Whig.* The political difference between himself and Steele was clear and unmistakable, but it could hardly have made a permanent breach in their friendship if Addison had lived. But he was dying, and the end came on the 17th of June 1719. He was only forty-seven years of age. He was buried by night (as the custom then was) in Westminster Abbey. He had been married in 1716 to Charlotte, Countess of Warwick, who survived him. Their only daughter, Charlotte, died in 1797. By precept and example—for his own life was pure—Addison greatly purified the morals and manners of that licentious time. "That man," said Swift, "had virtue enough to give reputation to an age."

Steele survived his friend ten years—as unrestful as all his previous years had been. Owing to his political action his patent of Drury Lane Theatre, granted in 1715, was withdrawn in 1720. The following year, however, it was restored. In 1722 he became M.P. for Wendover. Money troubles pursued him, and in 1724, by an arrangement with his creditors, he assigned his property, and retired first to Hereford and afterwards to Carmarthen, where, on the 1st of September 1729, he died.

During the fifty-seven years that he dwelt upon the earth Steele made many blunders and was guilty of many sins ; yet his errors were errors of the flesh and not the deadly errors of the spirit—cruelty and hypocrisy. Pleasure-loving as he was, he loved his fellow-men too well ever to wilfully wrong them for his own ends. His precept and practice were often at variance, but he never pretended to merit what he did not possess. He was not one of those who think they have discharged every obligation to virtue when they praise it. He said, "I shall not carry my humility so far as to call myself a vicious man ; but, at the same time, must confess my life is at best but pardonable" (*Tatler*, No. 271). Steele's esteem for women, his love for his wife and children, and the fact that a man of Addison's character valued him as a friend, testify to his intrinsic excellence.   He understood and appreciated virtue even when he failed to practice it, and the total result of his life was good.

The present volume is made up from the essays of Steele and Addison ; but it must not be forgotten that both authors won distinction in other branches of literature.   They wrote poems and dramas, and several of these works were highly successful at the time.   *Cato* is still famous.   Concerning it, Pope expressed the opinion that it had better not be put on the stage, but that Addison " would get reputation enough by only printing it."   The advice was not followed ; yet, though *Cato* was acted and applauded, Pope's judgment was not amiss ; for, in truth, Addison was no dramatist.   It is due to their essays alone that Steele and Addison rank among great men of letters to-day.

WALTER LEWIN.

BEBINGTON, CHESHIRE,
   29th October 1887.

TO

Sir *Samuel Garth*, M.D.

SIR,

S soon as I thought of making the *Lover* a
Present to one of my Friends, I resolved,
without farther distracting my Choice, to
send it *To the Best-natured Man.* You
are so universally known for this Character, that an
Epistle so directed would find its Way to You without
your Name, and I believe no Body but You yourself
would deliver such a Superscription to any other
Person.

This Propensity is the nearest akin to Love ; and
Good-nature is the worthiest Affection of the Mind,
as Love is the noblest Passion of it : While the latter
is wholly employed in endeavouring to make happy
one single Object, the other diffuses its Benevolence
to all the World.

As this is Your natural Bent, I cannot but con-
gratulate to You the singular Felicity that your
Profession is so agreeable to your Temper.   For
what Condition is more desirable than a constant

Impulse to relieve the Distressed, and a Capacity to administer that Relief? When the sick Man hangs his Eye on that of his Physician, how pleasing must it be to speak Comfort to his Anguish, to raise in him the first Motions of Hope, to lead him into a Persuasion that he shall return to the Company of his Friends, the Care of his Family, and all the Blessings of Being?

The Manner in which You practise this heavenly Faculty of aiding human Life, is according to the Liberality of Science, and demonstrates that your Heart is more set upon doing Good than growing Rich.

The pitiful Artifices which Empyricks are guilty of to drain Cash out of Valetudinarians, are the Abhorrence of your generous Mind; and it is as common with *Garth* to supply Indigent Patients with Money for Food, as to receive it from Wealthy ones for Physick. How much more amiable, Sir, would the Generosity which is already applauded by all that know You, appear to those whose Gratitude You every Day refuse, if they knew that You resist their Presents least You should supply those whose Wants you know, by taking from those with whose Necessities you are unacquainted?

The Families You frequent receive You as their Friend and Well-wisher, whose Concern, in their behalf, is as great as that of those who are related to them by the Tyes of Blood and the Sanctions of Affinity. This Tenderness interrupts the Satisfactions of Conversation, to which You are so happily turned, but we forgive You that our Mirth is often insipid to You, while You sit absent to what passes amongst us from your Care of such as languish in Sickness. We are sensible their Distresses, instead of being removed by Company, return more strongly to your Imagination by Comparison of their Condition to the Jollities of Health.

But I forget I am writing a Dedication ; and in an Address of this Kind, it is more usual to celebrate Mens great Talents, than those Virtues to which such Talents ought to be subservient : yet where the Bent of a Man's Spirit is taken up in the Application of his whole Force to serve the World in his Profession, it would be frivolous not to entertain him rather with Thanks for what he is, than Applauses for what he is capable of being. Besides, Sir, there is no Room for saying any thing to You as You are a Man of Wit and a great Poet ; all that can be spoken that is worthy an ingenuous Spirit, in the Celebration of such Faculties, has been incomparably said by your self to others, or by others to you : You have never been excelled in this Kind, but by those who have written in Praise of you : I will not pretend to be your Rival even with such an Advantage over you, but, assuring you, in Mr. *Codrington*'s * Words, that I do not know whether my Love or Admiration is greater,

I remain,

  SIR,

   Your most Faithful Friend,

   and most Obliged,

   Humble Servant,

    RICHARD STEELE.

* *Thou hast no Faults, or I no Faults can spy :*
Thou art all Beauty, or all Blindness I.
  Codrington to Dr. *Garth* before the *Dispensary.*

THE LOVER.

Written in Imitation of the TATLER.

By MARMADUKE MYRTLE, *Gent.*

No. 1. *Thursday, February* 25. 1714.

Virginibus Puerisque Canto. Hor.

THERE have been many and laudable Endeavours of late Years, by sundry Authors, under different Characters, and of different Inclinations and Capacities, to improve the World, by Half-sheet Advertisements, in Learning, Wit, and Politicks; but these Works have not attentively enough regarded the softer Affections of the Mind, which being properly raised and awakened, make way for the Operation of all good Arts.

AFTER mature Deliberation with my self upon this Subject, I have thought, that if I could trace the Passion or Affection of Love, through all its Joys and Inquietudes through all the Stages and Circumstances of Life, in both Sexes, with strict respect to Virtue and Innocence, I should, by a just Representation and History of that one Passion, steal into the Bosom of my Reader, and build upon it all the Sentiments and Resolutions which incline and qualify us for every thing that is truly Excellent, Great, and Noble.

ALL You, therefore, who are in the dawn of Life, as to Conversation with a faithless and artful World, attend to one who has passed through almost all the Mazes of it, and is familiarly acquainted with whatever can befal you in the pursuit of Love : If you diligently observe me, I will teach you to avoid the Temptations of lawless Desire, which leads to Shame and Sorrow, and carry you into the Paths of Love, which will conduct you to Honour and Happiness. This Passion is the Source of our Being, and as it is so, it is also the Support of it ; for all the Adventures which they meet with who swerve from Love, carry them so far out of the Way of their true Being, which cannot pleasingly pass on when it has deviated from the Rules of honourable Passion.

MY Purpose therefore, under this Title, is to Write of such things only which ought to please all Men, even as Men ; and I shall never hope for prevailing under this Character of *Lover* from my Force in the Reason offer'd, but as that Reason makes for the Happiness and Satisfaction of the Person to whom I address. My Reader is to be my Mistress, and I shall always endeavour to turn my Thoughts so as that there shall be nothing in my Writings too severe to be spoken before one unacquainted with Learning, or too light to be dwelt upon before one who is either fixed already in the Paths of Virtue, or desirous to walk in them for the future.

MY Assistants, in this Work, are Persons whose Conduct of Life has turned upon the Incidents which have occurred to them from this agreeable or lamentable Passion, as they respectively are apt to call it, from the Impression it has left upon their Imaginations, and which mingles in all their Words and Actions.

IT cannot be supposed the Gentlemen can be called by

their real Names, in so publick a manner as this is. But the Heroe of my Story, now in the full Bloom of Life, and seen every Day in all the Places of Resort, shall bear the Name of one of our *British* Rivers, which washes his Estate. As I design this Paper shall be a Picture of familiar Life, I shall avoid Words derived from learned Languages, or ending in Foreign Terminations: I shall shun also Names significant of the Person's Character of whom I talk; a Trick used by Play-wrights, which I have long thought no better a Device than that of underwriting the Name of an Animal on a Post, which the Painter conceived too delicately drawn to be known by common Eyes, or by his Delineation of its Limbs.

Mr. *SEVERN* is now in the twenty fifth Year of his Age, a Gentleman of great Modesty and Courage, which are the radical Virtues which lay the solid Foundation for a good Character and Behaviour both in publick and private. I will not, at this time, make the Reader any further acquainted with him than from this Particular, that he extreamly affects the Conversation of People of Merit who are advanced in Years, and treats every Woman of Condition, who is past being entertained on the foot of Homage to her Beauty, so respectfully, that in his Company she can never give her self the Compunction of having lost any thing which made her agreeable. This natural Goodness has gained him many Hearts, which have agreeable Persons to give with them: I mean, Mothers have a Fondness for him, and with that Fondness could be gratified by his Passion to their Daughters. Were you to visit him in a Morning, you would certainly find some awkard thing of Business, some old Steward, or distant Retainer to a great Family, who has a Proposal to make to him, not (you may be sure) coming from the Person who sent him, but only in general to know whether he is engaged.

Mr. *SEVERN* has at this time Patterns sent him of all the young Women in Town; and I, who am of his Council in these Matters, have read his Particulars of Women brought him, not from professed Undertakers that way, but from those who are under no Necessity of selling immediately, but such who have Daughters a good Way under Twenty, that can stay for a Market, and send in their Account of the Lady, in general Terms only; As that she is so Old, so Tall, worth so much down, and has two Batchelor Unkles (one a rich Merchant) that will never Marry; her Maiden-Aunt loves her mightily, and has very fine Jewels, and the like. I have observed in these Accounts, when the Fortune is not suitable, they subjoin a Postscript, she is very Handsome; if she is rich and Defective as to Charms, they add, she is very good.

BUT I was going to say, That Mr. *Severn* having the good Sense to affect the Conversation of those elder than himself, passes some Time at a Club, which (with himself) consists of Six; whom we shall names as follows.

Mr. *OSWALD*, a Widower, who has within these few Months buried a most agreeable Woman, who was his beloved Wife, and is indulged by this Company to speak of her in the Terms she deserved of him, with allowance to mingle Family-Tales concerning the Merit of his Children, and the Ways and Methods he designs to take, to Support a painful and lonely Being, after the loss of this Companion, which tempered all his Sorrows, and gave new Sense and Spirit to his Satisfactions.

Mr. *MULLET*, a Gentleman, who in the most plentiful Fortune, seems to taste very little of Life, because he has lost a Lady whom he passionately loved, and by whom he

had no Children; he is the last of a great House, and tho'
he wants not many Months of Fifty, is much sought by
Ladies as bright as any of the Sex; but as he is no Fool,
but is sensible they compare his Years with their own, and
have a mind to Marry him, because they have a mind to
Bury him, he is as froward, exceptious and humoursome as
e'er a Beauty of 'em all: I, who am intimate with *Mullet*
as well as *Severn*, know that many of the same Women have
been offered to him of Fifty, in case of losing him of Five
and Twenty; and some perhaps in hopes of having them
both: For they prudently judge, that when *Mullet* is dead, it
may then be time enough for *Severn* to Marry; and a Lady's
Maid can observe that many an unlikelier Thing has come
to pass, than this view of Marriage between her young
Mistress and both those Gentlemen.

Mr. *JOHNSON* is a Gentleman happy in the Conversation of an excellent Wife, by whom he has a numerous
Offspring; and the manner of subjecting his Desires
to his Circumstances, which are not too plentiful, may give
Occasion in my future Discourses to draw many Incidents
of Domestick Life, which may be as agreeable to the rest
of the young Men of this Nation, as they are to the well-
disposed Mr. *Severn*.

THE fifth Man of this little Assembly is Mr. *Wildgoose*,
an old Batchelor, who has lived to the 53d Year of his
Age, after being disappointed in Love at his 23d. That
Torment of Mind frets out in little Dissatisfactions and
Uneasinesses against every thing else, without administring
Remedy to the Ail it self, which still festers in his Heart,
and would be insupportable, were it not cooled by the
Society of the others abovementioned. A poor old Maid
is one, who has long been the Object of Ridicule, her
Humours and Particularities afford much Matter to the

Facetious; but the old Batchelor has ten times more of the splenatick and ridiculous, as he is conversant in larger Scenes of Life, and has more Opportunities to diffuse his Folly, and consequently can vex and delight People in more Views, than an ancient Virgin of the other Sex.

THE sixth and last of this Company, is my dear self, who oblige the World with this Work. But as it has been frequently observed, that the Fine Gentleman of a Play has always something in him which is of near Alliance to the real Character of the Author, I shall not pretend to be wholly above that Pleasure, but shall in the next Paper principally talk of my Self, and satisfie my Readers how well I am qualified to be the Secretary of Love. I had ordered my Bookseller to adorn the Head of my Paper with little pretty broken Arrows, Fans thrown away, and other Ensigns Armorial of the Isle of *Paphos*, for the Embellishment of my Work; but as I am a young Author, and pretend to no more but a happy Imitation of one who went before me, he would not be at that Charge; when I failed there, I desired him only to let the Paper be gilded; but he said that was a new Thing, and it would be taken to be written *By a Person of Quality*, which, I know not for what Reason, the *Bibliopoles* are also very averse to, and I was denied my second Request. However, this did not discourage me, and I was resolved to come out; not without some particular Hopes, that if I had not so many Admirers, I might possibly have more Customers than my Predecessor, whom I profess to imitate; for there are many more who can feel what will touch the Heart, than receive what would improve the Head.

I therefore design to be the Comfort and Consolation of all Persons in a languishing Condition, and will receive the Complaints of all the faithful Sighers in City, Town, or

Country ; firmly believing, that as bad as the World is, there are as Constant ones within the Cities of *London* and *Westminster*, as ever wandered in the Plains of *Arcadia.*

I shall in my next Paper, (as much as I can spare of it, from talking of my self) tell the World how to communicate their Thoughts to me, which will very properly come in with the Description of my Apartment, and the Furniture of it, together with the Account of my Person, which shall make up the second Paper or Chapter, and shall be placed before the *Errata* of this. I have nothing further to say now, but am willing to make an end of this Leaf as quaintly as possible, being the first ; and therefore would have it go off like an Act in a Play, with a Couplet ; but the Spirit of that will be wholly in the Power of the Reader, who must quicken his Voice hereabouts, like an Actor at his *Exit*, helping an empty Verse with lively Hand, Foot, and Voice, at once ; and if he is reading to Ladies, say briskly, That, with regard to the greatest Part of Mankind,

> *Foreign is every Character beside ;*
> *But that of Lover every Man has try'd.*

No. 2.   *Saturday, February* 27.

> ——*Mentis gratissimus Error.*   Hor.

I Cannot tell how many Years, Months, Hours, Days, or Minutes have passed away since I first saw Mrs. *Ann Page;* but certain I am, that they have ran by me, without my being much concerned in what was transacted in the World around me all that while. Mrs. *Page* being a Gentlewoman on whom I have ever doated to Distraction, has made me very particular in my Behaviour upon all the

Occurrences on this Earth, and negligent of those things in which others terminate all their Care and Study; insomuch, that I am very sensible it is only because I am harmless, that the busie World does not lock me up; for if they will not own themselves mad, they must conclude I am, when they see me cold to the Pursuits of Riches, Wealth and Power; and when People have been speaking of great Persons and Illustrious Actions, I close the whole with something about Mrs. *Page*, they are apt to think my Head turned, as well as I do theirs. However, I find Consolation in the Simplicity of my Distress, (which has banished all other Cares) and am reconciled to it. But however I may be looked upon by the silly Crowds who are toiling for more than they want, I am, without doubt, in my self the most innocent of all Creatures; and a Squirrel in a Chain, whose Teeth are cut out, is not more incapable of doing Mischief. Mrs. *Ann Page* had such a Turn with her Neck, when I, thinking no harm, first looked upon her, that I was soon after in a Fever, and had like to have left a World (which I ever since despised) and been at Rest. But as Mrs. *Ann's* Parents comply'd with her own Passion for a Gentleman of much greater Worth and Fortune than my self, all that was left for me was to lament or get rid of my Passion by all the Diversions and Entertainments I could. But I thank Mrs. *Ann* (I am still calling her by her Maiden Name), she has always been Civil to me, and permitted me to stand Godfather at the Baptism of one of her Sons.

THIS would appear a very humble Favour to a Man of ungovern'd Desire; but as for me, as soon as I found Mrs. *Ann* was engaged, I could not think of her with Hope any longer, any other ways than that I should ever be ready to express the Passion I had for her, by Civilities to any thing that had the most remote relation to her.   But alas! I am going on as if every Body living was acquainted with Mrs. *Ann Page* and my self, when there is indeed no occasion of mentioning either; but to inform the Reader, that it is from the Experience of a Patient, I am become a Physician in Love.   I have been in it thirty Years, just as long as the Learned *Sydenham* had the Gout; and tho' I cannot pretend to makes Cures, I can, like him, put you in a good Regimen when you are down in a Fit.   As I was saying, this Affection of mine left behind it a Scorn of every thing else; and having an Aversion to Business, I have passed my Time very much in Observation upon the Force and Influence this Passion has had upon other Men, and the different Turns it has given each respective Generation from the Cultivation or Abuse of it.   You'll say I fell into very unhappy Days for a Lover of my Complexion, who can be satisfied with distant Good-will from the Person beloved, and am contented that her Circumstances can allow me only her Esteem, when I acquaint you that my most vigorous Years were passed away in the Reign of the Amorous *Charles* the Second.   The Licences of that Court did not only make that Love, which the Vulgar call Romantick, the Object of Jest and Ridicule, but even common Decency and Modesty were almost abandoned as formal and unnatural.   The Writers for the Stage fell in with the Court, and the Theatre diffus'd the Malignity into the Minds of the Nobility and Gentry, by which means the Degeneracy spread it self through the whole People, and Shame it self was almost lost : Naked Innocence, that most charming of Beauties, was confronted by that most hideous of Monsters, barefaced Wickedness.

THIS made me place all my Happiness in Hours of Retirement; and as great Distresses often turn to Advantages, I impute it to the Wickedness of the Age, that I am a great Master of the Base-Viol.

WITH this instrument I have passed many a heavy Hour, and laid up Treasures of Knowledge, drawn from Contemplation, on what I had seen every Day in the World, during the Intervals from Musick and Reading, which took up the Principal Part of my Time. My Purpose, at present, is to be a Knight-Errant with the Pen, since that Order of Men who were so with their Swords, are quite laughed out of the World. My Business is to kill Monsters, and to relieve Virgins; but as it has been the Custom, time out of Mind, for Knights, who take upon them such laudable and hazardous Labours, to have a Castle, a Mote round it, and all other Conveniencies within themselves, it has luckily happened, that the spacious and magnificent Apartment, which the Ingenious Mr. *Powell* lately possessed in *Covent-Garden*, has lately been relinquished by him, upon some importunate Words and Menaces given him by a Gentleman who has the Sovereignty of it, by Vertue of some enchanted Rolls of Parchment which convey that Mansion unto the said chief Commander vulgarly called a Landlord. By this means, you are to understand, that the Apartment, wherein the little Kings and Queens lately diverted so many of our Nobility and Gentry, is now mine. This spacious Gallery, for such I have made it for my musings and wandrings of Thought, I have dignified with the Name of *the Lover's Lodge*, where, under fancied Skies, and painted Clouds, left by Mr. *Powel'*, I sit and read the true Histories of famous Knights and beautiful Damsels, which the Ignorant call Romances. To make my Walk more gloomy, and adapted both for Melody and Sadness, there lies before me, at present, a Death's Head, my Base-Viol, and the History of *Grand Cyrus.* I cannot tell by what Chance, I have also some Ridiculous Writers in my Study, for I have an Aversion for Comicks, and those they call pleasant Fellows, for they are insensible of Love. Those Creatures get into a Familiarity with Ladies, without respect on either side, and consequently can neither see what is amiable, or be the Objects of Love. I wonder how these Buffoons came into my Head. But I was going to intimate, that the Notions of Gallantry are turned topsie-turvey, and the Knight-Errantry of this profligate Age is destroying as many Women as they can. It is notorious, that a young Man of Condition does no more than is expected from him, if before he thinks of settling himself in the World, he is the Ruin of half a dozen Females, whose Fortunes are unequal to that which his laborious Ancestors, whether successful in Virtue or Iniquity, have left him.

THUS I every Day see Innocents abused, scorned, betrayed and neglected by Brutes, who have no Sense of any thing but what indulges their Appetites ; and can no longer suffer the more charming and accomplished Part of the Species to want a Friend and Advocate. I shall enquire, in due time, and make every Anti-Heroe in *Great Britain* give me an Account why one Woman is not as much as ought to fall to his Share ; and shall shew every abandoned Wanderer, that with all his blustering, his restless following every Female he sees, is much more ridiculous, than my constant, imaginary Attendance on my Fair One, without ever seeing her at all.

BUT the main Purpose of this Chapter I had like to have slipped over, to wit, the more exact Account of my Bower: As it is not natural for a Man in Love to sleep all Night, but to be a great Admirer of Walking, I am at the Charge of four Tapers burning all Night, and take my

Itinerations, with much gloomy Satisfaction, from one end to the other of my long Room, my Field-Bed being too small to interrupt my Passage, tho' placed in the middle of my Apartment.   No one who has not been polite enough to have visited Mr. *Powell's* Theatre, can have a Notion how I am accommodated; but if you will suppose a single Man had *Westminster-Hall* for his Bed-Chamber, and lay in a Truckle-Bed in the midst of it, it will give you a pretty good Idea of the Posture in which I dream (but with Honour and Chastity) of the incomparable Mrs. *Page.*

MY Predecessors in Knight-Errantry, who were, as I above observed, Men of the Sword, had their Lodgings adorned with burnished Arms round the Cornishes, Limbs of dryed Giants over their Heads and all about the Moat of their Castle, where they walked by Moon-light; but as I am a Pen-Champion and live in Town, and have quite another fort of People to deal with, to wit, the Criticks, Beaus and Rakes of *Covent-Garden*, I have nothing but Stand-dishes, Pens and Ink, and Paper, on little Tables at equal Distance, that no Thought may be lost as I am musing.   I am forced to comply, more than my Inclinations and high Passions would otherwise permit, and tell the World how to correspond with me, after their own Method, in the common Way: I am to signifie, therefore, that I am more accessible than any other Knights ever were before me, and in plain Terms, that there is a Coffee-house under my Apartment; nay further, that a Letter directed, to Mr. *Marmaduke Myrtle* at the *Lover's Lodge*, to be left at *Shanley's* Coffee-house *Covent-Garden*, will find the gentlest of Mortals, Your most Enamoured, Humble Servant.

Young Nobles, to my Laws Attention lend :
And all you Vulgar of my School, attend.
　　　　　　　　　　　Art of Love, Congreve.

Lovers-Lodge, March 2.

NOW I have told all the World my Name and Place of Abode, it is impossible for me to enjoy the Studious Retirement I promis'd my self in this place. For most of the People of Wit and Quality who frequented these Lodgings in Mr. *Powell's* time, have been here, and I having a silly Creature of a Footman who never lived but with private Gentlemen, and cannot sted-fastly Lie, they all see by his Countenance he does not speak Truth when he denies me, and will break in upon me. It is an unspeakable Pleasure that so many beauteous Ladies have made me Compliments upon my Design to favour and defend the Sex against all Pretenders without Merit, and those who have Merit, and use it only to deceive and betray. The principal Fair ones of the Town, and the most eminent Toasts, have sign'd an Address of Thanks to me, and in the Body of it laid before me some Grievances, among which the greatest are the evil Practices of a Sett of Persons whom they call in their Presentation the *Lover Vagabond*. There has been indeed, ever since I knew this Town, one Man of Condition or other, who has been at the Head, and, giving Example to this sort of Companions, been the Model for the Fashion. It would be a vain thing to pretend to Property in a Country where Thieves were tolerated, and it is as much so to talk of

Honour and Decency when the prevailing Humour runs directly against them. The *Lovers Vagabond* are an Order of Modern Adventurers, who seem to be the exact Opposite to that venerable and chaste Fraternity, which were formerly called Knights Errant. As a Knight Errant professed the Practice and Protection of all Virtues, particularly Chastity, a *Lover Vagabond* tramples upon all Rights Domestick, Civil, Human and Divine, to come at his own Gratification in the Corruption of Innocent Women. There are sometimes Persons of good Accomplishments and Faculties who commence secretly *Lovers Vagabond;* but tho' Amorous Stealths have been imputed by some Historians to the wisest and greatest of Mankind, yet none but superficial Men have ever publickly entered into the List of the Vagabond. A *Lover Vagabond,* considering him in his utmost Perfection and Accomplishment, is but a seeming Man. He usually has a Command of insignificant Words accompanied with easie Action, which passes among the sillier part of the Fair for Eloquence and fine Breeding. He has a Mein of Condescention, from the Knowledge that his Carriage is not absurd, which he pursues to the utmost Impudence. He can cover any Behaviour, or cloath any Idea with Words that to an unskilful Ear shall bear nothing of Offence. He has all the Sufficiency which little Learning, and general Notices of things give to giddy Heads, and is wholly exempt from that Diffidence which almost always accompanies great Sense and great Virtue in the Presence of the Admired. But the *Lover Vagabond* loving no Woman so much as to be distressed for the loss of her, his Manner is generally easie and janty, and it must be from very good Sense and Experience in Life, that he does not appear amiable. It happens unfortunately for him, tho' much to the Advantage of those whom I have taken under my Care, that the chief of this Order, at present, among us in *Great Britain*, is but a speculative *Debauchée*. He has the Language, the Air, the tender Glance; he can hang upon a Look, has most exactly the sudden Veneration of Face when he is catched ogling one whose Pardon he would beg for gazing, he has the Exultation at leading off a Lady to her Coach; can let drop an indifferent thing, or call her Servants with a Loudness, and a certain gay Insolence well enough; nay, he will hold her Hand too fast for a Man that leads her, and is indifferent to her, and yet come to that Gripe with such slow Degrees, that she cannot say he squeezed her Hand, but for any thing further he has no Inclination. This Chieftain, however, I fear will give me more Plague and Disturbance than any one Man with whom I am to engage, or rather whom I am to circumvent. He is busie in all Places; an ample Fortune and vigour of Life enable him to carry on a shew of great Devastation where-ever he comes. But I give him hereby fair Warning to turn his Thoughts to new Entertainments, upon pain of having it discovered that she is still a Virgin upon whom he made his last Settlement. The Secret, that he is more innocent than he seems, is preserved by great Charge and Expence on humble Retainers and Servants of his Pleasures. But some of the Women, who are above the Age of Novices, have found him out, and have in a private Gang given him the Nick-name of the *Blite*, for that they find themselves blasted by him, tho' they are not sensible of his Touch. It was the other Day said, at a Visit, Mr. such a one, naming the *Blite*, had ruined a certain young Lady; *No*, said a sensible Female, *If she says so, I am sure she wrongs him. He may*, continued she, with an Air of a disappointed Woman, between Rage and

Laughter, *hire Ruffians to abuse her, but many a Woman has come out of the* Blite's *Hands even safer than she wished. I know one to whom, at parting, with a thousand Poetical Repetitions, and pressing her Hands, he vowed he would tell no Body; but the Flirt, throwing out of his Arms, answered pertly,* I don't make you the same Promise.

THO' I shall from time to time display the *Lovers Vagabond* in their proper Colours, I here publish an Act of Indemnity to all Females who took them for fine Fellows 'till my Writings appeared, that is to say, (for in a publick Act we must be very clear) I shall not look back to any thing that happened before *Thursday* the 25th of *February* last past, that being the first Day of my Appearance in Publick.

I expect, therefore, to find that on that Day all vagrant Desires took their leave of the Cities of *London* and *Westminster*.

IN order to recover Simplicity of Manners without the Loss of true Gaiety of Life, I shall take upon me the Office of *Arbiter Elegantiarum.* I cannot easily put those two *Latin* into two as expressive *English* Words; but my Meaning is, to set up for a Judge of elegant Pleasures, and I shall dare to assert, in the first place, (to shew both the discerning and severity of a just Judge) that the greatest Elegance of Delights consists in the Innocence of them; I expect, therefore, a Seat to be kept for me at all Balls, and a Ticket sent, that by my self, or a subordinate Officer of mine, I may know what is done and said at all Assemblies of Diversion; I shall take care to substitute none, where I cannot be my self present, who are not fit for the best bred Society; in the Choice of such Deputies I shall have particular regard to their being accomplished in the little Usages of ordinary and common Life, as well as in noble and liberal Arts.

I have many Youths, who, in the intermediate Seasons between the Terms at the Universities, are under my Discipline, after being perfect Masters of the *Greek* and *Roman* Eloquence, to learn of me ordinary things, such as coming in, and going out of a Room. Mr. *Severn* himself, whom I now make the Pattern of Good-breeding, and my top fine Gentleman, was with me twice a Day for six Months upon his first coming to Town, before he could leave the Room with any tolerable Grace ; when he had a mind to be going he never could move without bringing in the Words, *Well Sir, I find I interrupt you;* or *Well I fear you have other Business;* or *Well I must be going;* hereupon I made him give me a certain Sum of Money down in Hand, under the Penalty of forfeiting Twenty Shillings every time upon going away he pronounced the Particle *well.* I will not say how much it cost him before he could get well out of the Room. Some silly Particle or other, as it were to tack the taking leave with the rest of the Discourse, is a common Error of young Men of good Education.

THO' I have already declared I shall not use Words of Foreign Termination, I cannot help it if my Correspondents do it. A Gentleman therefore who subscribes *Aronces*, and writes to me concerning some Regulations to be made among a Sett of Country Dancers, must be more particular in his Account. His general Complaint is, that the Men who are at the Expence of the Ball, bring People of different Characters together, and the Libertine and Innocent are huddled, to the Danger of the latter, and Encouragement of the former. I have frequently observed this kind of Enormity, and must desire *Aronces* to give me an exact Relation of the Airs and Glances of the whole Company, and particularly how Mrs. *Gatty* sets, when it happens that she is to pass by the *Lover Vagabond*, who, I find, is got into that Company by the Favour of his Cousin *Jenny*.   For I design to have a very strict Eye upon these Diversions, and it shall not suffice, that, according to the Author of *The Rape of the Lock*, all Faults are laid upon *Sylphs;* when I make my Enquiry, as the same Author has it,

> *What guards the Purity of melting Maids*
> *In courtly Balls and midnight Masquerades,*
> *Safe from the treacherous Friend and daring Spark,*
> *The Glance by Day and Whisper in the dark?*
> *When kind Occasion prompts their warm Desires,*
> *When Musick softens, and when Dancing fires?*

No. 4.   *Thursday, March 4.*

> *The Dancer joining with the tuneful Throng,*
> *Adds decent Motion to the sprightly Song.*
> *This Step denotes the careful Lover, This*
> *The hardy Warrior, or the drunken* Swiss.
> *His pliant Limbs in various Figures move,*
> *And different Gestures different Passions prove.*
> *Strange Art! that flows in silent Eloquence,*
> *That to the pleas'd Spectator can dispense*
> *Words without sound, and, without speaking, Sense.*
>   Weaver's *History of Dancing.*

THE great Work which I have begun for the Service of the more polite Part of this Nation, cannot be supposed to be carried on by the Invention and Industry of a single Person only: It is, therefore, necessary that I invite all other ingenious Persons to assist me.   Considering my Title is *The Lover*, and that a good Air and Mien is (in one who pretends to please the Fair) as useful as Skill

in all or any of the Arts and Sciences, I am mightily pleased
to observe, that the Art of Dancing is, of late, come to take
Rank in the Learned World, by being communicated in
Letters and Characters, as all other parts of Knowledge
have for some Ages been. I shall desire all those of the
Faculty of Dancing, to write me, from time to time, all the
new Steps they take in the Improvement of the Science.
I this Morning read, with unspeakable Delight, in *The
Evening Post*, the following Advertisement.

On Tuesday *last was publish'd,*

' The *Bretagne*, a *French* Dance, by Mr. *Pecour*, and
' Writ by Mr. *Siris;* Engraven in Characters and Figures,
' for the use of Masters, price 2*s.* 6*d*. *Note*, Mr *Siris*'s Ball-
' Dances are likewise Printed, and his original Art of
' Dancing by Characters and Figures. All Sold by *J.*
' *Walsh* at the *Harp* and *Hautboy* in *Catherine-Street* in
' the *Strand*.

TAKE this Dance in its full Extent and Variety, it is
the best I ever read, and tho' Mr. *Siris*, out of Modesty
may pretend that he has only translated it, I cannot but
believe, from the Stile, that he himself writ it; and if I
know any thing of Writing, he certainly penned the last
Coupée. This admirable Piece is full of Instruction, you
see it is called the *Bretagne*, that is to say, the *Britain*. It
is intended for a Festival Entertainment (like Mr. *Bays*'s
Grand Dance,) that, upon occasion of the Peace with
France and *Spain*, the whole Nation should learn a new
Dance together. Some of the best experienced Persons in
French Dancing, are to practise it at the great Room in
York-buildings, where, it seems, the Master of the Revels
lives. He, as it is usual, carries a White Wand in his

Hand, and at a Motion made with it to the Musick, the Dance is to begin. I am credibly informed, that out of Respect, and for Distinction-sake, he has ordered, that the first Person who shall be taken out, is to be the Censor of *Great Britain.* I do not think this at all unlikely, nor below the Gravity of that Sage; for it is well known, the Judges of the Land dance the first Day of every Term, and it is supposed, by some, they are to dance next after the Censor.

Mr. *Siris* has made the beginning of this Movement very difficult for any one who has not, from his natural Parts, a more than ordinary Qualification that way. The Dance is written in the Genius required by Mr. *Weaver* in his *History of Dancing.* *The Ancients* (says that more than Peripatetick Philosopher, Mr. *Weaver*) *were so fond of Dancing, that* Pliny *has given us Dancing Islands, which Passage of* Pliny, Cælius Rodiginus *quotes. There is also an Account,* says he, *that in the* Torrhebian *Lake, which is also called the* Nymphæan, *there are certain Islands of the Nymphs which move round in a ring at the sound of the Flutes, and are therefore called the* Calamine *Islands, from* Calamus, *a Pipe or Reed; and also the Dancing Islands, because at the sound of the Symphony they were moved by the beating of the Feet of the Singers.*

I appeal to all the learned Etymologists in *Great Britain,* whether it is possible to assign a Reason for calling this Grand Dance *The Britain,* if the *French* did not think to make this a dancing Island. The Stile of Mr. *Siris* is apparently Political, as any judicious Reader will find, if he peruses his *Siciliana,* which was writ to instruct another Dancing Island, taught by the *French.* Let any Man who has read *Machiavil,* and understands Dancing Characters, cast an Eye on Mr. *Siris's* second Page. It is Entituled,

The Siciliana, *Mr.* Siris's *new Dance for the Year* 1714. Mr. *Siris*, a Native of *France*, you may be sure, sees further into the *French* Motions for the ensuing Year than we heavy *Englishmen* do, or he would never say it was made for that more than any other Year, for all Authors believe their Works will last every Year after they are written to the Worlds end. I take it for a sly Satyr upon the awkard Imitation of all Nations which have not yet learned *French* Dances, that the very next Page to the *Siciliana* is called the *Baboons Minuet.* Then after that again, to intimidate the People who won't learn from the *French*, he calls the next the *Dragoons Minuet:* I wish all good Protestants to be aware of this *Movement*, for they tell me that when it is teaching, a Jesuit, in disguise, plays on the Kit.

BUT I forget that this is too elaborate for my Character. All that I have to say to the matter of Dancing, is only as it regards Lovers ; and as I would advise them to avoid dabbling in Politicks, I have explain'd these Political Dances, that the Motions we learn may never end in Warlike ones, like those which were performed by the Antients with clashing of Swords, described by Mr. *Weaver* (in the above-mentioned History) out of *Claudian*.

> *Here too, the Warlike Dancers bless our Sight,*
> *Their Artful Wandring, and their Laws of flight,*
> *An unconfus'd Return, and inoffensive Fight.*
> *Soon as the Master's Blow proclaims the Prize,*
> *Their moving Breasts in tuneful Changes rise,*
> *The Shields salute their Sides, or strait are shown*
> *In Air with waving, deep the Targets groan,*
> *Struck with alternate Swords, which thence rebound,*
> *And end the Consort, and the Sacred Sound.*

No. 5.   *Saturday, March 6.*

——*My Soul's far better Part,*
Cease weeping, nor afflict thy tender Heart.
For what thy Father to thy Mother was,
That Faith to thee, that Solemn Vow I pass!

                     Ar! of Love, Congreve.

AS I have fixed my Stand in the very Center of *Covent-Garden*, a Place for this last Century particularly famed for Wit and Love, and am near the Play-house, where one is represented every Night by the other, I think I ought to be particularly careful of what passes in my Neighbourhood; and as I am a profess'd Knight-Errant, do all that lies in my Power to make the Charming Endowment of Wit, and the prevailing Passion of Love, subservient to the Interests of Honour and Virtue. You are to understand, that having yesterday made an Excursion from my Lodge, there passed by me near St. *James*'s the Charmer of my Heart. I have, ever since her Parents first bestowed her, avoided all places by her frequented; but Accident once or twice in a Year brings the bright Phantom into my sight, upon which there is a flutter in my Bosom for many Days following; when I consider that during this Emotion I am highly exalted in my Being, and my every Sentiment improved by the effects of that Passion; when I reflect that all the Objects which present themselves to me, now are viewed in a different light from that in which they had appeared, had I not lately been exhilarated by her Presence; in fine, when I find in my self so strong an Inclination to oblige and entertain all whom I meet with, accompanied with such a readiness to receive kind Impressions of those I converse with, I am more and more convinced, that this Passion is in honest Minds the strongest Incentive that can move the Soul of Man to laudable Accomplishments. Is a Man Just? let him fall in Love and grow Generous; is a Man Good-natured? let him Love and grow Publick-spirited. It immediately makes the Good which is in him shine forth in new Excellencies, and the Ill vanish away without the Pain of Contrition, but with a sudden Amendment of Heart. This sort of Passion, to produce such Effects, must necessarily be conceived towards a modest and virtuous Woman; for the Arts to obtain her must be such as are agreeable to her, and the Lover becomes immediately possessed with such Perfections or Vices, as make way to the Object of his Desires. I have plenty of Examples to enforce these Truths, every Night that a Play is acted in my Neighbourhood; the noble Resolutions which Heroes in Tragedy take, in order to recommend themselves to their Mistresses, are no way below the Consideration of the wisest Men, yet, at the same time, Instructions the most probable to take Place in the Minds of the Young and Inconsiderate: But in our degenerate Age the Poet must have more than ordinary Skill to raise the Admiration of the Audience so high, in the more great and publick Parts of his Drama, to make a loose People attend to a Passion which they never, or that very faintly, felt in their own Bosoms. That perfect Piece, which has done so great Honour to our Nation and Language, called *Cato*, excels as much in the Passion of its Lovers, as in the sublime Sentiments of its Hero; their generous Love, which is more Heroick than any Concern in the Chief Characters of most Dramas, makes but subordinate Characters in this.

WHEN *Marcia* reproves *Juba* for entertaining her with

Love in such a Conjuncture of Affairs, wherein the Common Cause should take Place of all other Thoughts, the Prince answers in this noble Manner :

> *——— Thy Reproofs are just*
> *Thou Virtuous Maid ; I'll hasten to my Troops,*
> *And fire their languid Souls with* Cato's *Virtue.*
> *If e'er I lead them to the Field, when all*
> *The War shall stand ranged in its just Array,*
> *And dreadful Pomp: Then will I think on Thee !*
> *O lovely Maid, then will I think on Thee !*
> *And in the shock of charging Hosts, remember*
> *What glorious Deeds shou'd grace the Man, who hopes*
> *For* Marcia's *Love.*

IT has been observable, that the Stage in all times has had the utmost Influence on the Manners and Affections of Mankind ; and as those Representations of Human Life have tended to promote Virtue or Vice, so has the Age been improved or debauched. I doubt not but the frequent Reflections upon Marriage and innocent Love, with which our Theatre has long abounded, have been the great cause of our Corrupt Sentiments in this respect. It is not every Youth that can behold the fine Gentleman of the Comedy represented with a good Grace, leading a loose and profligate Life, and condemning Virtuous Affection as insipid, and not be secretly Emulous of what appears so amiable to a whole Audience. These gay Pictures strike strong and lasting Impressions on the Fancy and Imagination of Youth, and are hardly to be erased in riper Years, unless a Commerce between Virtuous and Innocent Lovers be painted with the same Advantage, and with as lovely Colours by the most Masterly Hands on the Theatre. I have said Masterly Hands, because they must be such who can run counter to our natural Propensity to inordinate

Pleasure; little Authors are very glad of Applause purchased any way; loose Appetites and Desires are easily raised, but there is a wide Difference between that Reputation and Applause which is obtained from our Wantonness, and that which flows from a Capacity of stirring such Affections which, upon cool Thoughts, contribute to our Happiness.

BUT I was going to give an Account of the Exultation which I am in, upon an accidental View of the Woman whom I had long loved, with a most pure, tho' ardent Passion; but as this is, according to my former Representations of the Matter, no way expedient for her to indulge me in, I must break the force of it by leading a Life suitable and analogous to it, and making all the Town sensible, how much they owe to her bright Eyes which inspire me in the Performance of my present Office, in which I shall particularly take all the Youth of both Sexes under my Care.

THE two Theatres, and all the Polite Coffee-houses, I shall constantly frequent, but principally the Coffee-house under my Lodge, *Button's*, and the Play-house in *Covent-Garden:* But as I set up for the Judge of Pleasures, I think it necessary to assign particular Places of Resort to my young Gentlemen as they come to Town, who cannot expect to pop in at Mr. *Button's*, on the first Day of their Arrival in Town. I recommend it, therefore, to young Men to frequent *Shanley's* some Days before they take upon them to appear at *Button's;* I have ordered that no one look in the Face of any New-Comer, and taken effectual Methods that he may possess himself of any empty Chair in the House without being stared at; but forasmuch as some who may have been in Town for some Months together heretofore, by long Absence have relapsed from the Audacity they had arrived at, into their first Bashfulness and Rusticity, I have given them the same Privilege of Obscure Entry for ten Days. I have directed also, that Books be kept of all that passes in Town in all the eminent Coffee-houses, that any Gentleman, tho' just arrived out of Exile from the most distant Counties in *Great Britain,* may as familiarly enter into the Town-Talk, as if he had lodged all that time in *Covent-Garden;* but above all things I have provided, that proper Houses for Bathing and Cup-ping may be ready for those Country Gentlemen, whose too healthy Visages give them an Air too Robust and importunate for this Polite Region of Lovers, who have so long avoided Wind and Weather, and have every Day been out-stripp'd by them in the Ground they have passed over by several Miles. As to the Orders under which I have put my Female Youth at Assemblies, Opera's, and Plays, I shall declare them in a particular Chapter under the Title of, *The Government of the Eye in Publick Places.*

No. 6.   *Tuesday, March 9.*

On Rows of homely Turf they sat to see,
Crown'd with the Wreaths of every common Tree.
There, while they sit in Rustick Majesty,
Each Lover has his Mistress in his Eye.

Art of Love.

CORRESPONDENTS begin to grow numerous, and indeed I cannot but be pleased with the Intelligence, which one of them sends me, for the Novelty of it. The Gentleman is a very great Antiquary, and tells me he has several Pieces by him, which are Letters from the *Sabine*

Virgins to their Parents, Friends and Lovers in their own Country, after the famous Rape which laid the Foundation of the *Roman* People. He thinks these very proper Memorials for one who writes an History under the Title of *Lover.* He has also Answers to those Letters, and pretends *Ovid* took the Design of his Epistles from having had these very Papers in his Hands. This you'll say is a very great Curiosity, and for that Reason I have resolved to give the Reader the following Account, which was written by a *Sabine* Lady to her Mother, within ten Days after that memorable mad Wedding, and is as follows.

Dear Mother,

' THIS is to acquaint you, that I am better pleased with
' a very good-natured Husband in this little Village
' here of *Rome,* than ever I was in all the State and
' Plenty at your House. When he first seized me, I
' must confess he was very rough and ungentle, but he
' grows much tamer every Day than other, and I do not
' question but we shall very soon be as orderly and sober a
' Couple as you and my Father. My Cousin *Lydia* no
' body knows of certainly, but the poor Girl had two or
' three Husbands in the Rout, and as she is very pretty,
' they say all contend for her still. *Romulus* has appointed
' a Day to fix the disputed Marriages ; but it is very
' remarkable, that several can neither agree to live together,
' or to part. For if one proposes it, that is taken so mortally
' ill, that the other will insist upon staying, at least till the
' other consents to stay, and then the Party who denied
' demands a Divorce, to be revenged of the same Inclination
' in the other. Thus they say, they cannot consent to
' cohabit till they are upon an Equality in having each
' refused the other. This you must believe will make a

'great perplexity; but *Romulus*, who expects a War, will
'have great regard to let none who do not like each other
'stay together, and makes it a Maxim, that a Robust Race
'is not to be expected to descend from Wranglers. Pray
'let me know how my Lover, who proposed himself to
'you, bears the loss of me. I must confess I could not but
'resent his being indifferent on this Occasion, after all the
'Vows and Protestations he made when you left us
'together. I don't question but he will make Jests upon
'the Poverty of the *Romans*; but they threaten here, that
'if you are not very well contented with what has passed,
'they will make you a Visit with Swords in their Hands,
'and demand Portions with your Daughters. When I was
'made Prize by my good Man, who is remarkably Valiant,
'(for which reason they left me undisputed in his Hands)
'he soon took off my first Terrors from my Observation
'of that his Preheminence, and a certain determinate
'Behaviour, with a dying Fondness that glowed in his
'Eyes. I told him from what I saw other People suffer, I
'could not but think my Lot very fortunate, that I had
'fallen into his Hands, and begged of him he would
'indulge my Curiosity in going with me to some Eminence,
'and observe what befel the rest of my Friends and
'Countrywomen. He did so, and from the Place we stood
'on, I observed what passed in all the hurlyburly, he
'observing to me the Quality and Merit of the Husbands,
'I giving to him an account of the Wives. How strangely
'Truth will out! *Hispulla*, as I saw, when they were
'strugling for her, has crooked Legs; *Chloe* laughed so
'violently when she was carried off, that I observed her
'Lover, as pretty as she is, hardly thought it a Purchase;
'while *Dictynna*, as homely as she is, by muffling her
'Face and shrieking, was contended for by twenty

' Rivals ; that arch Creature *Flora* has escaped by offering
' her self; as soon as she perceived what was intended,
' she got upon a little Hillock and cried out *Who*
' *will have me, who will have me ? Here I am ; come*
' *take me.* This forwardness made every Man think
' her a common Woman, and the Flirt is now safe
' under the Protection of *Romulus,* as a Woman not yet
' disposed of; but when her Character and Innocence is
' known, it is thought she will fall to the Lot of *Marcius,*
' for his generous Behaviour to *Thalestrina,* who you know
' was betrothed to *Cincinnatus : Marcius* and *Cincinnatus*
' have long been mortal Enemies, and met each other in
' Skirmishes of our different Nations, wherein sometimes
' one, sometimes the other has been successful. This noble
' Virgin, whose Beauty and Virtue distinguished her above
' all the *Sabine* Youth, fell into the Hands of *Marcius.*
' Our Apartments here are not very lofty, and Arbors and
' Grottoes, strewed with Rushes, Herbage and Flowers,
' make up the best Bridal Beds among the *Romans;* to
' such an Abode as this *Marcius* dragged the lovely
' *Thalestrina.* This People are not polite enough,
' especially on this Occasion, to express their Passion by
' Civility and ceremonious Behaviour : When *Thalestrina*
' was convinced of *Marcius's* immediate Purpose, she fell
' into a Swoon at his Feet, and with a Sigh in her Fall
' cryed, *Oh* Cincinnatus !

' *MARCIUS,* at the suddenness of the Accident, and
' the Name of his Enemy and Rival for Military Glory, was
' surprised with many different Passions and Resentments,
' which all ought to have given way to the Care of
' *Thalestrina* ; but in a Nation of Men only, and on the
' first Day wherein they had a Woman in their Common-
' wealth, he was much at a loss how to be assistant to her ;

' but as he saw Life revive in her, Nature and good Sense
' dictated rather to absent himself, than be present at the
' many Distortions of her Person in coming to her self.
' He retired, but entered the Place again when he thought
' she might be enough recovered to be capable of receiving
' what he had to say to her.

'HE approached as she leaned against a Tree which
' supported the Bower, and delivered himself in these
' Terms.

"*MADAM*, The Passion you were lately in, your noble
" Form, and the Person you called upon in your Distress,
" give me to understand you are *Thalestrina*. I am *Marcius*,
" and have no Debate with *Cincinnatus*, but on account of
" Glory ; were he a Stranger to me, your Passion for him
" should secure you ; were he my Friend, you should com-
" mand all in my Power, in spite of all the Charms I see in
" you ; and as he is my Enemy, I scorn to wound him in a
" Circumstance wherein he is not capable of making a
" Defence. You have common Humanity, and the
" Generosity of an Enemy for your Safeguard; I will
" return you to *Cincinnatus;* and I see, by the beautiful
" Gratitude which I now read in your Face, you will repre-
" sent this Conduct to the Advantage of the *Romans*, of
" whom there is not one who does not sacrifice his private
" Passions to the Service of his Country. I assure you, I
" know not whether it is more beholden to me this Day for
" the Offering which I make of my Anger, or my Love.

'HE did not put her to the Pain of long Acknowledg-
' ments of so great a Bounty as that of her very self, but
' conducted her into the Presence of *Romulus*, and told
' him, with a very joyous Air, he had resigned a fine Woman
' from his Bed, to purchase a Brave Man to his Country.

'I know *Cincinnatus* so well, that I doubt not but he

' will be a Friend to *Rome*, and interpose his good Offices
' for a Peace between us and the *Sabines:* I hope all will
' join in the same Mediation, who have Children here; for
' I already know not to which Party my Heart would wish
' Success, if a War should ensue; for I find a Wife is no
' longer a Daughter or any other Name, which comes in
' Competition with that Relation: But hope things will so
' end, that I may have the Pleasure to be the faithful
' Consort of an honest Man, without interfering with any
' other Character, especially that of,

Madam,

Your '*Dutiful Child,*

Miramantis.

No. 7.   *Thursday, March* 11.

———*halet & sua castra Cupido.*   Ov.

The Battle of EYES.

IT has been always my Opinion, that a Man in Love shou'd address himself to his Mistress with Passion and Sincerity; and that if this Method fails, it is in vain for him to have recourse to Artifice or Dissimulation, in which he will always find himself worsted, unless he be a much better Proficient in the Art than any Man I have yet been acquainted with.

THE following Letter is a very natural Exemplification of what I have here advanced. I have called it *The Battle of Eyes,* as it brought to my Mind several Combats of the same Nature, which I have formerly had with Mrs. *Ann Page.*

Sweet Mr. MYRTLE,

' I Have for some time been sorely smitten by Mrs. *Lucy*,
who is a Maiden Lady in the Twenty Eighth Year of
' her Age.   She has so much of the Coquette in her, that it
' supplies the place of Youth, and still keeps up the Girl in
' her Aspect and Behaviour.   She has found out the Art of
' making me believe that I have the first place in her
' Affection, and yet so puzzles me by a double Tongue,
' and an ambiguous Look, that about once a Fortnight I
' fancy I have quite lost her.   I was the other Night at the
' Opera, where seeing a place in the second Row of the
' Queen's Box kept by Mrs. *Lucy's* Livery, I placed my self
' in the Pit directly over-against her Footman, being deter-
' mined to ogle her most passionately all that Evening.   I
' had not taken my Stand there above a Quarter of an
' Hour, when *Enter Mrs.* Lucy.   At her first coming in I
' expected she would have cast her Eye upon her humble
' Servant; but, instead of that, after having dropp'd Curtsie
' after Curtsie to her Friends in the Boxes, she began to
' deal her Salutes about the Pit in the same liberal manner.
' Although I stood in the full Point of View, and, as I
' thought, made a better Figure than any body about me,
' she slid her Eye over me, Curtsied to the Right and to
' the Left, and would not see me for the space of three
' Minutes.   I fretted inwardly to find my self thus openly
' affronted on every side, and was resolved to let her know
' my Resentments by the first Opportunity.   This happened
' soon after; for Mrs. *Lucy* looking upon me, as tho' she
' had but just discovered me, she begun to sink in the first
' offer to a Curtsie; upon which, instead of making her
' any return, I cocked my Nose, and stared at the Upper
' Gallery; and immediately after raising my self on Tiptoe,

' stretched out my Neck, and bowed to a Lady who sate
' just behind her. I found, by my Coquette's Behaviour,
' that she was not a little nettled at this my Civility, which
' passed over her Head. She looked as pale as Ashes, fell
' a talking with one that sat next her, and broke out into
' several forced Smiles and Fits of Laughter, which I dare
' say there was no manner of occasion for. Being resolved
' to push my Success, I cast my Eye through the whole
' Circle of Beauties, and made my Bow to every one that I
' knew, and to several whom I never saw before in my Life.
' Things were thus come to an open Rupture, when the
' Curtain rising, I was forced to face about. I had not sat
' down long, but my Heart relented, and gave me several
' Girds and Twitches for the barbarous Treatment which I
' had shewn to Mrs. *Lucy*. I longed to see the Act ended,
' and to make Reparation for what I had done. At the
' first rising of the Audience, between the Acts, our Eyes
' met; but as mine begun to offer a Parley, the hard-hearted
' Slut conveyed her self behind an old Lady in such a man-
' ner, that she was concealed from me for several Moments.
' This gave me new matter of Indignation, and I begun to
' fancy I had lost her for ever. While I was in this per-
' plexity of Thought, Mrs. *Lucy* lifted her self up from
.' behind the Lady who shadowed her, and peeped at me
' over her right Shoulder. Nay, Madam, thinks I to my
' self, if those are your Tricks, I will give you as good as
' you bring; upon which I withdrew, in a great Passion,
' behind a tall broad-shouldered Fellow, who was very
' luckily placed before me. I here lay *Incog* for at least
' three Seconds; *Snug* was the Word; but being very un-
' easie in that Situation, I again emerged into open Candle-
' light, when looking for Mrs. *Lucy*, I could see nothing but
' the old Woman, who screened her for the remaining Part

' of the Interlude.   I was then forced to sit down to the
' Second Act, being very much agitated and tormented in
' Mind.   I was terribly afraid that she had discovered my
' Uneasiness, as well knowing, that if she caught me at
' such an Advantage, she would use me like a Dog.   For
' this Reason I was resolved to play the Indifferent upon
' her at my next standing up.   The Second Act, therefore,
' was no sooner finished, but I fastened my Eye upon a
' young Woman who sat at the further End of the Boxes,
' whispering at the same time, to one who was near me,
' with an Air of Pleasure and Admiration.   I gazed upon
' her a long time, when stealing a Glance at Mrs. *Lucy*, with
' a Design to see how she took it, I found her Face was
' turned another way, and that she was examining, from
' Head to Foot, a young well-dressed Rascal who stood be-
' hind her.   This cut me to the Quick, and notwithstanding
' I tossed back my Wig, rapped my Snuff-box, displayed my
' Handkerchief, and at last cracked a Jest with an Orange
' Wench, to attract her Eye, she persisted in her confounded
' Ogle, till Mrs. *Robinson* came upon the Stage to my
' Relief.   I now sate down sufficiently mortified, and
' determined, at the end of the Opera, to make my Sub-
' mission in the most humble Manner.   Accordingly, rising
' up, I put on a sneaking penitential Look, but, to my
' unspeakable Confusion, found her Back turned upon me.

    ' I had now nothing left for it but to make amends for
' all by handing her to her Chair.   I bustled through the
' Crowd, and got to her Box-door as soon as possible, when,
' to my utter Confusion, the young Puppy, I have been
' telling you of before, bolted out upon me with Mrs. *Lucy*
' in his Hand. .   I could not have started back with greater
' Precipitation if I had met a Ghost.   The malicious Gipsie
' took no Notice of me, but turning aside her Head said

' something to her Dog of a Gentleman-Usher, with a Smile
' that went to my Heart. I could not sleep all Night for it,
' and the next Morning writ the following Letter to her.

Madam,
" I Protest I meant nothing by what passed last Night,
   " and beg you will put the most candid Interpretation
" upon my Looks and Actions ; for however my Eyes may
" wander, there is none but Mrs. *Lucy* who has the entire
" Possession of my Heart.

    I am, Madam,
With a Passion that is not to be expressed either by Looks, Words, or
    Actions,
        Your most Unalienable,
          and most Humble Servant,
            Tom. Whiffle.

' AND now, Sir, what do you think was her Answer ?
' Why, to give you a true Notion of her, and that you may
· guess at all her cursed Tricks by this one——Here it is.

Mr. Whiffle,
" I Am very much surprized to hear you talk of any thing
   " that passed between us last Night, when to the best
" of my Remembrance I have not seen you these three days.
            Your Servant,
              L. T.

No. 8.   *Saturday, March* 13.

Linquenda Tellus & Domus & Placens Uxor.   Hor.

I N the Calculation of a Man's Happiness in Life, there is
    no one Circumstance which ought more carefully to be
considered, than the Object of one's Love. As that will

certainly take full Possession of the Heart, except it be resisted in time, it is the utmost Madness to let your Affection fix where you cannot expect the Approbation of your Reason. If a Man does not take this Precaution, his Days will pass away with frivolous Pleasures and solid Vexations; his own Reflections only must soften his Misfortunes and Afflictions; but he can have no recourse, no help from his cooler Thoughts, who dare not admit his Reason into his Council. We cannot look back upon the Pleasures which flow from loose Desire, but with Remorse and Contrition, and therefore the Mind cannot recur to them on occasions of Distress, to borrow Comfort; but honourable Love, tho' it has all the Softness and Tenderness which Imagination can form, can be admitted under the severest Affliction, and is the best Instrument to break its Force; but as it breaks the Force of Sorrow, it does not do it by wholly removing the Affliction, but rather by diversifying it. He that is under any great Calamity, loses the Sense of it, as it touches himself; and his Affliction, which, perhaps, would have had in it the Terrors of Fear and Shame, is, by the neglect of his own part in the Affair, turned only into Pity and Compassion for a tender Wife who participates it. This kind of Concern carries an Antidote to its Poison, and the Merit of her regard to him has something in it so pleasing, that the Soul feels a secret Consolation in the Happiness of being possessed of such a Companion, at the same time that he thinks her Participation is the greatest Article of his Distress. In all Ages Men who have differed from the Sentiments of the World, when they have been precipitated by Fury and Party, and been sacrificed to the Rage of their Enemies, have in Trials of this sort sunk under their Distresses, or behaved themselves decently in them, according to the Support which they have met with from the Domestick Partners of their Affliction. This is an Opportunity to vent the secret Pangs of Heart to one whose Love makes nothing ungrateful, or, to utter the Sense of Injuries, where that appears conscious Virtue, which to any other Audience would sound like Pride and Arrogance.

THERE are indeed very tender things to be recited from the Writings of Poetical Authors, which express the utmost Tenderness in an armorous Commerce; but indeed I never read any thing which, to me, had so much Nature and Love, as an Expression or two in the following Letter; but the Reader must be let into the Circumstance of the Matter, to have a right Sense of it. The Epistle was written by a Gentlewoman to her Husband, who was condemned to suffer Death: The unfortunate Catastrophe happened at *Exeter* in the Time of the late Rebellion. A Gentleman, whose Name was *Penruddock*, to whom the Letter was written, was Barbarously Sentenced to die without the least Appearance of Justice. He asserted the Illegality of his Enemies Proceedings, with a Spirit worthy his Innocence, and the Night before his Death his Lady writ to him the Letter which I so much admire, and is as follows:

Mrs. *Penruddock's* last Letter to her Husband.

My dear Heart,

' MY sad Parting was so far from making me forget you,
'that I scarce thought upon my self since, but
' wholly upon you. Those dear Embraces which I yet feel,
' and shall never lose, being the faithful Testimonies of an
'indulgent Husband, have charm'd my Soul to such a
' Reverence of your Remembrance, that were it possible, I

'would, with my own Blood, cement your dead Limbs to
'Life again ; and (with Reverence) think it no Sin to rob
'Heaven a little while longer of a Martyr.   Oh my Dear!
'you must now pardon my Passion, this being my last (oh
'fatal Word) that ever you will receive from me; and know,
'that until the last Minute that I can imagine you shall live,
'I will sacrifice the Prayers of a Christian, and the Groans
'of an afflicted Wife.   And when you are not (which sure
'by Sympathy I shall know) I shall wish my own Dissolu-
'tion with you, that so we may go Hand in Hand to
'Heaven.   'Tis too late to tell you what I have, or rather
'have not done for you ; how turn'd out of Doors because
'I came to beg Mercy; the Lord lay not your Blood to
'their Charge.   I would fain Discourse longer with you,
'but dare not ; Passion begins to drown my Reason, and
'will rob me of my *devoire*, which is all I have left to serve
'you.   Adieu therefore ten thousand times, my dearest
'Dear ; and since I must never see you more, take this
'Prayer ;   May your Faith be so strengthened that your
'Constancy may continue, and then I know Heaven will
'receive you ; whither Grief and Love will in a short time
'(I hope) translate,

My Dear,

Your sad, but constant Wife even to
love your Ashes when Dead,
Arundel Penruddock.

'*May* the 3d, 1655, 11 a-Clock at Night.   Your Chil-
'dren beg your Blessing, and present their Duties to you.

I do not know that I have ever read any thing so
affectionate as that Line, *Those dear Embraces which yet*
I feel.

Mr. *PENRUDDOCK*'s Answer has an equal Tenderness, which I shall recite also, that the Town may dispute whether the Man or the Woman expressed themselves the more kindly, and strive to imitate them in less Circumstances of Distress ; for from all, no Couple upon Earth are exempt.

Mr. *Penruddock*'s last Letter to his Lady.

Dearest best of Creatures,

' I HAD taken leave of the World when I received Yours : 'It did at once recal my Fondness for Life, and 'enable me to resign it. As I am sure I shall leave none 'behind me like you, which weakens my Resolution to part 'from you, so when I reflect I am going to a Place where 'there are none but such as you, I recover my Courage. 'But Fondness breaks in upon me ; and as I would not 'have my Tears flow to morrow, when your Husband, and 'the Father of our dear Babes, is a Publick Spectacle ; Do 'not think meanly of me, that I give way to Grief now in 'private, when I see my Sand run so fast, and I within few 'Hours am to leave you Helpless, and exposed to the 'Merciless and Insolent, that have wrongfully put me to a 'shameless Death, and will object that Shame to my poor 'Children. I thank you for all your Goodness to me, and 'will endeavour so to die, as to do nothing unworthy that 'Virtue in which we have mutually supported each other, 'and for which I desire you not Repine that I am first to 'be rewarded, since you ever preferred me to your self in 'all other things ; afford me, with Chearfulness, the 'Precedence in this.

' I desire your Prayers in the Article of Death, for my 'own will then be offered for You and Yours.

J. Penruddock.

No. 9.　　　　*Tuesday, March* 16.

Quantâ laboras in Charybdi !　　　　Hor.

UPON my opening the Lover's Box this Morning, I found nothing in it but the following Letter, made up very nicely, and sealed with a little *Cupid* holding a flaming Heart in each Hand, and circumscribed, *Love unites us.* I find, by the Contents of this Letter, that my Correspondent will soon change his Device, and perhaps make the Figure of *Hymen* perform that part which, at present, he has assigned to *Cupid.*

　　　SIR,

' AS you are a Man of Experience in the World, I beg
　　' your Advice in a Matter of great Importance to
' me.　I have, for some time, been engaged in close
' Friendship with a fine Woman: Your Knowledge of
' Mankind will easily inform you of the Purport of that
' Phrase.　In short, I have lived with her, as with a *She-*
' *Friend,* in the utmost Propriety of that Term ; but, at
' present, I am under a very great Embarass ; for having
' run out most of my Fortune, in the Course of my Con-
' versation with her, I find my self necessitated to go into a
' new way of Life, and by that means to make my self
' whole again.　A favourable Opportunity presents it self:
' A rich Widow (the common Refuge of us idle Fellows)
' has spoke kindly of me, and I have Reason to believe will
' very shortly put me in Possession of her Person and
' Jointure.　Tell me, dear Mr. *Myrtle,* how I shall com-
' municate this Affair to the poor Creature whom I am

' going to forsake. If I know her Temper, she loves me so
' well that she would rather see me beggar'd and undone,
' than in a State of Wealth and Ease with another Woman.
' She will call my Endeavours to make my self happy, being
' false to her. Nay, I don't know but she may be Fool
' enough to make away with her self; for the last time I
' talk'd to her, and mentioned this Affair at a distance, she
' seemed to show a cursed hankering after purling Streams.
' Let me Conjure thee, old *Marmaduke,* if thou wilt not
' give me some Advice, to give some to this Poor Woman;
' make her sensible that a Man does not take a Mistress
' for Better for Worse, and that there is some Difference
' between a Lover and a Husband : But you know better
' than I can tell you, what to say upon so nice a Subject.

I am,

Your most humble Servant,

W. T.

THERE is nothing which I more abhor, than that kind
of Wit which betrays a hardness of Heart. Inhumanity
is never so odious, as when it is practised with Mirth and
Wantonness. If I may make so free with my Correspondent, he seems to be a Man of this unlucky Turn. I shall
not fall into the same Fault which I condemn in him; but,
that I may be serious on such an Occasion, will desire my
Readers to consider throughly the Evils which they are
heaping up to themselves, when they engage in a Criminal
Amour. If they die in it, they know very well what must
be the dreadful Consequence. If either of them break
loose from the other, the Melancholy and Vexation that
are produced on such Occasions, are too dear a Payment for
those Pleasures which preceded, and are past, as though
they had never been.

THE Woman is generally the greatest Sufferer in Cases

of this Nature; for by the long Observations I have made on both Sexes, I have established this as a Maxim, that *Women dissemble their Passions better than Men, but that Men subdue their Passions better than Women.*

I have heard a Story to my present Purpose, which has very much affected me. The Gentleman, from whom I heard it, was an Eye-Witness of several parts of it.

ABOUT ten Years ago there lived at *Vienna* a *German* Count, who had long entertained a secret Amour with a young Lady of a considerable Family. After a Correspondence of Gallantries, which had lasted two or three Years, the Father of the young Count, whose Family was reduced to a low Condition, found out a very advantageous Match for him, and made his Son sensible that he ought, in common Prudence, to close with it. The Count, upon the first Opportunity, acquainted his Mistress very fairly with what had passed, and laid the whole matter before her, with such Freedom and Openness of Heart, that she seemingly consented to it. She only desired of him that they might have one Meeting more, before they parted for ever. The Place appointed for this their Meeting, was a Grove which stands at a little distance from the Town. They conversed together in this Place for some time, when on a sudden the Lady pulled out a Pocket-Pistol, and shot her Lover into the Heart, so that he immediately fell down Dead at her Feet. She then returned to her Father's House, telling every one she met what she had done. Her Friends, upon hearing her Story, wou'd have found out means for her to make her Escape; but she told 'em she had killed her dear Count, because she could not live without him; and that for the same Reason she was resolved to follow him by whatever way Justice should determine. She was no sooner seized, but she avowed her Guilt, rejected all Excuses that were made in her Favour, and only begged that her Execution might be speedy. She was sentenced to have her Head cut off, and was apprehensive of nothing but that the Interest of her Friends should obtain a Pardon for her. When the Confessor approached her, she asked him where he thought was the Soul of the dead Count? He replied, that his Case was very dangerous, considering the Circumstances in which he died. Upon this so desperate was her Frenzy, that she bid him leave her, for that she was resolved to go to the same place where the Count was. The Priest was forced to give her better hopes of the Deceased, from Considerations that he was upon the point of breaking off so Criminal a Commerce, and leading a new Life, before he could bring her Mind to a Temper fit for one who was so near her End. Upon the Day of her Execution she dressed her self in all her Ornaments, and walked towards the Scaffold more like an expecting Bride than a Condemned Criminal. My Friend tells me, that he saw her placed in the Chair, according to the Custom of that Place, where after having stretched out her Neck with an Air of Joy, she called upon the Name of the Count, which was the appointed Signal for the Executioner, who, with a single Blow of his Sword, severed her Head from her Body.

MY Reader may draw, without my Assistance, a suitable Moral out of so Tragical a Story.

No. 10.   *Thursday, March* 18.

———Magis illa placent quæ pluris emuntur.

I Have lately been very much teized with the Thought of Mrs. *Anne Page*, and the Memory of those many Cruelties which I suffered from that obdurate Fair one.

Mrs. *Anne* was in a particular manner very fond of *China* Ware, against which I had unfortunately declared my Aversion. I do not know but this was the first Occasion of her Coldness towards me, which makes me sick at the very Sight of a *China* Dish ever since. This is the best Introduction I can make for my present Discourse, which may serve to fill up a Gap till I am more at Leisure to resume the Thread of my Amours.

THERE are no Inclinations in Women which more surprise me than their Passions for Chalk and *China*. The first of these Maladies wears out in a little time; but when a Woman is visited with the second, it generally takes Possession of her for Life. *China* Vessels are Play-things for Women of all Ages. An old Lady of four-score shall be as busie in cleaning an *Indian* Mandarin, as her Great Grand Daughter is in dressing her Baby.

THE common way of purchasing such Trifles, if I may believe my Female Informers, is by exchanging old Suits of Cloaths for this brittle Ware. The Potters of *China* have, it seems, their Factors at this distance, who retail out their several Manufactures for cast Cloaths and superannuated Garments. I have known an old Petticoat metamorphosed into a Punch-Bowl, and a Pair of Breeches into a Tea-Pot. For this reason my Friend *Tradewell* in the City calls his great Room, that is nobly furnished out with *China*, his Wife's Wardrobe. In yonder Corner, says he, are above twenty Suits of Cloaths, and on that Scrutore above a hundred Yards of furbelow'd Silk. You cannot imagine how many Night-Gowns, Stays and Mantoes, went to the raising of that Pyramid. The worst of it is, says he, a Suit of Cloaths is not suffered to last half its time, that it may be the more vendible; so that in reality this is but a more dextrous way of picking the Husband's Pocket, who is often purchasing a great Vase of *China*, when he fancies that he is buying a fine Head, or a Silk Gown for his Wife. There is likewise another Inconvenience in this Female Passion for *China*, namely, that it administers to 'em great matter for Wrath and Sorrow. How much Anger and Affliction are produced daily in the Hearts of my dear Country-women, by the breach of this frail Furniture. Some of them pay half their Servants Wages in *China* Fragments, which their Carelessness has produced. *If thou hast a Piece of Earthen Ware, consider, says Epictetus, that it is a Piece of Earthen Ware, and by consequence very easie and obnoxious to be broken : Be not therefore so void of Reason as to be angry or grieved when this comes to pass.* In order, therefore, to exempt my fair Readers from such additional and supernumerary Calamities of Life, I wou'd advise them to forbear dealing in these perishable Commodities, till such time as they are Philosophers enough to keep their Temper at the fall of a Tea-Pot or a *China* Cup. I shall further recommend to their serious Consideration these three Particulars : First, That all *China* Ware is of a weak and transitory Nature. Secondly, That the Fashion of it is changeable : and Thirdly, That it is of no use. And first of the First : The Fragility of *China* is such as a reasonable Being ought by no means to set its Heart upon, tho' at the same time I am afraid I may complain with *Seneca* on the like occasion, that this very Consideration recommends them to our Choice ; our Luxury being grown so wanton, that this kind of Treasure becomes the more valuable, the more easily we may be deprived of it, and that it receives a Price from its Brittleness. There is a kind of Ostentation in Wealth, which sets the Possessor of it upon distinguishing themselves in those things where it is hard for the Poor to follow them. For this Reason I have often wondered that our Ladies have not taken Pleasure in Egg-shells, especially in those which are curiously stained and streaked, and which are so very tender that they require the nicest Hand to hold without breaking them. But as if the Brittleness of this Ware were not sufficient to make it Costly, the very Fashion of it is changeable, which brings me to my second Particular.

IT may chance that a Piece of *China* may survive all those Accidents to which it is by Nature liable, and last for some Years if rightly situated and taken care of. To remedy, therefore, this Inconvenience, it is so ordered that the Shape of it shall grow unfashionable, which makes new Supplies always necessary, and furnishes Employment for Life to Women of great and generous Souls who cannot live out of the Mode. I my self remember when there were few *China* Vessels to be seen that held more than a Dish of Coffee, but their Size is so gradually enlarged, that there are many, at present, which are capable of holding half a Hogshead. The Fashion of the Tea Cup is also greatly altered, and has run through a wonderful Variety of Colour, Shape and Size.

BUT, in the last place, *China* Ware is of no Use. Who would not laugh to see a Smith's Shop furnished with Anvils and Hammers of *China ?* The Furniture of a Lady's favourite Room is altogether as absurd : You see Jars of a prodigious Capacity that are to hold nothing. I have seen Horses and Herds of Cattel in this fine sort of Porselain, not to mention the several *Chinese* Ladies who, perhaps, are naturally enough represented in these frail Materials.

DID our Women take delight in heaping up Piles of Earthen Platters, brown Juggs, and the like useful Products of our *British* Potteries, there would be some Sense in it.

They might be ranged in as fine Figures, and disposed of in as beautiful Pieces of Architecture ; but there is an Objection to these which cannot be overcome, namely, that they would be of some Use, and might be taken down on all Occasions to be employed in Services of the Family; besides that they are intollerably cheap, and most shamefully durable and lasting.

No. 11.   *Saturday, March* 20.

Mæcenas Atavis edite regibus.

Bentley's Horace.

THE following Epistle is written to me from the Parish of *Gotham* in *Hereford-shire*, from one who had Credentials from me to be received as an humble Servant to a young Lady of the Family which he mentions ; because it may be an Instruction to all who Court great Alliances, I shall insert it Word for Word, as it came to my Hands.

Sweet Mr. MYRTLE,

' ACCORDING to your Persuasion I came down here
' into the Country, with a design to Ingraft my self
' into the Family to which you recommended me; but I
' wish you had thought a little more of it, before you gave
' me that Advice, for a Man is not always made happy by
' having settled himself in a powerful House ; for Riches
' and Honour are Ornamental to the Possessors of 'em, only
' when those Possessors have such Arts or Endowments

'which would render them Conspicuous without them;
'but these Creatures to whom you advised me to be allied
'are such, whose Interest it is to court Privacy, and are
'made up of so many Defects, that they could not better
'recommend themselves to the World, or consult their own
'Interest, than by hiding; but they are so little inclined to
'such a prudent Behaviour, that they seem to think that
'their Appearance upon all Occasions cannot chuse but be
'advantageous to them; and yet such is the force of
'Nature in biassing all its Instruments to the Uses for
'which she has made them most fit, that they are ever
'undertaking what would make the most beautiful of
'Human Race appear as ugly as themselves. Thus they
'take upon them to manage all things in this Country;
'and if any Man is to be Accused, Arrested, or Disgraced,
'one of these hideous Creatures has certainly a Hand in it.
'By these Methods and Arts they govern those who Con-
'temn them, and are perpetually followed by Crowds who
'hate them: At the same time there is I know not what
'excessively Comick and Diverting, to behold these very
'odd Fellows in their Magnificencies.

'YOU must know they set up extreamly for Genealogies,
'old Codes, and Mystick Writings, and knowing abundance
'of what was never worth knowing in the several Ages in
'which it was acted; but there is constantly, in all they
'pretend to, some Circumstance which secretly tends to
'raise the Honour and Antiquity of their Family. Thus
'they are not contented, as all we the rest of the World are,
'to become more Ancient every Day than other as Time
'passes on, but they grow old backwards, and every now
'and then they make some new Purchase of musty Rolls
'and Papers, which they tell you acquaints them with some
'new Matter concerning their further Antiquity. I met

' here, to my great Surprise, *Abednego* the *Jew*, who used to
' transfer Stock for me at *Change-Ally.* I was going to
' salute him, but he tipped me the Wink, and taking me
' apart at a proper Opportunity, desired me not to discover
' him, For, says he laughing, I am come down here as a
' Cheat; he explained himself further, that his way was to
' get some Paper that was Mouldy, Dusty, or Moth-eaten,
' and write upon it *Hebrew* Characters, which he sold to Sir
' *Anthony Crab-tree*'s Library; you must know there is no-
' thing so monstrous but they can make pass npon the
' People; so terrible are the *Crab-trees* in this County.
' The last Piece of Antiquity which they produced, was a
' Letter written, in *Noah*'s own Hand, to their Ancestor,
' and found upon a Mountain in *Wales*, (which, by the
' way, is said by them to be the oldest and highest Moun-
' tain in the World) directed to their Ancestor Sir *Robert*
' *Crab-tree*, an *Antediluvian* Knight. This, Sir, passes very
' currently here, and is well received, because all allow
' there have been no Faces like theirs in any other Family
' since the Flood.

' IT would be endless to give you a distinct Account of
' these Worthies in one Letter, but I will go as far as I can
' in it. I was, when I declared my Love, appointed an
' Hour in their great Hall, where were assembled all their
' Relations and Tenants; but instead of receiving me with
' Civility, as one who desired to be of their Family, as they
' know not how to shew Power and Greatness, but by
' doing things terrible and disagreeable, Mr. *Peter Brick-*
' *dust* stands up before all the Company, and enters into
' a downright Invective against me, to shew that I was
' not fit to be entertained among them. They call him
' here at *Gotham*, and in all these Parts, the *Accuser*, be-
' cause it is his natural Propensity to think the Worst of

'every Man.   Tho' the Implement has a very great Estate,
'the Poverty of his Soul is such, that he will do any thing
'for a further Penny.   He condescends to audit part of the
'Rents of Sir *Anthony*'s Estate, and, tho' born to a better
'Fortune than the Knight himself, is his utter Slave.   His
'Business about him is to find out some Body or other for
'him, from time to time, on whom to exercise his great
'Power and Interest.   *Peter* has the very Look of a
'Wicked one of low Practice.   *Peter* is made for a Lurcher,
'and as being a Creature of Prey, he rises to the Object he
'aims at, as if he were going to spring at some Game ; but
'he slinks, as you may have seen a Cur at once exert and
'check his little Anger when he sees a strange Mastiff.
'Naturalists say all Men have something in their Aspect of
'other Animals, which resemble them in Constitution.
'*Peter*'s Countenance discovers him a Creature of small
'Prey, it is a mixture of the Face of a Cat, and that of an
'Owl.   He has the spiteful Eagerness of the former,
'blended with the stupid Gravity of the latter.   He stood
'behind a Post all the while he was talking, and groped it
'as if he were feeling for Hobnails.   All that he said was so
'extravagant, wild, and groundless, and urged with a Mein
'so suitable to the Falshood and Folly of it, that I was
'rather diverted than offended at *Brickdust.*   When from
'another Quarter of the Hall, placed just under a Gallery,
'there stood up the Knight's Brother.   It is impossible to
'express the Particularity of this Gentleman.   His Mein is
'like that of a broken Tradesman the first Day he wears
'a Sword ; his Aspect was sad, but rather the Face of
'a Man incapable of Mirth, than under any Sorrow, and
'yet he does not look dull neither, but attentive to both
'Worlds at once, and has in his Brow both the Usurer and
'the Saint.   I observed great Respect paid to him ; but

‘ methought some Leavings of Conscience made him look
‘ somewhat abashed at the great Civilities which were paid
‘ him.   He roundly asserted I was not worth a Groat, and
‘ indeed made it out in a Moment; for by some Trick or
‘ other, he had got in his Custody all the Writings which
‘ make out the Title to my Estate.

‘ WHAT made this whole Matter the more extravagantly
‘ pleasant was, that there is an odd droning Loudness in the
‘ Brother's Voice, which made a large *Irish* Greyhound
‘ open at every Pause he made.   That great surly Creature
‘ made so docile and servile, was to me matter of much
‘ Entertainment and Curiosity.   The Knight's Brother,
‘ I assure you, spoke with a good steady Impudence, and
‘ having been long inur'd to Talk what he does not mean,
‘ he looks as if he meant what he said.

‘ THE Pleasantry of this excellent Farce is, that all these
‘ Fellows were bred Presbyterians, and are now set up for
‘ High Church-men.   They carry it admirably well, and
‘ the Partizans do not distinguish that there is a difference
‘ between those who are of neither side, from generous
‘ Principles, and those who are disinterested only from
‘ having no Principles at all.   The Knight himself was not
‘ in the Country, but is expected every Day; they say he is
‘ a precious one.   They make me expect he will treat me
‘ after another Way.   His manner is very drole ; he is very
‘ affable, and yet keeps you at a Distance ; for he talks to
‘ every Body, but will let no Body understand him.   Here
‘ is a Gentleman in the Country, a good intelligent Com-
‘ panion, that gives me a very pleasant Idea of him ; he
‘ says he has seen him go through his great Hall full of
‘ Company, and whisper every Man as he passed along ;
‘ when they have all had the Whisper, they have held up
‘ their Heads in a silly Amazement, like Geese when they

' are drinking : But perhaps more of this another time ;
' you would marry me into this goodly House,

I thank you for nothing, Dear SIR,

and am your Humble Servant for That.

' *P.S.* Here is a Story here that Mr. *What d'e-call* laughs
' at all they pretend to do against him, and is prepared for
' the Worst that can happen. To inure himself to be a
' publick Spectacle, they say, he rid an Hour and a half, at
' Noon-Day on *Wednesday* last, behind *Charles* the First at
' *Charing-Cross.*

No. 12.   *Tuesday, March 23.*

When Love's well tim'd, 'tis not a fault to Love,
The Strong, the Brave, the Virtuous, and the Wise
Sink in the soft Captivity together.   Portius *in* Cato.

THE following Letter, written in the finest *Italian*
Female Hand, as beautiful as a Picture or Draught
of a Letter, rather than the Work of a Pen, in the finest
small gilt Paper, when opened, diffused the most agreeable
Odours, which very suddenly seize the Brains of those who
have ever been Sick in Love. There is no Necessity on
such an occasion as this, that the Epistle should be filled
with sprightly Expressions. The fold of the Letter, the
care in Sealing it, and the Device on the Seal, are the great
Points in Favours of this kind from the Fair; for when it is
a Condescension to do any thing at all, every thing that is
not severe is gracious. As soon as I looked upon the

Hand, my poor fond Head would needs persuade it self that it came from Mrs. *Page;* but I read, and found it was the Acknowledgment of an Obligation, I have not Merit enough ever to be capable of laying upon any ; the Letter is thus,

March 19, 1714.

Mr. MYRTLE,

' SINCE you have taken upon your self the Province of 'Love, all Transactions relating to that Passion 'most properly belong to your Paper.   I beg the favour of 'you to insert this my Epistle in your very next, in order to 'give the earliest Notice possible of my having received 'very great Favour and Honour done to me, by some one 'to whom I am more obliged, than it can ever be in my 'Power to return.   I beg therefore that you will insert the 'following Advertisement, and you will oblige (tho' 'unknown,)

Your Servant, and great Admirer,

A. B.

' A certain Present, with a Letter from an unknown Hand, 'hath been very safely delivered to the Party to whom 'directed.

IT is the nicest part of Commerce in the World, that of doing and receiving Benefits.   Benefits are ever to be con- sidered rather by their Quality than Quantity, and there are so many thousand Circumstances, with respect to Time, Person and Place, which heighten and allay the Value, that even in ordinary Life it is almost an Impossibility to lay down Rules on this Subject ; because it alters in every individual Case that can happen, and there is something arises in it, which is so inexplicable, that none but the Persons concerned can judge of them, and those, as well as all other Persons, are incapable of giving Judgment in their own Case. All these Circumstances are still more intricate in that part of Life which is naturally above the Rules of any Laws, and must flow from the very Soul to be of any Regard at all, and are more exquisitely valuable and considerable, as they proceed more from Affection, without any manner of Respect to the intrinsick Worth of what is given, and it is indifferent whether it be a bit of Ribband or a Jewel. The Lover in the Comedy is not methinks absurd, where he prates of his Rules and Observations on this Subject.

YOU must entertain Women high, and bribe all about them. They talk of Ovid *and his Art of Loving; be liberal, and you out-do his Precepts——The Art of Love, Sir, is the Art of Giving——Be free to Women, they'll be free to you. Not every Open-handed Fellow hits it neither. Some give up Lap-fulls, and yet ne'er oblige. The Manner, you know, of doing a Thing, is more than the Thing its self—Some drop a Jewel which had been refus'd if bluntly offered.*

Some lose at Play what they design a Present.

The Skill is to be generous, and seem not to know it of your self, 'tis done with so much Ease; but a liberal Block-head presents a Mistress as he'd give an Alms——

I intend all this upon the Passion of Love within the strictest Rules; but Benefits and Injuries cannot touch to the Quick, 'till the Passion is arrived to such a height as to be mutual. Before that, all Presents and Services are only the Offerings of a Slave to a Tyrant; it is therefore necessary, to make them worthy to be received, to shew that they proceed from Affection, and that all your Talents are employed in subserviency to that Affection. The Skill and Address which is used on these Occasions in conveying Presents, or doing any other obliging thing, is for this reason much more regarded than the Presents or Actions themselves. I knew a Gentleman who affected making good Company chearful, and diverting himself with a whimsical way he had of laying particular Obligations upon several Ladies by the same Action, and making each believe it was done for her sake. Thus he would make a Ball, and tell one he wished she would give him leave to name for whom it was principally intended : Another, that he was overjoyed to see her there, for that he was sure had she not, nobody else would have been there that Evening. He would whisper a third, who was brought thither by a Relation, and without being named, And did your Cousin believe she introduced you hither; there is a Gentleman yonder said, she came with you, and not you with her. By this wily way he was by all esteemed the most obliging fine Gentleman ; that was so genteely said, and t'other thing so prettily contrived, that who but *Charles Myrtle* with all the fair and delightful, in his time. About his flourishing Years the Stage had a particular Liveliness owing to this Passion, but too often to this Passion abused and misrepresented. *Otway*, who writ then, exposed in his Play of *Venice preserved*, the Bounty of a silly disagreeable old Sinner, who at that time was a great Pretender to Politicks, in which he was the most ungainly Creature, and nothing could be more ridiculous than *Antonio* (for so he calls him) a Politician, except *Antonio* a Lover. This grim puzzled Leacher is thus treated by his *Aquilina*, whom he keeps and visits : In one of those lovely Moments she says to him, *I hate you, detest you, loath you, I am weary of you, I am sick of you——crazy in your Head, and lazy in your Body; you love to be medling with every thing, and if you had not Mony you are good for nothing.* This imperious Wench of this fribling Politician, was in the Interests of those who were then attempting to destroy his Country; she rates him in behalf of *Peirre*, who is her Favourite, and is then plotting the Destruction of *Venice.*——*Where's my Lord, my Happyness, my Love, my God, my Hero.* This contemptible Image represents in a very lively manner, how offensive every Endeavour to please is in the Man who is in himself disagreeable; poor *Antonio*, to satisfie an amorous Itch, must not only maintain his Wench, but support every Ruffian in her favour that is an Enemy to his Country; which will for ever be the Fate of those who attempt to be what Nature never designed them, Wits, Politicians and Lovers.

BUT I will break off this Discourse to oblige a Neighbour, who writes me the following Letter.

Good Mr. MYRTLE,

'AS I am your near Neighbour, within two Doors of the 'Lover's Lodge, and within the sound of your 'melodious Base-viol, I cannot better express my Gratitude 'for that Favour you do my Ears, large than by inviting 'you to divert your Eyes in my large Gallery, which is now 'garnisht, from top to bottom, with the finest Paintings '*Italy* has ever produced: I dare promise my self you will 'find such Variety, and such beautiful Objects, of both 'History and Landschape, Profane and Sacred, that it will 'not only be sufficient to please and recreate the Sight, but 'also to yield Satisfaction and Pleasure to your Mind, and 'instructive enough to inform and improve every Bodies 'else: When you have well viewed and considered the 'whole Collection, then I am to leave it to you, whether 'you will not think it may be of Use to the Readers of your '*Lover*, (which I understand is to come out to Morrow, 'very luckily for me the Day before my Sale begins) to

' recommend the viewing of my Collection to them, as a
' very agreeable and instructive Amusement to all Persons
' in Love.   But this and every thing else, that may concern
' me or my Collection, I leave to Mr. *Myrtle's* Judgment,
' and known Readiness to serve Mankind in their particular
' Stations of Life.

> *I am, SIR,*
>> *Your most Obedient,*
>>> *and Obliged Humble Servant,*

>>>> James Grame.

No. 13.　　*Thursday, March* 25.

Multi de Magnis, per Somnum, Rebu' loquuntur.　　Lucr.

THE strong Propensity that, from my Youth, I have had
to Love, hath betrayed me into innumerable Singularities, which the insensible Part of Mankind are apt to
turn into Ridicule. The astonishing Accounts of Sympathy,
Fascination, Errantry and Enchantments, are thereby
become so familiar to me, that my Conversation, upon
those Subjects, hath made several good People believe me
to be no better than I should be. My Behaviour hath
heretofore been suitable to my Opinions. I have lost great
Advantages by waiting for lucky Days, and have been
looked upon severely by fair Eyes, while I expected the
benign Aspect of my Stars. Many a time have I missed a
Ball, for the Pleasure of walking by a purling Stream ; and
chose to wander in unfrequented Solitudes, when I might
have been a King at *Questions and Commands.* It is well
known what a Prospect I had of rising by the Law, if I had

not thought it more noble to fill my Study with Poems and Romances, than with dull Records and mutable Acts of Parliament. I intend, at some convenient Season, to communicate to the Publick a Catalogue of my Books; and shall, every now and then, oblige the World with Extracts out of those Manuscripts, which Love and Leisure have drawn from my Pen. I have a Romance, in seven neat Folios, almost finished; besides Novels, Ditties, and Madrigals innumerable. The following Story is collected out of Writers in so learned a Language, that I am almost ashamed to own it. I must say for my Excuse, that it was compiled in my twentieth Year, upon my leaving the University, and is adapted to the Taste of those who are far gone in Romance; not to mention the several Morals that may be drawn from it. I have thought fit to call it,

The Dreams of ENDYMION.

THE Night was far advanced, and Sleep had sealed the Eyes of the most watchful Lovers, when on a sudden a confused Sound of Trumpets, Cymbals and Clarions made all the Inhabitants of *Heraclea* start from their Beds in Terror and Amazement. An Eclipse of the Moon was the Occasion of this Uproar; and a mixt Multitude of all Ages and Conditions ran directly to the Top of Mount *Latmos* with their Instruments of Musick to assist the fair Planet, which they imagined either to have fainted away, or to have been forced from her Sphere by the Power of Magical Incantations. As soon as they had restored her to her former Beauty, they returned home with Joy and Triumph, to take that benefit of Repose, which they thought their Piety deserved. Only *Cleander*, the Amorous *Cleander*, gave himself up to his Musings, and wandering through the Trees that cloath Mount *Latmos*, insensibly reached the

Summit of the Mountain. He was feeding his Eye with the fine Landskip that was spread before him, when he heard a languishing Voice utter these Words intermixt with Sighs: *Cruel Goddess, why wilt thou make me wretched by the Remembrance of my Happiness! Ye Powers,* said *Cleander* to himself, *is not that the Voice of* Endymion? He had no sooner said this, than he crept along whither the Voice directed him, and saw to his inexpressible Astonishment the following Spectacle. This strange Object was a Man stretched at length on a Declivity of the Mountain, with his Arms across his Breast, and his Eyes levelled at the Moon. *Thou fair Regent of the Moon,* said he, *after the Enjoyment of a Goddess, why wilt thou degrade thy Lover, and throw him back to Mount* Latmos *and Mortality?* *Ah Inconstant! thou thinkest no more of* Endymion. 'Tis he, 'tis he, cried *Cleander,* 'tis Endymion, *or the Ghost of my Friend.* With these Words he ran to him, and caught him in his Arms with the warmest Expressions of Transport. If *Cleander* was overjoyed, *Endymion* was no less, and their Endearments had lasted a long time, if *Cleander's* Curiosity had not spurred him to learn the Cause of *Endymion's* long Absence from *Heraclea,* his Adventures, and the reason of his odd Complaints. After repeated Intreaties, *Endymion* delivered himself in the following manner.

YOU may remember, that my frequent Contemplation of the Heavens had gained me the Reputation of a great Astronomer, amongst the Sages of *Heraclea.* But had there not been more powerful Motives, I had not, for Thirst of Knowledge, abandoned the good-natured Ladies of our City, with so much Youth and Vigour about me. You must know, that I had so often dreamt that *Diana* looked kindly on me, that I went to her Temple at *Ephesus* to learn the Will of the Goddess. I was surprised to find her

famous Statue there entirely to resemble the lovely Image
that had a thousand times smiled on me, in my Visions.
The succeeding Night I bribed the Priestess with a considerable Sum, to let me pass the time within the Temple.
After I had said whatever a violent Passion could inspire,
I fell in a Trance before the Shrine that encompassed her
Statue, and to my inexpressible Joy saw the Goddess
descend, and bid me ask her, with a Smile, whatever I
desired.   Bright Goddess, said I, were I to have my Wish,
' I would beg that the Pleasure, I now enjoy, might be
' eternal.   But since that is too much, give me, I pray thee,
' a Seat among the Stars that may place me ever in thy
' View, and nearest to thy Chariot.   Or if the number of
' the Stars be compleat, and the Destinies deny me this :
' Grant me at least to be wholly thine upon Earth, and
' disdain not the Present that I make thee of my self.
' Whether in Heaven, or in Earth, answered the Goddess,
' I will lose no Opportunity to gratifie thee.   Scarce had
she uttered these Words, but I lost the sight of her, and
only heard the Sound of her Quiver, as she turned and
glided away.

I related my Vision the next Morning to *Evadne* the
Priestess, · who expressed great Joy at my Success, and
having sprinkled me with Water from the Sacred Fountain,
and spoken mysterious Words, dismiss'd me with a Viol of
powerful Juices, and Instructions how to use it.   According
to her Commands I repaired to this Mountain, where
having drank off the Enchanted Draught, I lay stretched
upon the Ground, and fixed my Eyes with Delight on the
Moon.   Suddenly, methought, the Heavens were cleft, and
an Ivory Chariot drawn by Horses, or Dragons, took me
up, and whirled me over Cities, Rivers, Forests, and
Oceans, in a moment of time.   I was, at length, set down

in the middle of a Wood, where the Face of Nature was more delicious, than the Imagination of Poets or Painters have yet described. I had not walked long before I heard the Voices of Women, and at my drawing near I perceived *Diana* in the midst of her Nymphs. The beautiful Virgins were placed round her, under the Shadow of Trees: Some of them lay stretched on the Grass, others were viewing themselves in the Streams: Here was one sharpening the Point of an Arrow, there another was stroaking a Hound: Their Horns were hung upon the Boughs, and their Bows and Quivers were carelessly scattered upon the Ground. The Queen herself was less distinguished by her Golden Bow and Silver Crescent, than by that Beauty, which had long held me Captive. I russled a little too eagerly thro' the Boughs where I had concealed my self, when a Nymph that stood near her, casting a Look towards me, cried out, *a Man! a Man!* At that Word one of the oldest of the Virgins bent her Bow at me, and had shot me through the Heart, if *Diana* had not seasonably interposed. Hold, cried the Goddess, if he must die, let him die by my Hand. Give me, continued she, the Bundle of Arrows that *Cupid* presented me with the other Day, when we hunted in the *Idalian* Grove. A pretty young Nymph having put them in her Hands, she threw Arrow after Arrow at me, 'till I had received a hundred Wounds, which conveyed such a subtle Poison into my Blood, that I lost my Sight, staggered, and fell down dead. I had not lain long in that Condition, when, to my great Amazement, I found my self in the Arms of *Diana* drest after the manner of her Nymphs; and I saw the Light and her Eyes at the same time. I found, after that, she had used that seeming Cruelty to conceal our Loves; and thenceforward I passed for one of her Sex, and was looked upon as the Favourite Nymph of her Train. My Days were spent in those Sports which she takes Pleasure in: How often have we ranged the Desarts of *Hyrcania!* How agreeably have we wandered on the Banks of *Feneus*, or *Eurotas!* How many Lions have we coursed in *Getulia!* How have we panted after the swiftest Deer in *Creete*, and pursued the Tigers of *Armenia!* But our Nights——To what a pitch of Glory and Happiness was I raised! How much happier yet were my Lot, if the Mouth that tasted were allowed to reveal my Joys! But, oh *Cleander!* what shall we think of the other Sex, when I shall have assured thee, that Goddesses themselves are inconstant? It is in the Nature of Females to be suddenly hurried from one Extream to another. Love or Hate wholly possesses them; they have no third Passion. What they will, they will absolutely, and demand unlimited Obedience. They are ever prepared to show how little they can value their Lovers, and sacrifice what was once held dear, to their Ambition and thirst of Dominion. When they cease to love, they endeavour to persuade us, by Coldness and slighting Usage, that we never were beloved. But not being able to impose so far upon our Understanding, and to give the Lie to our Senses, they endeavour to make us lose the Memory, as they have lost the Desire of Possession. After so long a Course of Sighs, Vows, Fidelity, Submission, and whatever Lovers talk of, I was hurried away from the happy Regions I have described, in the same manner that I went; and, not many Hours since, found my Body extended on this Mountain, where the Goddess descended with a Veil over her Face; but upon hearing a Noise of Trumpets and Clarions, left me without speaking, and fled to the Moon in an Instant. The assurance that I was abandoned, made me vent those Complaints, which were still the more just, because after the Favour of a Goddess, I shall loath the faint Beauties of *Heraclea.*

ENDYMION had no sooner spoke these Words, than he and his Friend were surprised with a loud Laugh from behind a Bush that grew near them. Instantly started up three young Women, who had dogged *Cleander* in his solitary Walk, one of which was his Mistress. They ran so fast to *Heraclea,* that he could not over-take them; and before ten that Morning, all the Women of the Town had had a Fling at *Endymion.* Tho' they secretly believed his Amours to be real, they had the Malice to ridicule them, as the Visions of a distempered Imagination. Nay, these giggling Gipsies had Credit enough to get the poor Gentleman jested into a Proverb. Insomuch that if a Lover blabbs out the Secret, the *Heracleans* call him *a Lunatick;* they ask a pretty Fellow that conceals his Intreigues, if he hath *a Mistress in the Clouds?* and to boast of Favours is, with them, *to have the Dreams of* Endymion.

I could Dream on much longer with great delight to my self at least, but that I am awakened by the following Letter from a Gentleman, whom I have great reason to have an high Respect for, having frequently been an Eye-Witness of his Behaviour, both as to Love and Honour. I have seen him as a Lover win by fair Courtship at least fifty Ladies; and as a Soldier in open Field obtain compleat Victories always over superior Numbers, and sometimes observed the whole owing to his single Valour.

SIR,

' I Am to have a Benefit Play on *Monday* next, and the ' stress of the Story depending upon Love, I hope it ' will find a Room in your Paper.

' IT is the *Albion* Queens, with the Death of *Mary*
' Queen of *Scotland.*   Where that illustrious Lover, the
' Duke of *Norfolk*, rather than he will deny his Flame,
' gives up his Life.   Whenever I see you, I shall do you
' Honour, and am,

SIR,

Your most Humble Servant,

George Powel.

No. 14.   *Saturday, March 27.*

Oderint dum Metuant.
Motto on Sir Anthony Crabtree's *Coach.*

I Am to Day very busie, having a Wedding Suit for a
Gentleman, and the Knots of the Bride, offered to my
Consideration, and the Wedding itself to be on *Easter
Tuesday;* therefore the Reader must be contented with this
Letter, all which I do not my self understand, for the
Entertainment of this Day.

Mr. MYRTLE,

' READING the Letter in your *Lover* of the 20th from
' your Friend concerning the Family of the *Crab-*
' *trees*, I was pleased at the Non-reception of your Friend
' into that ridiculous Generation ; in which Family, as I am
' told, may be found an Antique Record in *Hebrew*, prov-
' ing their Original.   Sir *Anthony* is cautious of shewing the
' Manuscript, but his Secretary, with whom I'm well
' acquainted, and whose Knowledge is great in Crabbed
' Characters, does assure me it's writ in the Prophane
' Ignorant Stile used by the Phanaticks before the Restora-

‘ tion, and seems to be formed out of the Phrases of the
‘ *Revelations*, with many Periods ending with the Sight of
‘ the Beast, and the Image of the Beast, and the like.   I
‘ think your Friend ought to be thankful for his Deliver-
‘ ance :   However I can’t say Sir *Anthony* was always for
‘ destroying every thing, having once saved (not his
‘ Country, but) his House : The Story is thus related by a
‘ Servant then living in the Family.   It seems, in the Time
‘ of Sir *Ralph*, Father to this precious Stick *Anthony*, there
‘ was in the Family a Man that had lived long, but
‘ wickedly, under the Cloak of Religion ; but at length was
‘ discovered to have defiled the House with a Maid
‘ Servant who proved with Child, which was an Abomina-
‘ tion to Sir *Ralph*, who turned both out of Doors without
‘ paying them their Wages, being considerable, and ordered
‘ the Bed wherein the Crime had been committed, with the
‘ Furniture of that Room, to be burnt, which they were
‘ accordingly.   The Fellow thought by marrying the
‘ Woman, he might so far Ingratiate himself into his
‘ Master’s Favour, as to get their Wages ; but Sir *Ralph*
‘ was too Religious to allow that any thing could be due to
‘ the Wicked.   Upon which the Fellow resolved, since
‘ he was to be a Loser, his Master should be no Gainer ;
‘ therefore sent a Message to Sir *Ralph*, to let him know if
‘ he would pay him, he had something of moment to impart
‘ to him, which might be for the good of him and his
‘ Family : To this the old Gentleman gave Ear, and being
‘ ever apprehensive of some Plot or other against him (in
‘ which Sir *Anthony* takes much after him) resolved to pay
‘ the Fellow, and have him examined ; and when the great
‘ Secret came out, it was that he and the Maid had lain
‘ together upon every Bed in the House, and in every
‘ Room ; upon which the whole House and Furniture was

' condemned to be burnt on a certain Day ; but the Night
' before the Execution Sir *Anthony* came down to his
' Father's, and with a high Hand saved House and Goods.
' This is the plain well-known Matter of Fact, and this is
' the first House that I ever heard of to have been so near
' burning by the Fire of Love.   I can assure you, the
' Family is now grown much more polite, but having been
' bred in such Strictness and Formality, during the time of
' good Sir *Ralph*, both *Anthony* and his Brother *Zachariah*
' come into a Wenches Chamber with the same Air they
' used to enter their Congregations of Saints.   It is an hard
' thing to unlearn Gestures of the Body, and tho' *Anthony*
' has quite got over all the Prejudices of his Education, not
' only as to Superstition, but as to Religion also, he makes
' a very queer Figure, and the persecuted Sneak is still in
' his Face, tho' he now sets up for a Persecutor.

' IF the sower Behaviour and Hypocrisie, which the
' Enemies to Dissenters accuse them of, was utterly
' forgotten, and which by their Freedom and more open
' Communication with the rest of the World from the
' Toleration, is really at an End, I say, if all this were
' wholly out of the Memory of Man, all their Rancour,
' Spite, and Obstinacy might be revived among the *Crab-*
' *trees.*   This Particular however is to be more emphatically
' enlarged upon by those who shall write their History,
' which is, that they are impudent to a Jest.   They having
' as little Respect for Mankind, as Mankind has for them,
' they do not care how gross the thing is they attempt, so
' they can carry it.   Sir *Anthony* wanting a Cause, the
' last Circuit, to keep up the Face of his Grandeur, and to
' make himself popular, spoke to *Brickdust* to accuse some
' Body for Disrespect to an *Illustrious Family.*   They
' could not find such a one, but *Brickdust* told him of a

' Hawker who had Books about him writ in Favour of that
' House. Sir *Anthony* said, that would do as well, pro-
' vided they could persuade People to pronounce the Books
' were against that Interest. Well, they got the poor
' Hawker in amongst them, at a County Court, and in spite
' of all that the Gentlemen of greatest Honour, Quality and
' Estate could say, the Cry went against the Pedlar. There
' were indeed a great many People of Sense and Fashion,
' who are carryed away by the *Crabtrees*, sollicited to call
' out, that the Hawker should be turned out of the Place,
' when they saw, from the Appearance for Him, they could
' carry it no further. But they could procure no Body to
' do even this, but a natural Fool, who had made sport at a
' *Winchester* Wedding, and is every where as much known
' for an Ideot, as if he had his *Moorish* Dancers Habit and
' Bells on. Thus between Jest and Earnest they turned
' out the Pedlar, for the very contrary of what the Fellow
' had done. Sir *Anthony* says this was right, and still
' professes he is a Friend to that Family ; for, says that
' merry cunning Fellow, if I can bring it to that pass that
' no body shall dare to speak for them, without my leave, I
' shall easily manage that no body dare to be against them.
' This is, Mr. MYRTLE, the Logick of the *Crabtrees*. But I
' know not how to relate half the fine things I know of
' them ; read *Sancho Pancha*'s Government in *Barataria*,
' get *Hudibras* by heart, cast your Eye upon Books of
' Dreams, Incantations and Witchcrafts, and it will give you
' some faint Pictures of the Exotick and Comick Designs of
' this unaccountable Race, who are (according to their own
' different Accounts of their Parts and Births) occasionally
' *Syrians, Egyptians, Saxons, Arabians*, and every thing
' but *Welch, British, Scotch, Irish*, or any thing that is for
' the Interest of these Dominions. As you are the Patron

' of Love, I desire to know of you whether, after this faith-
' ful Representation of things, you ought to lament that
' your Friend has been rejected by the *Crabtrees.*

Your most humble Servant,

Ephraim Castlesoap.

No. 15.   *Tuesday, March* 31.

Crede mihi, quamvis contemnas murmura famæ,
Hic tibi pallori, Cynthia, versus erit.   Proper.

I Should be but a very ill Guide to others, in the Ways of
this Town, if I continually kept in my Lodge; I do
sometimes make Excursions and visit my Neighbours,
whose Manners and Characters cannot but be of great Use
to the Youth of this Kingdom, whom I propose to conduct
in Safety, if they will follow my Advice. It is the Business
of a Pilot to discover Shoals, Rocks and Quicksands, in
order to land his Passengers in Safety. I shall take Pains
to hang out Lights, but if those who Sail after me will
rather chuse to be stranded, (where I have given them a
Signal of Danger,) than follow my Course, their Shipwrack
is not to be imputed to me who lead them.

THERE are now in Town, among the Ladies who have
given up all other Considerations, to gratify themselves in
one sort of Delight, Three Eminent above the rest for their
Charms and Vices. The first can only please Novices; the
second seeks only Men of Business, and such of them as
are between Fools and Knaves; the third runs through the
whole Race of Men, and has Arts enough about her to
ensnare them all, as well as Desire enough to entertain

them all. These Ladies are professed Curtezans, and live upon it.

The first I shall give an Account of is *Jenny Lipsy*. All Creatures of Prey have their particular Game, and never dream of any other. *Jenny* never aims at any but Novices, and she makes her Advances with so much Skill, that she is seldom without two or three in pursuit of her, who are in their first Month of a Town-Life. I sate by her, a Week or two ago, at a Play; there was seated just before her a pretty snug Academick, who, I observed, was destined for her Entertainment that Evening. There sate by her a course Hoyden in a black Scarff, who seemed a Servant Maid stoln out with *Jenny* on this Frolick to a Play. *Jenny*, at every thing which passed in the Play that had little Sense in it, was so delighted as not to contain her self from loud Laughs, but particularly checked her self, with a well-acted Romp-like Confusion, when she was observed by the pretty young Gentleman; her Maid professing, in a lower Voice, she would never come abroad with her again. Many kind Looks however passed between my young Gentleman, and one he conceived as unskilled in the Town as himself. She begged his Pardon, two or three times, for pressing upon him negligently, and hoped there was no Offence, in such a Tone and Voice, and such a natural Impertinence, and want of Judgment, as would have deceived any Man in Town but *Roger Veterane*, who suspects every thing. My young Spark offered his Service, at the end of the Play, to see her out; *Jenny* said he was a Stranger to her, tho' he looked like a civil Body; but her Maid interposed and said, If the Gentleman will get us out of the Crowd, there can be no harm, since she would keep with her.

THE second Woman of Consideration is that artful shy Dame Madam *Twilight*. This Lady has got a Step or two in Age, Experience, and Address, beyond Miss *Jenny* abovementioned. She has been above these ten Years known for what she is, but she has preserved such a Decency in her Manners, and has so little Frolick in her Temper, that every Lover takes it she is as much pleased with him, as he with her. *Twilight* therefore has passed her ten Years Libertinism in short Marriages, rather than different Riots. The many Gallants, whose Relict she is, treat her with Civility and Respect where-ever they meet her, and every Man flatters himself it is the Necessity of her Affairs made her take such a loose, but she certainly loved no body but him. *Twilight*, as I said, is never outrageously joyful, but can comply with a Whisper, and retire very willingly with great Reluctance, seldom discovering Desire enough to overcome the Confusion to which her Compliance obliges her. But I must leave her Character half drawn, and in the Dress she often affects, a Veil, to hasten to her who gives me most disquiet of any of her Sex, when I am endeavouring to save the Free and Innocent from the Slavery to which she affects to reduce all Mortals, especially those of Merit.

THIS Lady, who is the Heroine of to-Day's Paper, as well acquainted with this Town as the Plains of *Arcadia*, dignified and distinguished among the loose Wanderers of Love by the Name of *Clidamira Dustgown*, is Mistress of the whole Art of Women; she can do what she pleases, with whom she pleases, and I have not yet known any one that cou'd save himself from her but by flight. She can, as Occasion serves, be termagant and haughty, if the Follower is in his Nature servile; then again so humble and resigning to those who love and admire none but themselves! She can lead the Conversation among raw Youths who are proud of being admitted into her Company, and will Lisp and grow so Girlish, and prevail upon hardened and experienced Rakes of the Town, who are above hurting any thing but Innocence. *Clidamira* is a Female Rake; the Male ones, I just now observed, affect mostly to have to do with the Innocent, and *Clidamira's* Passion is to deceive and bubble the Knowing. To indulge this Humour in herself, she has all the Learning of a Spark of the Town, is deep in Miscellany Poems, Plays, Novels and Romances; has the Copies of Verses, Scandals and Whispers all the Winter, which are brought forth in *London* and *Westminster;* all the Summer those produced at *Epsom, Tunbrige,* and the *Bath*; her Lewdness is as great, and her Understanding greater than that of any of her Admirers: By the force of the latter she is as much courted, even by those who have had her (as the Phrase is) as the finest Woman whose Charms are yet untasted; her Skill is such, that her Practice in Wickedness has not at all made her Hipocrisie of Innocence appear awkard or unlovely, but she can be any thing she ever was, to those who like what she was, better than what she is, the most accomplisht Frolick, and dissolute of all Wenches. What makes me have no Patience with Madam *Dustgown* is, that she is now laying all her Snares, and displaying all her Charms, to withdraw my Heart from Mrs. *Page.* But she shall die; I will sacrifice her, to gain a Smile for that Merit from my own incomparable Fair One.

CLI'DAMIRA has at this time three different Keepers; a rich Citizen, whom she has Orders, upon Occasion, to write to in the Stile of a Widow who wants his Charity; a Married Man of Quality, whom she is to address so, as that his Lady, who is as jealous as a Statesman, and admires her Lord for the finest Gentleman in the World, might read it; her third is a Gentleman learned in the

Laws, whom she writes to as his Client, when she has a mind to raise small Sums to support her lavish Gallant, who lives upon gratifying her real Passion, and sharing the Hire of her Prostitution.   It was necessary last Week her dear Comrade should have a fine Horse he had seen ; she levyed the Price of him upon her Slaves by the following Method.   She writes

To her City Friend.

SIR,

' DID I not know what Acts of Charity your Worship ' daily does, and that your good Lady is as inclined ' to do good as your self, I should not take this Liberty to ' move your Compassion to the Widow and Fatherless.   If ' your Worship's Business should divert you from taking ' Notice of this according to Direction here-under written, ' I shall presume to wait upon your Lady my self.

I am, &c.

THE latter Circumstance being a Threat, immediately produced a Largess above her ordinary Salary.

THE great Skill is to write Letters that may fall into any Hands, even a Wife's, and discover nothing.   Her Stile to my Lord was thus.

My Lord,

' IS it possible you can doat with so much Constancy on ' the Charms of a Wife, to be blind to the thousand ' nameless things that I do and say before you, even in her ' Presence, to reveal a Passion too strong to be smothered ?

MY Lady pouts ten Days after the intercepting such a Billet, misinterprets every Look and Sentence of every Friend she has, and keeps my Lord waking till he has dived into the Matter, and fined for his Quiet to *Clidamira.*

HER worthy Chamber Council is captivated at the prodigious Wit of the Creature, when she sends a bundle of old Parchments from Widow *Lackitt*, and has them lodged with his Clerk with a couple of Guineas, and underwrites she will give him his Brief at her own Lodgings. The busie Creature, who is in Joy when he is not actually taking Pains, is so exquisitely exalted at the Wit, Cunning and Address of deceiving that notable deep Discerner his own Clerk ; that, for fear of appearing too dull for an Hint himself, Cash is immediately conveyed to his Client, as left with him from the Person who is to lend the Mony upon the Mortgage. Thus the sly Thief shows, tho' he is a Man of Business, if he would give his Mind to it, he could be as notable a Gallant as the best. She is accommodated, and her Council is cheated in Raptures.

No. 16.	*Thursday, April* 1.

————Some Grains of Sense
Still mixt with Vollies of Impertinence.

Rochester's Poems.

THE Writer of the following Letter being a Person, if you will believe his own Story, the most impertinently crossed in Love that ever any Mortal was, and allowing his Letter to fit only for one Day in the Year, I have let him have his Will, and made it the Business of this.

Mr. MYRTLE,

' SINCE I writ my last to you, wherein I gave you some ' Account of the confounded Usage which I met ' with from the mischievous and ridiculous Race of the ' *Crab-trees*, I have made it my business to enquire into,

' and consider the Arts and Stratagems, by which a People
' so like in Genius to the *Cercopitheci*, should so long be
' suffered to impose upon many wise, brave and learned
' Gentlemen in this County.　After much Deliberation with
' my self I am come to this Resolution, That all their
' Successes are owing to a certain graceless Impudence in
' themselves, and an unmanly Modesty in others.　There is
' nothing but they will attempt from their want of Deference
' to the rest of the World ; and there is nothing but others
' seem ready to suffer from a too great Sensibility of what
' the World will think of them.　Among other the extra-
' ordinary Circumstances by which this Race is signalized,
' I am most diverted with their Superstition ; they are, you
' must know, great Observers of lucky and unlucky Days,
' and Sir *Anthony*, whose great Talent lies in making Fools
' of Mankind, chuses on the first of *April* to settle his
' Schemes for the ensuing Year ; and yet with all the hurry
' which he eternally appears in, he is the laziest Thief living.
' One of his Propositions for Management is to affect
' Bustle, and avoid Business : This, with several other as
' wise Maxims, is set down by his Secretary to be entered
' upon the 1st of *April* next.　The next to that, as I could
' gather it out of Mr. Secretary's *Coptick* Characters, is,
' Never to look before hand, but do as well as you can in
' the present Moment.

　' Sir *ANTHONY* has had great Success in following this
' latter Position ; but his Noddle is so full, by being always
' extricating himself from some present Difficulty, that he
' has not time to reflect, that tho' Men will bear some
' Hardships into which they are surprized, they may be
' roused by repeated Injuries.

　'THEY tell me most incredible Whimsies of him.
' Among the rest, that he shall take a Book of Humour and

' Ridicule, and take upon him to draw out a Scheme of
' Politicks hid under those seeming Pleasantries.　A
' notable Money Scrivener has informed me, that his
' Knighthood has conceived a mighty Opinion of *South*
' Sea Stock, not from the National and solid Security that
' is given to support the Interest thereof, but from the
' following memorable Passage in the 94th Page of a Book
' called *a Tale of a Tub.*　Most People agree that Piece
' was written for the advancement of Religion only ; but Sir
' *Anthony*, who sees more and less than any other Man
' living, will have it to be a Collection of Politicks ; and the
' Paragraph upon which he grounds his kind Conception of
' the Fund abovementioned, is as follows.

　' *THE first Undertaking of Lord* Peter *was to Purchase*
' *a large Continent lately said to have been discovered in*
' Terra Australis incognita.　*This Tract of Land he bought*
' *a very great Pennyworth from the Discoverers themselves*
' *(tho' some pretended to doubt whether they had ever been*
' *there) and then retailed it into several Cantons to certain*
' *Dealers, who carried over Colonies, but were all Ship-*
' *wreckt in the Voyage.　Upon which Lord* Peter *sold the*
' *said Continent to other Customers* again, *and* again, *and*
' again, *and* again *with the same Success.*

　'Mr. *MYRTLE*, if you Publish this Ribaldry I now
' send you, be sure you chuse the Day auspicious to the
' *Crabtrees* (to wit) the 1st of *April*, a Day wherein, time
' out of Mind, People have thought fit to divert themselves
' with passing upon their Neighbours Nonsense and Im-
' position for Wit and Art.　But to go on ; in order to
' amass a vast Sum of Money which he designs to place in
' the Fund, the Benefits of which are so mysteriously
' described in the above mentioned Political Discourse,
' Sir *Anthony* has resolved to part with the most valuable

' Manuscripts in his Library, which are actually sent to
' Town to be sold on the said 1st Day of *April*, and
' Catalogues given *gratis* to all the Fellows of the Royal
' Society.   The things which he expects most for, are as
' follows, *Fobor Camolanthi's Rudiments of Letters;* being
' the first Scrawls made by the said *Camolanthi* with his
' own Hand, before the Invention of Writing, wherein is to
' be seen the first B that ever was made.   The second
' Curiosity is the very white Wax which *John a Gant* had
' in his Hand, when he made the famous Conveyance by
' an Overt Act of biting, and the following Words,

> ' *In witness that this is Sooth,*
> ' *I bite the white Wax with my Tooth.*

'THE third is an *Egyptian Mummy*, very fresh, and fit
' to be kept as a Predecessor to any House which is so
' Ancient as to have lost the Records of its Ancestry.
'THE fourth is *the first hallowed Slipper which was
' kissed in honour of St.* Peter, who is reported by Hereticks
' to have worn none at all himself, but to have gone a
' fishing barefoot.   It would be endless to tell you all
' Circumstances of these prodigious Fellows, but *Zachariah*
' and *Brickdust* are gone Post to *London* to vouch for these
' Antiquities.   *Zachariah*, Sir *Anthony* says, has a very
' good Countenance to stand by the *Mummy* at the Sale, as
' well as to vouch for the *White Wax* in the Conveyance :
' I don't know what they may do with you *Londoners*, but
' they have quite lost themselves at *Gotham*, and the twelve
' wise Men are ashamed of them ; upon which the *Crabtrees*
' say they will have twelve others, but this is supposed to be
' only a Bounce ; for the *Gothamites* begin to perceive, tho'
' too late, that the *Crabtrees* are not such cunning Curs as
' they pretend, but are at the Bottom Fools, tho' they set

' up for the other Character   I suppose you must have
' heard the Story of the *Book-man*; falling upon that
' inconsiderable Fellow has explained them more than any
' thing that ever happened, and Sir *Anthony*, by all intelli-
' gent People, was reckoned a *Cudden* for medling with
' him; for, say they, there were a thousand ways of getting
' rid of him, and it was not worth doing it, whatever
' Chastisement they might put him to, at the rate of
' exposing themselves and their Affairs to the Examination
' which that impotent Vengeance brought upon them.

'THUS the *Crabtrees*, who indeed never had Sense,
' have now lost the Appearance of it; and Sir *Anthony*,
' for these ten Days last past, could not get any Body to
' whisper him : When he offers it, the Party attempted
' stands full before him, and there you see poor Sir
' *Anthony*, in a need to whisper, jerking and writhing his
' Noddle, and begging an Audience of a Starer who stands
' in the Posture of a Man stiff with Amazement, that he had
' not found him out before. If you'll turn to the next
' Page to that I quoted above, to wit, the next to the 94th,
' (which Phrase I own I steal from *Juvenal's Volveris à
' prima quæ proxima,*) you will find that Sir *Anthony* stole
' the manner of his Levy from Lord *Peter's* Invention of
' erecting *a whispering Office*, for the publick Good and
' Ease—of all—*Eves-droppers, Physicians, Midwives, small
' Politicians, Friends fallen out, repeating Poets, Lovers
' happy or in despair, Bawds, Privy-Councellors, Pages,
' Parasites* and *Buffoons.*——*An Asses Head was placed so
' conveniently, that the Party might easily with his Mouth
' accost either of the Animal's Ears.* The other Parts of
' that Paragraph are too course to be repeated. Sir
' *Anthony* is mightily afraid his dear Relations will hardly
' get safe back again to him, and therefore like the Country

' Fellow who said, *it was pity there was not an Act of*
' *Parliament against all Foreigners that should pretend to*
' *invade this Land,* he has given them a Pass which he
' thinks will be of as much Force all over *England,* as
' it would lately have been in this County where he is
' a Justice. There is one particular pleasant Clause in it,
' wherein he requires all People, notwithstanding their
' Looks, to let them pass for honest Men.

 ' *ZACHARIAH* disputed carrying that Clause, and said
' he was sure no Body could take him for any other; but
' Sir *Anthony* over-ruled him, and in his snearing way said,
' it could do him no harm to have it about him : Which is
' all at present,

From the most unfortunate of Lovers,

Ricardetto Languenti.

No. 17.   *Saturday, April* 3.

Who taught the Parrot humane Notes to try,
Or with a Voice endu'd the chatt'ring Pie ?
'Twas witty Want fierce Hunger to appease ;
Want taught their Masters, and their Masters these.
Dryden's Persius.

MRS. *Anne Page* was smiling very graciously upon me,
in a Dream between seven and eight yesterday
Morning, when three thundering Knocks at my Door drove
the fair Image from my Fancy, as *Diana* was hurried to the
Moon by the Cymbals and Trumpets of *Heraclea.* My
Servant came up to me, while I was cursing the rude Hand
that had disturbed me ; and delivered me a Letter, which
was given him, as he said, by a lusty flesh-coloured young

Man in an Embroidered Coat, who promised to call upon
me, two Days hence, at the same Hour. The dread of
such another Noise made me break open the Letter with
some Precipitation.

Mr. MYRTLE,

' MY Story in short is this. My Father kept me under,
'after I came from School, and snubbed me con-
' sumedly, till I was Five and twenty; and then he died,
' and left me Three thousand *per Annum.* I came to
' *London,* this Winter, where I am to be married to a fine
' young Lady, when I can get her in the Mind. But, I
' don't know how, there is no pleasing of her. She hath
' made my Heart ake so often, that I have resolved to
' follow somebody else; but she hath such a way with her
' Eyes, that I cannot do without her. When I first came
' to Town, I heard she should say, how that I was so
' *Rough!* Upon which I shaved every Day, and washed
' my Hands once in half an Hour, for a Week together.
' Being informed, that she hoped I might be *Polished* in
' time, I got a broad *French* Beaver, and an Embroider'd
' Coat, that cost me Threescore. Pound. I cannot indeed
' blame her for complaining that I have no *Taste,* for I
' have lost my Stomach; and I entirely agree with her that
' I want *Air,* for I am almost choaked in this smoaky
' Town. But this is not all. She hath given out, that she
' wishes I would Travel: And she told me no longer since
' than yesterday, that the Man she married should make
' the *Tour* of *Italy.* Now, Sir, I would be at any Expence,
' in Building, to please her; but as for going into Out-
' landish Countries, I thank her for That. In short, she
' would have me out of the way. For you must know, there
' is a little Snipper-snapper from *Oxford* that is mightily in

' her Books.   I don't know how it comes to pass; but
' though he hath but a plain grey Suit, he hath such a
' fawning way with him, that my Mind misgives me plaguily.
' He hath Words at his Fingers ends, and I can say no-
' thing but he has some Answer or another that puts me out;
' and yet he talks so, that one cannot be Angry neither.
' He always reads your LOVERS to her, and I hear her say
' often, that she should like such an ingenious Man as Mr.
' MYRTLE.   Now, what I desire is your Advice; for, as I
' told you before, I cannot do without her.   I am a hearty
' Fellow, and believe me, if you do me any Good, you shall
' have Gloves, and dance at my Wedding.

Your humble Servant to Command,

Timothy Gubbin.

IT falls out very luckily that I can recommend Mr.
Gubbin to a Person for his Purpose, without further risquing
my own Repose.   The following Letter, which I received a
Week ago, shall serve for an Answer to His.   And I
further declare, that I constitute the Author thereof my
Esquire, according to the Prayer of his Petition.   I have
accordingly assigned him an Apartment in *the Lover's
Lodge;* and shall further encourage him, as I find his
Merits answerable to his Pretensions.

Launcelot Bays *to* MARMADUKE MYRTLE.

Courteous Knight,
' A S you are a Professor and Patron of Love, I throw my
'   ' self at your Feet to beg a Boon of you.   When I
' have told you my Story, you will confess that I am the
' most Amorous and Chaste of Swains.   I am, Sir, by
' Profession, an Author, and the Scene of my Labours is a

'Garret. My Genuis leads me to Love, and I have a
'gentle manner. When I have occasion for Mony, I fancy
'to my self a Lady, and write such soft things, as you
'would bless your self to hear. But living at present in
'the City, where such Ware fetches but little, I shall, with-
'out your Assistance, fall shortly into great Poverty of
'Imagination. Would you believe it, Sir? I have lived
'this Month on a Posie for a Ring.

'MY Request is, that I may be transplanted from this
'barren Soil into *Covent-Garden.* My greatest Ambition
'is to be received in the Quality of Esquire to so courteous
'a Knight as you are; to carry your Pen in this your
'gentle Warfare, and do the Squirely Offices established in
'this Order of Chivalry. You may not perhaps find me
'unqualified to take some Drudgeries off your Hands,
'which you must otherwise undergo; and may possibly
'appoint me Sub-tutor to the *British* Savages, before they
'approach the Fair. It is thought sufficient that the Taylor
'and Dancing-master have managed an awkard Boy at his
'first coming to Town : Nay, upon the strength of a *fine*
'*Myrtle Barcelona*, a young Fellow, now-a-days, sets up for
'Love and Gallantry. The ill Success of such unformed
'Cavaliers, makes a Person of my Talents necessary in a
'civilized Country. You know, the Ladies will be attacked
'in form, before they listen to Terms; and though they do
'not absolutely insist upon Hanging or Drowning, they
'think it but decent, that such Attempts be made in Rhyme
'and Sonnet. I believe you will agree with me, that .
'no Woman of Spirit thinks a Man hath any Respect for
'her, 'till he hath plaid the Fool in her Service; and the
'mean Opinion that Sex hath of a Poet, makes any thing in
'Metre, from a Lover, an agreeable Sacrifice to their
'Vanity.

'NOW, since there are few Heads turned both for
'Dress and Politeness, since witty Sayings seldom break out
'from two Rows of fine Teeth, and true Spelling is not
'often the Work of a pretty Hand: I propose, for the good
'of my Country, to set up a Toy-shop of written Baubles,
'and Poetical Trinkets. The Perfumes of Flattery, the
'Cordials of Vows, the Salts of Wit, and the Washes of
'Panegyrick are ranged in due order, and placed in proper
'Receptacles to be retailed out at reasonable Prices. Here
'the Spark may be furnished with Satyrical Lashes, when
'he has lost his Clouded Cane. Here he may purchase
'Points, Conceits, and Repartees, as useful against an
'Enemy as the nicest Pushes his Fencing-Master can teach
'him. The most graceful Bow, he can learn, shall be still
'improved by a Compliment I can put in his Mouth ; and,
'to say no more, his Periwig shall by my Means, be the
'least valuable thing upon his Shoulders.

'NO generous Lover will repine at my good Fortune,
'when he hears that I get a warm Coat by that which gains
'him the Embraces of a Bride. While he feasts all his
'Senses, I shall content my self with the Luxury of some
'Meat, and much Drink. Thus, an equal Distribution
'will be made of Worldly Pleasures. As They become
'undoubtedly Happy, I shall grow undoubtedly Fat;
'Hearts will be at Rest, and Dunns be payed.

'THE following List of my Wares I desire you to
'advertise ; which will not fail, I hope, to bring Customers,
'and may lay a Foundation for the Commerce of Love in
'this Trading Island.

'LOVE-LETTERS and Sonnets, by the Quire, at five
'Guineas the Prose, and ten the Verse ; with Allowance to
'those that buy Quantities.

'A Sett of Rymes ready paired for any ordinary
' Amour; never used but twice.

' THE Art of Pleasing; or, Rules for Defamation; with
' a compleat Index.

' AN Apology for the Colour of a Lady's Hair; with a
' Word or two in defence of white Eye-lashes.

' A Treatise for, and another against growing Fat. Sharp
' Sayings against Faults which People cannot help; with
' Answers to each.

' A Compliment for a Masque, and a Repartee for a
' Rival.   Neither ever spoken before.

' AN Invective against embroidered Coats, for the Use
' of younger Brothers; to which is added an Appendix
' concerning Fringed Gloves.

' A List of the Heathen Goddesses, with the Colour of
' their Hair and Eyes; for the Assistance of young Gentle-
' men, that were never at the University.

' DOUBLE Entendres, and Feeling Language, collected
' from the Works of the most celebrated Poetesses of the
' Age.

' VOWS for young Virgins, to be sold by Number; and
' Flattery for old Maids by Weight.

' RAPTURES, Transports, and Exclamations, at a
' Crown a Dozen.

' TURTLES, Fountains, Grottoes, Forests, Roses,
' Tigresses, Rocks and Nightingales, at common Prices.

Parva leves capiunt animos.   Ovid.

I Was the other Night in the Box of the Gallery at Sir *Courtly Nice*, a Comedy I never miss for the Sake of the Knight himself, *Hothead* and *Testimony*, all Parts in themselves very diverting and Excellently performed by the Actors. Sir *Courtly*'s Character exposes to an extravagance those shallow Creatures, whose Imaginations are wholly taken up with Form and Outside, and labour only at an Excellence in indifferent things. To utter the Words, *Your humble Servant*, and Bow with a different Air each time they are repeated, makes up his whole Part in as pleasant a Scene as any of the Comedy. This puts me a musing upon the Force of being able to act fashionably in ordinary occasions, and filling up their part of the Room with a tolerable good Air, while there is nothing passing which engages the Attention of the Assembly or Company to any one other Point. It is monstrous to observe how few amongst us are able to do it, 'till half their Life is passed away, and then at last they rather get over it as a thing they neglect, than behave themselves in it as a thing they have ever regarded. This matter is no where so conspicuous as in an Assembly of Men of Parts, when they are got together upon any great Point, as at the College of Physicians, the Royal Society, or any other Place where you have had an Opportunity of seeing a good many *English* Gentlemen together. I have been mightily at a loss whether this proceeds from a too great Respect for themselves, or too great Deference to others; but, it seems to be partly one partly t'other. Whatever the Cause is, I have often seen the effect to a very great degree of Pleasantry. You shall, in the instant a Man is going to speak, see him stunt himself, and not rise within three Inches of his natural height, but lean on one side, as if taken with a sudden Sciatica; and 'tis ten to one whether he recovers, without danger of falling quite down with shifting Legs; and I have known it, when a very ingenious Gentleman has tried both his Legs, almost to tripping himself up, and then catched at himself with his Arms in the Air, turned pale, and finding by this time all his Speech stared out of his Head by a set of ill-natured Curs that rejoiced in his Confusion, sat down in a silence not to be broken during this Life. There is no Man knows, till he has tried, how prodigious tall he himself is: He cannot be let into this till he has attempted to speak in Publick; when he first does it, in an instant, from sitting to standing up, the Air is as much too fine for him, as if he had been conveyed to the top of the *Alps*. You see him gasp, heave and struggle like an Animal in an Air Pump, till he falls down into his Seat, but enjoys his Health well enough ever after, provided he can hold his Tongue. If the intended Orator stand upon the Floor, I have seen him miscarry by taking only too large a Step forward, and then in the Air of a Beggar, who is recommending himself with a lame Leg, speak such bold Truths, as have had an effect just equal to the Assurance with which they were uttered. A too great regard for doing what you are about with a good Grace, destroys your Capacity of doing it at all; but if Men would place their Ambition first upon the Virtue of the Action, and attempt things only because it is their Duty to attempt them, grace of Action and becoming Behaviour would naturally attend Truth of Heart and Honesty of Design; but when their

Imaginations are bent only upon recommending themselves, or imposing upon others, there is no wonder, that they are seized with such awkard Derelictions in the midst of their Vanity or Falshood. I remember when I was a young Fellow, there was a young Man of Quality that became an accomplished Orator in one Day. The Circumstance was this: A Gentleman who had chastised a Ruffian for an Insolence towards a Kinswoman of his, was attacked with outrageous Language in that Assembly; when his Friend's Name was ill treated from Man to Man, this ingenuous Youth discovered the utmost Pain to those that sat near him, and having more than once said, *I am sure I could fight for him, why can't I speak for him?* at last stood up. The Eyes of the whole Company were upon him, and tho' he appeared to have utterly forgot what he rose up to speak, yet the generous Motive which the whole Company knew he acted upon, procured him such an Acclamation of Voices to hear him, that he expressed himself with a Magnanimity and Clearness proceeding from the Integrity of his Heart, that made his very Adversaries receive him as a Man they wished their Friend. I mention this Circumstance to show, that the best way to do a thing as you ought, is to do it only because you ought. This thing happened soon after the Restoration, and I remember a set of Fellows they called the new Converts were the chief Speakers. It is true they always spoke against their Conscience; but having been longer used to do so in Publick, (as all are gifted at their Meetings) they excelled all other Prostitutes in firm Countenances and stiff Bodies. They were indeed ridiculous, but they could bear to be ridiculous, and carried their Points by having their Consciences seared, while that of others lay bleeding; but I am got into Chat upon Circumstances of a higher Nature than those of ordinary Life, Compliment and Ceremony. I was speaking of Sir *Courtly's Your humble Servant Madam.*

AS for my part, I always approve rather those who make the most of a little Understanding, and carry that as far as they can, than those who will not condescend to be perfect, if I may so speak, in the under Parts of their Character. Mrs. *Page* said very justly of me, one Day, (for you must know I am as mute as a Fish in her Presence,) If Mr. *Myrtle* can't speak for Love, and his Mistress can't speak out of Decency, their Affair must end as it began, only in dumb Show. I have a Cousin at the University who lately made me a Visit; I know him to want no Learning, Wit or Sense, if he would please to dispence it to us by Retail. He can make an Oration or write a Poem, but won't let us have any thing of his in small Parcels. He is come indeed to bear our rallying him upon it without being surly. I asked him, if he should talk with a Man who had a whole Language except the Conjunctions Copulative, how would he be able to understand him? Small Matters it is absolutely necessary to capacitate our selves for: Great Occasions do not occur every Moment. The *Jew* said very prettily, in defence of his frequent superstitious Washings, and the like outward Services; I do these because I have not always Opportunities to manifest my Devotion in Acts of Virtue. I had abundance to do to make my Cousin open his Mouth at all. He and I, one Evening, had sate together three Hours without uttering a Syllable; I was resolved to say nothing till he began the Discourse, but finding the Silence endless, I desired him to go down with me from my Lodge, and walk with me in the Piazza: we took two or three turns there in the dark in utter Silence; at last said I to him, Cousin *Tom*, this Taciturnity of thine, considering the Sense I know thou hast in thee, is a Vexation I can no longer endure with Patience ; we are now in the dark, and I can't see how you do it, but here give me your Hand, let me, while I hold you here, entreat you to exercise the Use of your Lips and Tongue, and oblige me so far as to utter, with as much Vehemence as you can, the Word *Coach.* My youth took my Friendship as I intended it, and, as well as he could in a laughing Voice, he cried C-o-a-c-h ; Very well Cousin, says I, try if you can speak it at once, with which he began to cry Coach, Coach, pulling himself out of my Hand ; No, says I, Cousin, you shall not go till you are perfect ; with that he called loudly and distinctly, insomuch that we had in an Instant all the Coaches from *Will's* and *Tom's* about the *Portico* or little Piazza ; the Fellows began to call Names, as thinking themselves abused since no one came to take Coach ; upon which one cryed out, What Rascals are those in the Piazza ? You Scoundrels, said I, what are you good for but to keep your Horses and selves in Exercise ? would you stare and stand idle at Coffee-house Doors all Night ? I went on with great Fluency, in the Language those Charioteers usually meet with, upon which they came down armed with Whips, and my Cousin complaining his Sword was borrowed of another College, and would not draw, wondered I would bring my self and him into such a Scrape ; he had not done speaking before a Whip Lash took him on the Cheek, upon which my young Gentleman snatched my Cane out of my Hand, and found every Limb about him as well as his Tongue. I stood by him with all my Might, and would fain have brought it to that, that my Cousin might be carried before a Justice, by way of Exercise in different Circumstances, rather than go on the insipid, dull, useless thing which an unmanly Bashfulness had made him ; but he improved daily after this Adventure of the Coachmen, and can be rough and civil as properly and with as good an Air as any Gentleman in Town. In a Word, his Actions are genteel, manly, and voluntary, which he owes to the Confidence into which I at first betrayed him, by the silly Adventure I have now related.

No. 19.   *Thursday, April* 8.

—quid deceat, non videt ullus amans.   Ovid.

I Shall be mightily in Arrear with my Correspondents, if I do not, for some time, appoint one Day in the Week to take into Consideration their Epistles.

THE first that falls into my Hands, out of a Bundle before me, is from an unhappy Man who is fallen in Love, but knows not with whom. Take his Case from his own Epistle.

Mr. MYRTLE,   *April* 3, 1714.

' I Am a young Gentleman of a moderate Fortune, have ' spent the greatest part of my Time for these two or ' three Years last past in what they call seeing the Town, ' but am now resolved to Marry, and forsake that unsettled ' kind of Life. My Thoughts are at present divided ' between two Sisters; and as they are both amiable, I ' can't as yet determine which to make my Addresses to, ' but must beg your Advice in this Critical Posture of ' Affairs. *Lucinda* has Sense enough, is very handsom, ' and excellently well shaped, her Eyes command Respect ' from all who behold them; it is impossible to see and not

' adore her; she dances to the greatest Perfection imagin-
' able, and is in short every way so well accomplish'd, that
' her Charms would be irresistible, had she not too great a
' mixture of Pride, and did not self-Admiration in some
' measure obscure the Lustre of her Beauty. *Celia* is not
' so handsome as her Sister, yet is very pretty; when she
' Talks she captivates her Hearers, yet seems wholly
' ignorant at the same time of her own Charms; and when
' the Eyes of the whole Company are fixt on her, she,
' with all the Innocence in the World, seems to wonder at
' their Attention, and rather apprehends that some Defect in
' her Person or Conversation, than any Perfection in either,
' is the cause of their earnest Observance. When I am
' with *Celia*, her agreeable easie Conversation and Good-
' humour ravish my Soul, and 'tis then I resolve with my
' self to fix my Thoughts on her alone; but when *Lucinda*
' approaches, all my Resolutions vanish, and I'm *Celia*'s no
' longer. I have endeavoured to search into my own
' Thoughts as nicely as possible, and have at last dis-
' covered that 'tis *Lucinda* I admire, but *Celia* I love; I
' would therefore beg your Advice which I ought to chuse,
' her, that by the delicacy of her Face and Shape, and
' stateliness of her Mien and Air, enforces my Adoration;
' or her that by the agreeableness of her Good-humour and
' Conversation engages my Love. An answer to this will
' be very acceptable to

Your humble Servant,

Charles Doubt.

THE Circumstance of this Gentleman puts me in mind
of a Paper of Verses in Sir *John Suckling*, upon two Sisters
whose Beauties were so equal and so like, that they

distracted the Choice and Approbation of their Beholders. While the Eyes of their Admirers were taken up in comparing their several Beauties, their Hearts were safe by being unresolved on whom of the two to fix. That witty Author on this Occasion concludes

> *He sure is happy'st that has hopes of either,*
> *Next him is he that sees them both together.*

MY Correspondent has not told me, that he has not easie Access to both his young Ladies; while he enjoys that, I cannot but propose the Expedient of seeing them both together, as an effectual Method towards coming to determination in this Case, tho' it had the contrary Effect in the Case of the Sisters reported by *Suckling.* If my Correspondent has stated the matter right, *Celia* will gain Ground of *Lucinda;* for Beauty palls by intimate Conversation, but good Humour and Affability gain new Strength the more frequently they discover themselves. I expect this Correspondent, provided he goes into my Method, should give me an Account how he finds himself, that I may note it in my Book of Receipts.

THE next Gentleman, I find, is extreamly high in his Feaver, for he starts from one thing to another in the present hurry of his Spirits, and makes it impossible for me to give any regular Judgment of his Condition. I find he is but lately fallen into it, and I must observe his future Letters very attentively, before I can be able to prescribe any thing for his Recovery. It is the Nature of his Disease, in the first Place, that the Patients think every Man delighted with their Ravings. The Stile of the Letter seems to me to be that which the Learned in Love distinguish by the Sublime Unintelligible; but take it from himself.

Oh ! *Mr.* MYRTLE,

'HAD you seen her for whom my Breast pants this
'Moment, your *Ann Page* had been as utterly no
'more as *Cleopatra* who ruined *Anthony,* or *Statira* who
'captivated *Alexander !* heedless Man that I was——But
'what could Wisdom have availed me after seeing her !
'As she is fair, she is also inexorable. Alas ! that what
'moves Passion should also be a check to our Desires, and
'how miserable is his Fate, who conceives Despair from the
'Merit of what inspires his Admiration ! Oh, dear Sir !
'send me your Advice, but I am sure I can't follow it, and
'I shall not have time to shew you how much I am

　　　Your humble Servant,

　　　　though I know I shall be Yours till Death,

　　　　　　　Cinthio Languissante.

I shall end to Day's Work with this notable piece of
Complaint from poor *Tim. Gubbin,* whose Lamentation you
must take in his own Words.

Mr. MYRTLE,

'SINCE I writ to you last, I have visited this Gentle-
'woman that I told you of, and whom I cannot be
'without every Day in the Week, except *Sundays.* You
'cannot imagine how very Proud she is, and Scornful, tho'
'at the same time she knows I am better born than her
'self ; but she loves none but Dissemblers. The young
'Spark who I complained to you was so much in her
'Favour, told her such a parcel of Lies t'other Day, that I
'told him to his Face I wonder'd he was not asham'd on
'it. You must know I believe most of what he says is out
'of a Book. I am loath to be quarrelsom, but if he Talks,

'and makes a Jest of me any longer, as I find he does, I'll
'make him understand that I am as good a Scholar at the
'Rapier as himself. I only speak it to you as a Case of
'Conscience, and ask you the Question, whether if a Man
'has more Wit than I, and uses it against me, I may not
'use what I think I have more than he against him?
'Therefore if I may have your leave, I would try my young
'Spark about the Business of Courage. I have told my
'Mistress as much, but I don't know what she means, but
'I think she has as mad a way of talking as he, and says
'the way to win her is to die for her my self; and if I
'won't do that, not to interrupt People who are better bred
'than my self, who are willing to die for her. Prethee,
'*Mr*. MYRTLE, tell me what all this means, for tho' I have
'a very good Estate, I am as unhappy as if I were not
'worth a Groat, and all for this proud Minx.

   I am, SIR,

     Your most Humble Servant,

       Timothy Gubbin.

No. 20.   *Saturday, April* 10.

She dropt a Tear, and Sighing seem'd to say,
Young Maidens Marry : Marry while you may.
         Flatman.

I AM apt to believe the Circumstances of the following
 Letter are unfeigned, and therefore shall not labour to
make them more entertaining by fabulous Ornaments. I
shall have, I dare say, enough to do in the Progress of the
Matter, to shew my Skill in Love ; therefore let the following

Letter lye before the Town, as a plain Narrative of what, I fear, will have more Incidents in it than it should have, were I my self either the Son or the Father in the Narration. I appeal to the Tea-Tables on the Matter.

Dear Mr. MYRTLE,

' I Have long had a secret (and I hope no Criminal) 'Ambition to appear in your Writings, and an equal ' Desire to be under your Direction. If therefore you have ' Kindness enough to gratifie the Vanity of an enamoured ' Female (who has a mind to be admired in Coffee-houses, ' and is willing to believe, that by a little of your Manage- ' ment she may make a tolerable figure among your ' Lovers ;) and to convince the World that you are resolved ' to be as good as your Word, by your readiness to give ' your Sage Advice to those who need it, and humbly sue ' for it ; I earnestly entreat you to Print me off to morrow, ' and at the same time to publish your Opinion of the ' following Case : For the Gentleman, who next my self is ' more concern'd in it, has perused the Letter I now ' presume to send you, and has positively declared he will ' stand to your Determination.

' Mr. *CARELESS* is a Gentleman of the *Middle-* ' *Temple:* He was sent thither very young to Study the ' Law. He has a Vivacity in all his Words and Actions, ' which has acquired him the Esteem and good Graces of a ' great many of our Sex. This kind of Happiness made ' him entirely neglect the chief Design which brought him ' up to *London. Cook* upon *Littleton* grew mouldy and ' dusty in his Solitary Study, while he shined among the ' Ladies in his Coat turned up with Velvet, and negligently ' grac'd with Oil and Powder. He better knew how to write ' a *Billet-doux* than to Engross a Bill, and he was much

' more expert in repeating Scraps of Plays, than in wording
' a Petition.　A certain Art he has of saying the most
' common things after an extraordinary manner, was of very
' great use to him in effectually recommending him to those
' Ladies, who are fond of that kind of Innocent Mirth
' which keeps Virtue always in danger, and consequently
' alarmed, and not in a stupid Security which tends neither
' to Virtue or Vice.——But alas ! where am I going ?——I
' ask ten thousand Pardons, dear Mr. MYRTLE, for this
' long Preamble.　What I am going to consult you in is
' this.　I am a young Woman who have been but Fourteen
' these 3 Years past (tho' to you I may venture to own, that
' I was Six and twenty the 1st Day of *May* last.)　My
' Father was an Officer in the Army, and tho' pretty well
' stricken in Years, yet no Man was a greater Encourager of
' Mirth and Diversion than himself; this Turn of Humour
' in the good old Man, made him extremely pleas'd with
' Mr. *Careless*, and unless the Business of his Family
' required his more serious Attention, he thought his Hours
' past slowly on, if young *Careless* happened to be absent
' from our House.　This Gentleman's close Intimacy with
' my Father, gave him frequent Opportunities of being in my
' Company; and he has often in gayety of Heart call me
' his *Maria*, his Mistress, his Charmer, and has told me a
' thousand times over he was in Love with me, in a way
' which goes for no more than *Madam I like your Company*.
' However, Mr. MYRTLE, you who seem no Stranger to the
' Weaknesses incident to our Sex, can't but imagine that a
' single Woman, and no profess'd Enemy to Matrimony,
' was not displeased at such like Declarations from a pretty
' Fellow that was young, lively, brisk, and did not want
' Wit.　Tho' he was thus agreeable, and I neither insensible
' of his Perfections, nor displeased at his Addresses to me,

' yet my Modesty laid too great a Restriction on me, to
' permit me to discover to him at first the secret Satisfac-
' tion I took in hearing him praise me, and how I was
' delighted when I listened to the Declaration of his
' Passion. What he pratled at last began to dwell upon
' me; I grew afraid that all his Professions of this Nature
' were meer Amusements to him, 'till one Evening when
' we were all very Merry in the Parlour, dancing Country
' Dances, and playing Plays, he said somewhat to me in
' Secret, which I fear I shall all my Life wish I had never
' heard.

' I remember we were engaged at a Play called Servants
' and Mistresses, when, among the Variety of Gentlemen
' which were given me to chuse out of, I pitched upon Mr.
' *Careless* as a Gentleman the most agreeable to my Fancy
' of any in the Company. Upon which he rose up, made
' me a very modest and respectful Bow; and when,
' according to the Custom of the Play, he had given a very
' graceful, and methought somewhat awful Salute, he
' whispered me and wished, with a Sigh, that he might be
' so happy as to be my Choice in earnest——I hear the
' Words still tingle in my Ear. I stole my Eye towards
' Mr. *Careless* the whole Night after; and if he happened
' to compliment any of the Ladies, I took particular Notice
' of her Countenance, I could not help thinking her very
' ugly, and that she did not at all deserve to have any thing
' said in her Praise : If he smiled at my Cousin, who was
' tolerably handsome, I was ready to cry; and when, in
' a fondling manner, he took my Sister *Sally* on his Knee,
' methought my poor Heart grew as heavy as Lead. Well !
' certainly my Inquietudes all that Night are not, and to
' Mr. *Myrtle* need not, be described——But, Mr. *Myrtle*,
' to make short of my Story, by mutual Endearments and a

' reciprocal Desire to please, Mr. *Careless* and I, from that
' time forward, became lovely and agreeable in each others
' Eyes. I thought my self happy in his Company, and a
' Sight of him never failed to fill me with the most ravishing
' Delight. He would often discourse to me of Marriage,
' and long till he was of Age that he might have me all his
' own. I convers'd with him as with the Man who was to
' have been my Companion for Life. I seldom dress'd but
' on the Day I expected a Visit from him——Thus we
' lived and loved, for some Months, till the malicious
' World talked of our Behaviour, and made Mr. *Carless*'s
' Father acquainted with our whole Proceedings. He
' sends for his Son. O, Mr. *Myrtle!* how shall I describe
' my Concern for his Departure? I dreaded his Father's
' Power over him, and trembled when I considered that his
' Father, who was able to leave him a good Fortune, might
' possibly awe him into a Neglect of me. Mr. *Careless*
' leaves me and *London*, in Obedience to his Father's
' Command. As soon as he got home, he sent me Word
' his Father severely menac'd him, and swore solemnly
' he would not leave him a Groat if he continu'd to love
' me, or entertained the least Thought of making me his
' Wife.

' IN Mr. *Careless*'s Absence my Father and Mother both
' die, and I survived them an Orphan of a very slender
' Fortune ; Mr. *Careless* writes a second Letter, wherein he
' lets me know, that his Father persists in his Resolution,
' however he assures me, that if I pleased he would post to
' *London* unknown to the old Man, and there marry me.
' I now had a difficult Card to play. I reasoned thus ;
' that if I took Mr. *Careless* at his Word, I should thereby
' prove the unhappy Instrument of making him guilty of
' Disobedience, and, by incurring his Father's Displeasure,

' put his Fortune in danger. I thought it would be no
' Argument of my Affection to involve the young Man I
' pretended to love, in these Dangers.   After some struggle
' my Passion gave way to Prudence, and I resolved to lose
' my Lover, rather than take him at the Expence of his
' Fame or Discretion. After I had wept heartily, I writ
' him a Letter in the Stile of one who had never loved; I
' told him I believed it most advisable to lay aside the
' Thoughts of a Match which was attended with many
' Difficulties, and could not but prove a very disadvan-
' tageous one to him, and, if his Father remained irrecon-
' cileable, to me too.   Mr. *Careless* followed my Advice, he
' commended my Freedom, ceased to be my Lover, but
' continued to be my Friend ever since.

' Mr. *CARELESS* is now at Age, unmarried, has
' attained to a plentiful Fortune without the Assistance of
' his Father: I am still unprovided for, and confess Mr.
' *Careless* is this Moment as much Master of my Heart as
' ever.   Dear Mr. *Myrtle*, be speedy in your Determination,
' and say what you think should be Mr. *Careless*'s Senti-
' ments towards me.   I wait with impatience for to-morrow's
' Paper, which is seriously to determine the Fate of your
' constant Reader,

Prudence Lovesick.

IT is a very hazardous Point to determine a Mater
attended with such nice Circumstances; but supposing
the Facts are honestly stated, if the Father of *Careless* has
any taste of Merit, he ought to give his Consent to a Lady
to whom he owes so generous a Refusal of his Son, rather
than be his Daughter, when it was incommodious to the
Circumstances of his Family; if an Accession of Wealth
is thrown in, which ought to be accounted as a Portion sent

by Providence to take off all prudential Objections that stood between the young Lady and her Happiness, I wont say what the Son should do, but if the Father does his Duty, it will have the same good Effect on the Lovers. Till that is refused, I shall not play the Casuist in a Case wherein no one can err, but with a Guilt which cannot but be obvious to any Man who has the least Sense of Humanity.

No. 21.   *Tuesday, April* 13.

Natio Comœda eft————   Juv.

IN hopes that People will trouble me no more with Accounts of the *Crabtrees*, I have admitted the following Letter, tho' I am sick of a People so eminently made the Objects of the contrary Passion to that of Love.

SIR,

' I Read in your Paper, the other Day, the Letter of
' *Richardetto Languenti,* concerning the ridiculous and
' mischievous Race of the *Crabtrees*. I must confess I
' never thought Words better put together or applied, than
' mischievous and ridiculous, for that unaccountable,
' lamentable, detestable, and every other Word ending
' in able, under tolerable. You may see, Sir, by the Hand,
' in which I write, that I am a Woman; and by the Stile
' and Passion, that I am an angry Woman; at the same
' time I don't know whether I may write my self Woman,
' only because I am of the Age of twenty nine, since I am
' still a Maid; but I am sure I should have been a Woman
' before now, if it had not been for this disagreeable, I

' would say execrable Race of the *Crabtrees.*   As fast, and
' as well as my Passion will let me, I will give you an
' Account of my Sufferings.

'I am the Daughter of a Gentleman of 400*l.* a Year,
' who has several other Children. Sir *Anthony* always
' giving himself out for a great Friend to the Landed
' Interest, as he calls it, has ever been in great Credit with
' my Father. To find Portions, Maintenance and Educa-
' tion for a numerous Family, my Father has practised that
' natural Improvement of a Country Gentleman's Estate,
' grazing Cattle, and driving them to the Market of *London.*
' He dealt for the whole with one eminent Butcher in St.
' *James*'s Market, with whom he Accompts once a Year,
' and takes the Payments which are made to the said
' Butcher in Ballance of their Accounts. You must know
' there is a great Lady in that Neighbourhood, eminent for
' her Justice and Charity, who uses Sir *Anthony* as her
' Steward : The Knight has got a great Estate by oppress-
' ing her Tenants, and terrifying all People in her Service
' with his great Power in her. The Lady above-mention'd
' owed my Father's Correspondent, the Butcher, a Sum of
' Mony which was to have been my Fortune in Marriage
' with an agreeable young Man, the Son of a Neighbouring
' Gentleman. My Father had so great a Respect for this
' Lady, that he engaged himself to take any Demands upon
' her in Payment without the least Scruple. By Sir
' *Anthony*'s Management a third part of the Lady's Debt
' to the Butcher is paid in a Coin I never heard of before,
' called Tin Tallies. My Father has written to Sir *Anthony*,
' and offered them to *Zachariah* his Brother, they being out
' of my Father's way to know what to do with ; but
' *Zachariah* has told the poor Butcher, who carried my
' Father's Letter, and written to my Father, that he can't

' meddle with them, but has gravely advised him to stick to
' the Landed Interest, and not mind Projects, for so the
' half-witted impudent Wretch calls receiving Mony for the
' Product of his Land. Thus, Sir, I have lost a good
' Husband by this Trick of Sir *Anthony*, and the whole
' Race of them wonder why our Family Curses them ; but,
' Sir, it is the Nature of the *Crabtrees* to be blind to the
' Evils they themselves commit, and don't think themselves
' guilty of Mischiefs, wherein they are the Original Causes,
' except they are the immediate Instruments. These gross
' Abuses the graceless Crew, by bragging of their Power,
' have committed against all the World without being found
' out and throughly explained, till the Devil, who owed
' them a Shame, prompted them to meddle with those that
' could draw their Pictures. I own'd to you, in the
' beginning of this Letter, that I was an angry Woman,
' and I think I have made it out that I have reason for it.
' I have nothing now left to divert my poor aking Heart
' from Reflection upon its Disappointment, but gratifying
' my Resentment against the Infamous Cause of it. When
' I reflect upon this Race, especially the Knight himself, I
' confess my Anger is immediately turned into Mirth ; for
' how is it possible that an ungainly Creature, who has what
' he is, writ in his Face, should impose upon any body?
' He looks so like a Cheat, that he passes upon People who
' do not know him from no other Advantage in the World,
' but that they are ashamed to be govern'd by so silly an
' Art as Physiognomy. With this mischievous Aspect there
' is something so awkard, so little, and briskly Comick in
' Sir *Anthony*'s Mein and Air, that one would think the
' Contempt of his Figure might save People from the
' Iniquity of his Designs ; but Sir *Anthony* has the Happi-
' ness next to a good Reputation, which is to be insensible

' of Shame, and therefore is as smug as he is ugly.   Forgive
' me personal Reflections, but ugly is a Woman's Word for
' Knavish.   I observe, Sir, you affect putting the Sentence
' of some Poet, *English* or *Latin*, at the top of your Paper;
' and as I desire you would let my Letter be as remarkable
' as possible, I beg you to put these Words out of Sir *John*
' *Suckling*'s Play of the Sad One, at the Head of this my
' Writing, except you would put in all my Letter, which I
' had much rather you would: The place in Sir *John*
' *Suckling* will agree well enough with the Knight; for tho'
' his Name is *Anthony*, and *Suckling* has used the Word
' *Robin*, every one of this Country will think him meant
' when you do but say *The Sad One*, for such indeed he is.
' The Passage is thus, A Poet and an Actor are introduced
' discoursing about Characters in a Play.   The Actor is
' telling the Author, that he wonders why he will represent
' what cannot be in Nature, an honest Lawyer : *Why*, says
' *Muliticarni*, (that is the Name of the Poet) *Dost think it*
' *impossible for a Lawyer to be honest ?*   The Actor answers,

> ' *As 'tis for a Lord-Treasurer to be poor,*
> ' *Or for a King not to be cozened :*
> ' *There's little* Robin, *in Debt within these three Years,*
> ' *Grown Fat and Full——*

' As for using the Words Treasurer instead of Steward,
' there is nothing in that, for Sir *Anthony*, in a snearing
' way calls himself so, and pretends he deserves that Word
' more than any one else who ever served her, tho' it's well
' known he has disparaged her more than any one that
' ever served any Body; and my Father says, since he has
' got me and the Tin Tallies lying upon his Hands, that he
' will send you an Account wherein he will prove, that if
' she had given him a Year's Income of all she has in the

' World to have nothing to say to him, she had saved above
' a Year's Revenue by it. But there is no dealing with
' him ; he has got all the Country to call the honest Man,
' who managed her Business before him, all the Names that
' Malice could invent ; so that whenever he is dismissed,
' he knows he cannot be worse used than the best Men
' have been before him. Thus Sir *Anthony* thinks himself
' secure against Defamation ; first, because he deserves all
' the Ill that can be said of him, and secondly, because the
' same thing has been said of those who deserve all the
' Praise which Language can bestow. I have a great deal
' more to say of the ugly Creature, but I had like to have
' forgot *Brickdust* and *Zachariah*. You must know they
' have different Apartments about Sir *Anthony*'s House, to
' examine every one who comes for Mony, or admit their
' Accounts. These Animals, if possible, are more hideous
' than Sir *Anthony* himself; they are both in Town, and
' they are as much desired in the Country as their Arrival
' in it formerly was feared and dreaded. The Presbyterian
' Ministers, in these Parts, have a very pleasant Tale of
' *Zachariah*, who, it seems, was made a Trustee in a
' Donation for Ministers dissenting from the Church of
' *England* ; the Description of Ministers dissenting from the
' Church of *England*, suits as well with Nonjurers as Dis-
' senters, and *Zachariah* being a new Convert, forsooth, to
' the Church, has a pious Compassion rather for those who
' were of our Church, and are gone higher, than to those
' who will not come up to it, and therefore, out of Scruple
' of Conscience, cheats the Dissenters. I desire you would
' be sure to print this, because it would be well that the
' Truth were known ; for some do not fail to say, that
' under the Notion of its being a Gift to pious Uses,
' *Zachariah* has reserved it for that good Christian himself.

' When *Zachariah* went through the Town of *Worcester*
' ——but that is a long Story——I had like to have forgot
' *Brickdust;* but what signifies talking of him——I remem-
' ber a whimsical Saying of one speaking of a silly Creature
' with a manly Aspect; he called him a *Cole-Black* silly
' Fellow, so I say *Brickdust* is a *soft ugly Cur,* he has a
' Phiz fit only for Accusation and Abuse; if he designed to
' commend, it would have that Effect; and it is Nonsense
' for you to set up for a *Lover,* when you let these Creatures
' go about to frighten Women with Child, and bear false
' Witness against honest Men. I fear I have said more
' than will come within your Paper, but pray don't leave
' any of it out, for my Lover was a very pretty Fellow, and
' was forced to leave me because of these cursed Tallies.

I am, dear Mr. MYRTLE,

very much Your Servant,

Susan Matchless.

Mr. MYRTLE,

' I Beg the Favour of you to acquaint the Town, that in
'   ' the   most   necessary   Earthen-Ware,   I have, with
' great Pains and Curiosity, wrought round the exterior
' Superficies of them, the true Effigies of Sir *Anthony*
' *Crabtree,* Mr. *Zachariah Crabtree,* and Mr. *Peter Brickdust.*
' They will be sold at all Potter's Shops within *London* and
' *Westminster* on the 19th Instant, and Country Customers
' may have them at a cheaper Rate.

Rubens Claywright.

No. 22.　　*Thursday, April* 15.

Secretum iter——　　　　　Hor.

THE Business of Love alters in every Family in *England*, and I must confess I did not sufficiently weigh the great Perplexity that I should fall into, from the vast Variety of Cases, when I undertook my present Province. The Author of the following Letters is in very whimsical Circumstances, which will be best represented by his Epistles.

　　SIR,

'AS I am about thirty, and of such a round untroubled 'Countenance as may make me appear not so much, 'I must complain to you of a general Calamity that 'obstructs or suspends the Advancement of the younger 'Men in the Pursuit of their Fortune. I now make Love 'to the Daughter of a Man of Business, who is so 'fantastical as to threaten to Marry the young Lady to a 'Contemporary of his own, I mean one of his own Years. 'He says no young Man can be good for any thing but 'filling an House full of Children, without being Wise 'enough to know how to provide for them. Now as I am 'to succeed in Love, as I can argue my Father-in-Law into 'an Opinion of my Ability for Business, give me leave to 'think it not Foreign to your Design, to Print my Thoughts 'concerning the Prejudices which Men in one Stage of Life 'have to those in another. The utmost Inconveniencies 'are owing to the Difficulty we meet with in being 'admitted into the Society of Men in Years, and adding 'thereby the early Knowledge of Men and Business to that

' of Books, for the reciprocal Improvement of each other.
' One of Fifty as naturally imagines the same Insufficiency
' in one of Thirty, as he of Thirty does in one of Fifteen,
' and each Age is thus left to instruct it self by the natural
' Course of its own Reflection and Experience. I am apt
' to think, that before Thirty a Man's natural and acquired
' Parts are at that Strength, as, with a little Experience, to
' enable him, (if ever he can be enabled) to acquit himself
' well in any Business or Conversation he shall be admitted
' into. As to the Objection, that those that have not been
' used to Business are consequently unfit for it, it might
' have been made one time or other against all Men that ever
' were born ; and is so general a one, that it is none at all.
' Besides, he that knew Man the best that ever any one did,
' says that *Wisdom cometh by Opportunity of Leisure, and he*
' *that hath little Business shall become Wise ;* and my Lord
' *Bacon* observes, that those Governments have been always
' the most happy, which have been administred by such as
' have spent part of their Life in Books and Leisure, and
' instances in the Governments of *Pius Quintus* and *Sixtus*
' *Quintus* about his own time ; who tho' they were
' esteemed but Pedantical Friars, proceeded upon truer
' Principles of State, than those who had had their Educa-
' tion in Affairs of State, and Courts of Princes. If this
' Rule holds in the dispatch of the most perplex'd Matters,
' as of Publick Politicks, it must of necessity in that of the
' common Divisions of Business, which every body knows
' are directed by Form, and require rather Diligence and
' Honesty, than great Ability in the Execution.

' A good Judgment will not only supply, but go beyond
' Experience ; for the latter is only a Knowledge that
' directs us in the Dispatch of Matters future, from the
' Consideration of Matters past of the same Nature ; but

' the former is a perpetual and equal Direction in every
' thing that can happen, and does not follow, but makes
' the Precedent that guides the other.

' THIS Everlasting Prejudice of the Old against the
' Young, heightens the natural Disposition of Youth to
' Pleasure, when they find themselves adjudged incapable
' of Business. Those among 'em therefore whose Circum-
' stances and way of Thinking will allow 'em such Free-
' dom, plunge themselves in all sensual Gratifications.
' Others of 'em, of a more regulated Turn of Thought, seek
' the Entertainment of Books and Contemplation, and are
' buried in these Pleasures. These Pursuits, during our
' middle Age, strengthen the Love of Retirement in the
' Sober Man, and make it necessary to the Libertine.
' They gain Philosophy enough by this time to be con-
' vinced 'tis their Interest to have as little Ambition as may
' be, and considering rather how much less they need to
' live happily, than how much more, can't conceive why
' they should trouble themselves about the raising a
' Fortune, which in the Pursuit must lessen their present
' Enjoyment, and in the Purchase cannot enlarge it.

' I confess the impious and impertinent way of Life and
' Conversation of Youth in general, exposes them to the
' just Disesteem of their Elders ; but where the contrary
' is found among any of them, it should be the more par-
' ticular Recommendation to their Patronage. There are
' some Observations, I have by Chance met with, so much
' in Favour of young Men, that I cannot supress them. As
' Sincerity is the chief Recommendation both in publick
' and private Matters, it is observed, that the Young are
' more sincere in the dispatch of Business, and Professions
' of Friendship, than those that are more advanc'd in
' Years : For they either prefer publick Reputation to

' private Advantage, or believe it the only way to it.   They
' are generally well-natur'd, as having not been acquainted
' with much Malice, or sower'd with Disappointment.   The
' less disposed to Pride or Avarice, as they have neither
' wanted or abounded.   They are unpractis'd in the ways
' of Flattery and Dissimulation, and think others practise it
' as little as themselves.   This arises from their Boldness,
' as having not been yet humbled by the Chances of Life,
' and their Credulity, as having not yet been often deceiv'd.
    ' I shall conclude by saying, 'tis very hard upon us young
' Fellows, that we are not to be trusted in Business and
' Conversation with those in Years, till due Age, together
' with its Consequences, ill Health and ill Humour, have
' mark'd us with a faded Cheek, a hollow Eye, a busie
' ruminating Forehead, and in short rendered us less cap-
' able of serving and pleasing them, than we were when we
' were thought unable to do either.   I beg your Pardon for
' so many serious Reflections, and your leave to add to
' them a Love-Letter to the Father, enclosed in one to the
' Daughter, and addressed to her for his Perusal.

I am, SIR,

Your most Humble Servant.

Madam,

'MY Life is wrapped up in you.   I disrelish every
     'Conversation, wherein there is not some mention
' made of you ; whenever you are named, I hear you com-
' mended, and that gives Ease to the Torment I am in,
' while I am forced to smother the Warmth of my Affection
' towards you.   You know your Father is not displeased
' that I Love you ; but I am, I know not how, to prefer
' your Interests to your self.   But all the Business of the

'World is Impertinence, and all its Riches Vexation, in
'comparison of the Joy there is in being understood.

  Madam,

   Your most Faithful,

     Most Devoted, Humble Servant.

'P.S. *When your Father asks whether I have writ, hide*
'*this, and show him the enclosed. Look displeased, and he*
'*will plead for me.*

  Madam,

' I Have a great Respect for you, but must beg you would
  'not take it amiss, if I can reckon no Woman a
'Beauty whose Father's Favour does not add to her other
'Qualifications. He is as I am, a Man of business, and I
'doubt not but he will acquaint you, that Business is to be
'minded ; your Declaration, joined with his in my Favour,
'will make me more frequent at your House, but till I
'know what I have to trust to, I do not think it is proper
'for me to intrude upon your Time and lose my own.

  I am, Madam,

   Your most humble Servant.

No. 23.   *Saturday, April* 17.

  Quod latet Arcanâ non enarrabile fibrâ. Pers.

Mr. MYRTLE,

'WHEN you first erected your Lodge, you then took
  'upon you to be a Patron of Lovers, and at the
'same time promised your Assistance to all those who
'shou'd address themselves to you for Advice, the better to
'conduct them thro' all those Paths of Love, which, it is to
'be presumed, you have often trod before them.

' IT is this Consideration which emboldens me to give

' you the trouble of this, without offering at any formal
' Apology for it.   It is a mighty Pleasure and a solid
' Satisfaction to a Man, to reflect that he has it in his
' Power to be serviceable to others ; and since I am con-
' fident of your Ability, if you deny me the Benefit of it, I
' shall grudge you the Possession of such an Advantage, and
' value you no more, tho' a Master in the Art of Love, than
' I would a Miser for his Wealth, when he poorly reserves
' it to himself, and can't find in his Soul to bestow the least
' part of it on the most needy and indigent.

'THAT you may be the better able to prescribe, I shall
' beg leave to lay my real Condition before you without
' Art or Dissimulation.   I am, in plain Terms, what you
' call a Rover, or a general Lover.   I am of the most
' perverse, untoward, amorous Constitution imaginable ; I
' have scarcely ever seen that Female who had not some
' Charm or other to catch my Heart with ; and I dare say
' I have been a Slave to more Mistresses than swell the
' Account of *Cowley's* Ballad called *The Chronicle.*   I have
' frequently been lost in Transports at the Sight of a *Chloe*
' or a *Sacharissa*, and have admired many an ugly *Corinna*
' for Wit or Humour.   *Myra* has charmed me ten thousand
' times with her Singing, and my Heart has leap'd for Joy
' when Miss *Aiery* has been dancing a Jig, or *Isabella* has
' moved a Minuet.   It has burnt and crackled like
' Charcoal at the flurt of a Fan, and I have sometimes fallen
' a Sacrifice to an hoop'd Petticoat.   In short, there is
' scarce a Woman, I ever laid my Eyes on, that I have not
' liked and loved, admired and wish'd for ; The Pretty, the
' Wise, the Witty, the Gay, the Prude and the Coquet, all, all
' from the fine Lady down to the dextrous *Molly* who waits
' with the Kettle at my Sister's Tea-Table, have made Scars
' or Wounds in my Heart.   And yet after all this——

' which is somewhat strange——My Heart is as whole
' as ever.——What I mean is this; that notwithstanding
' the Multiplicity of Darts which have been shot at me, yet
' they never made any lasting Impression on me, or have
' been able to throw me into an Humour serious enough to
' think of Marriage. Tho' I confess the Temper, I am
' now complaining of, has been exceeding troublesome to
' me, yet I could not help thinking Matrimony a Cure
' worse than the Disease. Beside, how shall I be certain I
' shan't be the same Latitudinarian in Love after I have
' swallowed the bitter Dose? It is for this Reason that I
' have long used my Endeavours to find out some other
' Remedy for my Distemper; and to that End I have had
' Recourse to all those famous Physicians who have pre-
' tended to write for the Good of those Persons who have
' been in my whimsical Circumstances——But, alas! after
' a long and tedious Consultation, among these mighty
' Professors, I could not perceive my self one Jot the
' better. I am convinced they are all a Parcel of Pretenders,
' and that I had no more Reason to expect any Benefit
' from them, than one afflicted with the Gout has to hope
' for an infallible Cure from your boasting sham Doctors
' who disperse their Bills and Advertisements thro' every
' Street in *London.*

' THE first I address'd myself to, was that *Galen* in
' Love, *Ovid.* The Fellow had a smooth Tongue, and
' really talked very prettily. He shew'd me a great many
' soft Letters of his own composing, told me some odd sur-
' prising Stories, made me sigh at his mournful Elegies, and
' promised me, that if I wou'd carefully observe his Rules,
' and follow those Directions laid down in his *Philo-dispen-*
' *satory,* or *Arte amandi,* I need not doubt but my Business
' was done. He delivered this with so serious an Air, that

'silly I began to believe him, and gather hopes of a perfect
'Recovery; till one Day, when I was giving great Atten-
'tion to him, I heard him break off in the midst of his
'Harangue, and immediately cry out in the Exclamatory
'Stile—

Hei mihi ! quòd nullis amor est medicabilis herbis.

'From that very Moment I thought him an ignorant
'Coxcomb, and never meddled with him since.

   'THE next I ventur'd upon was good *Abraham Cowley*,
'he was looked upon as a Proficient in his way, and was
'very much in Vogue among the Ladies, for gently hand-
'ling their Hearts, and easily getting at their Passions.
'His greatest Business lay among such as had but newly
'received their Wounds, and some expected great Refresh-
'ment from his balmy Compositions; but it has been said
'by others, that he was the worst in the World at a green
'Wound, and that whoever took him in hand when they
'were first hurt, they rather grew worse than better. How-
'ever, I was resolved to undergo one Course with him; I
'was introduced into his Company by a young Cousin of
'mine, who was at that time either in Love, or the Green-
'Sickness, and in a little time I was intimately acquainted
'with his *Mistress*. I was, I remember, mightily pleased
'to hear him tax the Ladies, and justifie his own Fickle-
'ness, by asking them, Cou'd they call the Shore Incon-
'stant, which kindly embraced every Wave?——Ah,
'think I ! This is a Doctor after my own Heart——his
'Case is exactly mine——But alas! I had not kept him
'Company long, before I discovered, that for all his Skill
'in Numbers, he was but an Ignorant Physician, since he
'cou'd not Cure himself. The third I went to was Mrs.
'*Behn*. She indeed, I thought, understood the Practick

' Part of Love better than the Speculative; but she was a
' dangerous Quack, for a sight of her always made my Dis-
' temper return upon me.   I liked some parts of her *Lovers*
' *Watch*, and wou'd have bought it from her: She told me
' she would hire the use out to me for a little time, but that
' she wou'd not sell it outright.

' THE last I advised with was the most renown'd *Isaac*
' *Bickerstaff*, Esq;   He was a Person of great Note and
' Fashion: Had very good Practice in this City for some
' Years: He had acquired a large Stock of Fame and
' Reputation for his Experience in the World, his Acquaint-
' ance with all the little Weaknesses and Infirmities
' incident to Human kind, and was more particularly had
' in Esteem for his Knowledge and Proficiency in the
' Occult Sciences.   From a Gentleman thus qualified, what
' might I not have hoped for ?   But, Sir, I soon understood
' that all his Predictions and Prophesies were but Dreams
' and Fables to amuse and divert us, and that he understood
' himself very well, when he called himself *Tatler.*

' AND now, Sir, after all these fruitless and repeated
' Enquiries, my last and only Refuge is in you.   You are
' certainly acquainted with all the Secret Springs of Love,
' and know the hidden Causes which make my Heart rise
' up to every She I meet.   You can't be ignorant how it
' comes to pass, that my Temper is so various ; and my
' Inclinations so floating and changeable, that one Object
' can't confine them, but like a wandring Bee they fly at
' every Flower.   I assure you, Mr. *Myrtle*, my present Dis-
' position is what gives me great Concern and Uneasiness.
' Tell me how I may reclaim this Volatile Heart of mine,
' this desultory Imagination, and keep it within bounds :
' Show me the way to fix it to one, or not Love at all.   I
' am not uneasie for your Answer, for I must own to you I

' feel but very little Pain ; but in some Distempers they say
' that is an ill Sign.

I am, SIR,

Your most Humble Servant,

Charles Lasie.

MY Correspondent is come already to the Condition he
desires; for what is not confined to one, is not Love at all;
and my Friend *Charles* needs not further Information in his
Case, but to be told, that he does not labour under the
Passion of Love, but the Vice of Wantonness.

No. 24   *Tuesday, April* 20.

There dwelt the Scorn of Vice, and Pity too.   Waller.

TRUE Virtue distinguishes it self by nothing more con-
spicuously than Charity towards those who are so
unhappy as to have, or be thought to have, taken a contrary
Course ; it is in the very Nature of Virtue to rejoice in all
new Converts towards its Interests, and bewail the Loss of
the most inconsiderable Votaries. It would perhaps be
thought a Severity to make Conclusions of the innate Goodness of Ladies at a Visit, by this Rule ; Beauty, Wit and
Virtue, in those Conversations, generally receive all the
Diminution imaginable ; and little Faults, Imperfections
and Misfortunes, are aggravated not without Bitterness.

DICTYNNA, tho' she is commended for singular Prudence and Oeconomy, appears in Conversation never to
have known what it is to be careful.

DECIA, who has no Virtue, or any thing like it but the
forbearance of Vice, cannot endure the Applause of

Dictynna. Ladies who are impatient of what is said to the Advantage of others, do not consider that they lay themselves open to all People of Discernment, who know that it is the want of good Qualities in themselves which makes People impatient of the Acknowledgment of them in others.

Among the many Advantages which one Sex has over the other, there is none so conspicuous, as, that the Fame of Men grows rather more just and certain by Examination; that of Women is almost irreparably lost by so much as a disadvantageous Rumour. This Case is so tender, that in order to the redress of it, it is more safe to try to dissuade the Aspersers from their Iniquity, than exhort the Innocent to such a Fortitude as to neglect their Calumny.

IT should, methinks, be a Rule to suspect every one who insinuates any thing against the Reputation of another, of the Vice with which they charge their Neighbour; for it is very unlikely it should flow from the Love of Virtue: The Resentment of the Virtuous towards those who are fallen, is that of Pity, and that is best exerted in Silence on the occasion. What then can be said to the numerous Tales that pass to and fro in this Town, to the Disparagement of those who have never offended their Accusers? As for my part, I always wait with Patience, and never doubt of Hearing in a little time for a Truth, the same Guilt of any Woman which I find she reports of another. It is, as I said, unnatural it should be otherwise; the Calumny usually flows from an Impatience of living under Severity, and they report the Sallies of others against the time of their own Escape. How many Women would be Speechless, if their Acquaintance were without Faults. There is a great Beauty in Town very far gone in this Vice. I have taken the Liberty to write her the following Epistle by the Penny-Post.

Madam,

'I Have frequently had the Honour of being in your
'Company, and should have had a great deal of
'delight in it, had you not pleased to imbitter that Happi-
'ness by the unmerciful Treatment you give all the rest of
'your Sex. Several of those I have heard you use
'unkindly were my particular Friends and Acquaintance.
'I can assure you, all the Advantage you had above those
'you lessened on these Occasions, was, that you were not
'absent, for the Company longed for the same Opportunity
'of speaking as freely of you. Believe me, your own Dress
'sits never the better on you, for tearing other People's
'Cloaths. While you are rifling every one that falls in
'your way, you cannot imagine how much that Fury dis-
'composes your own Figure. You believed you carried all
'before you the last time I had the Happiness to be where
'you were. As soon as your Cousin (whom you are too
'inadvertent to observe does not want Sense) had
'mentioned an agreeable young Lady which she met at a
'Visit in *Soho Square,* you immediately contradicted her,
'and told her you had seen the Lady, and were so unhappy
'that you could not observe those Charms in her. Her
'Name, says your Cousin, is Mrs. *Dulcett:* The same, said
'you. Your Cousin replied, She is Tall and Graceful; you
'again with a scornful Smile, She is Long and Confident:
'But, says your Kinswoman, I cannot but think her Eye
'has a fine Languor; I don't know but she might, said
'you, if one could see her awake, but that Sleepiness and
'Insensibility in them added to her Ungainliness, makes
'me doubt whether I ever saw her, but as walking in her
'Sleep. Well, but her Understanding has something in it
'very lively and diverting; Ay, says you, they that will
'Talk all, or have Memories, cannot but utter something

' now and then that is passable. Your Cousin seem'd at a
' loss what to say in support of one she had pronounced so
' agreeable, and therefore she retired to the Lady's Circum-
' stances (since you had disallowed every thing in her
' Person) and said, her Fortune would make up for all, for
' she had now ten thousand Pounds, and would, if her
' Brother died, have almost two thousand a Year. This
' too you knew the contrary of, and gave us to understand
' the utmost of her Fortune was four Thousand, and the
' Brother's Estate had a very heavy Mortgage, and when
' cleared would not be a neat Thousand a Year. Your
' Cousin, when you took so much Pains to contradict her
' Misrepresentations, grew grave with you, and told you,
' Since you were so Positive, you were the only one in
' Town who did not think Mrs. *Dulcett*, besides her being a
' considerable Fortune, a Woman of Wit, that danced
' gracefully, sang charmingly, has the best Mein, the
' prettiest way in every thing she did, that she had the least
' Affectation, the most Merit, was——Upon which you, with
' the utmost impatience, after ruffling your Fan, and riggling
' in your Seat, as if you had heard your Mother abused,
' rose up, and declaring you did not expect to be allowed
' one Word more in the Conversation, since your Cousin
' had once got the Discourse, left the Room. Your Cousin
' held the Lady of the House from following you out, and,
' instead of the Anger we thought her in when you were in
' the Room, fell into the most violent Laughter. When she
' came to her self, she prevented what we were going to say
' on the Occasion, by telling us, there was no such Creature
' in nature as Mrs. *Dulcett*, that she had laid this Plot
' against you for some Days, and was resolved to expose
' you for that scandalous Humour of yours, of allowing no
' Body to have any tolerable good Qualities but your self:

' You see, said she, how suddenly she made Objections,
' from the sort of Character I gave the Woman, assigning
' the proper Imperfection to the Quality in her according
' to my Commendation. I think we said all together,
' What, no such Woman in the World? What, said the
' Lady of the House, she to be so particular in the Estate
' mortgaged, and all those Dislikes to one she never saw, to
' one not in being, to one you had invented !—You may
' easily imagine what Raillery passed on the Occasion, and
' how you were used after such a Demonstration of your
' Censoriousness.

' I desire whenever hereafter you have the evil Spirit
' upon you to lessen any Body you hear commended, to
' think of Mrs. *Dulcett*: If you do not, you may assure
' your self, you will be told of her ; among your Acquaint-
' ance, whenever any one is spoken ill of, Mrs. *Dulcett* is
' the Word, and no one minds what you say after you have
' been thus detected. I advise you to go out of Town this
' Season, go into a Milk Diet, and when you return with
' Country Innocence in your Blood, I will do Justice to
' your good Humour, and am,

　　　Madam,

　　　Your most Obedient, Humble Servant,

　　　　　　　Marmaduke Myrtle.

THE painful manner Women usually receive favourable Accounts of one another, shows that the Ill-nature in
which this young Woman was detected, is not an uncommon
Infirmity. But let every Woman know, she cannot add to
her self what she takes from another ; but all that she
bestows upon another, will, by the discerning World, be
restored ten-fold ; and there can be no better Rule or
Description of a right Disposition than this,

There dwelt the Scorn of Vice, and Pity too.

The Scorn of it, in Virtuous Persons, is in respect to themselves, the Pity in regard to others.

No. 25. *Thursday, April* 22.

------ *Quid non mortalia pectora cogis* ---- Virg.

To Mr. MYRTLE.

SIR,

I Suppose that you begin to repent you Published my last Letter to you, since your late Indulgence to me occasions this frequent Trouble; I don't know, Sir, what it may be to you, but I am sure it is real Pleasure to me to embrace all Opportunities of shewing my self your humble Servant; therefore give me leave to talk before so great a Master of Love, and to use the Trite Simile of making a Declaration of War before *Hannibal.*

' AMONG all those Passions, to which the frailty and
' weakness of Man subject him, there is not any that
' extends such a boundless and despotick Empire over the
' whole Species, as that of Love. The Meek, the Mild,
' and the Humble are Strangers to Envy, Anger, and
' Ambition; but neither the Malicious, the Cholerick, or
' the Proud can say their Hearts have been always free
' from the Power of Love. This has subdued the exalted
' Minds of the most aspiring Tyrants, and has melted the
' most Sanguine Complexion into an effeminate Softness.
' An undaunted Hero has been known to tremble when he
' approached the Fair, and the mighty *Hercules* let fall his

'Club at a Woman's Feet.   The Scholar, the Statesman,
'and the Soldier have all been Lovers, and the most
'ignorant Swain has neglected both his Flocks and Pipe to
'woe *Daphne* or *Sylvia.*

'BUT tho' Love be a Passion which is thus common to
'all, yet how widely do its Votaries differ in their manner
'of Address?   The pleasing Enjoyment of the admired
'Object is what they all pursue, and yet few agree in the
'same Methods of obtaining their Ends, or accomplishing
'their Desires.   Every Lover has his particular Whim, and
'each resolves to follow his own way.   Some fancy Mony
'has a Sovereign Charm in it, and that no Rhetorick is so
'irresistibly prevailing as a Golden Shower.   Others think
'to take their Mistresses as they do Towns, by Bombard-
'ing or Undermining them ; if they can't beat them down
'by force of Arms, they'll try to blow them up with false
'Musick.   Some attempt to frighten their Mistresses into a
'Compliance, and threaten to hang or drown themselves, if
'they refuse to pity them.   Others turn Tragedians, and
'expect to move Compassion by a falling Tear, or a rising
'Sigh.   Some depend upon Dress, and conclude that if
'they can catch the Eye, they'll soon seize the Heart.   One
'Man affects Gravity, and another Levity, because some
'Women prefer the Solemnity of a *Spaniard* to the Gayety
'of a *Frenchman.*   An handsom Leg has found the way to
'a Widow's Bed, and a Coquette has been won by a Song
'or a Caper.   A Prude may be caught by a precise Look
'and a demure Behaviour, and a Platonick Lady has lain
'with her humble Servant out of a refin'd Friendship, when
'she would not listen to a Declaration of Love.   Some will
'be attacked in Mood and Figure ; and others will have it,
'that a great Scholar will never make a kind Husband.
'The witty *Clara* is delighted with Impertinence, and a

' celebrated Toast has languished for the beautiful Outside
' of a painted Butterfly. Some Women are allured by the
' resemblance of their own Follies ; and I have seen a Rake,
' by the help of a whining Accent, triumph over a sanctified
' Quaker.

 ' But of all the Arts which have been practised by the
' Men on the other Sex, I have not observed any kind of
' Address which has been so generally successful as Flattery.
' Whether it be, that by making a Woman in Love with her
' self, you thereby engage her to love the Person who
' makes her so ; as who would not be apt to be fond of the
' Cause which produces so agreeable an Effect? Or
' whether the Partiality and Self-Love, which most Women
' abound in, does the more readily induce them to believe,
' that all the Praise which is given them is really due to
' their Merit, and therefore they admire you for your
' Justice. Or whatever other Reason may possibly be
' assigned for this Weakness, I shall not now go about to
' enquire ; but so it is, that the shortest and surest way to a
' Woman's Heart is thro' the Road of skilful Flattery.
' This like a subtle Poyson insinuates it self almost into
' every Female, and a Dose of it rightly prepared seldom
' fails to produce an extraordinary Operation. Like a
' delicious Cordial it meets with an universal Acceptance
' and Approbation, while Sincerity and Plain-dealing are
' looked upon as nauseous and disgustful Physick. In
' Opposition to what I here advance, it may perhaps be
' said, we may love the Treason, and yet hate the Traitor.
' How true this Maxim may be in Politicks (Treachery
' being a Moral Evil, which, tho' of Use to us for our Safety,
' is yet sufficient to beget an Aversion in us towards the
' Wretch who is guilty of it) I shan't dispute ; but I am sure
' in Love Affairs it will scarcely hold. For she must be a

' Woman of uncommon Virtues and Qualifications, who can
' so nicely distinguish between the Gift and the Giver, as to
' refuse the one, and yet receive the other.   They do not
' think Flattery a Vice, and therefore can't be persuaded
' to dislike a Lover for being a Courtier; nay, tho' they are
' conscious of some of their own Imperfections, yet if their
' Admirers are not quick-sighted enough to discern them,
' they are willing to impute their Blindness to their Love;
' nay, tho' some Defects are grossly visible even to the
' Lover, yet if he will compliment his Mistress with what she
' really wants, I dare appeal to the whole Sex, whether
' either such Incense or the Offerer of it be one Jot nearer
' the losing their Favour, and whether they are not ever
' delighted with both the Delusion and the Deceiver.   But
' if they really believe themselves as amiable as the
' Flatterer tells them they are, then, in point of Gratitude,
' they conclude themselves obliged to think kindly of their
' Benefactor, that he is one, none can deny, since the
' greatest Kindness you can confer on a Mistress are Praise
' and Commendation.   These are those melting Sounds,
' that soft Musick which never sounds harshly in a
' Woman's Ear.   Before I conclude this Paper, I shall
' relate a Story which I know to be Fact.

' MISS *Witwou'd* was a young Gentlewoman of good
' Extraction and an handsome Fortune.   She was exactly
' shaped and very pretty: She dress'd and danc'd genteely,
' and sung sweetly : But notwithstanding these Advantages,
' (which one wou'd imagine were sufficient to make any one
' Woman satisfied) she had an insufferable Itch after the
' Reputation of a Wit.   She fancied she had as much Wit as
' she wanted (tho' indeed she wanted more than ever she'll
' have) and this Conceit made her fond of scribbling and shew-
' ing her Follies that way, as taking great Delight in Applause.

'MY Friend *Meanwell* is a Gentleman of good Sense
' and a sound Judgment, he is a professed Enemy to
' Flattery, and is of Opinion, that to commend without just
' Grounds, is to rob the Meritorious of that which only of
' Right belongs to them.　He says a Compliment is a
' modish Lie, and declares he wou'd not be guilty of so
' much Baseness as to cry up a beautiful Fool for Wit, not
' even in her own hearing, tho' he were sure to have his
' Falshood rewarded by the Enjoyment of his Mistress.
' Undeserved Applause is to him an Argument of either
' want of Judgment or of Insincerity, and he resolves he
' will never go about to establish another's Reputation at
' the Expence of his own.　With these honest useless
' Qualities he has made long but fruitless Courtship to
' young Miss *Witwou'd.　Ned Courtly* is a new but violent
' Pretender to the same Lady.　*Ned* is a shallow well
' dress'd Coxcomb : He was bred at Court, and is of a
' graceful and confident Behaviour, tempered with Civility.
' The shallow Thing can wait at a Distance, and look at
' her, and with a Smile approach her, and say, Your Lady-
' ship is divinely pretty.　He is wonderful happy also in
' particular Discoveries, and whenever he renews a Visit to
' his Mistress, she is sure of being presented with some
' additional Charm, which would have for ever lain con-
' ceal'd, had not *Ned* most luckily found it out.　*Ned*
' quickly perceiv'd Miss *Witwou'd's* weak side, and care-
' fully watch'd all Opportunities of making his Advantage of
' it.　Miss grows enamour'd of *Ned's* Company, and begins
' to despise *Meanwell* as an unpolish'd Clown.　She likes
' *Ned* as she does her Glass, and for the same Reason, that
' it always shows her her Beauties ; and she takes as much
' Pleasure in hearing him, injudiciously as he does it, give
' her also the Beauties of her Mind, as she does to see the

' Glass reflect those of her Body.   One Evening, last Week,
' *Meanwell* had the Honour to sup with her; the Cloth
' being taken away, she delivered him a Copy of Verses,
' which she said had been the Product of her leisure Hours,
' and desired the Opinion of so good a Judge.   My friend
' had the Patience to read them twice over, finds nothing
' extraordinary in them, so smilingly returns them with a
' silent Bow.   He was just going to speak his Mind
' impartially, when in came *Ned Courtly.*   He perused and
' hummed them over in a seeming Rapture, look'd at the
' Lady and then at the Paper for almost half an Hour in
' full Admiration——And then with a better Air than ever
' Critick spoke, he pronounced that the Author of those
' Verses had *Congreve*'s Wit and *Waller*'s Softness, and
' that there was nothing so compleatly perfect in all their
' Works.———The Consequence of this was——*Meanwell*
' was discarded, because he would be rigidly Honest in
' Trifles; and *Ned* made his Mistress his Wife, because in
' spite of Nature he allowed her a Poetess, or, perhaps, very
' justly, because he really thinks her so.

I am, SIR,

Your most humble Servant,

Vesuvius.

No. 25.   *Saturday, April* 24.

Durum ; sed levius fit patientiâ
Quicquid corrigere est nefas.   Hor.

SIR,

' I Find you are an Author who are more inclined to give
'   your Advice in Cases which raise Mirth in your
' Readers, than in those which are of a more serious and

' melancholy Nature. But you know very well, that in
' virtuous Love there are many unhappy Accidents which
' may lay a claim to your Compassion, and consequently to
' your Assistance. I my self am one of those distressed
' Persons, who may come in for my Share of your Concern.
' About eight Years ago I married a young Woman of great
' Merit, who was every way qualified for a Bosom Friend,
' that is, for advancing the innocent Pleasures of Life and
' alleviating its Misfortunes. She had all the good Sense I
' ever met with in any Male Acquaintance, with all that
' Sweetness of Temper which is peculiar to the most
' engaging of her Sex. Life was too happy with such a
' Companion in it ; for I must tell you, with Tears, that she
' was snatched away from me by a Feaver about twelve
' Months since. I was the more unable to bear this
' unspeakable Loss, as having conversed with very few
' besides her self during the whole Time of our Marriage.
' We were the whole World to one another, and whilst we
' lived together, tho' scarce either of us were ever in Com-
' pany, we were never alone. Being thus cut off from the
' Society of others, and from the Person who was most dear
' to me, I naturally betook my self to the reading of such
' Books as might tend to my Relief under this my great
' Calamity; after many others which I have perused upon
' this Occasion, I lately had the good Fortune to meet with
' a little Volume of Sermons, just Published, entitled, *Of*
' *Contentment, Patience, and Resignation to the Will of God,*
' *in several Sermons, by* Isaac Barrow, *D.D.*

  ' THE Duty of Contentment is so admirably explained,
' recommended, and enforced by Arguments drawn from
' Reason and Religion, that it is impossible to read what
' he has said on this Subject without being the better for it.
' I shall beg leave to transcribe two or three Passages,

‘ which more immediately affected me, as they came home
‘ to my own Condition.

‘ *THE Death of Friends doth, it may be, oppress thee with*
‘ *Sorrow. But canst thou lose thy best Friend? canst thou*
‘ *lose the Presence, the Conversation, the Protection, the*
‘ *Advice, the Succour of God? Is he not immortal, is he not*
‘ *immutable, is he not inseparable from thee? Canst thou be*
‘ *destitute of Friends, whilst he stands by thee? Is it not an*
‘ *Affront, an heinous Indignity to him, to behave thy self as*
‘ *if thy Happiness, thy Welfare, thy Comfort, had Depend-*
‘ *ance on any other but him? Is it not a great Fault to be*
‘ *unwilling to part with any thing, when he calleth for it?*
‘ *Neither is it a loss of thy Friend, but a separation for a*
‘ *small time; he is only parted from thee, as taking a little*
‘ *Journey, or going for a small time to Repose; within a*
‘ *while we shall be sure to meet again, and joyfully to con-*
‘ *gratulate, if we are fit, in a better Place, and more happy*
‘ *State;* Præmisimus, non amisimus; *we have sent him*
‘ *thither before, not quite lost him from us.*

‘ *THY Friend, if he be a good Man (and in such Friend-*
‘ *ships only, we can have a true Satisfaction) is himself in no*
‘ *bad Condition, and doth not want thee; thou canst not*
‘ *therefore reasonably grieve for him; and to grieve only for*
‘ *thy self, is perverse Selfishness and Fondness.*

‘ WHAT follows runs on in the same Vein of good
‘ Sense, tho’ it is a Consolation which I my self cannot
‘ make use of.

‘ *But thou hast lost a great Comfort of thy Life, and*
‘ *Advantage to thy Affairs here? Is it truly so? Is it*
‘ *indeed an irreparable Loss, even secluding the Consideration*
‘ *of God, whose Friendship repaireth all possible Loss?*
‘ *What is it, I pray, that was pleasant, convenient, or useful*
‘ *to thee in thy Friend, which may not in good measure be*

' *supplied here ?   Was it a Sense of hearty good Will, was it a*
' *sweet freedom of Conversation, was it sound Advice, or kind*
' *Assistance in thy Affairs ?   And mayst thou not find those*
' *which are alike able, and willing to minister those Benefits ?*
' *May not the same means, which knit him to thee, conciliate*
' *others also to be thy Friends ?   He did not alone surely pos-*
' *sess all the Good-nature, all the Fidelity, all the Wisdom in*
' *the World, nor hath carried them all away with him ?*
' *Other Friends therefore thou mayst find to supply his room ;*
' *all good Men will be ready, if thou art good, to be thy*
' *Friends : They will heartily love thee, they will be ready to*
' *chear thee with their sweet and wholsome Society, to yield*
' *thee their best Counsel and Help upon any Occasion.   Is it*
' *not therefore a fond and unaccountable Affection to a kind of*
' *Personality, rather than want of a real Convenience, that*
' *disturbeth thee ?*

' *IN fine, the same Reasons which in any other Loss may*
' *comfort us, should do it also in this ; neither a Friend, nor*
' *any other good thing we can enjoy under any Security of not*
' *soon losing it : Our Welfare is not annexed to one Man, no*
' *more than to any other inferior thing ; this is the Condition*
' *of all good things here, to be transient and separable from*
' *us, and accordingly we should be affected towards them.*

Fragile fractum est, mortale mortuum est.

' GIVE me leave to cite also out of this great Author
' a very agreeable Story which is taken from *Julian's*
' Epistles, and which perhaps pleases me the more, as it is
' applicable to my own case.
' *WHEN once a great King did excessively and obstinately*
' *grieve for the Death of his Wife, whom he tenderly loved, a*
' *Philosopher observing it, told him, that he was ready to*
' *comfort him, by restoring her to Life, supposing only that he*

' *would supply what was needful towards the performing it;*
' *the King said he was ready to furnish him with any thing;*
' *the Philosopher answered, that he was provided with all*
' *things necessary except one thing: What that was the King*
' *demanded; he replied, That if he would upon his Wife's*
' *Tomb inscribe the Names of three Persons who never*
' *mourned, she presently would revive. The King, after*
' *Enquiry, told the Philosopher that he could not find one*
' *such Man: Why then, O absurdest of all Men (said the*
' *Philosopher smiling) art thou not ashamed to moan as if*
 thou hadst alone fallen into so grievous a Case; when as
' *thou canst not find one Person that ever was free from*
' *such Domestick Affliction. So might the naming one Person,*
' *exempted from Inconveniences like to those we undergo, be*
' *safely proposed to us as a certain Cure of ours; but if we*
' *find the Condition impossible, then is the generality of the*
' *Case a sufficient ground of Content to us; then may we, as*
' *the wise Poet adviseth, Solace our own Evils by the Evils of*
' *others.*

 ' I have observed, Sir, in your Writings many Hints and
' Observations upon the most common Subjects which
' appeared new to me ; I should therefore beg of you to
' turn your Thoughts upon that melancholy Accident which
' is the Occasion of this Letter. If you can give me any
' additional Motives of Comfort, I shall receive them as
' a very great Piece of Charity, and I believe you may
' oblige many others who are under the same kind of
' Affliction, as well as,

    SIR,

      Your most humble Servant,

        R. B.

THIS Gentleman has too favourable an Opinion of me,
if he thinks me capable of adding any thing material to

what has been handled by the excellent Author whom he has mentioned in his Letter. That learned Man always exhausts his Subjects, and leaves nothing for those who come after him. He was not only a great Divine, but was perfectly well acquainted with all the ancient Writers of Morality, whose Thoughts he has every where digested into his Writings; and, at the same time, had a most inexhaustible Fund of Observation and good Sense in himself. He has scarce a Sermon that might not be spun out into a hundred modish Discourses from the Pulpit : For which Reason I am very glad to find, that we are likely to have a new Edition of his Works.

No. 27. *Tuesday, April 27.*

Ingenuas didicisse fideliter Artes
Emollit mores—— Ovid.

AMONG the many Letters of Correspondents, I have of late received but very few which are not mixed with Satyr. I am a little tired with such Ideas as the reading those Performances raise in the Mind; so are those who imagine they are alluded to by what has passed through my Hands, and I doubt not but my Readers in general cease also to be delighted with that kind of Reflections. When therefore it is irksom to us all, it is time to pass to more pleasing Arguments. But as I told the Town at my first setting out, that Mr. *Severn* was my Favourite of all the Characters which I have represented to compose our little Club mentioned in my first Paper, I shall declare my self further on this Subject, by Printing my Letter I have writ to Mr. *Severn*, which he will receive to Morrow Morning.

To Mr. Severn.

SIR,

'THIS comes with a Sett of *Latin* Authors just now
'Published by *Tonson.* You see they are in
'Twelves, and fit to be carried on Occasion in the Pocket.
'He sent me two Setts, one for my self, the other for the
'Gentleman whom I meant by Mr. *Severn.* You will please
'therefore to accept the Present he makes you. You need
'not be enjoined to be Partial to them as they are a Gift;
'for as you'll observe, Mr. *Maittaire* has had the Care of
'the Edition; you need not be further encouraged to
'recommend them to your Friends and Acquaintance.
'The Learned World is very much obliged to that Gentle-
'man for his useful Labours; and his elegant Addresses (to
'those to whom he Dedicates the Book) as well as to the
'Reader in general, show him a perfect Master in what he
'undertakes, for he introduces his Authors in a Stile as
'pure as their own. You know he had the good Fortune
'to live in the Favour, and, as it were, under the Patronage
'of the famous Dr. *Busby*, to whose great Talents and
'Knowledge in the Genius of Men we owe very great
'Ornaments of this Age, and the supply of Men of Letters
'and Capacity for many Generations, or rather Classes of
'remarkable Men during his long and eminent Life. I
'must confess, (and I have often reflected upon it) that I
'am of Opinion *Busby*'s Genius for Education had as great
'an Effect upon the Age he lived in, as that of any ancient
'Philosopher, without excepting one, had upon his Contem-
'poraries. Tho' I do not perceive that admirable Man is
'remembred by them, at least not recorded by them, with
'half the Veneration he deserves. I have known great Num-
'bers of his Scholars, and am confident, I could discover a
'Stranger who had been such, with a very little Conversation;

' Those of great Parts, who have passed through his Instruc-
' tion, have such a peculiar Readiness of Fancy and Delicacy
' of Taste, as is seldom found in Men educated elsewhere,
' tho' of equal Talents; and those who were of slower Capaci-
' ties, have an Arrogance (for Learning without Genius
' always produces that) that sets them much above greater
' Merit that grew under any other Gardiner. He had a
' Power of raising what the Lad had in him to the utmost
' height in what Nature designed him; and it was not his
' Fault, but the effect of Nature, that there were no indiffer-
' ent People came out of his Hands ; but his Scholars were
' the finest Gentlemen, or the greatest Pedants in the Age.
' The Soil which he manured always grew fertile, but it is
' not in the Planter to make Flowers of Weeds ; but what-
' ever it was under *Busby*'s Eye, it was sure to get forward
' towards the Use for which Nature designed it.

' BUT I forgot what I sate down to write upon, which
' was to hand to you these pretty Volumes of *Terence, Salust,*
' *Phædrus, Lucretius, Velleius Paterculus* and *Justin :* But it
' will be said how comes this matter to have at all a place in
' the *Lover ?* Why very properly ; for to you whose chief
' Art in recommending your self, is to Act and Speak like a
' Man of Virtue and Sense, that which contributes to make
' you wiser and better, is serviceable to you as you are a
' Gentleman and a Lover. Take my word for it, the oftener
' you take these Books in your Hand, you will find your
' Mind the more prepared for doing the most ordinary
' things with a good Grace and Spirit ; that is, the agreeable
' Thoughts of these Writers frequently employing your
' Imagination, will naturally and insensibly affect your
' Words and Actions. It will, in a greater degree, do what
' good Company does to all who frequent it, make you in
' your Air and Mein like those with whom you Converse.

‘ Mr. *Maittaire* has promised to go thro’ the best
‘ remaining Authors with the same Diligence : The large
‘ Indexes which lead with so much ease to any beautiful
‘ Passage one has a mind for, are of great Use and Pleasure.
‘ They are made with so much Judgment and Care, that
‘ they serve the purpose of an Abbreviation of the Book, and
‘ carry a secret Instruction, in that they lay the Sense of the
‘ Author still closer in Words of his own, or as good as his
‘ own. I am mighty well content with the Province of
‘ being esteemed but a Publisher, if I can be so happy as to
‘ quicken the Passage of useful Arts in the World ; and I
‘ wish this Paper’s coming, where otherwise Works of this
‘ kind would not be spoken of, may be of any Use to a Man
‘ who deserves so well of all Lovers of Learning as Mr.
‘ *Maittaire.* Perhaps a fond Mother may, by my Means,
‘ lighten her Son’s Satchel, and get him these little Volumes
‘ instead of the heavy Load the Boy was before encumbered
‘ with ; and her own Eyes may be judge, that this is a Print
‘ which cannot hurt the Childs.

   ‘ BUT I must leave these Ancients, and give a cast of my
‘ Office to a Living Writer, a Sister of the Quill.

   ‘ THE Sentiments and Inclinations of my Mind are so
‘ naturally turned to Love, that it is with a great deal of
‘ Pleasure I frequent the Play-house, where I have often an
‘ Opportunity of seeing this Passion represented in all its
‘ different Shapes. I have for some years been so constant
‘ a Customer to the Theatre, that I have got most of our
‘ celebrated Plays by heart ; for which reason it is with more
‘ than ordinary Pleasure that I hear the Actors give out a
‘ new one. It is no small Satisfaction to me, that I know
‘ we are to be entertained to Night with a Comedy from the
‘ same Hand that writ *the Gamester* and *the Busie Body*.
‘ The deserved Success these Plays met with, is a certain

' Demonstration that Wit alone is more than sufficient to
' supply all the Rules of Art. The Incidents in both those
' Pieces are so dexterously managed, and the Plots so
' ingeniously perplexed, as shew them at once to be the
' Invention of a Wit and a Woman. The Curious will
' observe the same happy Conduct in the Entertainment of
' this Night; and as we have but one *British* Lady who
' employs her Genius for the Drama, it would be a shameful
' Reflection on the Polite of both Sexes, should she want
' any Encouragement the Town can give her. I desire your
' Interest in her behalf, and am,

SIR,

Your most Obedient Servant,

Marmaduke Myrtle.

No. 28.   *Thursday, April* 29.

————*Nihil invitæ tristis custodia prodest:*
Quam peccare pudet, Cynthia, tuta sat est.

Propert.

MY Correspondents shall do my Business for me to Day.

Mr. MYRTLE,

' I Throw this Letter from two Pair of Stairs, with half a
' Crown with it, in an old Glove, in hopes he that
' takes it up (for I am watching till a Porter, or some such
' body passes by) will carry it to your *Lodge.* I have none
' to complain to but your self. I am locked up for fear of
' making my Escape to a Gentleman, whose Addresses I
' received by my Father's Approbation, tho' now his Pre-
' tensions are disallowed for the sake of a richer Man ; I

' have no help in this miserable Condition, nor Means to
' relieve my self, but by desiring you to Print the enclosed
' in your very next *Lover*.   The Gentleman who is to marry
' me, has visited me twice or thrice alone, and indeed I see
' such infallible Marks of the most unfeigned and respectful
' Passion towards me, that it is with great Anguish I write
' to him in the Sincerity of my Heart, which I know will be
' a sincere Affliction to him.   It is no matter for a Direc-
' tion by his Name ; he reads your Paper, and will too soon
' gather that the Circumstances of my Letter can concern
' only himself.

  SIR,
" IT is a very ill Return which I make to the Respect
   " you have for me, when I acknowledge to you, that,
" tho' the Day for our Marriage is appointed, I am incap-
" able of loving you ; you may have observed, in the long
" Conversations we have had at those times that we were
" lately left together, that some Secret hung upon my
" Mind : I was obliged to an ambiguous Behaviour, and
" durst not reveal my self further, because my Mother,
" from a Closet near the Place where we sate, could both
" hear and see our Conversation.   I have strict Commands
" from both my Parents to receive you, and am undone for
" ever, except you will be so kind and generous as to refuse
" me.   Consider, Sir, the Misery of bestowing your self upon
" one who can have no Prospect of Happiness but from
" your Death.   This is a Confession made perhaps with an
" offensive Sincerity, but that Conduct is much to be pre-
" ferred to a covert Dislike, which could not but pall all
" the Sweets of Life, by imposing on you a Companion that
" doats and languishes for another.   I will not go so far as
" to say, my Passion for the Gentleman whose Wife I am

" by Promise, would lead me to any thing criminal against
" your Honour; I know it is dreadful enough to a Man of
" your Sense to expect nothing but forced Civilities in
" return for tender Endearments, and cold Esteem for
" unreserved Love. If you will on this occasion let Reason
" take Place of Passion, I doubt not but Fate has in store
" for you some worthier Object of your Affection, in recom-
" pence of your Goodness to the only Woman that could
" be insensible of your Merit.

I am, SIR,

Your most humble Servant,

M. H.

Mr. Myrtle,

' I Am a young Woman perfectly at my own Liberty, Two
' and twenty, in the height and affluence of good
' Health, good Fortune, and good Humour; but I know
' not how, I must acknowledge there is something Solitary
' and Distrest in the very natural Condition of our Sex, till
' we have wholly rejected all thoughts of Marriage, or made
' our Choice. The Man has not yet appeared to these
' Eyes, whom I could like for a Husband. I therefore
' apply my self to you, to let the Town know there is, not
' many Furlongs from your *Lodge*, one that lives with too
' much Ease, and is undone for want of that acceptable
' kind of Uneasiness, the Importunity of Lovers. If you
' can send me half a dozen, I promise to take him who
' addresses me with most Gallantry and Wit, and to yeild
' to one of them within six Months after their first Declar-
' ation that they are my Servants; but at the same time I
' expect them to fight one another for me, and promise to
' be particularly Civil to him who first has his Arm in a
' Scarf for my Sake. I expect that they turn their Fury

'and Skill towards disarming, or slightly wounding, not
'killing one another; for I shall not take it for Respect to
'me to lessen the Number of my Slaves; at the same time
'the Conquered is to beg, and the Victor is to give Life for
'my Sake only. You must know, Sir, I value more being
'envied by Women, than loved by Men, and there is
'nothing proclaims a Beauty so effectually, as an Interview
'of her Lovers behind *Montague-house.* In hopes of a
'Serenade, soon after the Publication of this Letter, I rest
'in dull Tranquillity,

Your most Affectionate

Humble Servant,

Clidamira.

Mr. MYRTLE,

'YOU must know I am one of those Coxcombs who
'   'know my self to be abused, but have not Resolu-
'tion enough to resent it as I ought; to tell you plainly, I
'am a kind Keeper, and know my self to be the most ser-
'vile of Cuckolds, for I am wronged by a Woman whom I
'may part with when I please, but am afraid that when I
'please will never happen. As other People write Verses
'and Sonnets to deplore the Cruelty of their Mistress, I
'could think of nothing better this Morning than diverting
'my self, and soothing my Folly by the Example of Men of
'Wit, who have formerly been in my Condition. I was
'glad to meet an Epigram of a Gentleman I suppose your
'Worship is acquainted with, that hit my Condition; and
'make you a Present of it, as I have improved and trans-
'lated it in the janty Stile *of a Man of Wit and Pleasure about*
'*the Town.* Pray allow me to call her my Dear for the
'Rhyme sake; for I never writ Verses till she vexed me:

De Infamiâ suæ Puellæ.

Rumor ait crebro nostram peccare puellam ;
  Nunc ego me surdis auribus esse velim.
Crimina non hæc sunt nostro sine facta dolore :
  Quid miserum torques, rumor acerbe? tace.

The Town reports the Falshood of my Dear,
To which I cry, Oh that I could not hear !
I love her still, Peace then thou Babler Fame,
And let me rest contented in my Shame.

' Pray give my humble Service to Mrs. *Page;* you honour-
' able Lovers have a good Conscience to support you in
' your Vexations, but we alas——I am

Your humble Servant,

Giles Limberham.

No. 29.   *Saturday, May* 1.

Quis desiderio sit pudor aut modus
Tam chari Capitis?   Hor.

THE Reader may remember that in my first Paper I
described the Circumstances of the Persons, whose
Lives and Conversations my future Discourses should
principally describe. Mr. *Oswald,* who is a Widower,
and in the first Year of that distressed Condition, having
absented himself from our Meetings, I went to visit him
this Evening. My Intimacy made the Servant readily conduct me to him, though he had forbidden them to let any
body come at him. I found him leaning at a Table with a
Book before him, and saw, methoughts, a Concern in him
much deeper than that Seriousness which arises from

Reading only, though the matter upon which a Man has been employed has been never so weighty. He saw in me, I believe, a friendly Curiosity to know what put him into that Temper, and began to tell me that he had been looking over a little Collection of Books of his Wife's, and said it was an inexpressible Pleasure to him, that, tho' he thought her a most excellent Woman, he found, by perusing little Papers and Minutes among her Books, new Reasons for loving her; This, continued he, now in my Hand, is the *Contemplations Moral and Divine of Sir* Matthew Hale: She has turned down, and written little Remarks on the Margin as she goes on. In order to give you a Notion of her Merit and good Sense, pray give me leave to read three or four Paragraphs which she has marked with this Pencil. Here he looked upon the Pencil, till the Memory of some little Incident, of which it reminded him, filled his Eyes with Tears; which, to hide new Reasons for loving her, (but he only discovered his Grief the more) he began in a broken Voice to read Sir *Matthew's* second Chapter in his Discourse of Religion.

'THE Truth and Spirit of Religion comes in a narrow
'compass, though the Effect and Operation thereof are
'large and diffusive. *Solomon* comprehended it in a few
'Words, *Fear God, and keep his Commandments, for this
'is the whole Duty of Man:* The Soul and Life of Religion
'is the Fear of God, which is the Principle of Obedience;
'but Obedience to his Commands, which is an Act or
'Exercise of that Life, is various, according to the variety
'of the Commands of God: If I take a Kernel of an Acorn,
'the Principle of Life lies in it: The thing it self is but
'small, but the Vegetable Principle that lies in it takes up
'a less room than the Kernel it self, little more than the
'Quantity of a small Pins head, as is easie to be observed by

' Experiment; but the Exercise of that Spark of Life is
' large and comprehensive in its Operation; it produceth
' a great Tree, and in that Tree the Sap, the Body, the
' Bark, the Limbs, the Leaves, the Fruit; and so it is with
' the Principles of true Religion, the Principle it self lies in
' a narrow compass, but the Activity and Energy of it is
' diffusive and various.

' THIS Principle hath not only Productions that natur-
' ally flow from it, but where it is, it ferments and
' assimilates, and gives a kind of Tincture even to other
' Actions that do not in their own Nature follow from it,
' as the Nature and civil Actions of our Lives; under the
' former was our Lord's Parable of a Grain of Mustard-
' seed, under the latter of his Comparison of Leaven, just
' as we see in other things of Nature: Take a little Red
' Wine, and drop it into a Vessel of Water, it gives a new
' Tincture to the Water; or take a grain of Salt and put it
' into fresh Liquor, it doth communicate it self to the next
' adjacent part of the Liquor, and that again to the next,
' until the whole be fermented: So that small and little
' vital Principle of the Fear of God doth gradually and yet
' suddenly assimilate the Actions of our Life flowing from
' another Principle.   It rectifies and moderates our Affec-
' tions, and Passions, and Appetites, it gives Truth to our
' Speech, Sobriety to our Senses, Humility to our Parts,
' and the like.

' RELIGION is best in its *Simplicity* and *Purity*, but
' difficult to be retained so, without Superstitions and
' Accessions; and those do commonly in time *Stifle* and
' *Choak* the *Simplicity* of Religion, unless much Care and
' Circumspection be used: The Contemperations are so
' *many* and so *cumbersom*, that Religion loseth its *Nature*,
' or is strangled by them: Just as a Man that hath some

' Excellent Simple Cordial Spirit, and puts in Musk in it to
' make it smell sweet, and Honey to make it taste pleasant;
' and it may be *Cantharides* to make it look glorious. In-
' deed by the Infusions he hath given it a very *fine Smell,*
' and *Taste,* and *Colour,* but yet he hath so *clogg'd* it, and
' *sophisticated* it with Superadditions, that it may be he hath
' altered the Nature, and destroyed the Virtue of it.

HERE my Friend could go on no further, but reaching
to me the Book it self, he leaned on the Table, covering
his Eyes with his Hands, while I read the following Words
on the Margin, *Grant that this Superaddition which I make,
may be Love and Constancy to Mr.* Oswald. No one could
be unaffected with this Incident, nor could I forbear falling
into a kind of Consolatory Discourse, drawn from the Satisfaction it must needs be, to find new Proofs of the Virtue
of a Person he so tenderly loved; but observing his Concern too quick and lively for Conversation on that Subject,
I broke off with repeating only two Distichs of Mr. *Cowley*
to my Lady *Vandyke,* on the Death of her Husband,

> *Your Joys and Griefs were wont the same to be ;*
> *Begin not now, blest Pair, to disagree.*

I cannot but think it was a very right Sentiment in this
Lady, to make that Duty of Life in which she took pleasure,
the Superstructure upon the Motive of Religion ; for nothing can mend the Heart better than an honourable Love,
except Religion. It sweetens Disasters, and moderates
good Fortune, from a Benevolent Spirit that is naturally in
it, and extends it self to things the most remote. It cannot
be conceived by those who are involved in Libertine
Pleasures, the sweet Satisfactions that must arise from the
Union of two Persons who have left all the World, in order
to place their chief Delight in each other ; and to promote

that Delight by all the methods which Reason, urged by
Religion and Duty, forwarded by Passion, can intimate
to the Heart. Such a Pair give Charms to Virtue, and
make pleasant the ways of Innocence : A Deviation from
the Rules of such a Commerce would be courting Pain ; for
such a Life is as much to be preferred to any thing that can
be communicated by criminal Satisfactions, (to speak of it
in the mildest Terms) as Sobriety and elegant Conversation
are to Intemperance and Rioting.

No. 30.	*Tuesday, May* 4.

*Despicere unde queas alios, passimque videre
Errare, atque viam palanteis quærere vitæ.*   Luc.

IT is a very great Satisfaction to one who has put himself
upon the Platonick Foot, to look calmly on, while
Carnivorous Lovers run about howling for Hunger, which
the Intellectual and more abstracted Admirer is never gnaw'd
with. The following Letters give a lively Representation of
this matter.

Mr. Myrtle,

' IF ever any Man had reason to dispatch himself for
' Love, I am the Person ; I am lost to all Intents and
' Purposes, tho' I was the happiest Man in the World, and
' have no one to accuse but my self of my present Misfor-
' tunes, and yet I am not to be accused neither. To open
' this Riddle, you must know, Mr. *Myrtle*, that I am not
' now Twenty Years of Age ; I think that Circumstance
' necessary to tell you, for they say the Misfortune which
' befel me cannot happen but from the Height of Youth

'and Blood. I live in the Neighbourhood of a young
'Lady of Wealth, Wit and Beauty. I love her to Death,
'and she loves me with no less Ardour. We have had
'frequent Meetings by stealth, which are now interrupted
'by a very uncommon Accident. I have a Father who
'can never be enough satisfied that his House is not to be
'burned before next Morning; and for this reason, as well
'as, perhaps, other Jealousies, insists upon the Liberty of
'coming into my Chamber when I am asleep, to see
'whether my Candle is out. One Night he stole softly in,
'as indeed he always does, for fear of disturbing me, when
'I fast asleep was talking of my Mistress. As he has since
'told me, I named her, and then thought fit to go on as
'follows.

'THE Happiness we now enjoy is doubled by the
'Secrecy of it. I will come again to Morrow Night, and
'have ordered the Hackney Coachman to be ready to let
'me get up to your Window at the Hour appointed. Be
'ready to throw up the Sash when I tinkle with a Piece of
'Mony at the Glass. Your Letters I keep always in a Box
'under my Bed, and my Father can never come at them.
'Pray be sure to write; for the Day-time 'tis mighty sad
'shou'd be troubled with the Impertinence and Bustle of
'the World, and we never to meet or hear from each other
'but at Midnight.

'THE old Gentleman took my Key out of my Pocket,
'and by that means made himself Master of my Papers;
'and, in an hight Point of Honour, the next Day told the
'Parents of my Mistress the Danger their Daughter was in
'of being carried off by his Son, who had no Pretensions to
'a Woman of her Fortune; tho' he can do very handsomly
'for me.

'THIS matter has been very indiscreetly managed by

both our Parents; the Servants, and consequently the Neighbourhood, have the Story amongst them, and the innocentest Woman in the World is at the Mercy of busie Tongues: Now, Sir, I am not to judge of the Actions of my Father; but as he has a longer Purse then he will own, I desire you would lay before him, that he did not come at my Secret fairly, and that he ought, since he goes upon Punctilios, to have made no Use of what he arrived at by the Infirmity of a troubled Imagination. He says indeed for himself, that he had this Thought in his Head, and therefore had I owned the Thing to him when he taxed me, without shewing my Mistress's Letters, he should have been obliged, by the manner of getting the Secret, to have kept it; but since I had not owned it, had I not been confronted by her Letters, which he got by taking my Key out of my Pocket, I am under the same Degree of Favour as a Man who committed any other Crime would have been who had betrayed himself in the same manner. Mr. *Myrtle*, you are a great Casuist, and you see what a Jumble of unhappy Circumstances I am involved in, which I desire you to extricate me from by your best Advice, which will come very seasonably to two Families who are much your Friends, among whom none so much as the Lady concerned in the Story; and where she approves, you have an Admirer in,

SIR,

Your most Humble Servant,

Ulysses Transmarinus.

' I have Notice given me, that I must cross the Seas for this Business; but I am resolved to stay at least in the same Nation with my Fair One, till I hear further.

Mr. MYRTLE, *Friday, April* 30, 1714.

' YOU'LL oblige extremely your most humble Servant
' in inserting this in your next *Lover.*

Madam,

" DEATH would have been welcomer than your Letter
" in *Thursday's Lover;* for I must survive the
" Misery *that* would have ended. Your *Sincerity* is so far
" from being *Offensive,* that my Passion (were it now lawful
" to indulge it) is greater for you, and I cannot better prove
" the Truth of mine than by *refusing you,* and making you
" as happy in *your Choice,* as with *you* would have been the
" most unfortunate——

To Mr. MYRTLE.

SIR,

' THERE is a young Woman in our Neighbourhood
' that makes it her Business to disturb every body
' that passes by with her Beauty. She runs to the Window
' when she has a mind to do Mischief, and then when a
' Body looks up at her, she runs back, as tho' she had not
' a mind to be seen, tho' she came there on purpose. Her
' Hands and Arms you must know are very fine, for that
' reason she never lets them be unemployed, but is feeding
' a Squirrel, and catching People that pass by all Day long.
' She has a way of heaving out of the Window to see some-
' thing, so that one who stands in the Street just over
' against her, is taken with her side Face; one that is
' coming down fixes his Eyes at the Pole of her Neck till
' he stumbles ; and one coming up the Street is fixed
' Stock-still by her Eyes : She won't let any body go by in
' Peace. I am confident if you went that way your self, she
' would pretend to get you from Mrs. *Page.* As for my

'own part, I fear her not; but there are several of our
'Neighbours whose Sons are taken in her Chains, and
'several good Women's Husbands are always talking of
'her, and there is no quiet. I beg of you Sir, to take
'some Course with her, for she takes a delight in doing all
'this Mischief. It would be right to lay down some Rules
'against her; or if you please to appoint a time to come
'and speak to her, it would be a great Charity to our
'Street, especially to,

SIR,

Your most humble Servant,

Anthony Eyelid.

SIR,

'HERE is a young Gentlewoman in our Street, that I
'do not know at all, who looked full in my Face,
'and then looked as if she was mistaken, but looked so
'pretty, that I can't forget her; she does something or
'other to every one that passes by. I thought I would
'tell you of her.

Yours,

Ch. Busie.

SIR,

'HERE is a young Woman in our Street, that looks
'often melancholy out of the Window, as if she
'saw no Body, and no Body saw her, she is so intent. But
'she can give an Account of every thing that passes, and
'does it to Way-lay young Men. Pray say something
'about her.

Yours, unknown,

Tall-boy Gapeseed.

SIR,

'THERE is a young Woman in our Neighbourhood,
'that makes People with Bundles on their Back .

‘ stand as if they had none, and those who have none stand
‘ as if they had too heavy ones. Pray take her to your End
‘ of the Town, for she interrupts Business.

Your,

Ralph Doodle.

No. 31.   *Thursday, May 6.*

*Ridet hoc, inquam, Venus ipsa ; rident
Simplices Nymphæ, ferus & Cupido,
Semper ardentes acuens sagittas
         Cote cruentâ.*   Hor.

London, May 4.

Mr. MYRTLE,

‘ I Remember, some time ago, that I heard a Gentleman,
    ‘ who often talked out of a Book, speak of a King
‘ that was so fond of his Wife, that his Mind overflowed
‘ with the Happiness he had in the Possession of her
‘ Beauties. I remember it was just so that talking Fellow
‘ expressed himself; but all that I want of his Story is, that
‘ he shewed his Queen naked from a Chink in the Bed
‘ Chamber; and that the Queen, finding this out, resented
‘ it so highly, that she, after mature Deliberation, thought
‘ fit to plot against her Husband, and married the Man to
‘ whom he had exposed her Person. I have but a puzzled
‘ way of telling a Story; but this Circumstance, among such
‘ great People, may give you some Thoughts upon an
‘ Accident of the like kind, which happened to me a Man
‘ of middle Rank.

   ‘ THERE is a very gay, pleasant young Lady, whom
‘ I was well acquainted with, and had long known as being
‘ an Intimate of my Sister’s : We were the other Day a

riding out; the Women and Men on single Horses; it happened that this young Lady and I out-rid the Company, and in the Avenue of the Wood between *Hampstead* and *Highgate* her Horse threw her full upon her Head. She is a quick-witted Girl, and finding Chance had discovered more of her Beauty than ever she designed to favour me with, she in an Instant lay on the Turf in a decent manner, as in a Trance, before I could alight, and come to her Assistance. I fell in Love with her when she was Topsie Turvey, and from that Instant professed my self her Servant. She always laughed, and turned off the Discourse, and said she thought it must be so: The whole Family were mightily amazed how this Declaration came all of a sudden, and why, after two or three Years Intimacy, not a Word, and yet now I so very Eager. Well; the Father had no Exception to me, and the Wedding-day was named, when, all of a sudden, the Father has sent my Mistress to a distant Relation in the Country, and I am discarded. Now, Sir, what I desire of you is to insert this, that her Father may understand what she meant, when she said, *I shall be ashamed to be the Wife of any other Man;* and what I meant when I said that, *I know more of her already than any other Husband perhaps ever may.* These Expressions were let drop when the Father showed some Signs of parting us, and I appeal to you, whether, according to nice Rules, she is not to prefer me to all others. This is a serious matter in its Consequences, and I won't be choused; therefore pray insert it. The whole is humbly submitted by,

> *SIR,*
>
> > *Your most Unfortunate,*
> > *Humble Servant,*
> > > Tim. Pip.

To Mr. Marmaduke Myrtle.

SIR,

'OBSERVING you play the Casuist, the Doctor, nay
'often descend even to the Letter Carrier, for the
'Service of Lovers, I am apt to think my present Condition
'brings me within your Cognizance, and countenances this
'Application. Sir, I ever was a great Admirer of a single
'State, and my chief Study has been to collect Encomiums
'in its favour, and Instances of unhappy Marriages to con-
'firm me. I never could think my self the sad half of
'a Man, or, that my Cares wanted doubling. The best
'Exercise I ever performed at School was, a Translation of
'*Juvenal's* sixth Satyr. I remember my Master said smil-
'ing, Sirrah, you will die a Batchelor. Since I came to
'Man's Estate I have every Day talked over, with little
'variation, the common-place Sayings against Matrimony.
'I believe they've been more constant than my Prayers. I
'must now, Sir, acquaint you how I became disarmed of
'those Principles in an Instant, and how other Thoughts
'took place, so that I beg leave hereby to Recant, and
'protest against those damnable Doctrines. And further I
'humbly beseech all Ladies with whom I converse, to be-
'stow on me the Encouragement which new and true Con-
'verts generally meet with. I was riding in the Country
'last Spring; of all Days in the Week it was upon a
'*Tuesday*, when, on a sudden, I heard a Voice which
'guided my Sight to two young Women unknown to me:
'They were negligently, I won't say meanly drest, had
'large Staffs in their Hands, and were followed by Spaniels
'and Grey-hounds. One (whom I now see with the
'Lover's Telescope) wore a Bonnet. On her I cast my
'Eyes till the Brightness of hers made them fail me, that is,
'I have seen nothing in its true light since. I am a piece

' of a Scholar, yet am not able, Mr. *Myrtle*, to affirm what
' I saw, and how this Object struck the Organs of my Body,
' affected my Soul and Mind, and produced this lasting
' Idea.   The old Philosophers, you know, attributed a Soul
' to the Loadstone, when they cou'd not find out the
' Reason of its Union to Iron.   Whence shall I deduce the
' Cause of my Condition?   Shall I speak of an Impulse,
' Pressure of insensible Particles, secret Power, Destiny, the
' Stars, Magick; or shall I say in the Lawyers Terms, that
' every Feature had its Copies; or must I mention occult
' Quality, or as the genteel World translates it, *Je ne scay
' quoy?*   I should have told you I was a hunting when
' I saw this Object, that when it fled, my good-spirited
' Gelding refused the Gate that parted us, and run away
' with me.   This was as good as a second Game, for I who
' before was the greatest Sportsman in the Country, have
' ever since haunted the Woods to Sigh, not Hallow.   In
' lonely Shades by Day, and Moonshine Walks by Night
' (she ever by my Side) I have found my only Pleasure.
' This Condition I have suffered for a long Series of time;
' but wandering in the same Wood I saw a Country Girl
' in the same Bonnet in which I formerly beheld my great
' Calamity.   I followed her, and found the Aboad of her
' for whom I languish.   *Ma Charmante* is your constant
' Reader, who hereby will have some Notion of me and my
' Name.   I crave, Sir, your Assistance herein, and (to ease
' your self of another troublesome Letter) your Advice, in
' Case of a Denial to wait upon her.   I have abundance
' more to say, but desire you to say it to your self in behalf
' of,

     SIR,

       Your Enamoured Humble Servant.

No. 32. *Saturday, May 8.*

’Εν δικαιοσύνῃ συλλήβδην πᾶσ’ ἀξείή ἐsιν.   Aristot.

THE Task which I have enjoyned my self in these Papers, is to describe Love in all its Shapes : To warn the unwary of those Rocks, upon which so many in all Ages have split formerly, do split still, and will split hereafter, as long as Men and Women shall be what they now are ; and to delineate the true and unfeigned Delight, which virtuous Minds feel in the Enjoyment of their lawful and warranted Passions. This Task, the farther I go, I find grows the more upon my Hands. The dreadful Effects which have attended irregular Pursuits in this way, have led some shallow Philosophers to arrain that as simply unlawful, or at least as unbecoming a wise Man, which is certainly one of the first and fundamental Laws of Nature ; and they have seemed to look upon that as a Curse which rightly managed is the greatest Blessing that our Creator has given us here below ; and which is in Truth,

> *That Cordial Drop Heaven in our Cup has thrown,*
> *To make the nauseous Draught of Life go down.*

YET on the other Hand, when (comparatively speaking) so very many miscarry in this Particular, more than in any other single Circumstance belonging to human Life, one is tempted to cry out, with my Lord *Brooke* in his *Alaham,*

> *O wearisom Condition of Mortality*
> *Born to one Law, and to another bound ;*
> *Vainly begotten, yet forbidden Vanity ;*
> *Created Sick, commanded to be Sound !*
> *If Nature sure did not delight in Blood,*
> *She wou'd have found more easie ways to good.*

BUT since Complaints under most Pressures avail but little ; since in every Species of Actions there is a right and a wrong, which Circumstances only can determine ; since our Maker (for greater Reasons than those which our Laws ascribe to our Princes) cannot possibly do any wrong, or as the Divines speak, cannot be the Author of Sin ; since what was essential to Human Nature before the Fall, is in itself most certainly good, when rightly pursued ; and since one may observe that Mistakes and false Steps in this matter meet with harsher Censures, and are often more severely punished in this World, than many other Crimes which seem to be of a higher Nature : I have thought it worth while to enquire into this matter as exactly as I could, and to present the Publick with my Thoughts concerning the real Differences between the several sorts of Evil Actions, as I shall find opportunity, and as my importunate Correspondents, who are often in haste, and who must not be disobliged, will give me leave.

ONE Method, as I take it, to induce Men to avoid any Evil, is to know not only wherein it consists, but how great it is. The *Stoics* of old pretended that all Sins were equal ; that it was as great a Crime to steal a Pin, as to rob upon the Road. When their wise Man was once out of his way, he lost his Pretensions to Wisdom ; and when those were gone, whatsoever he did or said afterwards in that State of Aberration, it was all one. Sins were Sins, and where the Essence was the same, the Degrees mattered little. This contradicts human Nature, and common Sense ; and the Laws of all Nations distinguish in the Punishments which they inflict, between Crimes as they are more or less pernicious to the Society in and against which they are committed. That God does so too, we need not question. The Judge of the whole Earth must certainly do right.

When we know wherein the true Greatness of every Sin consists, we shall be able to judge of our own Faults, and sometimes of the Faults of others; we shall see why we ought to avoid them where there is room for Compassion; and where Punishment is necessary, we may be sure then to be severe in the right place; and by knowing how and when to forgive, may sometimes raise those that are sinking, and often save those from utter Destruction, who if abandoned would be irrecoverably lost. This is a large, and I think an useful Theme, and it is what I have not seen sufficiently enlarged upon in those Books of Morality which have come in my way. Now if in my Enquiries I have an Eye all along to the Christian Institution, and take a view of the Sins and Irregularities of Mankind in such a Light as is consistent with the Practice of our Saviour and his Apostles, I hope the softer and politer part of my Readers will not be upon that Account disgusted.

THE Aggravation of all Crimes is to be estimated either from the Persons injured or offended, or from the intrinsick Malice from whence those Injuries and Offences proceed. All Offences are against either our Maker, our Neighbour, or our selves. Offences against our Maker have this particular Aggravation, that they are committed against the Person to whom we have the greatest Obligations, and consequently do more immediately contradict the Light of our own Conscience. The Obligations of our original Being, and of our constant Preservation, during the whole Course of our Lives, which takes in all the Blessings that we daily receive from him, are so peculiarly due to God, that they are not communicable to any earthly Being. For tho' we may, and do hourly, receive Advantages from our Fellow-Creatures, yet those Advantages are ultimately to be referred to God, by whose good Providence those Fellow-Creatures are enabled to do us good. And besides, the good they do us is as much for their Sakes as for ours, since the Advantages they receive from us, and those we receive from them are reciprocal. But tho' our Creator is always doing good to us, we can do none to him, and upon that Score he has a Title to our Obedience, and that implicit, when once we are satisfied it is he that commands. This makes *Idolatry* to be so crying a Sin, because it is a Communication of that Honour to the Creature, (whether inanimate or animate it matters not) to which it can have no possible Title, and is due to the Creator only. Upon this account also *Irreligion* and *Atheism* are still worse, because they tear up all Religion by the Roots; and all Service and Worship is denyed to him to whom the utmost Service and Worship is justly due. This is so plain, that it needs neither Enlargement nor Proof.

THE second degree of Offences is of those which are committed against our Neighbours. They are equally God's Creatures as ourselves, and have an equal Title to his Protection, and we ought to think that they are equally dear to him. Offences against them may be comprehended under one common Title of *Injustice*. And what Divines usually call *Sins* against the *Second Table*, are, if strictly examined, but so many Sorts of Injuries against our Neighbours. The Pains, the Care, the Trouble, and above all, the Love, of Parents, demand Honour from their Children; and therefore when they do not meet with it, they are injured: This shews the Justice of the fifth Commandment. To take away our Neighbour's Life is the greatest Injury which can be done him, because it is absolutely irreparable. Next to that are Injuries done to his Bed, and for the same Reason too. The Goods we enjoy are the Means of our Subsistence here, and he that against our Wills takes them from us, does more or less, according to the greatness of our Loss, deprive us of our Subsistence. This shews the Justice of the sixth, seventh and eighth Commandments. And since none of those things to which by the original Grant from our common Maker we have a just Title, are secure, if Calumny and false Accusations are once allowed; therefore false witnessing is also forbidden in the ninth Commandment. And since a desire of possessing what is not our own, and what we see others enjoy, will, if encouraged, naturally lead Men to as many sorts of Injustice, as there are Sorts of Desires; therefore coveting what is not our own is fenced against by the tenth Commandment.

BY this Detail it plainly appears why I set Offences against our Neighbours in the second Place. When God gave the ten Commandments, he mention'd no Offences but those against himself and our Neighbours, and left the Sins which are immediately against our selves (which are properly Sins of Intemperance) to be forbidden by other Laws.

BUT then, tho' Sins against our selves ought, with respect to their Guilt, (which is what I here propose to consider) to be reckoned last; yet it does not follow from thence that they are not Sins, and consequently do not deserve Punishment. Whatsoever disables us in any Measure from doing our Duty to God or our Neighbour, is so far an *Injustice* towards them, and robs them of their due, and is so far a Crime. I say an *Injustice*, because, as I said before, all Faults in my Opinion are ultimately to be referred to that. Even *Uncharitableness* is *Injustice*, becau e our common Creator, who has made us all liable to Want, and consequently under a Necessity of desiring Assistance, expects we should be helpful to one another, because he is good to us. And when *Aristotle* says, in those Words that are the *Motto* of this Paper, that *all Virtues are contained in*

Justice, he states the true Notion of Good and Evil; and it is as applicable to Virtues considered in a Christian Light, as in a natural one. This then is the first Rule by which we are to weigh the different Degrees of Good and Evil.

No. 33.   *Tuesday, May* 11.

——Animum pictura puscit——   Virg.

I Went the other Day down the River, and dined with some Virtuosi Friends at *Greenwich*. The purpose of the Gentleman, who invited us, was to entertain us with a sight of that famous Cieling in the great Hall at *Greenwich* Hospital, painted by our Ingenious Countryman Mr. *Thornhill*, who has executed a great and noble Design with a Masterly Hand, and uncommon Genius. The Regularity, Symmetry, Boldness and Prominence of the Figures are not to be described, nor is it in the Power of Words to raise too great an Idea of the Work. As well as I could comprehend it from seeing it but twice, I shall give a plain Account of it.

IN the middle of the Cieling (which is about 106 Foot long, and 36 Foot wide, and near 50 Foot high) is a very large Oval Frame painted and carved in Imitation of Gold, with a great thickness rising in the inside to throw up the Figures to the greater heighth; the Oval is fastened to a great Suffeat adorned with Roses in Imitation of Copper. The whole is supported by eight gigantick Figures of Slaves, four on each Side, as though they were carved in Stone; between the Figures, thrown in Heaps into a covering, are all manner of Maritime Trophies in Metzorelievo; as Anchors, Cables, Rudders, Masts, Sails, Blocks, Capstals, Sea-guns, Sea-carriages, Boats, Pinnaces, Oars, Stretchers, Colours, Ensigns, Pennants, Drums, Trumpets, Bombs, Mortars, small Arms, Granadoes, Powder Barrels, Fire Arrows, grapling-Irons, Cross Staves, Quadrants, Compasses, &c.   All in Stone-Colours, to give the greater Beauty to the rest of the Cieling which is more significant.

ABOUT the Oval in the inside are placed the twelve Signs of the Zodiack, the six northern Signs, as *Aries, Taurus, Gemini, Cancer, Leo, Virgo,* are placed on the North side of the Oval ; and the six Southern Signs, as *Libra, Scorpio, Sagittarius, Capricornus, Aquarius, Pisces,* are to the South, with three of them in a Groupe which compose one quarter of the Year ; the Signs have their Attitudes,* and their Draperies are varied and adapted to the Seasons they possess, as the cool, the blue, and the tender green to the Spring, the yellow to the Summer, and the red and flame-Colour to the Dog Days and Autumnal Season, the white and cold to the Winter ; likewise the Fruits and the Flowers of every Season as they succeed each other.

IN the middle of the Oval are represented King *William* and Queen *Mary,* sitting on a Throne under a great

* Aries *is of a turbulent Aspect with little Winds and Rains hovering about him, his Drapery of a blewish Green, shadowed with dark Russet to denote the Changeableness of the Weather.*   April, *or* Taurus, *is more mild;* May, *or* Gemini, *in blue ;* June *a calm red ;* July *more reddish and as he leans upon his Lyon vails a little from the Sun.*   Virgo *almost naked and flying from the Heat of the Sun ;* Libra *in deep red ;* Scorpio *vails himself from the Scorching Sun in a flame Colour Mantle ;* Sagittarius *in red, less hot ;* December, *or* Capricorn, *blewish ;* Aquarius *in a waterish green ;* Pisces *in blue.*   Over Aries, Taurus, Gemini *presides* Flora ; *over* Cancer, Leo, Virgo *presides* Ceres ; *over* Libra, Scorpio, Sagittarius, Bacchus ; *and over* Capricorn, Aquarius, Pisces, Hyems *hovering over a brazen Pot of Fire.*

Pavilion or Purple Canopy, attended by the four Cardinal Vertues, as *Prudence, Temperance, Fortitude* and *Justice.*

OVER the Queen's Head is *Concord* with the *Fasces*, at her Feet two Doves, denoting mutual Concord and innocent Agreement, with *Cupid* holding the King's Scepter, while he is presenting *Peace* with the Lamb and Olive Branch, and *Liberty* expressed by the *Athenian* Cap, to *Europe*, who laying her Crowns at his Feet, receives them with an Air of Respect and Gratitude. The King tramples Tyranny under his Feet, which is exprest by a *French* Personage, with his Leaden Crown falling off, his Chains, Yoke and Iron Sword broken to pieces, Cardinal's Cap, triple crown'd Mitres, &c. tumbling down. Just beneath is *Time* bringing *Truth* to Light, near which is a Figure of Architecture, holding a large Drawing of part of the Hospital with the Cupola, and pointing up to the Royal Founders, attended by the little *Genii* of her Art. Beneath her is *Wisdom* and *Heroick Virtue*, represented by *Pallas* and *Hercules*, destroying *Ambition, Envy, Covetousness, Detraction, Calumny*, with other Vices, which seem to fall to the Earth, the place of their more natural Abode.

OVER the Royal Pavilion is shewn at a great heighth *Apollo* in his Golden Chariot, drawn by four white Horses, attended by the *Horæ*, and Morning Dews falling before him, going his Course through the twelve Signs of the Zodiack, and from him the whole Plafond or Cieling is enlightened.

EACH end of the Cieling is raised in Perspective, with a Ballustrade and Eliptick Arches, supported by Groupes of Stone Figures, which form a Gallery of the whole breadth of the Hall ; in the middle of which Gallery, (as tho' on the Stock) going into the upper Hall, is seen in Perspective the Tafferil of the *Blenheim* Man of War, with all her Galleries,

Port-holes open, *&c.* to one side of which is a Figure of *Victory* flying, with Spoils taken from the Enemy, and putting them aboard the *English* Man of War. Before the Ship is a Figure representing the City of *London,* with the Arms, Sword and Cap of Maintenance, supported by *Thame* and *Isis,* with other small Rivers offering up their Treasures to her. The River *Tine* pouring forth Sacks of Coals. In the Gallery on each side the Ship are the Arts and Sciences that relate to Navigation, with the great *Archimedes,* many old Philosophers consulting the Compass, *&c.*

AT the other end, as you return out of the Hall, is a Gallery in the same manner, in the middle of which is the Stern of a beautiful Gally filled with *Spanish* Trophies. Under which is the *Humber* with his Pigs of Lead : The *Severn,* with the *Avon* falling into her, with other lesser Rivers. In the North end of the Gallery is the famous *Ticho Brahe,* that noble *Danish* Knight, and great Ornament of his Profession and Human Nature ; near him is *Copernicus* with his *Pythagorean* System in his Hand ; next to him is an old Mathematician holding a large Table, and on it are described two Principal Figures, of the incomparable Sir *Isaac Newton,* on which many extraordinary things in that Art are built. On the other end of the Gallery, to the South, is our learned Mr. *Flamstead,* Reg. Astron. Profess. with his ingenious Disciple Mr. *Tho. Weston.* In Mr. *Flamstead*'s Hand is a large Scroll of Paper, on which is drawn the great Eclipse of the Sun that will happen on *April*   1715 ; near him is an old Man with a Pendulum counting the Seconds of Time, as Mr. *Flamstead* makes his Observations with his great Mural Arch and Tube on the Descent of the Moon on the *Severn,* which at certain times form such a Roll of the Tides as the Sailors corruptly call the *Higre,* instead of the *Eager,* and is very dangerous to all Ships in its way. This is also exprest by Rivers tumbling down by the Moon's Influence into the *Severn.* In this Gallery are more Arts and Sciences relating to Navigation.

ALL the great Rivers, at each end of the Hall, have their proper Product of Fish issuing out of their Vases.

IN the four great Angles of the Cieling, which are over the Arches of the Galleries, are the four Elements, as *Fire, Air, Earth* and *Water,* represented by *Jupiter, Juno, Cybele* and *Neptune,* with their lesser Deities accompanying, as *Vulcan, Iris,* the *Fauni, Amphitrite,* with all their proper Attitudes, *&c.*

AT one end of the great Oval is a large Figure of *Fame* descending, riding on the Winds, and sounding forth the Praises of the Royal Pair.

ALL the Sides of the Hall are adorned with fluted Pillasters, Trophies of Shells, Corals, Pearls ; the Jambs of the Windows ornamented with Roses impannel'd, or the *Opus reticulamium* heightened with green Gold.

THE whole raises in the Spectator the most lively Images of Glory and Victory, and cannot be beheld without much Passion and Emotion.

N. B. Sir *James Bateman* was the first proposer, and the first Benefactor to this Cieling.

No. 34.   *Thursday, May* 13.

—— *Waking Life appears a Dream.*

Rosamond.

REPROACH is of all things the most painful to Lovers, especially to Us of the Platonick kind ; this makes it excessively grievous to me, that a Paper, tho' a very dull one called the *Monitor*, accuses me of Writing obscenely. He is a stupid Fellow, and does not understand, that the same Object, according to the Artist who represents it, may be decent, or unfit to be looked at. Naked Figures, by a Masterly Hand, are so drawn, sometimes, as to be incapable of exciting Immodest Thoughts. I have, in my Paper of *May* the 6th, spoken of an Amour that owes its beginning, and makes it self necessary to be lawfully consummated, from an Accident of a Lady's falling Topsie-turvie: Upon which this heavy Rogue says, *Is this suffered in a Christian Country?* Yes it is, and may very lawfully, but not when such awkard Tools as he pretend to meddle with the same Subject: None but Persons extremely well-bred ought to touch Ladies Petticoats; but I aver, that I have said nothing to offend the most Chast and Delicate, and all who read that Passage may be very Innocent; and the Lady of the Story may be a very good Christian, though she did not in her Appearance differ from an Heathen, when she fell upon her Head. We who follow *Plato*, or are engaged in the High Passion, can see a Lady's Ankle with as much Indifference as her Wrist: We are so inwardly taken up, that the same Ideas do not spring in our Imaginations, as do with the common World; we are made gentle, soft, courteous, and harmless, from the Force of the *belle* Passion; of which Coarse Dunces, with an Appetite for Women, like that they have for Beef, have no Conception.

AS I gave an Account the other Day of my passing a Day at *Greenwich* with much delight in beholding a Piece of Painting of Mr. *Thornhill's*, which is an Honour to our Nation; I shall now give an Account of my passing yesterday Morning, an Hour before Dinner, in a Place where People may go and be very well entertained, whether they have, or have not, a good Taste. They will certainly be well pleased, for they will have unavoidable Opportunities of seeing what they most like, in the most various and agreeable Shapes and Positions, I mean their own dear selves. The Place I am going to mention is Mr. *Gumley's* Glass-Gallery over the *New Exchange.* I little thought I should ever in the *Lover* have occasion to talk of such a thing as Trade; but when a Man walks in that Illustrious Room, and reflects what incredible Improvement our Artificers of *England* have made in Manufacture of Glass in thirty Years time, and can suppose such an Alteration of our Affairs in other parts of Commerce, it is demonstrable that the Nations who are possessed of Mines of Gold, are but Drudges to a People, whose Arts and Industry, with other Advantages natural to us, may make it self the Shop of the World. We are arrived at such Perfection in this Ware, of which I am speaking, that it is not in the Power of any Potentate in *Europe,* to have so beautiful a Mirror as he may purchase here for a Trifle, by all the Cost and Charge that he can lay out in his Dominions. It is a modest Computation, that *England* gains fifty .thousand Pounds a Year by exporting this Commodity for the Service of Foreign Nations: The whole owing to the Inquisitive and Mechanick, as well as liberal Genius of the late Duke of *Buckingham.* This prodigious Effect by the Art of Man, from Parts of Nature that are as unlikely to produce it, as one would suppose a Man could burn common Earth to a Tulip, opens a Field of Contemplation which would lead me too far from my Purpose, which is only to celebrate the agreeable Oeconomy of placing the several Wares to Sale, in the Gallery of which I am talking. No Imagination can work up a more pleasing Assemblage of beautiful things, to set off each other, than are here actually laid together. In the midst of the Walk are set in

Order a long Row of rich Tables, on many of which lie Cabinets inlaid or wholly made of Corals, Conchs, Ambers, or the like parts of Matter which Nature seems to have formed wholly to shew the Beauty of her Works, and to have thrown and distinguished from the Mass of Earth as she does by great Gifts and Endowments those Spirits and Persons of Men and Women whom she designs to make Instruments of great Consideration in the Crowd of her People. When I walked here, I could not but lament to my Companion, that this Method was not taken up when the *Indian* Kings were lately in *England.* The Surprise such Appearances as these would put them into, would have been as great as a new Sense added to one of us. To see the things about us so placed, as that three or four Persons can to the Eye, in an Instant, become a large Assembly ! You cannot move or do any the least indifferent Action, in any Limb or part of your Body, but you vary the Scene around with additional Pleasure : Among other Circumstances, I could not but be pleased to see a Lap-Dog at a Loss, for an Instant, for his Lady, and beginning to run to the Image of her in a Glass, till he was driven back by himself, whom he saw running towards him. The poor Animal corrected his Mistake, by tracing her Footsteps by his Sense less subject to Mistake, and arrived at her Feet, to the no small Diversion of the Company who saw it, and the Envy of several fine Gentlemen, whom the odd Accident diverted from looking at themselves, to behold the beauteous *Bellamira.*

IT would be an Arrogance to pretend to convey distinctly by the Ear, a Pleasure that should come in at the Eye; but my gentle Reader will thank me for many pleasing Thoughts he or she had not ever had before, in a Place more new than he could arrive at by landing in a

Foreign Nation. About forty Years ago it was the Fashion for all the Gallants of the Town, the Wits and the Braves, to walk in the *New Exchange* below, to shew themselves. What an Happiness have those whose Fortunes and Humours are capable of receiving Gratifications in this Place, that such a Scene was displayed in their Life-time! The Learned have not more Reason to rejoice, that they live in the same Days with *Newton*, than the Gay, the Delicate, and the Curious in Luxury of Dress and Furniture have, that there has appeared in their time my honest Friend and polite Director of Artificers, Mr. *Gumley*.

No. 35.   *Saturday, May* 15.

> ————*'tis confest,*
> *The Men who flatter highest, please us best.*
> Helen *to* Paris, Ovid's *Epistles.*

I Shall make the following Letters the Entertainment of this Day, and recommend the Contents of the first in a more particular manner to the serious Consideration of all my Female Readers.

Dear MARMADUKE,

' THO' you have treated the Fair Sex with an Air of
' Distinction suitable to the Character you bear, I
' presume you will make no Scruple to admonish them of
' any Faults, by the Amendment of which they may still
' become more amiable. What I complain to you of, is
' from my own Experience. My Case is this.

' *MIRANDA* is in the bloom of Sixteen, and shines in
' all the Beauties of her Sex. Her Face, her Shape, her
' Mein, her Wit, surprise and engage all who have the
' Happiness to know her. *Miranda* is the Idol of my
' Heart, the Object of all my Hopes and Fears. None of
' her Actions are indifferent to me. Every Look and
' Motion gives me either Pleasure or Pain. I have omitted
' no reasonable Methods to convince her of the Greatness
' of my Passion, yet as she is one with whom I propose to
' pass the Remainder of my Life, I cannot forbear mixing
' the Sincerity of the Friend with the Tenderness of the
' Lover. In short, Sir, I am one of those unfortunate Men,
' who think young Women ought to be treated like Rational
' Creatures. I forbear therefore to launch out into all the
' usual Excesses of Flattery and Romance; to make her a
' Goddess, and my self a Madman; to give up all my Senses
' and Reason to be moulded and informed as she thinks
' proper.

' FROM hence arise all our Differences. *Miranda* is
' one of those fashionable Ladies, who, expecting an im-
' plicit Faith from their Admirers, are impatient and
' affronted at the least shew of Contradiction.

' AS she was lately reading the Works of a celebrated
' Author, who has thought fit to represent himself in his
' Writings under the Character of an old Man, she was
' pleased to observe, that it was very uncommon to see
' a Person at Fourscore have so lively a Fancy, and so brisk
' an Imagination. I could not help informing her upon
' this Occasion, that I had frequently had the Honour to
' Drink a Glass with the Gentleman, and that to my certain
' Knowledge he was not yet turned of Forty. Instead of
' thanking me for setting her right in this particular, she
' immediately took Fire, and asked me with a Frown,

' *Whether that was my Breeding to contradict a Lady?* You
' must know, Sir, this Question usually puts an end to all
' our Disputes.   A little while after she desired my Opinion
' of her Lap-dog, and I had no sooner unfortunately
' observed, that his Ears were somewhat of the shortest,
' than she roundly asked me, *Whether I designed that for a
' Compliment?*   I took the freedom from hence, in an
' honest plain way, to expose the Weakness and Folly
' of being delighted with Flattery, to tell her that Ladies
' ought not always to be complimented, to enumerate the
' Inconveniences it often leads them into, to make her
' sensible of the ill Designs Men generally aim at by it, and
' the mean Opinion they must entertain of those who are
' delighted with it.   All this would not do ; I could not get
' one kind Look from her that Night.

' I have told you already, that I have used all reasonable
' Methods to convince her of my Passion, and I am sure I
' have the Preference in her Esteem to all other Pre-
' tenders.   She knows I love, and, in spight of all her Arts
' to hide it, I know I am beloved : Yet, from these little
' Differences, and a certain Coquet Humour which makes
' her delight to see her Lover uneasie, tho' at the same
' time she torments her self, I have often despaired of our
' ever coming together.   I thought however the following
' Verses, which I presented to her Yesterday, made some
' Impression on her ; and if she sees you think them toler-
' able enough to allow them a Place in your Paper, I am in
' hopes they may help to hasten the happy Day.

I.

Tell me, Miranda, *why should I
Lament and languish, pine and die?
While you, regardless of my Pain,
Seem pleas'd to hear your Slave complain.*

II.

Dame Eve, unskill'd in Female Arts
And modern ways of tort'ring Hearts,
No sooner saw her Spark than lov'd,
Confess'd her Flame, and his approv'd.

III.

Nature still breaks through all Disguise,
Glows in your Cheeks, and rules your Eyes.
Love trembles in your Hands and Heart,
Your panting Breasts proclaim his Dart.

IV.

No more, Miranda, then be coy,
No longer keep us both from Joy ;
No longer study to conceal
What all your Actions thus reveal.

I am, Dear *Marmaduke*,

Your most Obedient Humble Servant.

Mr. Myrtle,

' I Send you the enclosed Letter, which I have lately
' received from a young *Templar* who is my Humble
' Servant.   I desire you would inform me, whether what he
' asserts be Law or Equity.   His Letter runs thus.

Madam,

" HAPPENING lately to be in Company with a vener-
" able Lady who has a very large Fortune, I was
" so complaisant to ask her if she would allow me to do her
" the Honour to make her a Wife? She was so kind
" to ask me again, whether I was in jest or earnest?   Upon
" my repeating the Question, she returned my Civility, and
" told me, she thought I was mad. But upon my third
" Application she consented, that is, she told me positively

"she would never have me. This I take for an absolute
" Promise, having been frequently informed, that Womens
" Answers in such Cases are to be interpreted backwards.

" I have consulted a Proctor in *Doctors Commons*, who
" seems to be of Opinion, that it has the full Force
" of a Contract, and that (having Witness of it) I might
" recover half her Fortune, should she offer to marry any
" one else.

" I mention this, Madam, not only to let you see that
" I can have the same Encouragement elsewhere which you
" give me, but to admonish you how much Care you ought
' to take of promising any other Man Marriage, by declar-
" ing positively that you will never have him, except

Your most Obedient, Humble Servant,

Tom. Truelove.

No. 36.   *Tuesday, May* 18.

Concubitu prohibere vago——   Hor.

I Have heard it objected, by several Persons, against my
Papers, that they are apt to kindle Love in young
Hearts, and inflame the Sexes with a Desire for one
another: I am so far from denying this Charge, that I
shall make no Scruple to own it is the chief End of my
Writing. *Love* is a Passion of the Mind (perhaps the
noblest) which was planted in it by the same Hand that
created it. We ought to be so far, therefore, from endeavouring to root it out, that we should rather make it our Business to keep it up and cherish it. Our chief Care must be
to fix this, as well as our other Passions, upon proper
Objects, and to direct it to a right End.

FOR this Reason, as I have ever shewn my self a Friend to Honourable Love, I have constantly discountenanced all vicious Passions. Tho' the several Sorts of these are each of them highly Criminal, yet that which leads us to defile another Man's Bed is by far of the blackest dye.

THE excellent Author of *The whole Duty of Man*, has given us a very lively Picture of this Crime, with all those melancholly Circumstances that must necessarily attend it. One must indeed wonder to see it punished so lightly among civilized Nations, when even the most Barbarous have regarded it with the utmost Horror and Detestation. I was lately entertained with a Story to this Purpose, which was told me by one of my Friends who was himself upon the Place when the thing happened.

IN an Out-Plantation, upon the Borders of *Potuxen* a River in *Maryland*, there lived a Planter, who was Master of a great Number of *Negro* Slaves. The Increase of these poor Creatures is always an Advantage to the Planters, their Children being born Slaves; for which Reason the Owners are very well pleased, when any of them marry. Among these *Negroes* there happened to be two; who had always lived together and contracted an intimate Friendship, which went on for several Years in an uninterrupted Course. Their Joys and their Griefs were mutual; their Confidence in each other was intire; Distrust and Suspicion were Passions they had no Notion of. The one was a Batchelor; the other married to a Slave of his own Complexion, by whom he had several Children. It happened that the Head of this small Family rose early one Morning, on a leisure Day, to go far into the Woods a hunting, in order to entertain his Wife and Children at Night with some Provisions better than ordinary. The Batchelor Slave, it seems, had for a long time entertained a Passion for his

Friend's Wife ; which, from the Sequel of the Story, we may conclude, he had endeavoured to stifle, but in vain. The Impatience of his Desires prompted him to take this Opportunity, of the Husband's Absence, to practise upon the Weakness of the Woman ; which accordingly he did, and was so unfortunate as to succeed in his Attempt. The Hunter, who found his Prey much nearer home than usual, returned some Hours sooner than was expected, loaden with the Spoils of the Day, and full of the pleasing Thoughts of feasting and rejoycing, with his Family, over the Fruits of his Labour. Upon his entring his Shed, the first Objects that struck his Eyes were, his Wife and his Friend asleep in the Embraces of each other. A Man acquainted with the Passions of human Nature will easily conceive the Astonishment, the Rage, and the Despair, that overpower'd the poor *Indian* at once : He burst out into Lamentations and Reproaches ; and tore his Hair like one Distracted. His Cries and broken Accents awakened the guilty Couple ; whose Shame and Confusion were equal to the Agonies of the injured. After a considerable Pause of Silence on both Sides, he expostulated with his Friend in Terms like these : My Wrongs are greater than I am able to express ; and far too great for me to bear. My Wife——But I blame not her. After a long and lasting Friendship, exercised under all the Hardships and Severities of a most irksome Captivity ; after mutual repeated Instances of Affection and Fidelity ; could I suspect my Friend, my bosom-Friend should prove a Traitor ? I thought my self happy, even in Bondage, in the Enjoyment of such a Friend and such a Wife ; but cannot bear the Thoughts of Life with Liberty, after having been so basely betrayed by both. You both are lost to me, and I to you. I soon shall be at Rest ; live and enjoy your Crime. Adieu. Having said this, he turned away and went out, with a Resolution to dye immediately.　The guilty *Negro* followed him, touched with the quickest Sense of Remorse for his Treachery.　'Tis I alone, (said he) that am guilty; and I alone, who am not fit to live.　Let me intreat you to forgive your Wife, who was overcome by my Importunities.　I promise never to give either of you the least Disquiet for the future: Live and be happy together, and think of me no more.　Bear with me but for this Night; and to Morrow you shall be satisfied. Here they both wept, and parted.　When the Husband went out in the Morning to his Work, the first thing he saw was his Friend hanging upon the Bough of a Tree before the Cabbin-Door.

IF the Wretches of this Nation, who set up for Men of Wit and Gallantry, were capable of feeling the generous Remorse of this poor Slave, upon the like Occasions, we should, I fear, have a much thinner appearance of Equipage in Town.

METHINKS there should be a general Confederacy amongst all honest Men to exclude from Society, and to Brand with the blackest Note of Infamy, those Miscreants, who make it the Business of their Lives to get into Families, and to estrange the Affections of the Wife from the Husband.　There is something so very base and so Inhuman in this modish Wickedness, that one cannot help wishing the honest Liberty of the *Ancient Comedy* were restor'd; and that Offenders in this kind might be exposed by their Names in our publick Theatres.　Under such a Discipline, we should see those who now Glory in the Ruin of deluded Women, reduced to withdraw themselves from the just Resentments of their Country-men and Fellow-Citizens.

No. 37.   *Thursday, May* 20.

What Pains! what racking Thoughts he proves,
Who lives remov'd from her he loves.   Congreve.

MY own unhappy Passion for Mrs. *Page* has made me extremely sensible of all the Distresses occasioned by Love. I have often reflected what could be the Cause, that while we see the most worthless part of Mankind every Day succeeding in their Attempts, while we see those Wretches whose Hearts are utterly incapable of this noble Passion, appear stupid and senseless amidst the Caresses of the Fair; we cannot but observe, that the noblest and greatest Flames which have been kindled in the Breasts of Men of Sense and Merit, have seldom met with a due Return.

AS the Thoughts of those who have been throughly in Love are frequently wild and extravagant, I have been sometimes tempted to think, that Providence, never designing we should fix our thoughts of Happiness altogether here, will not allow us to taste so large a Share of it as we must necessarily do in the Enjoyment of an Object on which all the Passions of our Soul have been placed, and to which all the Faculties of our Mind have been long aspiring.

IT is certain, however, that without having Recourse to a superior Power, there are several Accidents which naturally happen on these Occasions, and from whence we may generally give a pretty good Account why the greatest Passions are usually unsuccessful. It has been long since observed by a celebrated *French* Writer, that it is much easier for a Man to succeed who only feigns a Passion, than for one who is truly and desperately in Love. The first is still Master of himself, and can watch all the Turns and Revolutions in the Temper of her whom he would engage. The latter is too much taken up with his own Passion to attend any thing else: It is with difficulty he can even perswade himself to speak, when he finds every thing he can say so short of what he feels, and that his Conceptions are too tender to be expressed by Words. The Fair, generally speaking, are not sufficiently sensible of the Value they ought to put upon such a Passion, nor consider how strong that Love must be which shall throw the most Eloquent into the utmost Confusion before them. *Flavia* is an unhappy Instance of what I am observing; she was courted at once by *Tom Trifle*, and *Octavio;* the first could entertain her with his Love, with the same Indifference he talked on any other Occasion, and with great Serenity of Mind make a Digression from what he was saying, either to play with her Lap-Dog, or give his Opinion of a Suit of Knots. *Octavio*, when Fortune favoured him with an Opportunity of declaring himself, was often struck Speechless in the midst of a Sentence, and could for some time express himself no other way than by pressing her Hand and dropping a Tear. *Flavia* having duly weighed the Merit of both, married *Trifle.* His Unkindness to her after Marriage, his Inability for any thing of Business, and Carelessness in relation to his Fortune, soon plunged her into so many unhappy Circumstances, that she had long since sunk under the weight of them, had she not been constantly supported by the Interest and Assistance of the generous *Octavio.*

BUT besides the Reasons I have already assigned for the ill Success of the most deserving Passions, there is one which I must not omit. It is the Unhappiness of too many Women of Fortune and Merit (from a distrust of their own Judgment) to submit themselves entirely to the Direction of others, and rely too much on those Friendships they have contracted with some of their own Sex. These Female Acquaintance either immediately form some Design of their own upon them, in order to accomplish which every other Proposal is discouraged, or from a Spice of Envy, too incident to the Sex, cannot endure to see them ardently beloved, or think of having them pass their Days in the Arms of a Man who they are sensible would make it the Business of his Life to oblige them.

I have been led more particularly into the Subject of my present Paper, by the unhappy Passion of poor *Philander*. *Philander*, tho' of an Age which the greatest part of our Youth think fit to waste in all the Excesses of Luxury and Debauchery, has laid it out in furnishing his Mind with the most noble and manly Notions of Wisdom and Virtue. He has not at the same time forgot to make himself Master of all those little Accomplishments which the Polite have agreed to think necessary for a well-bred Man ; and is equally qualified for the most important Affairs, or the most gay Conversation. A perfect Knowledge of the World has made him for a long time look with the utmost Contempt on that insipid part of the Female Sex, who are skilled in nothing but Dress and Vanity. His Heart remained untouched amidst a thousand Beauties, till a particular Accident first brought him to the Knowledge of the lovely, the virtuous *Emilia*. *Emilia*, with a Fortune that might command the Vanities of Life, has shewn that she has a Mind infinitely above them. Her Beauty serves but as the Varnish to her Virtues, while with a graceful Innocence peculiar to her, she declares, that if ever she becomes a Wife, she has no Ambition to be a Gawdy Slave, but shall prefer substantial Happiness to empty Shew. *Philander* saw and loved her with a Passion equal to so much Desert: His Birth and Fortune must have entitled him at least to a favourable hearing, had not his Love given the Alarm to the Designs of a She Friend. There is something at all times highly barbarous in aspersing the absent, even where the Case is doubtful; but the malicious Creature, who takes it upon her to be *Emilia's* Directress, is foolish enough to charge *Philander* with being deficient in those very things for which he is more remarkably conspicuous: As I am a constant Patron to virtuous Love, I am in hopes however, that should this Paper reach *Emilia*, she will be so just to her self, to be her own Judge in a Cause of this Consequence; since, as a celebrated Author observes, it is very certain, that a generous and constant Passion, in an agreeable Lover, is the greatest Blessing that can happen to the most deserving of her Sex; and if overlooked in one, may perhaps never after be found in another.

No. 38.   *Saturday, May* 22.

——Scribere Jussit Amor.   Ovid.

I Shall make this Paper consist of one or two letters. The first is from *Philander* to *Emilia*, but was probably intercepted by the Good-natured Directress whom I mentioned in my last. There is so much Love and Sincerity through the whole, as must have affected the most stubborn temper.

Philander *to* Emilia.

Madam,

' IF you judge of my Passion only by what I said, when I 'had last the Honour to see you, you very much

' injure a Heart like mine, that is filled with Sentiments
' too lively, too tender to be expressed. I hardly know
' indeed what I said. What I very well remember is, that
' I was all Love and all Confusion, that I found it more
' difficult to speak before the Woman I was born to
' admire, than I have formerly done before the largest
· Assemblies.

' AT the same time I must confess, I was not a little
' amazed at being so often interrupted by a Creature,
' whom the most common Rules of Civility ought to have
' kept at a much greater Distance. I must own, Madam, I
' was perfectly at a Loss how to behave my self on such an
' Occasion, and whether I ought to stifle my Resentments,
' or give way to them, while I was so near a Person whom
' I had rather die than offend.

' AS to the business of Fortune between us, I have no
' other Proposal to make, but that I may put my whole
' Estate into the Hands of your Council, to be settled after
· any manner which you think will make you most easie.
' I hope I have long since resolved that my Carriage shall
' be such, if ever I have the Honour to be called your
' Husband, as shall unite our interests by the surest Tie, I
' mean that of *Affection.* Give me leave to assure you,
' Madam, with a Freedom which I think my self obliged to
' use on so serious an Occasion, that even as beautiful as
' you are, I could never be contented with your Person
' without your *Heart.* All I desire is, that I may have
' leave to try if my utmost Endeavours to please and
' deserve you, can make any Impression on it. I only beg
' I may be allowed to explain my self at large on this
' Head, though at the same time, to confess the Truth,
' Madam, I cannot help entertaining a vain Hope, that
' Providence had a much more than ordinary Influence in

' my first seeing you, and that I shall act with so much
' Truth and Sincerity in my Pretensions to you, as may
' possibly move you to think, that tho' I can never fully
' deserve you, I am much too sincere to be slighted.
' Vouchsafe, Madam, to hear me, and either root out this
' foolish Notion by a frank and generous Denial, or bless
' me with an Opportunity of dedicating my whole Life to
' your Service, and doing whatever the Heart of Man can
' be inspired with, when it is filled at once with *Gratitude*
' and *Love.*   I am,

  Madam,

   With infinite Passion, .
    Your most Devoted,
     Most Obedient, Humble Servant, &c.

THE next Letter was sent me last Week by a Lady
whose Case is truly deplorable, if it is really such as she
here represents it.   I shall insert it, as she desires, for the
sake of the Moral at the end of it.

 SIR,

' I Am perhaps the most unfortunate Woman living.   My
' Story in short is this.   *Cinthio*——Pardon those
' Tears that will fall upon this Paper at the sight of his
' Name——I would tell you that I was long and passion-
' ately beloved by him——But how can I describe the
' Greatness, the Sincerity of his Passion !   What Pains did
' he not take ?   What Method did he omit to shew how
' much he valued me ?   I must have been the worst, the
' most foolish of my Sex, to have been insensible to so
' much Truth and Merit.   I loved the dear, the unhappy
' Youth, with a Passion not inferior to his own ; but out of
' a foolish Reserve, which our silly Sex seldom know when

‘ they ought to keep up, and when lay aside, I rather chose
‘ to receive his Messages, and send him his Answers, by a
‘ Female Confident, than to see him my self. *Doria* (for so
‘ I shall call the Wretch) had long been a common Friend
‘ to us both ; she had a thousand times talked to me of
‘ *Cinthio* with all those Praises he so truly deserved ; when
‘ one Day she came to me, and with a seeming Anguish of
‘ Mind told me, that Cinthio *was the worst of Men, and had
‘ basely betrayed me.* It would be too tedious to give you
‘ an Account of the Fact she charged him with. I shall
‘ only inform you, that there happened at that time to be
‘ so many unlucky Circumstances, which made what she
‘ had told me look like Truth, that I could not help believ-
‘ ing her. She found the way to work up my Passion to
‘ such a height, that I made a Vow never to see him or
‘ receive a Message from him more ; and within a Fort-
‘ night after, by her Instigation, took a Man for my
‘ Husband whom I could neither Love nor Hate. I was
‘ no sooner Married, than I was fully convinced my *Cinthio*
‘ had been abused. After I had for some Days endured
‘ the sharpest Pangs of Rage, Despair, Jealousie and Love,
‘ I composed my self just enough to send him word that I
‘ was satisfied of his Innocence ; but conjured him, if he
‘ had ever loved, to avoid seeing me. I was this Afternoon
‘ obliged to go to a near Relation’s. The first Person I
‘ fixed my Eyes on when I came into the Room was
‘ *Cinthio*, who immediately burst into a Flood of Tears,
‘ made a low Bow, and retired.

‘ I had much ado to forbear Fainting, but am got home,
‘ and am this moment enduring such Torments as no
‘ Words can give a Notion of. I am undone ; but before
‘ my Senses are quite lost, I send you this, that it may for
‘ the future be observed as a constant Rule by my unhappy

' Sex, *Never to condemn a Lover, however guilty he may at*
' *first appear, till they have at least given him an Opportunity*
' *of justifying himself.*

I am, SIR,

The most unhappy of Women,

J. C.

P.S. ' I had like to have omitted informing you, that
' when I sent a Letter, in the Anguish of my Soul, to the
' Wretch above described, to desire I might know why she
' had ruined me, I received the following Answer.

Dear Jenny,

" THE Fellow you mention talked so perpetually about
" you, and took so little Notice of any Body else,
" that I could at last no longer endure him. I plainly
" foresaw, that if you had ever come together, you would
" have been Company for none but your selves; for which
" Reason I took Care to have you marry a Man with
" whom, if I am not mistaken, you may live as other
" Women generally do with their Husbands.

I am, Yours, &c.

No. 39.   *Tuesday, May* 25.

Nec Verbum Verbo curabis reddere fidus
Interpres————

Hor.

SINCE I have given Publick Notice of my Abode, I
have had many Visits from unfortunate Fellow-
Sufferers who have been crossed in Love as well as my self.
WILL. WORMWOOD, who is related to me by my

Mother's side, is one of those who often repair to me for my Advice. *Will.* is a Fellow of good Sense, but puts it to little other use than to torment himself. He is a Man of so refined an Understanding, that he can set a Construction upon every thing to his own disadvantage, and turn even a Civility into an Affront. He groans under imaginary Injuries, finds himself abused by his Friends, and fancies the whole World in a kind of Combination against him. In short, poor *Wormwood* is devoured with the Spleen: You may be sure a Man of this Humour makes a very whimsical Lover. Be that as it will, he is now over Head and Ears in that Passion, and by a very curious Interpretation of his Mistress's Behaviour, has in less than three Months reduced himself to a perfect Skeleton. As her Fortune is inferior to his, she gives him all the Encouragement another Man could wish, but has the Mortification to find that her Lover still Sowers upon her Hands. *Will.* is dissatisfied with her, whether she Smiles or Frowns upon him ; and always thinks her either too reserved, or too coming. A kind Word, that would make another Lover's Heart dance for Joy, pangs poor *Will.* and makes him lie awake all Night——As I was going on with *Will. Wormwood*'s Amour, I received a Present from my Bookseller, which I found to be *The Characters of* Theophrastus, Translated from the *Greek* into *English* by Mr. *Budgell.*

IT was with me, as I believe it will be with all who look into this Translation ; when I had begun to peruse it, I could not lay it by, till I had gone thro' the whole Book ; and was agreeably surprised to meet with a Chapter in it, Entitled, *A Discontented Temper*, which gives a livelier Picture of my Cousin *Wormwood*, than that which I was drawing for him my self. It is as follows,

CHAP. XVII.

A Discontented Temper.

' A Discontented Temper, is *A frame of Mind which sets*
' *a Man upon Complaining without reason.* When one of
' his Neighbours who makes an Entertainment, sends a
' Servant to him with a Plate of any thing that is Nice,
' *What,* says he, *your Master did not think me good enough*
' *to Dine with him?* He complains of his Mistress at the
' very time she is caressing him ; and when she redoubles
' her Kisses and Endearments, I *wish,* says he, *all this*
' *came from your Heart.* In a dry Season he grumbles
' for want of Rain, and when a Shower falls, mutters to
' himself, *Why could not this have come sooner?* If he
' happens to find a Purse of Mony, *Had it been a Pot of*
' *Gold,* says he, *it would have been worth stooping for.* He
' takes a great deal of pains to beat down the Price of a
' Slave ; and after he has paid his Money for him, *I am sure,*
' says he, *Thou art good for nothing, or I should not have*
' *had thee so cheap.* When a Messenger comes with great
' Joy to acquaint him that his Wife is brought to Bed of a
' Son, he answers, *That is as much as to say, Friend, I am*
' *poorer by half to day than I was Yesterday.* Tho' he
' has gain'd a Cause with full Costs and Damages, he com-
' plains that his Council did not insist upon the most
' material Points. If after any Misfortune has befallen
' him, his Friends raise a voluntary Contribution for him,
' and desire him to be Merry, *How is that possible,* says he,
' *when I am to pay every one of you his Money again, and be*
' *obliged to you into the bargain?*

THE Instances of a Discontented Temper which
Theophrastus has here made use of, like those which he

singles out to illustrate the rest of his Characters, are chosen with the greatest Nicety, and full of Humour. His Strokes are always fine and exquisite, and tho' they are not sometimes violent enough to affect the Imagination of a course Reader, cannot but give the highest Pleasure to every Man of a refined Taste, who has a thorough Insight into Human Nature.

AS for the Translation, I have never seen any of a Prose Author which has pleased me more. The Gentleman who has obliged the Publick with it, has followed the Rule which *Horace* has laid down for Translators, by preserving every where the Life and Spirit of his Author, without servilely copying after him Word for Word. This is what the *French*, who have most distinguished themselves by Performances of this Nature, so often inculcate when they advise a Translator to find out such particular Elegances in his own Tongue, as bear some Analogy to those he sees in the Original, and to express himself by such Phrases as his Author would probably have made use of, had he written in the Language into which he is translated. By this means, as well as by throwing in a lucky Word, or a short Circumstance, the Meaning of *Theophrastus* is all along explained, and the Humour very often carried to a greater height. A Translator, who does not thus consider the different Genius of the two Languages in which he is concerned, with such parallel Turns of Thoughts and Expression as correspond with one another in both of them, may value himself upon being a *faithful Interpreter;* but in Works of Wit and Humour will never do Justice to his Author, or Credit to himself.

AS this is every where a judicious and a reasonable Liberty, I see no Chapter in *Theophrastus* where it has been so much indulged, and in which it was so absolutely

necessary, as in the Character of the *Sloven.* I find the
Translator himself, tho' he has taken Pains to qualifie it, is
still apprehensive that there may be something too gross in
the Description. The Reader will see with how much
Delicacy he has touched upon every Particular, and cast
into Shades every thing that was shocking in so Nauseous a
Figure.

CHAP. XIX.

A SLOVEN.

' SLOVENLINESS is *Such a Neglect of a Man's Person,*
' *as makes him Offensive to other People.* The Sloven
' comes into Company with a dirty pair of Hands, and a
' sett of long Nails at the end of them, and tells you for an
' Excuse, that his Father and Grandfather used to do so
' before him. However, that he may out-go his Fore-
' Fathers, his Fingers are covered with Warts of his own
' raising. He is as hairy as a Goat, and takes care to let
' you see it. His Teeth and Breath are perfectly well-
' suited to one another. He lays about him at Table after
' a very extraordinary manner, and takes in a Meal at a
' Mouthful ; which he seldom disposes of without offending
' the Company. In Drinking he generally makes more
' haste than good speed. When he goes into the Bath, you
' may easily find him out by the scent of his Oyl, and dis-
' tinguish him when he is dress'd by the spots in his Coat.
' He does not stand upon Decency in Conversation, but
' will talk Smut, tho' a Priest and his Mother be in the
' Room. He commits a Blunder in the most solemn
' Offices of Devotion, and afterwards falls a laughing at it.
' At a Consort of Musick he breaks in upon the Perform-
' ance, hums over the Tune to himself, or if he thinks it
' long, asks the Musicians *Whether they will never have*

'*done?* He always spits at random, and if he is at an
' Entertainment, 'tis ten to one but it is upon the Servant
' who stands behind him.

THE foregoing Translation brings to my Remembrance
that excellent Observation of my Lord *Roscommon*'s.

> *None yet have been with* Admiration *read,*
> *But who (beside their* Learning) *were* Well-bred.
> *Lord* Roscommon's *Essay on Translated Verse.*

IF after this the Reader can endure the filthy Representation of the same Figure exposed in its worst Light, he
may see how it looks in the former *English* Version, which
was Published some Years since, and is done from the
French of *Bruyere.*

Nastiness or *Slovenliness.*

' SLOVENLINESS is a lazy and beastly Negligence of
' a Man's own Person, whereby he becomes so sordid, as to
' be offensive to those about him. You'll see him come
' into Company when he is cover'd all over with a Leprosy
' and Scurf, and with very long Nails, and says, those
' Distempers were hereditary, that his Father and Grand-
' father had them before him. He has Ulcers in his
' Thighs, and Boils upon his Hands, which he takes no
' care to have cured, but lets them run on till they are gone
' beyond Remedy. His Arm-pits are all hairy, and most
' part of his Body like a Wild Beast. His Teeth are black
' and rotten, which makes his Breath stink so that you
' cannot endure him to come nigh you ; he will also snuff
' up his Nose and spit it out as he eats, and uses to speak
' with his Mouth cramm'd full, and lets his Victuals come
' out at both Corners. He belches in the Cup as he is
' drinking, and uses nasty stinking Oyl in the Bath. He

' will intrude into the best Company in sordid ragged
' Cloaths. If he goes with his Mother to the Southsayers,
' he cannot then refrain from wicked and prophane Ex-
' pressions. When he is making his Oblations at the
' Temple, he will let the Dish drop out of his Hand, and
' fall a laughing, as if he had done some brave Exploit.
' At the finest Consort of Musick he can't forbear clapping
' his Hands, and making a rude Noise; will pretend to
' Sing along with them, and fall a Railing at them to leave
' off. Sitting at Table, he spits full upon the Servants who
' waited there.

I cannot close this Paper without observing, That if
Gentlemen of Leisure and Genius would take the same
Pains upon some other *Greek* or *Roman* Author, that has
been bestowed upon this, we should no longer be abused
by our Booksellers, who set their Hackney-Writers at Work
for so much a Sheet. The World would soon be convinced,
that there is a great deal of difference between putting an
Author into *English,* and *Translating* him.

No. 40.   *Thursday, May* 27.

> ———*Nec tarda senectus*
> *Debilitat vires*———   Virg.

THE Bosom into which Love enters, enclines the Person
who is inspired with it, with a Goodness towards all
with whom he converses, more extensive than even that
which is instilled by Charity. I pretend to so much of this
noble Passion, as seldom to overlook the Excellencies of
other Men ; and I forgive Mrs. *Page* all the Pangs my Passion has given me, since, though I am never to have her,

all other Persons are become more agreeable to me, from the large good Will, the beginning of which I owe to the Admiration of her. There are no Excellencies of Mind or Body in any Person that comes before me, which escape my Observation, and I take great Pleasure in divulging my Sense of them.

I must confess, Entertainments of the Neighbouring Theatre frequently engage my Evenings ; I do not take it to be a Condescension, that some of my Papers are but Paraphrases upon Play Bills. I have grown old in the Observation of the Feats of Activity and Genius for intelligent Movements, which I have always loved in my old Acquaintance *Jo. Prince*, who is to entertain us on *Monday* next with several new Inventions, wherein he has expressed the Compass and Variety of his excellent Talent. One of those Diversions he calls the *Rattle*, from the *Harlequin*, irregular and comick Movements with which it is performed ; another, which he hath termed *the Loobey*, is performed by himself, bearing a *Prong*, and Mrs. *Bicknall* managing a *Rake* with as much Beauty (tho' a little higher Dancing) as an *Arcadian* Shepherdess. The next Dance he will give us is very aptly called *the Innocent*, to be performed by Mrs. *Younger*, a genteel Movement, consisting of a Sarabrand and Jigg, to represent both the Simplicity and Gaiety of that Character.

THE fourth Act will be followed by a Motion contrived to represent the Midnight Mirth of Linkboys ; the Dance is very Humorous, and well imagined.

HIS Play concludes with what they call a Figure Dance, performed by an Elegant Assembly of Gentlemen and Ladies, and is as much different from any of the preceding Movements, as the Stile of a Poem is above that of a Ballad

BUT I must turn my Thoughts from this Performer, to a Person who has also diverted many different Generations on the Theatre, but in a much higher Sphere ; to wit, in the Character of a Poet.   The Person whom I am about to mention is the Celebrated Mr. *d'Urfey*, who has had the Fate of all great Authors, to have met with much Envy and Opposition ; but the sagacious part of Mankind ward (as soon as they begin to grow conspicuous) themselves against the Envious, by representing the Nobility of their Birth ; and I do not know why I may not as well defend the Writings of my Friend against the Malice of Criticks, by shewing how Ancient a Gentleman he is from whom they pretend to detract.   I will undertake to show those who pretend to Cavil at my Friend's Writings, that his Ancestors made a greater Figure in the World, nay in the Learned World, than their own.

Monsieur Perrault, *the famous* French *Academist, in his Memoirs of the Worthies of* France, *gives this Testimony of the House of* d'Urfey.

' HONORIUS *d'Urfey*, says he, Cadet of the Illustrious
' House of *d'Urfey*, in the Province of *Forrest*,
' was chosen Knight of *Malta*, and discharged the *devoirs*
' of his Profession, with all the Bravery and all the
' Exactness it could require.

  ' HE had two Brothers, the Eldest of which married the
' Heiress of *Chatteaumorant ;* but the Marriage afterwards
' being declared Null, by Reason of his Insufficiency, he
' became Religious, and died Prior of *Mountverdon*, and
' Dean of the Chapter of St. *John de Mountbrisson.*

  ' THE second Brother was Master of the Horse to the
' Duke of *Savoy*, and liv'd to be above one hundred Years
' old.

' *HONORIUS* was very much admired for many noble
' and witty Performances; but what principally obliges
' us to put him into the Number of our Illustrious Men,
' was the Beauty and Fertility which appears with so much
' Splendor in *Astrea,* the Romance he has left us, in which
' are lively Pictures of all the Conditions of human Life, in so
' genuine a Manner, that the Idea he gives of them has not
' only for above fifty Years past charmed all *France,* but all
' *Europe.*

' WHATEVER Veneration we are obliged to have for
' the admirable Poems of *Homer,* which have been the
' Delight of all Ages, yet, I believe, it may be said, that to
' consider them on the Score of Invention, Manners,
' Passion and Character, Monsieur *d'Urfey's Astrea,* tho'
' Prose, deserves no less the Name of a Poem, and not in
' the least Inferior to *Homer's* ; this is the Judgment of very
' learned Men, *viz.* Cardinal *Richlieu,* Mr. *Waller, Cowley,*
' &c. And those, who have been very much prepossest for
' the Ancients against the Moderns.

' OF this excellent Romance we mention, tho' finisht by
' another (he dying before the last *Tome* was written) yet he
' left enough from his own Hand to establish his Fame ;
' nor was it found to be meerly Romance, but an enigmati-
' cal Contexture of his own principal Adventures, before he
' set out for his noble Station at *Malta,* where he remained
' several Years.

' HE had conceived a Love for Madamoiselle *de*
' *Chatteaumorant,* sole Heiress of her Family, beautiful,
' rich and haughty, but of that noble Haughtiness which is
' commonly inspired by great Virtues ; in his Absence, she
' was married to his eldest Brother, more upon a political
' Account than any united Affection, as will thus appear.

' THE Houses of *d' Urfey* and *Chatteaumorant,* the two

' greatest of the whole Province, were always at Enmity
' with one another, and their Interests had divided all the
' Nobility of the Country, so that the Parents on both sides
' were willing by this Alliance to dry up the Source of the
' Quarrels and Misfortunes, which usually happened every
' Moment.

' *D'URFEY*, at his Return from *Malta*, found his
' Mistress married to his Brother, yet still he could not
' cease to love her ; and in all likelihood was not ignorant
' of his secret Defect, who, after ten Years Marriage,
' confessing at last his Impotence, was divorc'd ; and then
' the Chevalier (obtaining a Dispensation of his Vow)
' after he had surmounted several Difficulties, espoused
' Madamoiselle *Chatteaumorant.*

' THESE Adventures gave Occasion to those of *Celadon*,
' *Silvander*, *Astrea* and *Diana*, who are the mystical Images
' of them ; divers Affairs of Persons of the best Quality at
' Court, in his Time, having also furnisht Matter for the
' ingenious Construction of the Work.

So far Perrault.

' *SEVERINUS d' Urfey*, his near Kinsman, the before-
' mentioned Chevalier being his great Unkle, for the
' Extravagancy of his Youth, or some other Reason which
' has always been a Secret to those about him, was dis-
' inherited some time before he came into *England;*
' where being excellently well gifted in all Gentleman-like
' Qualities, tho' undoing all by his immoderate Vice of
' Gaming, he married a Gentlewoman of *Huntingtonshire*
' of the Family of the *Marmions*, from whom descended
' *Thomas d' Urfey*, the Ornament of this Paper.

THERE seems to be no Blot in this Pedigree, but that

of the Insufficiency of the Gentleman who married the Heiress of *Chatteaumorant ;* but as he could by reason of that Defect have no Descendants, the Heralds of *Germany, Scotland* and *Wales* all agree, that Insufficiency in a Collateral Line cannot affect the Heirs General ; so that thus my Friend and his Writings are safe against the most malicious Criticks in this particular.

MONSIEUR *Menage* reports, that the *d'Urfeys* descended from the Emperors of *Constantinople* on the Father's side, and the Viceroy of *Naples* on the Mother's. I shall put *Menage's* Words by way of Advertisement at the end of my to-Days Work. This long Account I have inserted, that the Ignorant of Mr. *d'Urfey's* Quality may know how to receive him, when on the seventh of next Month he shall appear (as he designs) in Honour of the Ladies, to speak an Oration by way of Prologue to the *Richmond Heiress.*

THAT Gentleman has so long appeared in the Cities of *London* and *Westminster,* attended only by one Servant, and him all along under Age, that the Generality have too familiar a Conception of him ; but it is to be hoped, that the Ladies, for whose Sake only he appears in Publick, will Smile upon him, as if he himself were a Knight of *Malta,* and receive him as if they beheld *Honorius* and *Severinus* in their professed Servant *Thomas d'Urfey.* It is recommended to all the fine Spirits, and beautiful Ladies, to possess themselves of Mr. *d'Urfey's* Tickets, least a further Account, which we shall shortly give of his Family and Merit, may make the Generality Purchase them, and exclude those whom he most desires for his Audience.

Extract from Menage.

MESSIRE *d'Urfey se noment Lascuris en leur nom de Family, et Pretendent etre issus des Anciens Lascuris*

Empereurs de Constantinople, le dernier Marqui d' Urſey qui avoit epouse une dalegre, disoit a son fils qui etoit exempt des Gardes, Mon fils, vous avez de grands Examples a suivre tant du Cote Paternel que Maternel de mon Cote vos Ancêtres etoient Empereurs d' Orient, et du Cote de vôtre Mere vous venes de Viceroie de Naples. Le fils repondit, il faut, Monsieur, que ce soient de pauvres gens, de n'avoir pu faire qu'un miserable exempt de Gardes, d'on vient qu'ils ne m'ont laisi ni l' Emp.re ni leur Viceroyaute.

I N D E X

TO THE

L O V E R .

A.

ABEDNEGO the *Jew*, how he bubbled Sir *Anthony Crabtree* with a pretended Manuscript, No. 11.

Advertisement about written Dances, N. 4.

Adultery, the great Crime of it, N. 36. How punished in a Negro in *Virginia, ib.*

Amours, Criminal, the Evils heaped up in them, N. 9. An Instance in the Story of a *German* Count and his Mistress, *ibid.*

Ancestry, how fond the *Crabtrees* are of it, No. 11, 16.

Antonio, in *Venice* preserv'd, betrays his Country for the Sake of a Woman that hates him, N. 12. A grim puzled Leacher, *ib.*

April, First of, a Day auspicious to the *Crabtrees*, N. 16.

Arbiter Elegantiarum, the Lover's Office, N. 3.

Aristotle, his Saying of Justice, 32.

Aronces, his Complaint about Country Dances, N. 3.

Authors, Half-sheet, their Care to improve Mankind, N. 1. Little ones glad of Applause on any Account, 5. Must not take Mony, 39. It makes 'em translate ill, *ib.*

B.

B*Acon*, Lord, his Saying of the Happiness of Governments in employing Men of Books and Leisure, N. 22.

Barrow, Dr. his Discourse of Contentment recommended, N. 26.   His great Merit, *ib.*

Bateman, Sir *James*, the first Proposer of the fine Cieling at *Greenwich* Hospital, N. 33.

Bays, Lancelot, his Letter and Petition to be the Lover's Esquire, N. 17.   His Toyshop of written Baubles, *ib.*

Behn, Mrs. understood the Practick Part of Love better than the Speculative, N. 23.

Benefits, the doing and receiving them the nicest Part of Commerce, N. 12.

Bickerstaff, Isaac, Esq ; rightly termed the Tatler, N. 23.

Blite, Leader of the Lovers Vagabond, N. 3.

Bookman, Sir *Anthony Crabtree*'s Quarrel with him, N. 16.

Bretagne, the Dance so called, N. 4.

Brickdust, Peter, a Kinsman of the *Crabtrees*, has the Face of a Cat and an Owl, N. 11.   His vile Character, *ib.*   Sir *Anthony Crabtree*'s Accuser, *ib.* & 14. and Voucher, 16. more hideous if possible than Sir *Anthony Crabtree*, 21.   What his Phiz is fit for, *ib.*

Britain, designed for a Dancing Island by the *French*, N. 4.

Brook, Lord, what he said of the wearisome Condition of Mortality, N. 32.

Brittleness, Things valued by the Ladies for it, N. 10.

Buckingham, late Duke of, the great Improver of the Manufacture of Glass in *England*, N. 34.

Busby, Dr. his Genius for Education, N. 27.

Budgell, Mr. his Translation of the Characters of *Theophrastus* recommended, N. 39.

Butcher, of St. *James's* Market, how Sir *Anthony Crabtree* paid him what his Lady ow'd him, N. 21.

C.

C*ARELESS*, (Mr.) of the *Middle Temple*, his Character, N. 20.

 Castlesoap, (*Ephraim*) his Letter about the *Crabtrees*, N. 14.

Cato, (Tragedy of) its Perfection, N. 5.

Censor of *Great Britain*, by whom to be taken out to dance, N. 4.

Censoriousness, how it exposes itself, N. 24.

Cercopitheci, the *Crabtrees* like them, N. 16.

Charles II, the Licenses of his Court, N. 2.

China Ware, the Folly of being fond of it, N. 10.

Claudian, of Dancing, N. 4.

Claywright, (*Rubens*) his Letter about the Pictures of the *Crabtrees* on his Potters Ware, N. 21.

Clidamira, her Letter to desire her Lovers might fight for her, N. 28

Coach, an Adventure upon calling one, N. 18.

Comedy, (fine Gentleman of) how dangerous a Character, N. 5.

Conjugal Affection, the great Relief of it in Distress, N. 8.

Contentment, the Duty of it, N. 26.

Country Gentlemen have too healthy Countenances, N. 5.

Courtly, (*Ned*) a Coxcomb, preferred to *Meanwell*, a Man of Wit, by a Lady, and why, N. 25.

Cowley, (*Abraham*) an ill Doctor in Love, N. 23.

Crabtrees, a mischievous ridiculous Family in *Herefordshire*, N. 11. &c. Their ugly Faces, *ib.* Bred Presbyterians, turn High Church-men, *ib.* Hated, 14, 21. Their Logick, *ib.* A most unaccountable Race, *ib.* Like the *Circopitheci*, 16. How fond of Ancestry, *ib.* First of *April* their auspicious Day, *ib.* An execrable Race, 21. A graceless Crew, *ib.* Where their Effigies are to be seen, *ib.* Sir *Anthony*, what an Antiquary he is, *ib.* Vide *Antonio* in *Venice* preserv'd, N. 12. His Motto, 14. How he saved the House of Sir *Ralph* his Father, *ib.* His sneaking Look, *ib.* His Behaviour towards an Illustrious Family, *ib.* His Superstition, 16. Why he form'd the South Sea Project, *ib.* His Curiosities, *ib.* He quarrels with the Bookman, and loses his Whisperers, *ib.* What his Levées were made up of, *ib.* How he cheated a Lady that employed him, *Susan Matchless* and her Father, 21. What an ungainly Creature, *ib.* His awkward little and briskly comick Air, *ib.* Insensible of Shame, and as smug as he is ugly, *ib.* What the Lady who employed him lost by him, *ib.* Sir *Ralph* would burn his House because Fornication had been committed in it, 11. Sir *Robert* a Knight before the Flood, 11. *Zachariah*'s clumsey Character, 11. How he comes into a Wenches Chamber, 14. A rare Voucher in the Business of Conveyances, 16. An half-witted impotent Wretch, 21. More hideous than Sir *Anthony*, *ib.* What a rare Trustee he is, *ib.*

Crimes, how aggravated, N. 32.
Curiosities, Sir *Anthony Crabtree*'s Collection, N. 16.

D.

DANCES, written, N. 4.
    Dancing (promiscuous) its Danger, N. 3.
Desires (loose) their own Punishment, N. 8.
Diana, her Amour with *Edymion*, N. 13.
Discontented Temper, taken out of *Theophrastus*'s Characters, N. 39.
Doubt, (*Charles*) his Letter for Advice in the Choice of his Mistress,
    N. 10.
Dreams of *Endymion*, N. 13.
D'Urfey (Mr. the Celebrated) has met with Envy as well as Opposition,
    N. 40. How related to the Marquis *d'Urfey*, the Author of the
    French Romance called *Astrea*, *ib.*
D'Urfeys, the Family of them in *France*, N. 40.
Dulcet, (Mrs.) how she was abused in Conversation, tho' a Fictitious
    Person, N. 24.
Dustgown, (*Clidamira*) her Character, N. 15.

E.

EMILIA and *Philander*, their Amour, N. 37.
    Endymion's Dreams, N. 13.
Epictetus, his Saying of Brittle Ware, N. 10.
Evil, a good Method to avoid it, N. 32.
Eyelid (*Anthony*) his Letter of Complaint against a Lady or looking
    out at Window, N. 7.

F

FLATTERY the most successful way of winning Women, N. 25.
    Flavia, her ill Choice in Marriage, N. 37.

G.

GALLANTRY, (Modern) nothing but Debauchery, N. 36.
    Giving, the Art of it in Lovers, N. 12.
Glass, (Manufacture of) by whom and how improved in *England*,
    N. 34.

Gotham, the Habitation of the *Crabtrees* in *Herefordshire*, N. 11.

Gothamites at last find out the *Crabtrees* to be no cunning Curs, N. 16.

Grame, (*James*) his Letter about his Pictures, N. 12.

Greenwich Hospital, the excellent Painting there, N. 33.

Gubbin, (*Timothy*) his Letter for Advice in his Amour, N. 17, 19.

Gumley, (Mr.) his Glass Gallery described, N. 34.

H.

HALE, (Sir *Matthew*) his Discourse of Religion, N. 29. Heart, to speak from it in Publick the surest way of Success, N. 18. How mended by honourable Love, 29.

I.

IDOLATRY, what makes it a crying Sin, N. 32. *Jenny Lipsy*, her Character, N. 15.

Inhumanity, how odious with Wantonness, N. 9.

Injustice, the great Sin of it with Respect to our Neighbours and ourselves, N. 32.

Johnson, (Mr.) one of the Lovers Assistants, his Character, N. 1.

Islands, dancing ones, N. 4.

Judges, their dancing, N. 4.

Judgment goes beyond Experience, N. 22.

Justice, all Virtues contained in it, N. 32.

K.

KING, grieving for his Wife's Death, how reproved by a Philosopher, N. 26.

King *William*, and Queen *Mary*, their Pictures at *Greenwich* Hospital described, N. 33.

Knight Errantry, how corrupted, N. 2.

L.

LANGUENTI, (*Ricardetto*) his Letter about the Crabtrees, N. 16.

Languissante, (*Cinthio*) his sublime unintelligible Letter, N. 19.

Lasie, (*Charles*) the Rover, his Letter, N. 23.

Letter, from a *Sabine* Lady to her Mother, a little while after the famous Rape of the *Romans*, N. 6.   About the Battle of the Eyes, 7. From Mrs. *Penruddock* to her Husband, the Day before he was to suffer Death, 8.   Mr. *Penruddock*'s Answer, *ib.*   From a Man leaving his Mistress to marry, 9.   From *Gotham* in *Herefordshire*, about the mischievous and ridiculous Family of the *Crabtrees*, 11.   A nice one from a Lady, 12.   From *James Grame* about his Pictures, *ib.*   From *George Powel*, 13.   From *Ephraim Castlesoap* about the *Crabtrees*, 14.   Madam *Dust gown*'s to her Lover, 15.   From *Ricardetto Languenti* about the *Crabtrees*, 16.   From *Timothy Gubbins*, 17, 19. From *Lancelot Bays*, 17.   From *Charles Doubt*, 19.   From *Cinthio Languissante*, *ib.*   From *Prudence Lovesick*, 20.   From *Susan Matchless* about the *Crabtrees*, 21.   From *Rubens Claywright* about the *Crabtrees* Pictures on his Potters Ware, *ib.*   About the fittest Age and Qualifications for Business, 22.   Two Letters from a Lover to his Mistress, one to be read by herself, and another by her Father, *ib.*   From *Charles Lasie*, 23.   *Marmaduke Myrtle*'s to a censorious Lady, 24.   From *Vesuvius* of the Power of Love, 25.   From a Gentleman about afflicting ones self for the Death of a Wife, 26. Mr. *Myrtle* to Mr. *Severn* on Mr. *Maittaire*'s new Edition of the Classicks in 12*mo.* 27.   From a Lady to desire her Lover to refuse her, 28.   The Answer, 30.   From *Clidamira*, *ib.*   From *Giles Limberham* about his inconstant Mistress, 28.   From *Ulysses Transmarinus*, 30.   From *Anthony Eyelids*, *Ch. Busie*, *Tallboy Gapeseed*, and *Ralph Doodle*, about staring Ladies, *ib.*   From *Tim. Pip*, 31.   From an old Batchelor fallen in Love, 31.   About *Miranda*'s Love of Flattery, 35.   From *Tom. Truelove*, 35.   From *Philander* to *Emilia*, 38.   From a Lady betrayed by a she Friend, *ib.*

Lodge, (Lovers) where *Powell*'s Puppet-Show was, N. 2. described, *ib.*

Levées, Sir *Anthony Crabtree*'s described, N. 16.

Limberham, (*Giles*) his Letter of Complaint against his kept Mistress, N. 28.

Love, (Passion of) leads to every Thing truly excellent, great and noble, N. 1, 5.   Instance out of *Cato*, *ib.*   Its Power over all Sorts of Men, 15.   When Honourable how it mends the Heart, 29.   One of the fundamental Laws of Nature, 32.   The chief End of the *Lover*, 36. Feign'd more likely to succeed than true, 37.

Lover, the Design of that Paper, N. 1.   The Characters of the Author's

Assistants, *ib.* of himself, *ib.* An Account of his Passion for Mrs. *Ann Page*, 2. He meets her, 5. Disappointments he has met with by it, 14.

Lovers Vagabond, an Order of Adventurers, N. 3. Their Leaders Character, *ib.*

Lovesick, (*Prudence*) her Letter, N. 20. Her Generosity to her Lover, *ib.*

M.

M*AITTAIRE*, (Mr.) his new Edition of the Classicks in *12mo* recommended, N. 27.

Marcius resigns *Thalestrina* to his Rival, N. 6.

Matchless, (*Susan*) her Letter about the *Crabtrees*, N. 21

Meanwell loses his Mistress for his Sincerity, N. 25.

Minuets, with Meanings, N. 4.

Miramantis the *Sabine*, her Letter to her Mother, N. 6.

Miranda's Character, N. 35.

Mischievous and ridiculous, Words made for the Family of the *Crabtrees*, N. 21.

Monitor, a horrid Paper, N. 34. The Author a heavy Rogue, *ib.*

Mortality, the wearisom Condition of it, N. 32.

Motto, a notable one on Sir *Anthony Crabtree*'s Coach, N. 14.

Myrtle, (*Marmaduke*) Author of the *Lover*, N. 2. His Lodging, *ib.* His Letter to a censorious Lady, 24.

N.

N*EGRO*, the Tragical Story of an Adulterous one in *Virginia*, N. 36.

Neighbours, the Sin of injuring them, N. 32.

Nice, (Sir *Courtly*) the Mirrour of Fops, N. 18.

O.

O*SWALD*, (Mr.) the Widower, his Character, N. 1. His Love for his Wife's Memory, 29.

Ovid, the *Galen* of Love, N. 23.

P.

PAGE, (Mrs. *Ann*) the Author's Love for her, N. 2.
  Paintings of *Greenwich* Hospital described, N. 33.
Peace, the whole Nation to learn to dance upon it, N. 4.
Pedlar, an honest one, how abused by Sir *Anthony Crabtree*, N. 14.
Penruddock, (Mrs.) her Letter to her Husband condemned to dye, N.
  8.   His Answer, *ib.*
Philander and *Emilia*, their Amour, N. 37.   His Letter to her, 38.
Pip, (*Tim.*) his Pretensions to a Lady from seeing her Topsie Turvey,
  N. 31.
Platonick Lovers, their Indifference, N. 34.
Potters Ware of *Britain*, its Use, N. 10.   The effigies of the *Crabtree*
  to be seen on some of it, 22.
Powell, (*George*) his Behaviour as to Love and Honour, N. 13.
Prince, (*Jo.*) his Entertainments in Dancing, N. 40.
Publick, (speaking in it) with what Confusion *Englishmen* do it, N. 18.
  The Cause of it, *ib.*

R.

RAPE, (*Sabine*) the Behaviour of some of the Ladies then, N. 6.
  Religion, Sir *Matthew Hale*'s Discourse of it, N. 29.
Reproach, the most painful Thing to Lovers, N. 34.
Robin the Treasurer, what *Suckling* says of him, N. 21.
Romans, their Publick Spirit, N. 26.
Room, how to leave it handsomely, N. 3.

S.

SABINE Lady, her Letter to her Mother from *Rome*, after the
  famous Rape by the *Romans*, N. 6.
Scandal a Fault in the Ladies, N. 24.
Severn (Mr.) his Character, N. 1.   *Marmaduke Myrtle*'s Letters to
  him about Mr. *Maittaire*'s Edition of the *Classicks* in 12*mo.* 27.
Sins of the Second Table, N. 32.
Sloven (Character of one) out of *Theophrastus*, N. 39.
Stage debauch'd in *Charles* II. Reign, N. 2.   Its Influence on
  Manners, 5.

T.

TACITURNITY, when a Fault, N. 18.
    Tale of a Tub, written for the Advancement of Religion, N. 16.
Sir *Anthony Crabtree* borrows his *South-Sea* Project from it, *ib.*
Theophrastus's Characters well Translated by Mr. *Budgel*, N. 39.
Thornhill, his excellent Painting at *Greenwich*, N. 33.
Tin Tallies, a Coin much in Use by the *Crabtrees*, N. 21.
Transmarinus Ulysses, his Letter about his Father's betraying him in an Amour, N. 30.
Town, how to qualify ones self for it, N. 5.
Toyshop, (Poetical) *Lancelot Bays*'s, N. 17.
Translation, Rules for it, N. 39.
True-Love, (*Tom.*) his Letter to his Mistress, not to promise her self by Denial, N. 35.
Twilight, (Madam) her Character, N. 15.

V.

VERSES on Dancing, N. 4.
    Vesuvius, his Letter of the Power of Love, N. 24.

W.

WHIFFLE, (*Tom.*) his Letter about the Battle of the Eyes, N. 7.
    Whispers, Sir *Anthony Crabtree's* Politicks made up of them, N. 11. He is at a sad Loss for want of them, 16.
Wildgoose, (Mr.) one of the *Lover*'s Assistants, his Character, N. 1.
Witwood (Miss) her Affectation of Wit, N. 25.
Women, the greatest Sufferers in Criminal Amours, N. 9. The several Ways Men take to gain them, 25. Won by Flattery, *ib.* Apt to prefer feign'd Love, to true, 37. And to be directed by others in their Choice of Husbands, *ib.*
Wormwood, (*Will.*) his Character, N. 39.

Addison's

Papers on *Milton*'s *Paradise Lost*,

from the *Spectator*.

MILTON'S PARADISE LOST.*

I.

Cedite Romani Scriptores cedite Graii.—Propert.

THERE is nothing in Nature more irksome than general Discourses, especially when they turn chiefly upon Words. For this Reason I shall wave the Discussion of that Point which was started some Years since, whether *Milton's Paradise Lost* may be called an Heroick Poem? Those who will not give it that Title, may call it (if they please) a *Divine Poem*. It will be sufficient to its Perfection, if it has in it all the Beauties of the highest kind of Poetry; and as for those who alledge it is not an Heroick Poem, they advance no more to the Diminution of it, than if they should say *Adam* is not *Æneas*, nor *Eve Helen*.

I shall therefore examine it by the Rules of Epic Poetry, and see whether it falls short of the *Iliad* or *Æneid*, in the Beauties which are essential to that kind of Writing. The first thing to be considered in an Epic Poem, is the Fable, which is perfect or imperfect, according as the Action which it relates is more or less so. This Action should have three Qualifications in it. First, It should be but One Action. Secondly, It should be an entire Action; and, Thirdly, It should be a great Action. To consider the Action of the *Iliad*, *Æneid*, and *Paradise Lost*, in these three several Lights. *Homer* to preserve the Unity of his Action hastens into the Midst of Things, as *Horace* has observed: Had he gone up to *Leda's* Egg, or begun much later, even at the Rape of *Helen*, or the Investing of *Troy*, it is

* Originally printed in the Saturday *Spectators*, from January 5 to May 3, 1712

manifest that the Story of the Poem would have been a Series of several Actions.   He therefore opens his Poem with the Discord of his Princes, and artfully interweaves, in the several succeeding Parts of it, an Account of every Thing material which relates to them and had passed before that fatal Dissension.   After the same manner, *Æneas* makes his first Appearance in the *Tyrrhene* Seas, and within Sight of *Italy*, because the Action proposed to be celebrated was that of his settling himself in *Latium*.   But because it was necessary for the Reader to know what had happened to him in the taking of *Troy*, and in the preceding Parts of his Voyage, *Virgil* makes his Hero relate it by way of Episode in the second and third Books of the *Æneid*. The Contents of both which Books come before those of the first Book in the Thread of the Story, tho' for preserving of this Unity of Action they follow them in the Disposition of the Poem.   *Milton*, in imitation of these two great Poets, opens his *Paradise Lost* with an Infernal Council plotting the Fall of Man, which is the Action he proposed to celebrate ; and as for those great Actions, which preceded, in point of Time, the Battle of the Angels, and the Creation of the World, (which would have entirely destroyed the Unity of his principal Action, had he related them in the same Order that they happened) he cast them into the fifth, sixth, and seventh Books, by way of Episode to this noble Poem.

Aristotle himself allows, that *Homer* has nothing to boast of as to the Unity of his Fable, tho' at the same time that great Critick and Philosopher endeavours to palliate this Imperfection in the *Greek* Poet, by imputing it in some measure to the very Nature of an Epic Poem.   Some have been of opinion, that the *Æneid* also labours in this Particular, and has Episodes which may be looked upon as Excrescencies rather than as Parts of the Action.   On the contrary, the Poem, which we have now under our Consideration, hath no other Episodes than such as naturally arise from the Subject, and yet is filled with such a Multitude of astonishing Incidents, that it gives us at the same time a Pleasure of the greatest Variety, and of the greatest Simplicity ; uniform in its Nature, tho' diversified in the Execution.

I must observe also, that as *Virgil*, in the Poem which was designed to celebrate the Original of the *Roman* Empire, has described the Birth of its great Rival, the *Carthaginian* Commonwealth : *Milton*, with the like Art, in his Poem on the *Fall of Man*, has related the Fall of those Angels who are his professed Enemies.   Besides the many other Beauties in such an

Episode, its running parallel with the great Action of the Poem hinders it from breaking the Unity so much as another Episode would have done, that had not so great an Affinity with the principal Subject. In short, this is the same kind of Beauty which the Criticks admire in *The Spanish Frier*, or *The Double Discovery*, where the two different Plots look like Counter-parts and Copies of one another.

The second Qualification required in the Action of an Epic Poem, is, that it should be an *entire* Action : An Action is entire when it is complete in all its Parts; or, as *Aristotle* describes it, when it consists of a Beginning, a Middle, and an End. Nothing should go before it, be intermixed with it, or follow after it, that is not related to it. As on the contrary, no single Step should be omitted in that just and regular Progress which it must be supposed to take from its Original to its Consummation. Thus we see the Anger of *Achilles* in its Birth, its Continuance and Effects ; and *Æneas's* Settlement in *Italy*, carried on thro' all the Oppositions in his Way to it both by Sea and Land. The Action in *Milton* excels (I think) both the former in this Particular ; we see it contrived in Hell, executed upon Earth, and punished by Heaven. The Parts of it are told in the most distinct Manner, and grow out of one another in the most natural Order.

The third Qualification of an Epic Poem is its *Greatness*. The Anger of *Achilles* was of such Consequence, that it embroiled the Kings of *Greece*, destroyed the Heroes of *Troy*, and engaged all the Gods in Factions. *Æneas's* Settlement in *Italy* produced the *Cæsars*, and gave Birth to the *Roman* Empire. *Milton's* Subject was still greater than either of the former ; it does not determine the Fate of single Persons or Nations, but of a whole Species. The united Powers of Hell are joined together for the Destruction of Mankind, which they effected in part, and would have completed, had not Omnipotence it self interposed. The principal Actors are Man in his greatest Perfection, and Woman in her highest Beauty. Their Enemies are the fallen Angels : The Messiah their Friend, and the Almighty their Protector. In short, every thing that is great in the whole Circle of Being, whether within the Verge of Nature, or out of it, has a proper Part assigned it in this noble Poem.

In Poetry, as in Architecture, not only the Whole, but the principal Members, and every Part of them, should be Great. I will not presume to say, that the Book of Games in the *Æneid*, or that in the *Iliad*, are not of this Nature, nor to reprehend

Virgil's Simile of the Top, and many other of the same kind in the *Iliad*, as liable to any Censure in this Particular ; but I think we may say, without derogating from those wonderful Performances, that there is an unquestionable Magnificence in every Part of *Paradise Lost*, and indeed a much greater than could have been formed upon any Pagan System.

But *Aristotle*, by the Greatness of the Action, does not only mean that it should be great in its Nature, but also in its Duration, or in other Words that it should have a due Length in it, as well as what we properly call Greatness. The just Measure of this kind of Magnitude, he explains by the following Similitude. An Animal, no bigger than a Mite, cannot appear perfect to the Eye, because the Sight takes it in at once, and has only a confused Idea of the Whole, and not a distinct Idea of all its Parts ; if on the contrary you should suppose an Animal of ten thousand Furlongs in length, the Eye would be so filled with a single Part of it, that it could not give the Mind an Idea of the Whole. What these Animals are to the Eye, a very short or a very long Action would be to the Memory. The first would be, as it were, lost and swallowed up by it, and the other difficult to be contained in it. *Homer* and *Virgil* have shewn their principal Art in this Particular ; the Action of the *Iliad*, and that of the *Æneid*, were in themselves exceeding short, but are so beautifully extended and diversified by the Invention of *Episodes*, and the Machinery of Gods, with the like poetical Ornaments, that they make up an agreeable Story, sufficient to employ the Memory without over-charging it. *Milton's* Action is enriched with such a Variety of Circumstances, that I have taken as much Pleasure in reading the Contents of his Books, as in the best invented Story I ever met with. It is possible, that the Traditions, on which the *Iliad* and *Æneid* were built, had more Circumstances in them than the History of *the Fall of Man*, as it is related in Scripture. Besides, it was easier for *Homer* and *Virgil* to dash the Truth with Fiction, as they were in no danger of offending the Religion of their Country by it. But as for *Milton*, he had not only a very few Circumstances upon which to raise his Poem, but was also obliged to proceed with the greatest Caution in every thing that he added out of his own Invention. And, indeed, notwithstanding all the Restraints he was under, he has filled his Story with so many surprising Incidents, which bear so close an Analogy with what is delivered in Holy Writ, that it is capable of pleasing the most delicate Reader, without giving Offence to the most scrupulous.

The modern Criticks have collected from several Hints in the *Iliad* and *Æneid* the Space of Time, which is taken up by the Action of each of those Poems ; but as a great Part of *Milton's* Story was transacted in Regions that lie out of the Reach of the Sun and the Sphere of Day, it is impossible to gratify the Reader with such a Calculation, which indeed would be more curious than instructive; none of the Criticks, either Ancient or Modern, having laid down Rules to circumscribe the Action of an Epic Poem with any determin'd Number of Years, Days or Hours.

This Piece of Criticism on Milton's Paradise Lost *shall be carried on in the following* Saturdays *Papers.*

II.

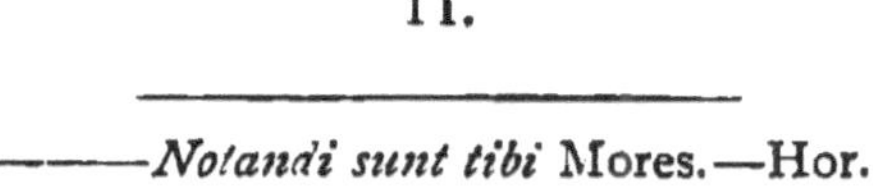

———*Notandi sunt tibi* Mores.—Hor.

HAVING examined the Action of *Paradise Lost*, let us in the next place consider the Actors. This is *Aristotle's* Method of considering, first the Fable, and secondly the Manners ; or, as we generally call them in *English*, the Fable and the Characters.

Homer has excelled all the Heroic Poets that ever wrote, in the Multitude and Variety of his Characters. Every God that is admitted into this Poem, acts a Part which would have been suitable to no other Deity. His Princes are as much distinguished by their Manners, as by their Dominions ; and even those among them, whose Characters seem wholly made up of Courage, differ from one another as to the particular kinds of Courage in which they excel. In short, there is scarce a Speech or Action in the *Iliad*, which the Reader may not ascribe to the Person that speaks or acts, without seeing his Name at the Head of it.

Homer does not only outshine all other Poets in the Variety, but also in the Novelty of his Characters. He has introduced among his *Grecian* Princes a Person who had lived thrice the Age of Man, and conversed with *Theseus, Hercules, Polyphemus,* and the first Race of Heroes. His principal Actor is the Son of a Goddess, not to mention the Offspring of other Deities, who have likewise a Place in his Poem, and the venerable *Trojan* Prince, who was the Father of so many Kings and

Heroes. There is in these several Characters of *Homer*, a certain Dignity as well as Novelty, which adapts them in a more peculiar manner to the Nature of an Heroic Poem. Tho' at the same time, to give them the greater Variety, he has described a *Vulcan*, that is a Buffoon among his Gods, and a *Thersites* among his Mortals.

Virgil falls infinitely short of *Homer* in the Characters of his Poem, both as to their Variety and Novelty. *Æneas* is indeed a perfect Character, but as for *Achates*, tho' he is stiled the Hero's Friend, he does nothing in the whole Poem which may deserve that Title. *Gyas, Mnesteus, Sergestus*, and *Cloanthus*, are all of them Men of the same Stamp and Character.

——*Fortemque Gyan, fortemque Cloanthum.*

There are indeed several very Natural Incidents in the Part of *Ascanius*; as that of *Dido* cannot be sufficiently admired. I do not see any thing new or particular in *Turnus*. *Pallas* and *Evander* are remote Copies of *Hector* and *Priam*, as *Lausus* and *Mezentius* are almost Parallels to *Pallas* and *Evander*. The Characters of *Nisus* and *Eurialus* are beautiful, but common. We must not forget the Parts of *Sinon, Camilla*, and some few others, which are fine Improvements on the *Greek* Poet. In short, there is neither that Variety nor Novelty in the Persons of the *Æneid*, which we meet with in those of the *Iliad*.

If we look into the Characters of *Milton*, we shall find that he has introduced all the Variety his Fable was capable of receiving. The whole Species of Mankind was in two Persons at the Time to which the Subject of his Poem is confined. We have, however, four distinct Characters in these two Persons. We see Man and Woman in the highest Innocence and Perfection, and in the most abject State of Guilt and Infirmity. The two last Characters are, indeed, very common and obvious, but the two first are not only more magnificent but more new than any Characters either in *Virgil* or *Homer*, or indeed in the whole Circle of Nature.

Milton was so sensible of this Defect in the Subject of his Poem, and of the few Characters it would afford him, that he has brought into it two Actors of a Shadowy and Fictitious Nature, in the Persons of *Sin* and *Death*, by which means he has wrought into the Body of his Fable a very beautiful and well-invented Allegory. But notwithstanding the Fineness of this Allegory may attone for it in some measure; I cannot think that Persons of such a Chymerical Existence are proper Actors in an Epic Poem ; because there is not that measure of Probability annexed to them, which is requisite in Writings of this kind, as I shall shew more at large hereafter.

Virgil has, indeed, admitted *Fame* as an Actress in the *Æneid,* but the Part she acts is very short, and none of the most admired Circumstances in that Divine Work. We find in Mock-Heroic Poems, particularly in the *Dispensary* and the *Lutrin,* several Allegorical Persons of this Nature which are very beautiful in those Compositions, and may, perhaps, be used as an Argument, that the Authors of them were of Opinion, such Characters might have a Place in an Epic Work. For my own part, I should be glad the Reader would think so, for the sake of the Poem I am now examining, and must further add, that if such empty unsubstantial Beings may be ever made use of on this Occasion, never were any more nicely imagined, and employed in more proper Actions, than those of which I am now speaking.

Another Principal Actor in this Poem is the great Enemy of Mankind. The Part of *Ulysses* in *Homer's Odyssey* is very much admired by *Aristotle,* as perplexing that Fable with very agreeable Plots and Intricacies, not only by the many Adventures in his Voyage, and the Subtility of his Behaviour, but by the various Concealments and Discoveries of his Person in several Parts of that Poem. But the Crafty Being I have now mentioned, makes a much longer Voyage than *Ulysses,* puts in practice many more Wiles and Stratagems, and hides himself under a greater Variety of Shapes and Appearances, all of which are severally detected, to the great Delight and Surprize of the Reader.

We may likewise observe with how much Art the Poet has varied several Characters of the Persons that speak to his infernal Assembly. On the contrary, how has he represented the whole Godhead exerting it self towards Man in its full Benevolence under the Three-fold Distinction of a Creator, a Redeemer and a Comforter !

Nor must we omit the Person of *Raphael,* who amidst his Tenderness and Friendship for Man, shews such a Dignity and Condescension in all his Speech and Behaviour, as are suitable to a Superior Nature. The Angels are indeed as much diversified in *Milton,* and distinguished by their proper Parts, as the Gods are in *Homer* or *Virgil.* The Reader will find nothing ascribed to *Uriel, Gabriel, Michael,* or *Raphael,* which is not in a particular manner suitable to their respective Characters.

There is another Circumstance in the principal Actors of the *Iliad* and *Æneid,* which gives a peculiar Beauty to those two Poems, and was therefore contrived with very great Judgment. I mean the Authors having chosen for their Heroes, Persons who were so nearly related to the People for whom they wrote. *Achilles* was a *Greek,* and *Æneas* the remote Founder of *Rome.* By this means their Countrymen (whom they principally proposed to themselves for their Readers) were particularly attentive to all the Parts of their Story, and sympathized with their Heroes in all their Adventures. A *Roman* could not but rejoice in the Escapes, Successes and Victories of *Æneas,* and be grieved at any Defeats, Misfortunes or Disappointments that befel him ; as a *Greek* must have had the same Regard for *Achilles.* And it is plain, that each of those Poems have lost this great Advantage, among those Readers to whom their Heroes are as Strangers, or indifferent Persons.

Milton's Poem is admirable in this respect, since it is impossible for any of its Readers, whatever Nation, Country or People he may belong to, not to be related to the Persons who are the principal Actors in it ; but what is still infinitely more to its Advantage, the principal Actors in this Poem are not only our Progenitors, but our Representatives. We have an actual Interest in every thing they do, and no less than our utmost Happiness is concerned, and lies at Stake in all their Behaviour.

I shall subjoin as a Corollary to the foregoing Remark, an admirable Observation out of *Aristotle,* which hath been very much misrepresented in the Quotations of some Modern Criticks. ' If a Man of perfect and consummate Virtue falls into ' a Misfortune, it raises our Pity, but not our Terror, because we ' do not fear that it may be our own Case, who do not resemble ' the Suffering Person.' But as that great Philosopher adds, ' If ' we see a Man of Virtue mixt with Infirmities, fall into any ' Misfortune, it does not only raise our Pity but our Terror ; ' because we are afraid that the like Misfortunes may happen ' to our selves, who resemble the Character of the Suffering ' Person.

I shall take another Opportunity to observe, that a Person of an absolute and consummate Virtue should never be introduced in Tragedy, and shall only remark in this Place, that the foregoing Observation of *Aristotle,* tho' it may be true in other Occasions, does not hold in this ; because in the present Case, though the Persons who fall into Misfortune are of the most perfect and consummate Virtue, it is not to be considered as what may possibly be, but what actually is our own Case ; since we are embarked with them on the same Bottom, and must be Partakers of their Happiness or Misery.

In this, and some other very few Instances, *Aristotle's* Rules for Epic Poetry (which he had drawn from his Reflections upon *Homer*) cannot be supposed to quadrate exactly with the Heroic Poems which have been made since his Time ; since it is plain his Rules would still have been more perfect, could he have perused the *Æneid* which was made some hundred Years after his Death.

In my next, I shall go through other Parts of Milton's *Poem ; and hope that what I shall there advance, as well as what I have already written, will not only serve as a Comment upon* Milton, *but upon* Aristotle.

III.

Reddere personæ scit convenientia cuique.—Hor.

WE have already taken a general Survey of the Fable and Characters in *Milton's Paradise Lost.* The Parts which remain to be considered, according to *Aristotle's* Method, are the *Sentiments* and the *Language.* Before I enter upon the first of these, I must advertise my Reader, that it is my Design as soon as I have finished my general Reflections on these four several Heads, to give particular Instances out of the Poem which is now before us of Beauties and Imperfections which may be observed under each of them, as also of such other Particulars as may not properly fall under any of them. This I thought fit to premise, that the Reader may not judge too hastily of this Piece of Criticism, or look upon it as Imperfect, before he has seen the whole Extent of it.

The Sentiments in an Epic Poem are the Thoughts and Behaviour which the Author ascribes to the Persons whom he introduces, and are *just* when they are conformable to the Characters of the several Persons. The Sentiments have likewise a relation to *Things* as well as *Persons*, and are then perfect when they are such as are adapted to the Subject. If in either of these Cases the Poet endeavours to argue or explain, to magnify or diminish, to raise Love or Hatred, Pity or Terror, or any other Passion, we ought to consider whether the Sentiments he makes use of are proper for those Ends. *Homer* is censured by the Criticks for his Defect as to this Particular in several parts of the *Iliad* and *Odyssey*, tho' at the same time those, who have treated this great Poet with Candour, have attributed this Defect to the Times in which he lived. It was the Fault of the Age, and not of *Homer*, if there wants that Delicacy in some of his Sentiments which now appears in the Works of Men of a much inferior Genius. Besides, if there are Blemishes in any particular Thoughts, there is an infinite Beauty in the greatest Part of them. In short, if there are many Poets who would not have fallen into the Meanness of some of his Sentiments, there are none who could have risen up to the Greatness of others. *Virgil* has excelled all others in the Propriety of his Sentiments. *Milton* shines likewise very much in this Particular : Nor must we omit one Consideration which adds to his Honour and Reputation. *Homer* and *Virgil* introduced Persons whose Characters are commonly known among Men, and such as are to be met with either in History, or in ordinary Conversation. *Milton's* Characters, most of them, lie out of Nature, and were to be formed purely by his own Invention. It shews a greater Genius in *Shakespear* to have drawn his *Calyban*, than his *Hotspur* or *Julius Cæsar:* The one was to be supplied out of his own Imagination, whereas the other might have been formed upon Tradition, History and Observation. It was much easier therefore for *Homer* to find proper Sentiments for an Assembly of *Grecian* Generals, than for *Milton* to diversify his infernal Council with proper Characters, and inspire them with a Variety of Sentiments. The Lovers of *Dido* and *Æneas* are only Copies of what has passed between other Persons. *Adam* and *Eve*, before the Fall, are a different Species from that of Mankind, who are descended from them ; and none but a Poet of the most unbounded Invention, and the most exquisite Judgment, could have filled their Conversation and Behaviour with so many apt Circumstances during their State of Innocence.

Nor is it sufficient for an Epic Poem to be filled with such Thoughts as are *Natural*, unless it abound also with such as are *Sublime*. *Virgil* in this Particular falls short of *Homer*. He has not indeed so many Thoughts that are Low and Vulgar ; but at the same time has not so many Thoughts that are Sublime and Noble. The Truth of it is, *Virgil* seldom rises into very astonishing Sentiments, where he is not fired by the *Iliad*. He every where charms and pleases us by the Force of his own Genius ; but seldom elevates and transports us where he does not fetch his Hints from *Homer*.

Milton's chief Talent, and indeed his distinguishing Excellence, lies in the Sublimity of his Thoughts.   There are others of the Moderns who rival him in every other part of Poetry; but in the Greatness of his Sentiments he triumphs over all the Poets both Modern and Ancient, *Homer* only excepted.   It is impossible for the Imagination of Man to distend itself with greater Ideas, than those which he has laid together in his first, second, and sixth Books.   The seventh, which describes the Creation of the World, is likewise wonderfully Sublime, tho' not so apt to stir up Emotion in the Mind of the Reader, nor consequently so perfect in the Epic Way of Writing, because it is filled with less Action.   Let the judicious Reader compare what *Longinus* has observed on several Passages in *Homer*, and he will find Parallels for most of them in the *Paradise Lost.*

From what has been said we may infer, that as there are two kinds of Sentiments, the Natural and the Sublime, which are always to be pursued in an Heroic Poem, there are also two kinds of Thoughts which are carefully to be avoided.   The first are such as are affected and unnatural; the second such as are mean and vulgar.   As for the first kind of Thoughts, we meet with little or nothing that is like them in *Virgil:* He has none of those trifling Points and Puerilities that are so often to be met with in *Ovid*, none of the Epigrammatick Turns of *Lucan*, none of those swelling Sentiments which are so frequent in *Statius* and *Claudian*, none of those mixed Embellishments of *Tasso*.   Every thing is just and natural.   His Sentiments shew that he had a perfect Insight into human Nature, and that he knew every thing which was the most proper to affect it.

Mr. *Dryden* has in some Places, which I may hereafter take notice of, misrepresented *Virgil's* way of thinking as to this Particular, in the Translation he has given us of the *Æneid.* I do not remember that *Homer* any where falls into the Faults above-mentioned, which were indeed the false Refinements of later Ages.   *Milton*, it must be confest, has sometimes erred in this Respect, as I shall shew more at large in another Paper; tho' considering how all the Poets of the Age in which he writ were infected with this wrong way of thinking, he is rather to be admired that he did not give more into it, than that he did sometimes comply with the vicious Taste which still prevails so much among Modern Writers.

But since several Thoughts may be natural which are low and groveling, an Epic Poet should not only avoid such Sentiments as are unnatural or affected, but also such as are mean and vulgar.   *Homer* has opened a great Field of Raillery to Men of more Delicacy than Greatness of Genius, by the Homeliness of some of his Sentiments.   But, as I have before said, these are rather to be imputed to the Simplicity of the Age in which he lived, to which I may also add, of that which he described, than to any Imperfection in that Divine Poet. *Zoilus*, among the Ancients, and Monsieur *Perrault*, among the Moderns, pushed their Ridicule very far upon him, on account of some such Sentiments.   There is no Blemish to be observed in *Virgil* under this Head, and but a very few in *Milton*.

I shall give but one Instance of this Impropriety of Thought in *Homer*, and at the same time compare it with an Instance of the same Nature, both in *Virgil* and *Milton*.   Sentiments which raise Laughter, can very seldom be admitted with any Decency into an Heroic Poem, whose Business it is to excite Passions of a much nobler Nature.   *Homer*, however, in his Characters of *Vulcan* and *Thersites*, in his Story of *Mars* and *Venus*, in his Behaviour of *Irus*, and in other Passages, has been observed to have lapsed into the Burlesque Character, and to have departed from that serious Air which seems essential to the Magnificence of an Epic Poem.   I remember but one Laugh in the whole *Æneid*, which rises in the fifth Book, upon *Monœtes*, where he is represented as thrown overboard, and drying himself upon a Rock.   But this Piece of Mirth is so well timed, that the severest Critick can have nothing to say against it ; for it is in the Book of Games and Diversions, where the Reader's Mind may be supposed to be sufficiently relaxed for such an Entertainment.   The only Piece of Pleasantry in *Paradise Lost*, is where the Evil Spirits are described as rallying the Angels upon the Success of their new invented Artillery. This Passage I look upon to be the most exceptionable in the whole Poem, as being nothing else but a String of Punns, and those too very indifferent ones.

> ————*Satan beheld their Plight,*
> *And to his Mates thus in Derision call'd.*
> *O Friends, why come not on those Victors Proud?*
> *Ere-while they fierce were coming, and when we,*
> *To entertain them fair with open Front,*
> *And Breast, (what could we more?) propounded terms*
> *Of Composition, straight they chang'd their minds,*
> *Flew off, and into strange Vagaries fell*
> *As they would dance: yet for a Dance they seem'd*
> *Somewhat extravagant, and wild; perhaps*

For Joy of offer'd Peace ; but I suppose
If our Proposals once again were heard,
We should compel them to a quick Result.
   To whom thus Belial *in like gamesome Mood :*
Leader, the Terms we sent were Terms of Weight,
Of hard Contents, *and full of force urg'd home ;*
Such as we might perceive amus'd them all,
And stumbled *many : who receives them right,*
Had need, from Head to Foot, well understand ;
Not understood, *this Gift they have besides,*
They shew us when our Foes walk not upright.
   Thus they among themselves in pleasant vein
Stood Scoffing————

IV.

———

Ne, quicunque Deus, quicunque adhibebitur heros,
Regali conspectus in auro nuper et ostio,
Migret in Obscuras humili sermone tabernas :
Aut, dum vitat humum, nubes et inania captet.—Hor.

———

HAVING already treated of the Fable, the Characters, and Sentiments in the *Paradise Lost,* we are in the last Place to consider the *Language ;* and as the Learned World is very much divided upon *Milton* as to this Point, I hope they will excuse me if I appear particular in any of my Opinions, and encline to those who judge the most advantageously of the Author.

It is requisite that the Language of an Heroic Poem should be both Perspicuous and Sublime. In proportion as either of these two Qualities are wanting, the Language is imperfect. Perspicuity is the first and most necessary Qualification ; insomuch that a good-natur'd Reader sometimes overlooks a little Slip even in the Grammar or *Syntax,* where it is impossible for him to mistake the Poet's Sense. Of this Kind is that Passage in *Milton,* wherein he speaks of *Satan.*

    ————God and his Son except,
Created thing nought valu'd he nor shunn'd.

And that in which he describes *Adam* and *Eve.*

> Adam *the goodliest Man of Men since born*
> *His Sons, the fairest of her Daughters* Eve.

It is plain, that in the former of these Passages according to the natural *Syntax*, the Divine Persons mentioned in the first Line are represented as created Beings ; and that, in the other, *Adam* and *Eve* are confounded with their Sons and Daughters. Such little Blemishes as these, when the Thought is great and natural, we should, with *Horace*, impute to a pardonable Inadvertency, or to the Weakness of human Nature, which cannot attend to each minute Particular, and give the last Finishing to every Circumstance in so long a Work. The Ancient Criticks therefore, who were acted by a Spirit of Candour, rather than that of Cavilling, invented certain Figures of Speech, on purpose to palliate little Errors of this nature in the Writings of those Authors who had so many greater Beauties to attone for them.

If Clearness and Perspicuity were only to be consulted, the Poet would have nothing else to do but to cloath his Thoughts in the most plain and natural Expressions. But since it often happens that the most obvious Phrases, and those which are used in ordinary Conversation, become too familiar to the Ear, and contract a kind of Meanness by passing through the Mouths of the Vulgar, a Poet should take particular Care to guard himself against Idiomatick Ways of Speaking. *Ovid* and *Lucan* have many Poornesses of Expression upon this Account, as taking up with the first Phrases that offered, without putting themselves to the Trouble of looking after such as would not only have been natural, but also elevated and sublime. *Milton* has but few Failings in this Kind, of which, however, you may meet with some Instances, as in the following Passages.

> *Embrios and Idiots, Eremites and Fryars,*
> White, Black, *and* Grey, *with all their* Trumpery,
> *Here Pilgrims roam*————
> ————*A while discourse they hold,*
> No fear lest Dinner cool ; *when thus began*
> *Our Author*————
> *Who of all Ages to succeed, but feeling*
> *The Evil on him brought by me, will curse*
> *My Head, ill fare our Ancestor impure,*
> For this we may thank Adam————

The Great Masters in Composition, knew very well that many an elegant Phrase becomes improper for a Poet or an Orator, when it has been debased by common Use. For this Reason the Works of Ancient Authors, which are written in dead Languages, have a great Advantage over those which are written in Languages that are now spoken. Were there any mean Phrases or Idioms in *Virgil* and *Homer*, they would not shock the Ear of the most delicate Modern Reader, so much as they would have done that of an old *Greek* or *Roman*, because we never hear them pronounced in our Streets, or in ordinary Conversation.

It is not therefore sufficient, that the Language of an Epic Poem be Perspicuous, unless it be also Sublime. To this end it ought to deviate from the common Forms and ordinary Phrases of Speech. The Judgment of a Poet very much discovers it self in shunning the common Roads of Expression, without falling into such ways of Speech as may seem stiff and unnatural; he must not swell into a false Sublime, by endeavouring to avoid the other Extream. Among the *Greeks*, *Æschylus*, and sometimes *Sophocles*, were guilty of this Fault; among the *Latins*, *Claudian* and *Statius;* and among our own Countrymen, *Shakespear* and *Lee.* In these Authors the Affectation of Greatness often hurts the Perspicuity of the Stile, as in many others the Endeavour after Perspicuity prejudices its Greatness.

Aristotle has observed, that the Idiomatick Stile may be avoided, and the Sublime formed, by the following Methods. First, by the Use of Metaphors: Such are those of *Milton.*

> Imparadised *in one another's Arms.* .
> ———*And in his Hand a Reed*
> *Stood waving* tipt *with Fire.*———
> *The grassie Clods now* calv'd,— ——
> Spangled *with Eyes*————

In these and innumerable other Instances, the Metaphors are very bold but just; I must however observe that the Metaphors are not so thick sown in *Milton*, which always savours too much of Wit; that they never clash with one another, which, as *Aristotle* observes, turns a Sentence into a kind of an Enigma or Riddle; and that he seldom has recourse to them where the proper and natural Words will do as well.

Another way of raising the Language, and giving it a Poetical Turn, is to make use of the Idioms of other Tongues. *Virgil* is full of the *Greek* Forms of Speech, which the Criticks call *Hellenisms*, as *Horace* in his Odes abounds with them much more than *Virgil.* I need not mention the several Dialects which *Homer* has made use of for this end. *Milton*, in conformity with the Practice of the Ancient Poets, and with *Aristotle's* Rule, has infused a great many *Latinisms*, as well as *Græcisms*, and sometimes *Hebraisms*, into the Language of his Poem ; as towards the Beginning of it.

> Nor *did they* not *perceive the evil Plight*
> *In which they were,* or *the fierce Pains not feel.*
> *Yet to their Gen'ral's Voice they soon obey'd.—*
> ————*Who shall tempt with wand'ring Feet*
> *The dark unbottom'd Infinite Abyss,*
> *And through the* palpable Obscure *find out*
> *His uncouth way, or spread his airy Flight*
> *Upborn with indefatigable Wings*
> *Over the* vast Abrupt!
>
> ————*So both ascend*
> *In the Visions of God*————   Book 2.

Under this Head may be reckon'd the placing the Adjective after the Substantive, the Transposition of Words, the turning the Adjective into a Substantive, with several other Foreign Modes of Speech which this Poet has naturalized to give his Verse the greater Sound, and throw it out of Prose.

The third Method mentioned by *Aristotle* is what agrees with the Genius of the *Greek* Language more than with that of any other Tongue, and is therefore more used by *Homer* than by any other Poet. I mean the lengthning of a Phrase by the Addition of Words, which may either be inserted or omitted, as also by the extending or contracting of particular Words by the Insertion or Omission of certain Syllables. *Milton* has put in practice this Method of raising his Language, as far as the Nature of our Tongue will permit, as in the Passage above-mentioned, *Eremite*, for what is Hermit, in common Discourse. If you observe the Measure of his Verse, he has with great Judgment suppressed a Syllable in several Words, and shortned those of two Syllables into one, by which Method, besides the above-mentioned Advantage, he has given a greater Variety to his Numbers. But this Practice is more particularly remarkable in the Names of Persons and of Countries, as *Beëlzebub, Hessebon,* and in many other Particulars, wherein he has either changed the Name, or made use of that which is not the most commonly known, that he might the better depart from the Language of the Vulgar.

The same Reason recommended to him several old Words, which also makes his Poem appear the more venerable, and gives it a greater Air of Antiquity.

I must likewise take notice, that there are in *Milton* several Words of his own coining, as *Cerberean*, *miscreated*, *Hell-doom'd*, *Embryon* Atoms, and many others. If the Reader is offended at this Liberty in our *English* Poet, I would recommend him to a Discourse in *Plutarch*, which shews us how frequently *Homer* has made use of the same Liberty.

Milton, by the above-mentioned Helps, and by the Choice of the noblest Words and Phrases which our Tongue would afford him, has carried our Language to a greater Height than any of the *English* Poets have ever done before or after him, and made the Sublimity of his Stile equal to that of his Sentiments.

I have been the more particular in these Observations on *Milton's* Stile, because it is that Part of him in which he appears the most singular. The Remarks I have here made upon the Practice of other Poets, with my Observations out of *Aristotle*, will perhaps alleviate the Prejudice which some have taken to his Poem upon this Account ; tho' after all, I must confess that I think his Stile, tho' admirable in general, is in some places too much stiffened and obscured by the frequent Use of those Methods, which *Aristotle* has prescribed for the raising of it.

The Redundancy of those several Ways of Speech, which *Aristotle* calls *foreign Language*, and with which *Milton* has so very much enriched, and in some Places darkned the Language of his Poem, was the more proper for his use, because his Poem is written in Blank Verse. Rhyme, without any other Assistance, throws the Language off from Prose, and very often makes an indifferent Phrase pass unregarded ; but where the Verse is not built upon Rhymes, there Pomp of Sound, and Energy of Expression, are indispensably necessary to support the Stile, and keep it from falling into the Flatness of Prose.

Those who have not a Taste for this Elevation of Stile, and are apt to ridicule a Poet when he departs from the common Forms of Expression, would do well to see how *Aristotle* has treated an Ancient Author called *Euclid*, for his insipid Mirth upon this Occasion. Mr. *Dryden* used to call these sort of Men his Prose-Criticks.

I should, under this Head of the Language, consider *Milton's* Numbers, in which he has made use of several Elisions, which are not customary among other *English* Poets, as may be particularly observed in his cutting off the Letter *Y*, when it precedes a Vowel. This, and some other Innovations in the Measure of his Verse, has varied his Numbers in such a manner, as makes them incapable of satiating the Ear, and cloying the Reader, which the same uniform Measure would certainly have done, and which the perpetual Returns of Rhime never fail to do in long Narrative Poems. I shall close these Reflections upon the Language of *Paradise Lost*, with observing that *Milton* has copied after *Homer* rather than *Virgil* in the length of his Periods, the Copiousness of his Phrases, and the running of his Verses into one another.

V.

——Ubi plura nitent in carmine, non ego paucis
Offendor maculis, quas aut Incuria fudit,
Aut Humana parum oavit Natura——   Hor.

I HAVE now considered *Milton's Paradise Lost* under those four great Heads of the Fable, the Characters, the Sentiments, and the Language ; and have shewn that he excels, in general, under each of these Heads. I hope that I have made several Discoveries which may appear new, even to those who are versed in Critical Learning. Were I indeed to chuse my Readers, by whose Judgment I would stand or fall, they should not be such as are acquainted only with the *French* and *Italian* Criticks, but also with the Ancient and Moderns who have written in either of the learned Languages. Above all, I would have them well versed in the *Greek* and *Latin* Poets, without which a Man very often fancies that he understands a Critick, when in Reality he does not comprehend his Meaning.

It is in Criticism, as in all other Sciences and Speculations ; one who brings with him any implicit Notions and Observations which he has made in his reading of the Poets, will find his own Reflections methodized and explained, and perhaps several little Hints that had passed in his Mind, perfected and improved in the Works of a good Critick ; whereas one who has not these previous Lights is very often an utter Stranger to what he reads, and apt to put a wrong Interpretation upon it.

Nor is it sufficient, that a Man who sets up for a Judge in Criticism, should have perused the Authors above mentioned, unless he has also a clear and Logical Head. Without this Talent he is perpetually puzzled and perplexed amidst his own

Blunders, mistakes the Sense of those he would confute, or if he chances to think right, does not know how to convey his Thoughts to another with Clearness and Perspicuity. *Aristotle*, who was the best Critick, was also one of the best Logicians that ever appeared in the World.

Mr. *Lock's* Essay on Human Understanding would be thought a very odd Book for a Man to make himself Master of, who would get a Reputation by Critical Writings ; though at the same time it is very certain, that an Author who has not learned the Art of distinguishing between Words and Things, and of ranging his Thoughts, and setting them in proper Lights, whatever Notions he may have, will lose himself in Confusion and Obscurity. I might further observe, that there is not a *Greek* or *Latin* Critick who has not shewn, even in the Style of his Criticisms, that he was a Master of all the Elegance and Delicacy of his Native Tongue.

The Truth of it is, there is nothing more absurd, than for a Man to set up for a Critick, without a good Insight into all the Parts of Learning ; whereas many of those who have endeavoured to signalize themselves by Works of this Nature among our *English* Writers, are not only defective in the above-mentioned Particulars, but plainly discover, by the Phrases which they make use of, and by their confused way of thinking, that they are not acquainted with the most common and ordinary Systems of Arts and Sciences. A few general Rules extracted out of the *French* Authors, with a certain Cant of Words, has sometimes set up an Illiterate heavy Writer for a most judicious and formidable Critick.

One great Mark, by which you may discover a Critick who has neither Taste nor Learning, is this, that he seldom ventures to praise any Passage in an Author which has not been before received and applauded by the Publick, and that his Criticism turns wholly upon little Faults and Errors. This part of a Critick is so very easie to succeed in, that we find every ordinary Reader, upon the publishing of a new Poem, has Wit and Ill-nature enough to turn several Passages of it into Ridicule, and very often in the right Place. This Mr. *Dryden* has very agreeably remarked in those two celebrated Lines,

> *Errors, like Straws, upon the Surface flow ;*
> *He who would search for Pearls must dive below.*

A true Critick ought to dwell rather upon Excellencies than Imperfections, to discover the concealed Beauties of a Writer, and communicate to the World such things as are worth their Observation. The most exquisite Words and finest Strokes of an Author are those which very often appear the most doubtful and exceptionable to a Man who wants a Relish for polite Learning ; and they are these, which a sower undistinguishing Critick generally attacks with the greatest Violence. *Tully* observes, that it is very easie to brand or fix a Mark upon what he calls *Verbum ardens*, or, as it may be rendered into *English, a glowing bold Expression,* and to turn it into Ridicule by a cold ill-natured Criticism. A little Wit is equally capable of exposing a Beauty, and of aggravating a Fault ; and though such a Treatment of an Author naturally produces Indignation in the Mind of an understanding Reader, it has however its Effect among the Generality of those whose Hands it falls into, the Rabble of Mankind being very apt to think that every thing which is laughed at with any Mixture of Wit, is ridiculous in it self.

Such a Mirth as this is always unseasonable in a Critick, as it rather prejudices the Reader than convinces him, and is capable of making a Beauty, as well as a Blemish, the Subject of Derision. A Man, who cannot write with Wit on a proper Subject, is dull and stupid, but one who shews it in an improper Place, is as impertinent and absurd. Besides, a Man who has the Gift of Ridicule is apt to find Fault with any thing that gives him an Opportunity of exerting his beloved Talent, and very often censures a Passage, not because there is any Fault in it, but because he can be merry upon it. Such kinds of Pleasantry are very unfair and disingenuous in Works of Criticism, in which the greatest Masters, both Ancient and Modern, have always appeared with a serious and instructive Air.

As I intend in my next Paper to shew the Defects in *Milton's Paradise Lost,* I thought fit to premise these few Particulars, to the End that the Reader may know I enter upon it, as on a very ungrateful Work, and that I shall just point at the Imperfections, without endeavouring to enflame them with Ridicule. I must also observe with *Longinus,* that the Productions of a great Genius, with many Lapses and Inadvertencies, are infinitely preferable to the Works of an inferior kind of Author, which are scrupulously exact and conformable to all the Rules of correct Writing.

I shall conclude my Paper with a Story out of *Boccalini,* which sufficiently shews us the Opinion that judicious Author entertained of the sort of Criticks I have been here mentioning. A famous Critick, says he, having gathered together all the

Faults of an eminent Poet, made a Present of them to *Apollo*, who received them very graciously, and resolved to make the Author a suitable Return for the Trouble he had been at in collecting them. In order to this, he set before him a Sack of Wheat, as it had been just threshed out of the Sheaf. He then bid him pick out the Chaff from among the Corn, and lay it aside by it self. The Critick applied himself to the Task with great Industry and ·Pleasure, and after having made the due Separation, was presented by *Apollo* with the Chaff for his Pains.

VI.

————————————————————*velut si*
Egregio inspersos reprendas corpore nævos.—Hor.

AFTER what I have said in my last *Saturday's* Paper, I shall enter on the subject of this without further Preface, and remark the several Defects which appear in the Fable, the Characters, the Sentiments, and the Language of *Milton's Paradise Lost;* not doubting but the Reader will pardon me, if I alledge at the same time whatever may be said for the Extenuation of such Defects. The first Imperfection which I shall observe in the Fable is that the Event of it is unhappy.

The Fable of every Poem is, according to *Aristotle's* Division, either *Simple* or *Implex.* It is called Simple when there is no change of Fortune in it : Implex, when the Fortune of the chief Actor changes from Bad to Good, or from Good to Bad. The Implex Fable is thought the most perfect ; I suppose, because it is more proper to stir up the Passions of the Reader, and to surprize him with a greater Variety of Accidents.

The Implex Fable is therefore of two kinds : In the first the chief Actor makes his Way through a long Series of Dangers and Difficulties, till he arrives at Honour and Prosperity, as we see in the Story of *Ulysses.* In the second, the chief Actor in the Poem falls from some eminent Pitch of Honour and Prosperity, into Misery and Disgrace. Thus we see *Adam* and *Eve* sinking from a State of Innocence and Happiness, into the most abject Condition of Sin and Sorrow.

The most taking Tragedies among the Ancients were built on this last sort of Implex Fable, particularly the Tragedy of *Œdipus*, which proceeds upon a Story, if we may believe

Aristotle, the most proper for Tragedy that could be invented by the Wit of Man. I have taken some Pains in a former Paper to shew, that this kind of Implex Fable, wherein the Event is unhappy, is more apt to affect an Audience than that of the first kind; notwithstanding many excellent Pieces among the Ancients, as well as most of those which have been written of late Years in our own Country, are raised upon contrary Plans. I must however own, that I think this kind of Fable, which is the most perfect in Tragedy, is not so proper for an Heroic Poem.

Milton seems to have been sensible of this Imperfection in his Fable, and has therefore endeavoured to cure it by several Expedients; particularly by the Mortification which the great Adversary of Mankind meets with upon his Return to the Assembly of Infernal Spirits, as it is described in a beautiful Passage of the Tenth Book; and likewise by the Vision wherein *Adam* at the close of the Poem sees his off-spring triumphing over his great Enemy, and himself restored to a happier *Paradise* than that from which he fell.

There is another Objection against *Milton's* Fable, which is indeed almost the same with the former, tho' placed in a different Light, namely, That the Hero in the *Paradise Lost* is unsuccessful, and by no means a Match for his Enemies. This gave Occasion to Mr. *Dryden's* Reflection, that the Devil was in reality *Milton's* Hero. I think I have obviated this Objection in my first Paper. The *Paradise Lost* is an Epic or a Narrative Poem, and he that looks for an Hero in it, searches for that which *Milton* never intended; but if he will needs fix the Name of an Hero upon any Person in it, 'tis certainly the *Messiah* who is the Hero, both in the Principal Action, and in the chief Episodes. Paganism could not furnish out a real Action for a Fable greater than that of the *Iliad* or *Æneid*, and therefore an Heathen could not form a higher Notion of a Poem than one of that kind, which they call an Heroic. Whether *Milton's* is not of a sublimer Nature I will not presume to determine: It is sufficient that I shew there is in the *Paradise Lost* all the Greatness of Plan, Regularity of Design, and masterly Beauties which we discover in *Homer* and *Virgil*.

I must in the next Place observe, that *Milton* has interwoven in the Texture of his Fable some Particulars which do not seem to have Probability enough for an Epic Poem, particularly in the Actions which he ascribes to *Sin* and *Death*, and the Picture which he draws of the *Limbo of Vanity*, with other Passages in the second Book. Such Allegories rather

savour of the Spirit of *Spenser* and *Ariosto*, than of *Homer*
and *Virgil.*

In the Structure of his Poem he has likewise admitted of too
many Digressions.   It is finely observed by *Aristotle*, that the
Author of an Heroic Poem should seldom speak himself, but
throw as much of his Work as he can into the Mouths of those
who are his Principal Actors.   *Aristotle* has given no reason
for this Precept ; but I presume it is because the Mind of the
Reader is more awed and elevated when he hears *Æneas* or
Achilles speak, than when *Virgil* or *Homer* talk in their own
Persons.   Besides that assuming the Character of an eminent
Man is apt to fire the Imagination, and raise the Ideas of the
Author.   *Tully* tells us, mentioning his Dialogue of Old Age,
in which *Cato* is the chief Speaker, that upon a Review of it he
was agreeably imposed upon, and fancied that it was *Cato*, and
not he himself, who uttered his Thoughts on that Subject.

If the Reader would be at the Pains to see how the Story of
the *Iliad* and the *Æneid* is delivered by those Persons who act
in it, he will be surprized to find how little in either of these
Poems proceeds from the Authors.   *Milton* has, in the general
disposition of his Fable, very finely observed this great Rule ;
insomuch that there is scarce a third Part of it which comes
from the Poet ; the rest is spoken either by *Adam* and *Eve*, or
by some Good or Evil Spirit who is engaged either in their
Destruction or Defence.

From what has been here observed it appears, that Digressions are by no means to be allowed of in an Epic Poem.   If
the Poet, even in the ordinary course of his Narration, should
speak as little as possible, he should certainly never let his
Narration sleep for the sake of any Reflections of his own.   I
have often observed, with a secret Admiration, that the longest
Reflection in the *Æneid* is in that Passage of the Tenth Book,
where *Turnus* is represented as dressing himself in the Spoils
of *Pallas*, whom he had slain.   *Virgil* here lets his Fable stand
still for the sake of the following Remark.   *How is the Mind of
Man ignorant of Futurity, and unable to bear prosperous Fortune with Moderation?   The Time will come when* Turnus
shall wish that he had left the Body of Pallas *untouched, and
curse the Day on which he dressed himself in these Spoils.*   As
the great Event of the *Æneid*, and the Death of *Turnus*, whom
Æneas slew because he saw him adorned with the Spoils of
Pallas, turns upon this Incident, *Virgil* went out of his way to
make this Reflection upon it, without which so small a Circumstance might possibly have slipped out of his Reader's Memory.

Lucan, who was an Injudicious Poet, lets drop his Story very frequently for the sake of his unnecessary Digressions, or his *Diverticula*, as *Scaliger* calls them.   If he gives us an Account of the Prodigies which preceded the Civil War, he declaims upon the Occasion, and shews how much happier it would be for Man, if he did not feel his Evil Fortune before it comes to pass ; and suffer not only by its real Weight, but by the Apprehension of it.   *Milton's* Complaint for his Blindness, his Panegyrick on Marriage, his Reflections on *Adam* and *Eve's* going naked, of the Angels eating, and several other Passages in his Poem, are liable to the same Exception, tho' I must confess there is so great a Beauty in these very Digressions, that I would not wish them out of his Poem.

I have, in a former Paper, spoken of the *Characters* of *Milton's Paradise Lost*, and declared my Opinion, as to the Allegorical Persons who are introduced in it.

If we look into the *Sentiments*, I think they are sometimes defective under the following Heads : First, as there are several of them too much pointed, and some that degenerate even into Punns.   Of this last kind I am afraid is that in the First Book, where speaking of the Pigmies, he calls them,

> ————*The small* Infantry
> *Warr'd on by Cranes*———— ——

Another Blemish that appears in some of his Thoughts, is his frequent Allusion to Heathen Fables, which are not certainly of a Piece with the Divine Subject, of which he treats. I do not find fault with these Allusions, where the Poet himself represents them as fabulous, as he does in some Places, but where he mentions them as Truths and Matters of Fact.   The Limits of my Paper will not give me leave to be particular in Instances of this kind ; the Reader will easily remark them in his Perusal of the Poem.

A third fault in his Sentiments, is an unnecessary Ostentation of Learning, which likewise occurs very frequently.   It is certain that both *Homer* and *Virgil* were Masters of all the Learning of their Times, but it shews it self in their Works after an indirect and concealed manner.   *Milton* seems ambitious of letting us know, by his Excursions on Free-Will and Predestination, and his many Glances upon History, Astronomy, Geography, and the like, as well as by the Terms and Phrases he sometimes makes use of, that he was acquainted with the whole Circle of Arts and Sciences.

If, in the last place, we consider the *Language* of this great Poet, we must allow what I have hinted in a former Paper, that it is often too much laboured, and sometimes obscured by old Words, Transpositions, and Foreign Idioms. *Seneca's* Objection to the Style of a great Author, *Riget ejus oratio, nihil in eâ placidum nihil lene,* is what many Criticks make to *Milton:* As I cannot wholly refuse it, so I have already apologized for it in another Paper ; to which I may further add, that *Milton's* Sentiments and Ideas were so wonderfully Sublime, that it would have been impossible for him to have represented them in their full Strength and Beauty, without having recourse to these Foreign Assistances. Our Language sunk under him, and was unequal to that Greatness of Soul, which furnished him with such glorious Conceptions.

A second Fault in his Language is, that he often affects a kind of Jingle in his Words, as in the following Passages, and many others :

> *And brought into the* World *a* World *of Woe.*
> ——*Begirt th' Almighty throne*
> Beseeching *or* besieging——
> *This* tempted *our* attempt——
> *At one slight* bound *high overleapt all* bound.

I know there are Figures for this kind of Speech, that some of the greatest Ancients have been guilty of it, and that *Aristotle* himself has given it a place in his Rhetorick among the Beauties of that Art. But as it is in its self poor and trifling, it is I think at present universally exploded by all the Masters of Polite Writing.

The last Fault which I shall take notice of in *Milton's* Style, is the frequent use of what the Learned call *Technical Words,* or Terms of Art. It is one of the great Beauties of Poetry, to make hard things intelligible, and to deliver what is abstruse of it self in such easy Language as may be understood by ordinary Readers : Besides, that the Knowledge of a Poet should rather seem born with him, or inspired, than drawn from Books and Systems. I have often wondered how Mr. *Dryden* could translate a Passage out of *Virgil* after the following manner.

> *Tack to the Larboard, and stand off to Sea.*
> *Veer Star-board Sea and Land.*——

Milton makes use of *Larboard* in the same manner. When he is upon Building he mentions *Doric Pillars, Pilasters, Cornice, Freeze, Architrave.* When he talks of Heavenly Bodies, you meet with *Eccliptic* and *Eccentric,* the *trepidation, Stars dropping from the Zenith, Rays culminating from the Equator.* To which might be added many Instances of the like kind in several other Arts and Sciences.

I shall in my next Papers give an Account of the many particular Beauties in *Milton,* which would have been too long to insert under those general Heads I have already treated of, and with which I intend to conclude this Piece of Criticism.

VII.

——volet hæc sub luce videri,
*Judicis argutum quæ non formidat acumen.—*Hor.

I HAVE seen in the Works of a Modern Philosopher, a Map of the Spots in the Sun. My last Paper of the Faults and Blemishes in *Milton's Paradise Lost,* may be considered as a Piece of the same Nature. To pursue the Allusion: As it is observed, that among the bright Parts of the Luminous Body above mentioned, there are some which glow more intensely, and dart a stronger Light than others; so, notwithstanding I have already shewn *Milton's* Poem to be very beautiful in general, I shall now proceed to take Notice of such Beauties as appear to me more exquisite than the rest. *Milton* has proposed the Subject of his Poem in the following Verses.

> *Of Man's first disobedience, and the fruit*
> *Of that forbidden tree, whose mortal taste*
> *Brought Death into the World and all our woe,*
> *With loss of* Eden, *till one greater Man*
> *Restore us, and regain the blissful Seat,*
> *Sing Heavenly Muse——*

These Lines are perhaps as plain, simple and unadorned as any of the whole Poem, in which Particular the Author has conformed himself to the Example of *Homer* and the Precept of *Horace.*

His Invocation to a Work which turns in a great measure upon the Creation of the World, is very properly made to the Muse who inspired *Moses* in those Books from whence our

Author drew his Subject, and to the Holy Spirit who is therein represented as operating after a particular manner in the first Production of Nature. This whole Exordium rises very happily into noble Language and Sentiment, as I think the Transition to the Fable is exquisitely beautiful and natural.

The Nine Days Astonishment, in which the Angels lay entranced after their dreadful Overthrow and Fall from Heaven, before they could recover either the use of Thought or Speech, is a noble *Circumstance*, and very finely imagined. The Division of Hell into Seas of Fire, and into firm Ground impregnated with the same furious Element, with that particular Circumstance of the Exclusion of *Hope* from those Infernal Regions, are Instances of the same great fruitful Invention.

The Thoughts in the first Speech and Description of *Satan*, who is one of the Principal Actors in this Poem, are wonderfully proper to give us a full Idea of him. His Pride, Envy and Revenge, Obstinacy, Despair and Impenitence, are all of them very artfully interwoven. In short, his first Speech is a Complication of all those Passions which discover themselves separately in several other of his Speeches in the Poem. The whole part of this great Enemy of Mankind is filled with such Incidents as are very apt to raise and terrifie the Reader's Imagination. Of this nature, in the Book now before us, is his being the first that awakens out of the general Trance, with his Posture on the burning Lake, his rising from it, and the Description of his Shield and Spear.

Thus Satan *talking to his nearest Mate,*
With head up-lift above the wave, and eyes
That sparkling blaz'd, his other parts beside
Prone on the Flood, extended long and large,
Lay floating many a rood————
Forthwith upright he rears from off the pool
His mighty Stature ; on each hand the flames
Driv'n backward slope their pointing Spires, and rowl'd
In Billows, leave i' th' midst a horrid vale.
Then with expanded wings he steers his flight
Aloft, incumbent on the dusky Air
That felt unusual weight————
————His pondrous Shield
Ethereal temper, massie, large and round,
Behind him cast ; the broad circumference
Hung on his Shoulders like the Moon, whose orb
Thro' Optick Glass the Tuscan *Artist views*

> *At Ev'ning, from the top of* Fesole,
> *Or in* Valdarno, *to descry new Lands,*
> *Rivers, or Mountains, on her spotted Globe.*
> *His Spear (to equal which the tallest pine*
> *Hewn on* Norwegian *Hills to be the Mast*
> *Of some great Ammiral, were but a wand)*
> *He walk'd with, to support uneasie Steps*
> *Over the burning Marl*————

To which we may add his Call to the fallen Angels that lay plunged and stupified in the Sea of Fire.

> *He call'd so loud, that all the hollow deep*
> *Of Hell resounded*————

But there is no single Passage in the whole Poem worked up to a greater Sublimity, than that wherein his Person is described in those celebrated Lines :

> ————*He, above the rest*
> *In shape and gesture proudly eminent*
> *Stood like a Tower,* &c.

His Sentiments are every way answerable to his Character, and suitable to a created Being of the most exalted and most depraved Nature. Such is that in which he takes Possession of his Place of Torments.

> ————*Hail Horrors! hail*
> *Infernal World! and thou profoundest Hell*
> *Receive thy new Possessor, one who brings*
> *A mind not to be changed by place or time.*

And afterwards,

> ————*Here at least*
> *We shall be free; th' Almighty hath not built*
> *Here for his envy, will not drive us hence :*
> *Here we may reign secure; and in my choice*
> *To reign is worth Ambition, tho' in Hell :*
> *Better to reign in Hell, than serve in Heav'n.*

Amidst those Impieties which this Enraged Spirit utters in other places of the Poem, the Author has taken care to introduce none that is not big with absurdity, and incapable of shocking a Religious Reader ; his Words, as the Poet himself describes them, bearing only a *Semblance of Worth, not Substance.* He is likewise with great Art described as owning his Adversary to be Almighty. Whatever perverse Interpretation he puts on the Justice, Mercy, and other Attributes of the Supreme Being, he frequently confesses his Omnipotence, that being the Perfection he was forced to allow him, and the only Consideration which could support his Pride under the Shame of his Defeat.

Nor must I here omit that beautiful Circumstance of his bursting out in Tears, upon his Survey of those innumerable Spirits whom he had involved in the same Guilt and Ruin with himself.

> ——*He now prepared*
> *To speak ; whereat their doubled ranks they bend*
> *From wing to wing, and half enclose him round*
> *With all his Peers : Attention held them mute.*
> *Thrice he assay'd, and thrice in spite of Scorn*
> *Tears such as Angels weep, burst forth*——

The Catalogue of Evil Spirits has abundance of Learning in it, and a very agreeable turn of Poetry, which rises in a great measure from its describing the Places where they were worshipped, by those beautiful Marks of Rivers so frequent among the Ancient Poets. The Author had doubtless in this place *Homer's* Catalogue of Ships, and *Virgil's* List of Warriors, in his View. The Characters of *Moloch* and *Belial* prepare the Reader's Mind for their respective Speeches and Behaviour in the second and sixth Book. The Account of *Thammuz* is finely Romantick, and suitable to what we read among the Ancients of the Worship which was paid to that Idol.

> ——Thammuz *came next behind,*
> *Whose annual Wound in* Lebanon *allur'd*
> *The* Syrian *Damsels to lament his fate,*
> *In am'rous Ditties all a Summer's day,*
> *While smooth* Adonis *from his native Rock*
> *Ran purple to the Sea, suppos'd with Blood*
> *Of* Thammuz *yearly wounded : the Love tale*
> *Infected* Zion's *Daughters with like Heat,*
> *Whose wanton Passions in the sacred Porch*
> Ezekiel *saw, when by the Vision led*
> *His Eye survey'd the dark Idolatries*
> *Of alienated* Judah.——

The Reader will pardon me if I insert as a Note on this beautiful Passage, the Account given us by the late ingenious

Mr. *Maundrell* of this Ancient Piece of Worship, and probably the first Occasion of such a Superstition. 'We came to a fair 'large River—doubtless the Ancient River *Adonis*, so famous 'for the Idolatrous Rites performed here in Lamentation of '*Adonis*. We had the Fortune to see what may be supposed 'to be the Occasion of that Opinion which *Lucian* relates, con-'cerning this River, *viz.* That this Stream, at certain Seasons 'of the Year, especially about the Feast of *Adonis*, is of a 'bloody Colour ; which the Heathens looked upon as proceed-'ing from a kind of Sympathy in the River for the Death of '*Adonis*, who was killed by a wild Boar in the Mountains, out 'of which this Stream rises. Something like this we saw 'actually come to pass ; for the Water was stain'd to a 'surprizing Redness ; and, as we observ'd in Travelling, had 'discolour'd the Sea a great way into a reddish Hue, occasion'd 'doubtless by a sort of Minium, or red Earth, washed into the 'River by the Violence of the Rain, and not by any Stain from '*Adonis's* Blood.

The Passage in the Catalogue, explaining the manner how Spirits transform themselves by Contractions or Enlargement of their Dimensions, is introduced with great Judgment, to make way for several surprizing Accidents in the Sequel of the Poem. There follows one, at the very End of the first Book, which is what the *French* Criticks call *Marvellous*, but at the same time *probable* by reason of the Passage last mentioned. As soon as the Infernal Palace is finished, we are told the Multitude and Rabble of Spirits immediately shrunk themselves into a small Compass, that there might be Room for such a numberless Assembly in this capacious Hall. But it is the Poet's Refinement upon this Thought which I most admire, and which is indeed very noble in its self. For he tells us, that notwithstanding the vulgar, among the fallen Spirits, contracted their Forms, those of the first Rank and Dignity still preserved their natural Dimensions.

Thus incorporeal Spirits to smallest Forms
Reduc'd their Shapes immense, and were at large,
Though without Number, still amidst the Hall
Of that Infernal Court. But far within,
And in their own Dimensions like themselves,
The great Seraphick Lords and Cherubim,
In close recess and secret conclave sate,
A thousand Demy-Gods on Golden Seats,
Frequent and Full———

The Character of *Mammon,* and the Description of the *Pandæmonium,* are full of Beauties.

There are several other Strokes in the first Book wonderfully poetical, and Instances of that Sublime Genius so peculiar to the Author.   Such is the Description of *Azazel's* Stature, and of the Infernal Standard, which he unfurls ; as also of that ghastly Light, by which the Fiends appear to one another in their Place of Torments.

> *The Seat of Desolation, void of Light,*
> *Save what the glimm'ring of those livid Flames*
> *Casts pale and dreadful————*

The Shout of the whole Host of fallen Angels when drawn up in Battel Array :

> *————The universal Host up sent*
> *A Shout that tore Hell's Concave, and beyond*
> *Frighted the reign of* Chaos *and old* Night.

The Review, which the Leader makes of his Infernal Army :

> *————He thro' the armed files*
> *Darts his experienc'd eye, and soon traverse*
> *The whole Battalion views, their Order due,*
> *Their Visages and Stature as of Gods.*
> *Their Number last he sums ; and now his Heart*
> *Distends with Pride, and hard'ning in his strength*
> *Glories————— .*

The Flash of Light which appear'd upon the drawing of their Swords :

> *He spake : and to confirm his words outflew*
> *Millions of flaming Swords, drawn from the thighs*
> *Of mighty* Cherubim ; *the sudden Blaze*
> *Far round illumin'd Hell————*

The sudden Production of the *Pandæmonium :*

> *Anon out of the Earth a Fabrick huge*
> *Rose like an Exhalation, with the Sound*
> *Of dulcet Symphonies and Voices sweet.*

The Artificial Illuminations made in it :

> ————————*From the arched Roof*
> *Pendent by subtle Magick, many a Row*
> *Of Starry Lamps and blazing Crescets, fed*
> *With* Naphtha *and* Asphaltus, *yielded Light*
> *As from a Sky*————————

There are also several noble Similes and Allusions in the First Book of *Paradise Lost*. And here I must observe, that when *Milton* alludes either to Things or Persons, he never quits his Simile till it rises to some very great Idea, which is often foreign to the Occasion that gave Birth to it. The Resemblance does not, perhaps, last above a Line or two, but the Poet runs on with the Hint till he has raised out of it some glorious Image or Sentiment, proper to inflame the Mind of the Reader, and to give it that sublime kind of Entertainment, which is suitable to the Nature of an Heroick Poem. Those who are acquainted with *Homer's* and *Virgil's* way of Writing, cannot but be pleased with this kind of Structure in *Milton's* Similitudes. I am the more particular on this Head, because ignorant Readers, who have formed their Taste upon the quaint Similes, and little Turns of Wit, which are so much in Vogue among Modern Poets, cannot relish these Beauties which are of a much higher Nature, and are therefore apt to censure *Milton's* Comparisons in which they do not see any surprizing Points of Likeness. Monsieur *Perrault* was a Man of this viciated Relish, and for that very Reason has endeavoured to turn into Ridicule several of *Homer's* Similitudes, which he calls *Comparaisons a longue queue, Long-tail'd Comparisons*. I shall conclude this Paper on the First Book of *Milton* with the Answer which Monsieur *Boileau* makes to *Perrault* on this Occasion ; 'Comparisons, says he, in Odes and Epic Poems, 'are not introduced only to illustrate and embellish the Dis- 'course, but to amuse and relax the Mind of the Reader, by 'frequently disengaging him from too painful an Attention to 'the Principal Subject, and by leading him into other agreeable 'Images. *Homer*, says he, excelled in this Particular, whose 'Comparisons abound with such Images of Nature as are 'proper to relieve and diversifie his Subjects. He continually 'instructs the Reader, and makes him take notice, even in 'Objects which are every Day before our Eyes, of such Cir- 'cumstances as we should not otherwise have observed. *To this he adds, as a Maxim universally acknowledged,* ' That it is 'not necessary in Poetry for the Points of the Comparison to 'correspond with one another exactly, but that a general

' Resemblance is sufficient, and that too much Nicety in this
' Particular favours of the Rhetorician and Epigrammatist.

In short, if we look into the Conduct of *Homer*, *Virgil* and
Milton, as the great Fable is the Soul of each Poem, so to give
their Works an agreeable Variety, their Episodes are so many
short Fables, and their Similes so many short Episodes ; to
which you may add, if you please, that their Metaphors are so
many short Similes. If the Reader considers the Comparisons
in the first Book of *Milton*, of the Sun in an Eclipse, of the
Sleeping *Leviathan*, of the Bees swarming about their Hive, of
the Fairy Dance, in the view wherein I have here placed them,
he will easily discover the great Beauties that are in each of
those Passages.

VIII.

Di, quibus imperium est animarum, umbræque silentes,
Et Chaos, et Phlegethon, loca nocte silentia late ;
Sit mihi fas audita loqui ! sit numine vestro
Pandere res alta terra et caligine mersas.—Virg.

I HAVE before observed in general, that the Persons whom
Milton introduces into his Poem always discover such Sentiments and Behaviour, as are in a peculiar manner conformable
to their respective Characters. Every Circumstance in their
Speeches and Actions is with great Justness and Delicacy
adapted to the Persons who speak and act. As the Poet very
much excels in this Consistency of his Characters, I shall beg
Leave to consider several Passages of the Second Book in this
Light. That superior Greatness and Mock-Majesty, which is
ascribed to the Prince of the fallen Angels, is admirably preserved in the Beginning of this Book. His opening and closing
the Debate ; his taking on himself that great Enterprize at the
Thought of which the whole Infernal Assembly trembled ; his
encountering the hideous Phantom who guarded the Gates of
Hell, and appeared to him in all his Terrors, are Instances of
that proud and daring Mind which could not brook Submission
even to Omnipotence.

> Satan *was now at hand, and from his Seat*
> *The Monster moving onward came as fast*
> *With horrid strides, Hell trembled as he strode,*

> *Th' undaunted Fiend what this might be admir'd,*
> *Admir'd, not fear'd——*

The same Boldness and Intrepidity of Behaviour discovers it self in the several Adventures which he meets with during his Passage through the Regions of unformed Matter, and particularly in his Address to those tremendous Powers who are described as presiding over it.

The Part of *Moloch* is likewise in all its Circumstances full of that Fire and Fury which distinguish this Spirit from the rest of the fallen Angels. He is described in the first Book as besmeared with the Blood of Human Sacrifices, and delighted with the Tears of Parents and the Cries of Children. In the Second Book he is marked out as the fiercest Spirit that fought in Heaven: and if we consider the Figure which he makes in the Sixth Book, where the Battle of the Angels is described, we find it every way answerable to the same furious enraged Character.

> *——Where the might of* Gabriel *fought,*
> *And with fierce Ensigns pierc'd the deep array*
> *Of* Moloc, *furious King, who him defy'd,*
> *And at his chariot wheels to drag him bound*
> *Threaten'd, nor from the Holy one of Heav'n*
> *Refrain'd his tongue blasphemous; but anon*
> *Down cloven to the waste, with shatter'd arms*
> *And uncouth pain fled bellowing.——*

It may be worth while to observe, that *Milton* has represented this violent impetuous Spirit, who is hurried only by such precipitate Passions, as the *first* that rises in that Assembly, to give his Opinion upon their present Posture of Affairs. Accordingly he declares himself abruptly for War, and appears incensed at his Companions, for losing so much Time as even to deliberate upon it. All his Sentiments are Rash, Audacious and Desperate. Such is that of arming themselves with their Tortures, and turning their Punishments upon him who inflicted them.

> *——————No, let us rather chuse,*
> *Arm'd with Hell flames and fury, all at once*
> *O'er Heavens high tow'rs to force resistless way,*
> *Turning our tortures into horrid arms*
> *Against the Torturer; when to meet the Noise*

> *Of his almighty Engine he shall hear*
> *Infernal Thunder, and for Lightning see*
> *Black fire and horror shot with equal rage*
> *Among his Angels; and his throne it self*
> *Mixt with* Tartarean *Sulphur, and strange Fire,*
> *His own invented Torments——*

His preferring Annihilation to Shame or Misery, is also highly suitable to his Character; as the Comfort he draws from their disturbing the Peace of Heaven, that if it be not Victory it is Revenge, is a Sentiment truly Diabolical, and becoming the Bitterness of this implacable Spirit.

Belial is described in the first Book, as the Idol of the Lewd and Luxurious. He is in the Second Book, pursuant to that Description, characterised as timorous and slothful; and if we look in the Sixth Book, we find him celebrated in the Battel of Angels for nothing but that scoffing Speech which he makes to *Satan*, on their supposed Advantage over the Enemy. As his Appearance is uniform, and of a Piece, in these three several Views, we find his Sentiments in the Infernal Assembly every way conformable to his Character. Such are his Apprehensions of a second Battel, his Horrors of Annihilation, his preferring to be miserable rather than *not to be*. I need not observe, that the Contrast of Thought in this Speech, and that which precedes it, gives an agreeable Variety to the Debate.

Mammon's Character is so fully drawn in the First Book, that the Poet adds nothing to it in the Second. We were before told, that he was the first who taught Mankind to ransack the Earth for Gold and Silver, and that he was the Architect of *Pandæmonium*, or the Infernal Place, where the Evil Spirits were to meet in Council. His Speech in this Book is every way suitable to so depraved a Character. How proper is that Reflection, of their being unable to taste the Happiness of Heaven were they actually there, in the Mouth of one, who while he was in Heaven, is said to have had his Mind dazled with the outward Pomps and Glories of the Place, and to have been more intent on the Riches of the Pavement, than on the Beatifick Vision. I shall also leave the Reader to judge how agreeable the following Sentiments are to the same Character.

> *——This deep World*
> *Of Darkness do we dread? How oft amidst*
> *Thick cloud and dark doth Heav'ns all-ruling Sire*
> *Chuse to reside, his Glory unobscured,*

> *And with the Majesty of Darkness round*
> *Covers his Throne; from whence deep Thunders roar*
> *Mustering their Rage, and Heav'n resembles Hell?*
> *As he our Darkness, cannot we his Light*
> *Imitate when we please?   This desart Soil*
> *Wants not her hidden Lustre, Gems and Gold;*
> *Nor want we Skill or Art, from whence to raise*
> *Magnificence; and what can Heav'n shew more?*

Beelzebub, who is reckoned the second in Dignity that fell, and is, in the First Book, the second that awakens out of the Trance, and confers with *Satan* upon the Situation of their Affairs, maintains his Rank in the Book now before us.   There is a wonderful Majesty described in his rising up to speak.   He acts as a kind of Moderator between the two opposite Parties, and proposes a third Undertaking, which the whole Assembly gives into.   The Motion he makes of detaching one of their Body in search of a new World is grounded upon a Project devised by *Satan*, and cursorily proposed by him in the following Lines of the first Book.

> *Space may produce new Worlds, whereof so rife*
> *There went a Fame in Heav'n, that he erelong*
> *Intended to create, and therein plant*
> *A Generation, whom his choice Regard*
> *Should favour equal to the Sons of Heav'n:*
> *Thither, if but to pry, shall be perhaps*
> *Our first Eruption, thither or elsewhere:*
> *For this Infernal Pit shall never hold*
> *Celestial Spirits in Bondage, nor th' Abyss*
> *Long under Darkness cover.   But these Thoughts*
> *Full Counsel must mature:* ——

It is on this Project that *Beelzebub* grounds his Proposal.

> —— *What if we find*
> *Some easier Enterprize?   There is a Place*
> *(If ancient and prophetick Fame in Heav'n*
> *Err not) another World, the happy Seat*
> *Of some new Race call'd* MAN, *about this Time*
> *To be created like to us, though less*
> *In Power and Excellence, but favour'd more*
> *Of him who rules above; so was his Will*
> *Pronounc'd among the Gods, and by an Oath,*
> *That shook Heav'n's whole Circumference, confirm'd*

The Reader may observe how just it was not to omit in the First Book the Project upon which the whole Poem turns : As also that the Prince of the fallen Angels was the only proper Person to give it Birth, and that the next to him in Dignity was the fittest to second and support it.

There is besides, I think, something wonderfully Beautiful, and very apt to affect the Reader's Imagination in this ancient Prophecy or Report in Heaven, concerning the Creation of Man. Nothing could shew more the Dignity of the Species, than this Tradition which ran of them before their Existence. They are represented to have been the Talk of Heaven, before they were created. *Virgil*, in compliment to the *Roman* Commonwealth, makes the Heroes of it appear in their State of Preexistence ; but *Milton* does a far greater Honour to Mankind in general, as he gives us a Glimpse of them even before they are in Being.

The rising of this great Assembly is described in a very Sublime and Poetical Manner.

> *Their rising all at once was as the Sound*
> *Of Thunder heard remote———*

The Diversions of the fallen Angels, with the particular Account of their Place of Habitation, are described with great Pregnancy of Thought, and Copiousness of Invention. The Diversions are every way suitable to Beings who had nothing left them but Strength and Knowledge misapplied. Such are their Contentions at the Race, and in Feats of Arms, with their Entertainment in the following Lines.

> *Others with vast* Typhæan *rage more fell*
> *Rend up both Rocks and Hills, and ride the Air*
> *In Whirlwind; Hell scarce holds the wild Uproar.*

Their Musick is employed in celebrating their own criminal Exploits, and their Discourse in sounding the unfathomable Depths of Fate, Free-will and Fore-knowledge.

The several Circumstances in the Description of Hell are finely imagined ; as the four Rivers which disgorge themselves into the Sea of Fire, the Extreams of Cold and Heat, and the River of Oblivion. The monstrous Animals produced in that Infernal World are represented by a single Line, which gives us a more horrid idea of them, than a much longer Description would have done.

> ——————————*Nature breeds,*
> *Perverse, all monstrous, all prodigious Things,*
> *Abominable, inutterable, and* worse,
> Than Fables yet have feign'd, or Fear conceiv'd,
> *Gorgon's, and Hydra's, and Chimera's dire.*

This Episode of the fallen Spirits, and their Place of Habitation, comes in very happily to unbend the Mind of the Reader from its Attention to the Debate. An ordinary Poet would indeed have spun out so many Circumstances to a great Length, and by that means have weakned, instead of illustrated, the principal Fable.

The Flight of Satan to the Gates of Hell is finely imaged.

I have already declared my Opinion of the Allegory concerning *Sin* and *Death*, which is however a very finished Piece in its kind, when it is not considered as a Part of an Epic Poem. The Genealogy of the several Persons is contrived with great Delicacy. *Sin* is the Daughter of *Satan*, and *Death* the Offspring of *Sin*. The incestuous Mixture between *Sin* and *Death* produces those Monsters and Hell-hounds which from time to time enter into their Mother, and tear the Bowels of her who gave them Birth. These are the Terrors of an evil Conscience, and the proper Fruits of *Sin*, which naturally rise from the Apprehensions of *Death*. This last beautiful Moral is, I think, clearly intimated in the Speech of *Sin*, where complaining of this her dreadful Issue, she adds,

> Before mine Eyes in Opposition sits
> Grim *Death* my Son and Foe, who sets them on,
> *And me his Parent would full soon devour*
> *For want of other Prey, but that he knows*
> *His End with mine involv'd————*

I need not mention to the Reader the beautiful Circumstance in the last Part of this Quotation. He will likewise observe how naturally the three Persons concerned in this Allegory are tempted by one common Interest to enter into a Confederacy together, and how properly *Sin* is made the Portress of Hell, and the only Being that can open the Gates to that World of Tortures.

The descriptive Part of this Allegory is likewise very strong, and full of Sublime Ideas. The Figure of *Death*, the Regal Crown upon his Head, his Menace of *Satan*, his advancing to the Combat, the Outcry at his Birth, are Circumstances too noble to be past over in Silence, and extreamly suitable to this *King of Terrors.* I need not mention the Justness of Thought which is observed in the Generation of these several Symbolical Persons ; that *Sin* was produced upon the first Revolt of *Satan,* that *Death* appear'd soon after he was cast into Hell, and that the Terrors of Conscience were conceived at the Gate of this Place of Torments. The Description of the Gates is very poetical, as the opening of them is full of *Milton's* Spirit.

> ————*On a sudden open fly*
> *With impetuous Recoil and jarring Sound*
> *Th' infernal Doors, and on their Hinges grate*
> *Harsh Thunder, that the lowest Bottom shook*
> *Of* Erebus. *She open'd, but to shut*
> *Excell'd her Pow'r ; the Gates wide open stood,*
> *That with extended Wings a banner'd Host*
> *Under spread Ensigns marching might pass through*
> *With Horse and Chariots rank'd in loose Array ;*
> *So wide they stood, and like a Furnace Mouth*
> *Cast forth redounding Smoak and ruddy Flame.*

In *Satan's* Voyage through the *Chaos* there are several Imaginary Persons described, as residing in that immense Waste of Matter. This may perhaps be conformable to the Taste of those Criticks who are pleased with nothing in a Poet which has not Life and Manners ascribed to it ; but for my own Part, I am pleased most with those Passages in this Description which carry in them a greater Measure of Probability, and are such as might possibly have happened. Of this kind is his first mounting in the Smoke that rises from the Infernal Pit, his falling into a Cloud of Nitre, and the like combustible Materials, that by their Explosion still hurried him forward in his Voyage ; his springing upward like a Pyramid of Fire, with his laborious Passage through that Confusion of Elements which the Poet calls

The Womb of Nature, and perhaps her Grave.

The Glimmering Light which shot into the *Chaos* from the utmost Verge of the Creation, with the distant discovery of the Earth that hung close by the Moon, are wonderfully Beautiful and Poetical.

IX.

Nec deus intersit, nisi dignus vindice nodus
Inciderit———— Hor.

HORACE advises a Poet to consider thoroughly the Nature and Force of his Genius. *Milton* seems to have known perfectly well, wherein his Strength lay, and has therefore chosen a Subject entirely conformable to those Talents, of which he was Master. As his Genius was wonderfully turned to the Sublime, his Subject is the noblest that could have entered into the Thoughts of Man. Every thing that is truly great and astonishing, has a place in it. The whole System of the intellectual World ; the *Chaos*, and the Creation ; Heaven, Earth and Hell ; enter into the Constitution of his Poem.

Having in the First and Second Books represented the Infernal World with all its Horrors, the Thread of his Fable naturally leads him into the opposite Regions of Bliss and Glory.

If *Milton's* Majesty forsakes him any where, it is in those Parts of his Poem, where the Divine Persons are introduced as Speakers. One may, I think, observe that the Author proceeds with a kind of Fear and Trembling, whilst he describes the Sentiments of the Almighty. He dares not give his Imagination its full Play, but chuses to confine himself to such Thoughts as are drawn from the Books of the most Orthodox Divines, and to such Expressions as may be met with in Scripture. The Beauties, therefore, which we are to look for in these Speeches, are not of a Poetical Nature, nor so proper to fill the Mind with Sentiments of Grandeur, as with Thoughts of Devotion. The Passions, which they are designed to raise, are a Divine Love and Religious Fear. The Particular Beauty of the Speeches in the Third Book, consists in that Shortness and Perspicuity of Style, in which the Poet has couched the greatest Mysteries of Christianity, and drawn together, in a regular Scheme, the whole Dispensation of Providence, with respect to Man. He has represented all the abstruse Doctrines of Predestination, Free-Will and Grace, as also the great Points of Incarnation and Redemption, (which naturally grow up in a Poem that treats of the Fall of Man) with great Energy of Expression, and in a clearer and stronger Light than I ever met with in any

other Writer.   As these Points are dry in themselves to the
generality of Readers, the concise and clear manner in which
he has treated them, is very much to be admired, as is likewise
that particular Art which he has made use of in the interspersing
of all those Graces of Poetry, which the Subject was capable of
receiving.

The Survey of the whole Creation, and of every thing that is
transacted in it, is a Prospect worthy of Omniscience ; and as
much above that, in which *Virgil* has drawn his *Jupiter*, as the
Christian Idea of the Supreme Being is more Rational and
Sublime than that of the Heathens.   The particular Objects on
which he is described to have cast his Eye, are represented in
the most beautiful and lively Manner.

> *Now had th' Almighty Father from above,*
> *(From the pure Empyrean where he sits*
> *High thron'd above all height) bent down his Eye,*
> *His own Works and their Works at once to view.*
> *About him all the Sanctities of Heav'n*
> *Stood thick as Stars, and from his Sight receiv'd*
> *Beatitude past utt'rance : On his right*
> *The radiant Image of his Glory sat,*
> *His only Son.   On earth he first beheld*
> *Our two first Parents, yet the only two*
> *Of Mankind, in the happy garden plac'd,*
> *Reaping immortal fruits of Joy and Love ;*
> *Uninterrupted Joy, unrival'd Love*
> *In blissful Solitude.   He then survey'd*
> *Hell and the Gulph between, and* Satan *there*
> *Coasting the Wall of Heaven on this side Night,*
> *In the dun air sublime ; and ready now*
> *To stoop with wearied wings, and willing feet*
> *On the bare outside of this world, that seem'd*
> *Firm land imbosom'd without firmament ;*
> *Uncertain which, in Ocean or in Air.*
> *Him God beholding from his prospect high,*
> *Wherein past, present, future he beholds,*
> *Thus to his only Son foreseeing spake.*

Satan's Approach to the Confines of the Creation, is finely
imaged in the beginning of the Speech, which immediately
follows.   The Effects of this Speech in the blessed Spirits, and
in the Divine Person to whom it was addressed, cannot but
fill the Mind of the Reader with a secret Pleasure and
Complacency.

> *Thus while God spake, ambrosial fragrance fill'd*
> *All Heav'n, and in the blessed Spirits elect*
> *Sense of new Joy ineffable diffus'd.*
> *Beyond compare the Son of God was seen*
> *Most glorious, in him all his Father shone*
> *Substantially express'd, and in his face*
> *Divine Compassion visibly appear'd,*
> *Love without end, and without measure Grace.*

I need not point out the Beauty of that Circumstance, wherein the whole Host of Angels are represented as standing Mute ; now shew how proper the Occasion was to produce such a Silence in Heaven. The Close of this Divine Colloquy, with the Hymn of Angels that follows upon it, are so wonderfully Beautiful and Poetical, that I should not forbear inserting the whole Passage, if the Bounds of my Paper would give me leave.

> *No sooner had th' Almighty ceas'd, but all*
> *The multitudes of Angels with a shout*
> *(Loud as from numbers without number, sweet*
> *As from blest Voices) utt'ring Joy, Heav'n rung*
> *With Jubilee, and loud Hosanna's fill'd*
> *Th' eternal regions; &c. &c.——*

Satan's Walk upon the Outside of the Universe, which, at a Distance, appeared to him of a globular Form, but, upon his nearer Approach, looked like an unbounded Plain, is natural and noble : As his Roaming upon the Frontiers of the Creation between that Mass of Matter, which was wrought into a World, and that shapeless unformed Heap of Materials, which still lay in Chaos and Confusion, strikes the Imagination with something astonishingly great and wild. I have before spoken of the *Limbo of Vanity*, which the Poet places upon this outermost Surface of the Universe, and shall here explain my self more at large on that, and other Parts of the Poem, which are of the same Shadowy Nature.

Aristotle observes, that the Fable of an Epic Poem should abound in Circumstances that are both credible and astonishing; or as the *French* Criticks chuse to phrase it, the Fable should be filled with the Probable and the Marvellous. This Rule is as fine and just as any in *Aristotle's* whole Art of Poetry.

If the Fable is only Probable, it differs nothing from a true History ; if it is only Marvellous, it is no better than a Romance. The great Secret therefore of Heroic Poetry is to relate such

Circumstances, as may produce in the Reader at the same time both Belief and Astonishment. This is brought to pass in a *well-chosen* Fable, by the Account of such things as have really happened, or at least of such things as have happened according to the received Opinions of Mankind. *Milton's* Fable is a Masterpiece of this Nature ; as the War in Heaven, the Condition of the fallen Angels, the State of Innocence, and Temptation of the Serpent, and the Fall of Man, though they are very astonishing in themselves, are not only credible, but actual Points of Faith.

The next Method of reconciling Miracles with Credibility, is by a happy Invention of the Poet ; as in particular, when he introduces Agents of a superior Nature, who are capable of effecting what is wonderful, and what is not to be met with in the ordinary course of things. *Ulysses's* Ship being turned into a Rock, and *Æneas's* Fleet into a Shoal of Water Nymphs ; though they are very surprising Accidents, are nevertheless probable, when we are told that they were the Gods who thus transformed them. It is this kind of Machinery which fills the Poems both of *Homer* and *Virgil* with such Circumstances as are wonderful, but not impossible, and so frequently produce in the Reader the most pleasing Passion that can rise in the Mind of Man, which is Admiration. If there be any Instance in the *Æneid* liable to Exception upon this Account, it is in the Beginning of the Third Book, where *Æneas* is represented as tearing up the Myrtle that dropped Blood. To qualifie this wonderful Circumstance, *Polydorus* tells a Story from the Root of the Myrtle, that the barbarous Inhabitants of the Country having pierced him with Spears and Arrows, the Wood which was left in his Body took Root in his Wounds, and gave Birth to that bleeding Tree. This Circumstance seems to have the Marvellous without the Probable, because it is represented as proceeding from Natural Causes, without the Interposition of any God, or other Supernatural Power capable of producing it. The Spears and Arrows grow of themselves, without so much as the Modern Help of an Enchantment. If we look into the Fiction of *Milton's* Fable, though we find it full of surprizing Incidents, they are generally suited to our Notions of the Things and Persons described, and tempered with a due Measure of Probability. I must only make an Exception to the *Limbo of Vanity*, with his Episode of *Sin* and *Death*, and some of the imaginary Persons in his *Chaos*. These Passages are astonishing, but not credible ; the Reader cannot so far impose upon himself as to see a Possibility in them ; they are the

Description of Dreams and Shadows, not of Things or Persons. I know that many Criticks look upon the Stories of *Circe*, *Polypheme*, the *Sirens*, nay the whole *Odyssey* and *Iliad*, to be Allegories ; but allowing this to be true, they are Fables, which considering the Opinions of Mankind that prevailed in the Age of the Poet, might possibly have been according to the Letter. The Persons are such as might have acted what is ascribed to them, as the Circumstances in which they are represented, might possibly have been Truths and Realities. This Appearance of Probability is so absolutely requisite in the greater kinds of Poetry, that *Aristotle* observes the Ancient Tragick Writers made use of the Names of such great Men as had actually lived in the World, tho' the Tragedy proceeded upon Adventures they were never engaged in, on purpose to make the Subject more Credible. In a Word, besides the hidden Meaning of an Epic Allegory, the plain litteral Sense ought to appear Probable. The Story should be such as an ordinary Reader may acquiesce in, whatever Natural, Moral, or Political Truth may be discovered in it by Men of greater Penetration.

Satan, after having long wandered upon the Surface, or outmost Wall of the Universe, discovers at last a wide Gap in it, which led into the Creation, and is described as the Opening through which the Angels pass to and fro into the lower World, upon their Errands to Mankind. His Sitting upon the Brink of this Passage, and taking a Survey of the whole Face of Nature that appeared to him new and fresh in all its Beauties, with the Simile illustrating this Circumstance, fills the Mind of the Reader with as surprizing and glorious an Idea as any that arises in the whole Poem. He looks down into that vast Hollow of the Universe with the Eye, or (as *Milton* calls it in his first Book) with the Kenn of an Angel. He surveys all the Wonders in this immense Amphitheatre that lye between both the Poles of Heaven, and takes in at one View the whole Round of the Creation.

His Flight between the several Worlds that shined on every side of him, with the particular Description of the Sun, are set forth in all the Wantonness of a luxuriant Imagination. His Shape, Speech and Behaviour upon his transforming himself into an Angel of Light, are touched with exquisite Beauty. The Poet's Thought of directing *Satan* to the Sun, which in the vulgar Opinion of Mankind is the most conspicuous Part of the Creation, and the placing in it an Angel, is a Circumstance very finely contrived, and the more adjusted to a Poetical Probability, as it was a received Doctrine among the most famous

Philosophers, that every Orb had its *Intelligence;* and as an Apostle in Sacred Writ is said to have seen such an Angel in the Sun. In the Answer which this Angel returns to the disguised evil Spirit, there is such a becoming Majesty as is altogether suitable to a Superior Being. The Part of it in which he represents himself as present at the Creation, is very noble in it self, and not only proper where it is introduced, but requisite to prepare the Reader for what follows in the Seventh Book.

> *I saw when at his Word the formless Mass,*
> *This World's material Mould, came to a Heap:*
> *Confusion heard his Voice, and wild Uproar*
> *Stood rul'd, stood vast Infinitude confin'd,*
> *Till at his second Bidding Darkness fled,*
> *Light shon, &c.*

In the following Part of the Speech he points out the Earth with such Circumstances, that the Reader can scarce forbear fancying himself employed on the same distant View of it.

> *Look downward on the Globe whose hither Side*
> *With Light from hence, tho' but reflected, shines;*
> *That place is Earth, the Seat of Man, that Light*
> *His Day, &c.*

I must not conclude my Reflections upon this Third Book of *Paradise Lost,* without taking Notice of that celebrated Complaint of *Milton* with which it opens; and which certainly deserves all the Praises that have been given it; tho' as I have before hinted, it may rather be looked upon as an Excrescence, than as an essential Part of the Poem. The same Observation might be applied to that beautiful Digression upon Hypocrisie, in the same Book.

X.

Nec satis est pulchra esse poemata, dulcia sunto.   Hor.

THOSE, who know how many Volumes have been written on the Poems of *Homer* and *Virgil,* will easily pardon the Length of my Discourse upon *Milton.* The *Paradise Lost* is looked upon, by the best Judges, as the greatest Production, or at least the noblest Work of Genius in our Language, and therefore deserves to be set before an *English* Reader in its full Beauty. For this Reason, tho' I have endeavoured to give a general Idea of its Graces and Imperfections in my Six First Papers, I thought my self obliged to bestow one upon every Book in particular. The Three first Books I have already dispatched, and am now entering upon the Fourth. I need not acquaint my Reader that there are Multitudes of Beauties in this great Author, especially in the Descriptive Parts of his Poem, which I have not touched upon, it being my Intention to point out those only, which appear to me the most exquisite, or those which are not so obvious to ordinary Readers. Every one that has read the Criticks who have written upon the *Odyssey*, the *Iliad* and the *Æneid*, knows very well, that though they agree in their Opinions of the great Beauties in those Poems, they have nevertheless each of them discovered several Master-Strokes, which have escaped the Observation of the rest. In the same manner, I question not, but any Writer who shall treat of this Subject after me, may find several Beauties in *Milton*, which I have not taken notice of. I must likewise observe, that as the greatest Masters of Critical Learning differ among one another, as to some particular Points in an Epic Poem, I have not bound my self scrupulously to the Rules which any one of them has laid down upon that Art, but have taken the Liberty sometimes to join with one, and sometimes with another, and sometimes to differ from all of them, when I have thought that the Reason of the thing was on my side.

We may consider the Beauties of the Fourth Book under three Heads. In the first are those Pictures of Still-Life, which we meet with in the Description of *Eden*, *Paradise*, *Adam's* Bower, *&c.* In the next are the Machines, which comprehend the Speeches and Behaviour of the good and bad Angels. In the last is the Conduct of *Adam* and *Eve*, who are the Principal Actors in the Poem.

In the Description of *Paradise*, the Poet has observed *Aristotle's* Rule of lavishing all the Ornaments of Diction on the weak unactive Parts of the Fable, which are not supported by the Beauty of Sentiments and Characters. Accordingly the Reader may observe, that the Expressions are more florid and elaborate in these Descriptions, than in most other Parts of the Poem. I must further add, that tho' the *Drawings* of Gardens, Rivers, Rainbows, and the like dead Pieces of Nature, are justly censured in an Heroic Poem, when they run out into an unnecessary length; the Description of *Paradise* would have been faulty, had not the Poet been very particular in it, not only as it is the Scene of the Principal Action, but as it is requisite to give us an Idea of that Happiness from which our first Parents fell. The Plan of it is wonderfully Beautiful, and formed upon the short Sketch which we have of it in Holy Writ. *Milton's* Exuberance of Imagination has poured forth such a Redundancy of Ornaments on this Seat of Happiness and Innocence, that it would be endless to point out each Particular.

I must not quit this Head, without further observing, that there is scarce a Speech of *Adam* or *Eve* in the whole Poem, wherein the Sentiments and Allusions are not taken from this their delightful Habitation. The Reader, during their whole Course of Action, always finds himself in the Walks of *Paradise.* In short, as the Criticks have remarked, that in those Poems, wherein Shepherds are Actors, the Thoughts ought always to take a Tincture from the Woods, Fields and Rivers, so we may observe, that our first Parents seldom lose Sight of their happy Station in any thing they speak or do ; and, if the Reader will give me leave to use the Expression, that their Thoughts are always *Paradisiacal.*

We are in the next place to consider the Machines of the Fourth Book. *Satan* being now within Prospect of *Eden,* and looking round upon the Glories of the Creation, is filled with Sentiments different from those which he discovered whilst he was in Hell. The Place inspires him with Thoughts more adapted to it : He reflects upon the happy Condition from which he fell, and breaks forth into a Speech that is softned with several transient Touches of Remorse and Self-accusation : But at length he confirms himself in Impenitence, and in his Design of drawing Man into his own State of Guilt and Misery. This Conflict of Passions is raised with a great deal of Art, as the opening of his Speech to the Sun is very bold and noble.

> *O thou that with surpassing Glory crown'd,*
> *Look'st from thy sole Dominion like the God*
> *Of this new World ; at whose Sight all the Stars*
> *Hide their diminish'd Heads ; to thee I call,*
> *But with no friendly Voice, and add thy name,*
> *O Sun ! to tell thee how I hate thy beams,*
> *That bring to my Remembrance from what State*
> *I fell, how glorious once above thy Sphere.*

This Speech is, I think, the finest that is ascribed to *Satan* in the whole Poem. The Evil Spirit afterwards proceeds to make his Discoveries concerning our first Parents, and to learn

after what manner they may be best attacked. His bounding
over the Walls of *Paradise;* his sitting in the Shape of a Cormorant upon the Tree of Life, which stood in the Center of it,
and overtopped all the other Trees of the Garden, his alighting
among the Herd of Animals, which are so beautifully represented as playing about *Adam* and *Eve*, together with his
transforming himself into different Shapes, in order to hear
their Conversation, are Circumstances that give an agreeable
Surprize to the Reader, and are devised with great Art, to con-
nect that Series of Adventures in which the Poet has engaged
this Artificer of Fraud.

The Thought of *Satan's* Transformation into a Cormorant,
and placing himself on the Tree of Life, seems raised upon
that Passage in the *Iliad,* where two Deities are described, as
perching on the Top of an Oak in the shape of Vulturs.

His planting himself at the Ear of *Eve* under the form of a
Toad, in order to produce vain Dreams and Imaginations, is a
Circumstance of the same Nature ; as his starting up in his
own Form is wonderfully fine, both in the Literal Description,
and in the Moral which is concealed under it. His Answer
upon his being discovered, and demanded to give an Account
of himself, is conformable to the Pride and Intrepidity of his
Character.

> *Know ye not then, said* Satan, *fill'd with Scorn,*
> *Know ye not Me ? ye knew me once no mate*
> *For you, there sitting where you durst not soar ;*
> *Not to know Me argues your selves unknown,*
> *The lowest of your throng ;——*

Zephon's Rebuke, with the Influence it had on *Satan*, is
exquisitely Graceful and Moral. *Satan* is afterwards led away
to *Gabriel*, the chief of the Guardian Angels, who kept watch in
Paradise.   His disdainful Behaviour on this Occasion is so
remarkable a Beauty, that the most ordinary Reader cannot
but take Notice of it. *Gabriel's* discovering his Approach
at a Distance, is drawn with great strength and liveliness of
Imagination.

> *O Friends, I hear the tread of nimble Feet*
> *Hasting this Way, and now by glimps discern*
> Ithuriel *and* Zephon *through the shade ;*
> *And with them comes a third of Regal Port,*
> *But faded splendor wan ; who by his gait*
> *And fierce demeanor seems the Prince of Hell ;*

Not likely to part hence without contest :
Stand firm, for in his look defiance lours.

The Conference between *Gabriel* and *Satan* abounds with
Sentiments proper for the Occasion, and suitable to the Persons
of the two Speakers.   *Satan* cloathing himself with Terror
when he prepares for the Combat is truly sublime, and at least
equal to *Homer's* Description of Discord celebrated by *Lon-*
ginus, or to that of Fame in *Virgil*, who are both represented
with their Feet standing upon the Earth, and their Heads
reaching above the Clouds.

> *While thus he spake, th' Angelic Squadron bright*
> *Turn'd fiery red, sharpning in mooned Horns*
> *Their Phalanx, and began to hem him round*
> *With ported Spears, &c.*
> ———*On th' other side* Satan *alarm'd,*
> *Collecting all his might dilated stood*
> *Like* Teneriff, *or* Atlas, *unremov'd.*
> *His Stature reach'd the Sky, and on his Crest*
> *Sat horror plum'd ;*———

I must here take notice, that *Milton* is every where full of
Hints and sometimes literal Translations, taken from the
greatest of the *Greek* and *Latin* Poets.   But this I may reserve
for a Discourse by it self, because I would not break the Thread
of these Speculations, that are designed for *English* Readers,
with such Reflections as would be of no use but to the
Learned.

I must however observe in this Place, that the breaking off
the Combat between *Gabriel* and *Satan,* by the hanging out of
the Golden Scales in Heaven, is a Refinement upon *Homer's*
Thought, who tells us, that before the Battle between *Hector* and
Achilles, Jupiter weighed the Event of it in a pair of Scales.
The Reader may see the whole Passage in the 22nd *Iliad.*

Virgil, before the last decisive Combat, describes *Jupiter* in
the same manner, as weighing the Fates of *Turnus* and *Æneas.*
Milton, though he fetched this beautiful Circumstance from the
Iliad and *Æneid,* does not only insert it as a Poetical Embellishment, like the Authors above-mentioned ; but makes an artful
use of it for the proper carrying on of his Fable, and for the
breaking off the Combat between the two Warriors, who were
upon the point of engaging.   To this we may further add, that
Milton is the more justified in this Passage, as we find the same

noble Allegory in Holy Writ, where a wicked Prince, some few Hours before he was assaulted and slain, is said to have been *weighed in the Scales, and to have been found wanting.*

I must here take Notice under the Head of the Machines, that *Uriel's* gliding down to the Earth upon a Sunbeam, with the Poet's Device to make him *descend,* as well in his return to the Sun, as in his coming from it, is a Prettiness that might have been admired in a little fanciful Poet, but seems below the Genius of *Milton.* The Description of the Host of armed Angels walking their nightly Round in *Paradise,* is of another Spirit.

> *So saying, on he led his radiant files,*
> *Dazling the Moon;——*

as that Account of the Hymns which our first Parents used to hear them sing in these their Midnight Walks, is altogether Divine, and inexpressibly amusing to the Imagination.

We are, in the last place, to consider the Parts which *Adam* and *Eve* act in the Fourth Book. The Description of them as they first appeared to *Satan,* is exquisitely drawn, and sufficient to make the fallen Angel gaze upon them with all that Astonishment, and those Emotions of Envy, in which he is represented.

> *Two of far nobler Shape erect and tall,*
> *God-like erect! with native honour clad*
> *In naked Majesty, seem'd lords of all;*
> *And worthy seem'd: for in their looks divine*
> *The image of their glorious Maker shon,*
> *Truth, Wisdom, Sanctitude severe and pure;*
> *Severe, but in true filial freedom plac'd:*
> *For contemplation he and valour form'd,*
> *For softness she and sweet attractive grace;*
> *He for God only, she for God in him.*
> *His fair large front, and eye sublime, declar'd*
> *Absolute rule; and* Hyacinthin *Locks*
> *Round from his parted forelock manly hung*
> *Clustring, but not beneath his Shoulders broad.*
> *She, as a Veil, down to her slender waste*
> *Her unadorned golden tresses wore*
> *Dis-shevel'd, but in wanton ringlets wav'd.*
> *So pass'd they naked on, nor shun'd the Sight*
> *Of God or Angel, for they thought no ill:*
> *So hand in hand they pass'd, the loveliest pair*
> *That ever since in love's embraces met.*

There is a fine Spirit of Poetry in the Lines which follow, wherein they are described as sitting on a Bed of Flowers by the side of a Fountain, amidst a mixed Assembly of Animals.

The Speeches of these two first Lovers flow equally from Passion and Sincerity.   The Professions they make to one another are full of Warmth : but at the same time founded on Truth.   In a Word, they are the .Gallantries of *Paradise :*

> ——— *When* Adam *first of Men*———
> *Sole partner and sole part of all these joys,*
> *Dearer thy self than all ;*———
> *But let us ever praise him, and extol*
> *His bounty, following our delightful Task,*
> *To prune these growing plants, and tend these flow'rs ;*
> *Which were it toilsome, yet with thee were sweet.*
>
>   *To whom thus* Eve *reply'd, O thou for whom,*
> *And from whom I was form'd, flesh of thy flesh,*
> *And without whom am to no end, my Guide*
> *And Head, what thou hast said is just and right.*
> *For we to him indeed all praises owe,*
> *And daily thanks ; I chiefly, who enjoy*
> *So far the happier Lot, enjoying thee*
> *Præeminent by so much odds, while thou*
> *Like consort to thy self canst no where find,* &c.

The remaining part of *Eve's* Speech, in which she gives an Account of her self upon her first Creation, and the manner in which she was brought to *Adam,* is I think as beautiful a Passage as any in *Milton,* or perhaps in any other Poet whatsoever.   These Passages are all worked off with so much Art, that they are capable of pleasing the most delicate Reader, without offending the most severe.

> *That Day I oft remember, when from Sleep,* &c.

A Poet of less Judgment and Invention than this great Author, would have found it very difficult to have filled these tender Parts of the Poem with Sentiments proper for a State of Innocence ; to have described the Warmth of Love, and the Professions of it, without Artifice or Hyperbole : to have made the Man speak the most endearing things, without descending from his natural Dignity, and the Woman receiving them without departing from the Modesty of her Character ; in a Word, to adjust the Prerogatives of Wisdom and Beauty, and make each appear to the other in its proper Force and Loveliness. This mutual Subordination of the two Sexes is wonderfully kept up in the whole Poem, as particularly in the Speech of *Eve* I have before mentioned, and upon the Conclusion of it in the following Lines.

> *So spake our general Mother, and with eyes*
> *Of Conjugal attraction unreproved,*
> *And meek surrender, half embracing lean'd*
> *On our first father ; half her swelling breast*
> *Naked met his under the flowing Gold*
> *Of her loose tresses hid : he in delight*
> *Both of her beauty and submissive charms*
> *Smil'd with superior Love.———*

The Poet adds, that the Devil turned away with Envy at the sight of so much Happiness.

We have another View of our first Parents in their Evening Discourses, which is full of pleasing Images and Sentiments suitable to their Condition and Characters. The Speech of *Eve*, in particular, is dressed up in such a soft and natural Turn of Words and Sentiments, as cannot be sufficiently admired.

I shall close my Reflections upon this Book, with observing the Masterly Transition which the Poet makes to their Evening Worship in the following Lines.

> *Thus at their shady Lodge arriv'd, both stood,*
> *Both turn'd, and under open Sky, ador'd*
> *The God that made both Sky, Air, Earth and Heaven,*
> *Which they beheld, the Moon's resplendent Globe,*
> *And Starry Pole :* Thou also mad'st the Night,
> Maker Omnipotent, and thou the Day, &c.

Most of the Modern Heroick Poets have imitated the Ancients, in beginning a Speech without premising, that the Person said thus or thus ; but as it is easie to imitate the Ancients in the Omission of two or three Words, it requires Judgment to do it in such a manner as they shall not be missed, and that the Speech may begin naturally without them. There is a fine Instance of this Kind out of *Homer*, in the Twenty Third Chapter of *Longinus*.

XI.

——*Major rerum mihi nascitur ordo.*—Virg.

WE were told in the foregoing Book how the evil Spirit practised upon *Eve* as she lay asleep, in order to inspire her with Thoughts of Vanity, Pride, and Ambition. The Author, who shews a wonderful Art throughout his whole Poem, in preparing the Reader for the several Occurrences that arise in it, founds upon the above-mention'd Circumstance, the first Part of the fifth Book. *Adam* upon his awaking finds *Eve* still asleep, with an unusual Discomposure in her Looks. The Posture in which he regards her, is describ'd with a Tenderness not to be express'd, as the Whisper with which he awakens her, is the softest that ever was convey'd to a Lover's Ear.

> *His wonder was, to find unwaken'd* Eve
> *With Tresses discompos'd, and glowing Cheek,*
> *As through unquiet Rest: he on his side*
> *Leaning half-rais'd, with Looks of cordial Love*
> *Hung over her enamour'd, and beheld*
> *Beauty, which whether waking or asleep,*
> *Shot forth peculiar Graces: then, with Voice*
> *Mild, as when* Zephyrus *on* Flora *breathes,*
> *Her Hand soft touching, whisper'd thus: Awake*
> *My Fairest, my Espous'd, my latest found,*
> *Heav'n's last best Gift, my ever-new Delight!*
> *Awake: the Morning shines, and the fresh Field*
> *Calls us, we lose the Prime, to mark how spring*
> *Our tended Plants, how blows the Citron Grove,*
> *What drops the Myrrh, and what the balmy Reed,*
> *How Nature paints her Colours, how the Bee*
> *Sits on the Bloom, extracting liquid Sweets,*
>   *Such whispering wak'd her, but with startled Eye*
> *On* Adam, *whom embracing, thus she spake:*
>   *O Sole, in whom my Thoughts find all Repose,*
> *My Glory, my Perfection! glad I see*
> *Thy Face, and Morn return'd——*

I cannot but take notice that *Milton*, in the Conferences between *Adam* and *Eve*, had his Eye very frequently upon the Book of *Canticles*, in which there is a noble Spirit of Eastern

Poetry ; and very often not unlike what we meet with in *Homer*, who is generally placed near the Age of *Solomon*. I think there is no question but the Poet in the preceding Speech remember'd those two Passages which are spoken on the like occasion, and fill'd with the same pleasing Images of Nature.

> *My beloved spake, and said unto me, Rise up, my Love, my Fair one, and come away ; for lo the Winter is past, the Rain is over and gone, the Flowers appear on the Earth, the Time of the singing of Birds is come, and the Voice of the Turtle is heard in our Land. The Fig-tree putteth forth her green Figs, and the Vines with the tender Grape give a good Smell. Arise my Love, my Fair-one and come away.*

> *Come, my Beloved, let us go forth into the Field ; let us get up early to the Vineyards, let us see if the Vine flourish, whether the tender Grape appear, and the Pomegranates bud forth.*

His preferring the Garden of *Eden*, to that

> ———*Where the* Sapient *King*
> *Held Dalliance with his fair* Egyptian *Spouse,*

shews that the Poet had this delightful Scene in his mind.

Eve's Dream is full of those *high Conceits engendring Pride*, which, we are told, the Devil endeavour'd to instill into her. Of this kind is that Part of it where she fancies herself awaken'd by *Adam* in the following beautiful Lines.

> *Why sleep'st thou* Eve ? *now is the pleasant Time,*
> *The cool, the silent, save where Silence yields*
> *To the night-warbling Bird, that now awake*
> *Tunes sweetest his love-labour'd Song ; now reigns*
> *Full orb'd the Moon, and with more pleasing Light*
> *Shadowy sets off the Face of things : In vain,*
> *If none regard. Heav'n wakes with all his Eyes,*
> *Whom to behold but thee, Nature's Desire,*
> *In whose sight all things joy, with Ravishment,*
> *Attracted by thy Beauty still to gaze !*

An injudicious Poet would have made *Adam* talk thro' the whole Work in such Sentiments as these : But Flattery and Falshood are not the Courtship of *Milton's Adam*, and could not be heard by *Eve* in her State of Innocence, excepting only in a Dream produc'd on purpose to taint her Imagination.

Other vain Sentiments of the same kind in this Relation of her Dream, will be obvious to every Reader. Tho' the Catastrophe of the Poem is finely presag'd on this Occasion, the Particulars of it are so artfully shadow'd, that they do not anticipate the Story which follows in the ninth Book. I shall only add, that tho' the Vision it self is founded upon Truth, the Circumstances of it are full of that Wildness and Inconsistency which are natural to a Dream. *Adam*, conformable to his superior Character for Wisdom, instructs and comforts *Eve* upon this occasion.

> *So chear'd he his fair Spouse, and she was chear'd,*
> *But silently a gentle Tear let fall*
> *From either Eye, and wiped them with her hair;*
> *Two other precious Drops, that ready stood*
> *Each in their chrystal Sluice, he ere they fell*
> *Kiss'd, as the gracious Sign of sweet Remorse*
> *And pious Awe, that fear'd to have offended.*

The Morning Hymn is written in Imitation of one of those Psalms, where, in the overflowings of Gratitude and Praise, the Psalmist calls not only upon the Angels, but upon the most conspicuous Parts of the inanimate Creation, to join with him in extolling their common Maker. Invocations of this nature fill the Mind with glorious Ideas of God's Works, and awaken that Divine Enthusiasm, which is so natural to Devotion. But if this calling upon the dead Parts of Nature, is at all times a proper kind of Worship, it was in a particular manner suitable to our first Parents, who had the Creation fresh upon their Minds, and had not seen the various Dispensations of Providence, nor consequently could be acquainted with those many Topicks of Praise which might afford Matter to the Devotions of their Posterity. I need not remark the beautiful Spirit of Poetry, which runs through this whole Hymn, nor the Holiness of that Resolution with which it concludes.

Having already mentioned those Speeches which are assigned to the Persons in this Poem, I proceed to the Description which the Poet gives of *Raphael.* His Departure from before the Throne, and the Flight thro' the Choirs of Angels, is finely imaged. As *Milton* every where fills his Poem with Circumstances that are marvellous and astonishing, he describes the Gate of Heaven as framed after such a manner, that it open'd of it self upon the Approach of the Angel who was to pass through it.

> ———*'Till at the Gate*
> *Of Heav'n arriv'd, the Gate self-open'd wide,*
> *On golden Hinges turning, as by Work*
> *Divine, the Sovereign Architect had framed.*

The Poet here seems to have regarded two or three Passages in the 18th *Iliad*, as that in particular, where speaking of *Vulcan*, *Homer* says, that he had made twenty *Tripodes* running on Golden Wheels; which, upon occasion, might-go of themselves to the Assembly of the Gods, and, when there was no more Use for them, return again after the same manner. *Scaliger* has rallied *Homer* very severely upon this Point, as M. *Dacier* has endeavoured to defend it. I will not pretend to determine, whether in this particular of *Homer* the Marvellous does not lose sight of the Probable. As the miraculous Workmanship of *Milton's* Gates is not so extraordinary as this of the *Tripodes*, so I am persuaded he would not have mentioned it, had not he been supported in it by a Passage in the Scripture, which speaks of Wheels in Heaven that had Life in them, and moved of themselves, or stood still, in conformity with the Cherubims, whom they accompanied.

There is no question but *Milton* had this Circumstance in his Thoughts, because in the following Book he describes the Chariot of the *Messiah* with *living* Wheels, according to the Plan in *Ezekiel's* Vision.

> ———*Forth rush'd with Whirlwind sound*
> *The Chariot of paternal Deity*
> *Flashing thick flames, Wheel within Wheel undrawn,*
> *Itself instinct with Spirit*———

I question not but *Bossu*, and the two *Daciers*, who are for vindicating every thing that is censured in *Homer*, by something parallel in Holy Writ, would have been very well pleased had they thought of confronting *Vulcan's Tripodes* with *Ezekiel's* Wheels.

Raphael's Descent to the Earth, with the Figure of his Person, is represented in very lively Colours. Several of the *French*, *Italian* and *English* Poets have given a Loose to their Imaginations in the Description of Angels: But I do not remember to have met with any so finely drawn, and so comformable to the Notions which are given of them in Scripture, as this in *Milton*. After having set him forth in all his Heavenly Plumage, and represented him as alighting upon the

Earth, the Poet concludes his Description with a Circumstance, which is altogether new, and imagined with the greatest Strength of Fancy.

> *————Like* Maia's *Son he stood,*
> *And shook his Plumes, that Heav'nly Fragrance fill'd*
> *The Circuit wide.————*

Raphael's Reception by the Guardian Angels; his passing through the Wilderness of Sweets; his distant Appearance to *Adam*, have all the Graces that Poetry is capable of bestowing. The Author afterwards gives us a particular Description of *Eve* in her Domestick Employments.

> *So saying, with dispatchful Looks in haste*
> *She turns, on hospitable Thoughts intent,*
> *What Choice to chuse for Delicacy best,*
> *What order, so contriv'd, as not to mix*
> *Tastes, not well join'd, inelegant, but bring*
> *Taste after Taste, upheld with kindliest Change;*
> *Bestirs her then, &c.————*

Though in this, and other Parts of the same Book, the Subject is only the Housewifry of our first Parent, it is set off with so many pleasing Images and strong Expressions, as make it none of the least agreeable Parts in this Divine Work.

The natural Majesty of *Adam*, and at the same time his submissive Behaviour to the Superior Being, who had vouchsafed to be his Guest; the solemn Hail which the Angel bestows upon the Mother of Mankind, with the Figure of *Eve* ministring at the Table, are Circumstances which deserve to be admired.

Raphael's Behaviour is every way suitable to the Dignity of his Nature, and to that Character of a sociable Spirit, with which the Author has so judiciously introduced him. He had received Instructions to converse with *Adam*, as one Friend converses with another, and to warn him of the Enemy, who was contriving his Destruction: Accordingly he is represented as sitting down at Table with *Adam*, and eating of the Fruits of *Paradise*. The Occasion naturally leads him to his Discourse on the Food of Angels. After having thus entered into Conversation with Man upon more indifferent Subjects, he warns him of his Obedience, and makes natural Transition to the History of that fallen Angel, who was employ'd in the Circumvention of our first Parents.

Had I followed Monsieur *Bossu's* Method in my first Paper of *Milton*, I should have dated the Action of *Paradise Lost* from the Beginning of *Raphael's* Speech in this Book, as he supposes the Action of the *Æneid* to begin in the second Book of that Poem.   I could allege many Reasons for my drawing the Action of the *Æneid* rather from its immediate Beginning in the first Book, than from its remote Beginning in the second ; and shew why I have considered the sacking of *Troy* as an *Episode*, according to the common Acceptation of that Word.   But as this would be a dry unentertaining Piece of Criticism, and perhaps unnecessary to those who have read my first Paper, I shall not enlarge upon it.   Whichever of the Notions be true, the Unity of *Milton's* Action is preserved according to either of them ; whether we consider the Fall of Man in its immediate Beginning, as proceeding from the Resolutions taken in the infernal Council, or in its more remote Beginning, as proceeding from the first Revolt of the Angels in Heaven.   The Occasion which *Milton* assigns for this Revolt, as it is founded on Hints in Holy Writ, and on the Opinion of some great Writers, so it was the most proper that the Poet could have made use of.

The Revolt in Heaven is described with great Force of Imagination and a fine Variety of Circumstances.   The learned Reader cannot but be pleased with the Poet's Imitation of *Homer* in the last of the following Lines.

> *At length into the Limits of the North*
> *They came, and Satan took his Royal Seat*
> *High on a Hill, far blazing, as a Mount*
> *Rais'd on a Mount, with Pyramids and Tow'rs*
> *From Diamond Cuarries hewn, and Rocks of Gold,*
> *The Palace of great* Lucifer, (*so call*
> *That Structure in the Dialect of Men*
> *Interpreted*)————

Homer mentions Persons and Things, which he tells us in the Language of the Gods are call'd by different Names from those they go by in the Language of Men.   *Milton* has imitated him with his usual Judgment in this particular Place, wherein he has likewise the Authority of Scripture to justifie him.   The Part of *Abdiel*, who was the only Spirit that in this infinite Host of Angels preserved his Allegiance to his Maker, exhibits to us a noble Moral of religious Singularity.   The Zeal of the Seraphim breaks forth in a becoming Warmth of Sentiments and Expressions, as the Character which is given us of him denotes that generous Scorn and Intrepidity which attends Heroic Virtue. The Author doubtless designed it as a Pattern to those who live among Mankind in their present State of Degeneracy and Corruption.

> *So spake the Seraph* Abdiel, *faithful found*
> *Among the faithless, faithful only he;*
> *Among innumerable false, unmov'd,*
> *Unshaken, unseduc'd, unterrify'd;*
> *His Loyalty he kept, his Love, his Zeal:*
> *Nor Number, nor Example with him wrought*
> *To swerve from Truth, or change his constant Mind,*
> *Though single. From amidst them forth he pass'd,*
> *Long way through hostile Scorn, which he sustain'd*
> *Superior, nor of Violence fear'd ought;*
> *And, with retorted Scorn, his Back he turn'd*
> *On those proud Tow'rs to swift Destruction doom'd.*

XII.

> ————*vocat in Certamina Divos.*—Virg.

WE are now entering upon the Sixth Book of *Paradise Lost,* in which the Poet describes the Battel of Angels; having raised his Reader's Expectation, and prepared him for it by several Passages in the preceding Books. I omitted quoting these Passages in my Observations on the former Books, having purposely reserved them for the opening of this, the Subject of which gave occasion to them. The Author's Imagination was so inflam'd with this great Scene of Action, that wherever he speaks of it, he rises, if possible, above himself. Thus where he mentions Satan in the Beginning of his Poem:

> ————————*Him the Almighty Power*
> *Hurl'd headlong flaming from th' Ethereal Sky,*
> *With hideous ruin and combustion, down*
> *To bottomless Perdition, there to dwell*
> *In Adamantine Chains and penal Fire,*
> *Who durst defy th' Omnipotent to Arms.*

We have likewise several noble Hints of it in the Infernal Conference.

> *O Prince ! O Chief of many throned Powers,*
> *That led th' imbattel'd Seraphim to War,*
> *Too well I see and rue the dire Event,*
> *That with sad Overthrow and foul Defeat*
> *Hath lost us Heav'n, and all this mighty Host*
> *In horrible Destruction laid thus low.*
> *But see ! the angry Victor has recall'd*
> *His Ministers of Vengeance and Pursuit,*
> *Back to the Gates of Heav'n : The sulph'rous Hail*
> *Shot after us in Storm, o'erblown, hath laid*
> *The fiery Surge, that from the Precipice*
> *Of Heaven receiv'd us falling: and the Thunder,*
> *Wing'd with red Lightning and impetuous Rage,*
> *Perhaps hath spent his Shafts, and ceases now*
> *To bellow through the vast and boundless Deep.*

There are several other very sublime Images on the same Subject in the First Book, as also in the Second.

> *What when we fled amain, pursu'd and strook*
> *With Heav'n's afflicting Thunder, and besought*
> *The Deep to shelter us; this Hell then seem'd*
> *A Refuge from those Wounds——*

In short, the Poet never mentions anything of this Battel but in such Images of Greatness and Terror as are suitable to the Subject.   Among several others I cannot forbear quoting that Passage, where the Power, who is described as presiding over the Chaos, speaks in the Third Book.

> *Thus Satan; and him thus the Anarch old*
> *With faultring Speech, and Visage incompos'd,*
> *Answer'd, I know thee, Stranger, who thou art,*
> *That mighty leading Angel, who of late*
> *Made Head against Heaven's King, tho' overthrown.*
> *I saw and heard, for such a numerous Host*
> *Fled not in silence through the frighted Deep*
> *With Ruin upon Ruin, Rout on Rout,*
> *Confusion worse confounded; and Heav'n's Gates*
> *Pour'd out by Millions her victorious Bands*
> *Pursuing——*

It requir'd great Pregnancy of Invention, and Strength of Imagination, to fill this Battel with such Circumstances as should raise and astonish the Mind of the Reader ; and at the same time an Exactness of Judgment, to avoid every thing that might appear light or trivial.   Those who look into *Homer*, are surprized to find his Battels still rising one above another, and improving in Horrour, to the Conclusion of the *Iliad. Milton's* Fight of Angels is wrought up with the same Beauty.   It is usher'd in with such Signs of Wrath as are suitable to Omnipotence incensed.   The first Engagement is carry'd on under a Cope of Fire, occasion'd by the Flights of innumerable burning Darts and Arrows, which are discharged from either Host.   The second Onset is still more terrible, as it is filled with those artificial Thunders, which seem to make the Victory doubtful, and produce a kind of Consternation even in the good Angels. This is follow'd by the tearing up of Mountains and Promontories ; till, in the last place, the Messiah comes forth in the Fulness of Majesty and Terror.   The Pomp of his Appearance amidst the Roarings of his Thunders, the Flashes of his Lightnings, and the Noise of his Chariot-Wheels, is described with the utmost Flights of Human Imagination.

There is nothing in the first and last Day's Engagement which does not appear natural, and agreeable enough to the Ideas most Readers would conceive of a Fight between two Armies of Angels.

The second Day's Engagement is apt to startle an Imagination, which has not been raised and qualify'd for such a Description, by the reading of the ancient Poets, and of *Homer* in particular.   It was certainly a very bold Thought in our Author, to ascribe the first Use of Artillery to the Rebel Angels.   But as such a pernicious Invention may be well suppos'd to have proceeded from such Authors, so it entered very properly into the Thoughts of that Being, who is all along describ'd as aspiring to the Majesty of his Maker.   Such Engines were the only Instruments he could have made use of to imitate those Thunders, that in all Poetry, both sacred and profane, are represented as the Arms of the Almighty.   The tearing up the Hills, was not altogether so daring a Thought as the former.   We are, in some measure, prepared for such an Incident by the Description of the Giants' War, which we meet with among the Ancient Poets.   What still made this Circumstance the more proper for the Poe 's Use, is the Opinion of many learned Men, that the Fable of the Giants' War, which makes so great a noise in Antiquity, and gave birth to the sublimest Description in *Hesiod's* Works was an Allegory founded upon this very Tradition of a Fight between the good and bad Angels.

It may, perhaps, be worth while to consider with what Judgment *Milton*, in this Narration, has avoided every thing that is mean and trivial in the Descriptions of the *Latin* and *Greek* Poets; and at the same time improved every great Hint which he met with in their Works upon this Subject. *Homer* in that Passage, which *Longinus* has celebrated for its Sublimeness, and which *Virgil* and *Ovid* have copy'd after him, tells us, that the Giants threw *Ossa* upon *Olympus*, and *Pelion* upon *Ossa*. He adds an Epithet to *Pelion* (εἰνοσίφυλλον) which very much swells the Idea, by bringing up to the Reader's Imagination all the Woods that grew upon it. There is further a great Beauty in his singling out by Name these three remarkable Mountains, so well known to the *Greeks*. This last is such a Beauty as the Scene of *Milton's* War could not possibly furnish him with. *Claudian*, in his Fragment upon the Giants' War, has given full scope to that Wildness of Imagination which was natural to him. He tells us, that the Giants tore up whole Islands by the Roots, and threw them at the Gods. He describes one of them in particular taking up *Lemnos* in his Arms, and whirling it to the Skies, with all *Vulcan's* Shop in the midst of it. Another tears up Mount *Ida*, with the River *Enipeus*, which ran down the Sides of it; but the Poet, not content to describe him with this Mountain upon his Shoulders, tells us that the River flow'd down his Back, as he held it up in that Posture. It is visible to every judicious Reader, that such Ideas savour more of Burlesque, than of the Sublime. They proceed from a Wantonness of Imagination, and rather divert the Mind than astonish it. *Milton* has taken every thing that is sublime in these several Passages, and composes out of them the following great Image.

> *From their Foundations loos'ning to and fro,*
> *They pluck'd the seated Hills, with all their Load,*
> *Rocks, Waters, Woods; and by the shaggy Tops*
> *Up-lifting bore them in their Hands———*

We have the full Majesty of *Homer* in this short Description, improv'd by the Imagination of *Claudian*, without its Puerilities.

I need not point out the Description of the fallen Angels seeing the Promontories hanging over their Heads in such a dreadful manner, with the other numberless Beauties in this Book, which are so conspicuous, that they cannot escape the Notice of the most ordinary Reader.

There are indeed so many wonderful Strokes of Poetry in

this Book, and such a variety of Sublime Ideas, that it would have been impossible to have given them a place within the bounds of this Paper. Besides that, I find it in a great measure done to my hand at the End of my Lord *Roscommon's* Essay on Translated Poetry. I shall refer my Reader thither for some of the Master Strokes in the Sixth Book of *Paradise Lost*, tho' at the same time there are many others which that noble Author has not taken notice of.

Milton, notwithstanding the sublime Genius he was Master of, has in this Book drawn to his Assistance all the Helps he could meet with among the Ancient Poets. The Sword of *Michael*, which makes so great a havock among the bad Angels, was given him, we are told, out of the Armory of God.

> ————*But the Sword*
> *Of* Michael *from the Armory of God*
> *Was giv'n him temper'd so, that neither keen*
> *Nor solid might resist that Edge : It met*
> *The Sword of Satan, with steep Force to smite*
> *Descending, and in half cut sheer————*

This Passage is a Copy of that in *Virgil*, wherein the Poet tells us, that the Sword of *Æneas*, which was given him by a Deity, broke into Pieces the Sword of *Turnus*, which came from a mortal Forge. As the Moral in this Place is divine, so by the way we may observe, that the bestowing on a Man who is favour'd by Heaven such an allegorical Weapon, is very conformable to the old Eastern way of Thinking. Not only *Homer* has made use of it, but we find the *Jewish* Hero in the Book of *Maccabees*, who had fought the Battels of the chosen People with so much Glory and Success, receiving in his Dream a Sword from the Hand of the Prophet *Jeremiah*. The following Passage, wherein Satan is described as wounded by the Sword of *Michael*, is in imitation of *Homer*.

> *The griding Sword with discontinuous Wound*
> *Pass'd thro' him ; but th' Ethereal Substance clos'd*
> *Not long divisible ; and from the Gash*
> *A Stream of Nectarous Humour issuing flow'd*
> *Sanguine, (such as celestial Spirits may bleed)*
> *And all his Armour stain'd————*

Homer tells us in the same manner, that upon *Diomedes* wounding the Gods, there flow'd from the Wound an *Ichor*, or pure kind of Blood, which was not bred from mortal Viands; and that tho' the Pain was exquisitely great, the Wound soon closed up and healed in those Beings who are vested with Immortality.

I question not but *Milton* in his Description of his furious *Moloch* flying from the Battel, and bellowing with the Wound he had received, had his Eye on *Mars* in the *Iliad;* who, upon his being wounded, is represented as retiring out of the Fight, and making an Outcry louder than that of a whole Army when it begins the Charge. *Homer* adds, that the *Greeks* and *Tro-jans*, who were engaged in a general Battel, were terrify'd on each side with the bellowing of this wounded Deity. The Reader will easily observe how *Milton* has kept all the Horrour of this Image, without running into the Ridicule of it.

> ——*Where the Might of* Gabriel *fought,*
> *And with fierce Ensigns pierc'd the deep Array*
> *Of* Moloch, *furious King! who him defy'd,*
> *And at his Chariot-wheels to drag him bound*
> *Threaten'd, nor from the Holy One of Heav'n*
> *Refrain'd his Tongue blasphemous: but anon*
> *Down cloven to the Waste, with shatter'd Arms*
> *And uncouth Pain fled bellowing.*——

Milton has likewise raised his Description in this Book with many Images taken out of the poetical Parts of Scripture. The Messiah's Chariot, as I have before taken notice, is formed upon a Vision of *Ezekiel*, who, as *Grotius* observes, has very much in him of *Homer's* Spirit in the Poetical Parts of his Prophecy.

The following Lines in that glorious Commission which is given the Messiah to extirpate the Host of Rebel Angels, is drawn from a Sublime Passage in the Psalms.

> *Go then thou Mightiest in thy Father's Might!*
> *Ascend my Chariot, guide the rapid Wheels*
> *That shake Heav'n's Basis; bring forth all my War,*
> *My Bow, my Thunder, my Almighty Arms,*
> *Gird on thy Sword on thy puissant Thigh.*

The Reader will easily discover many other Strokes of the same nature.

There is no question but *Milton* had heated his Imagination with the Fight of the Gods in *Homer*, before he enter'd upon this Engagement of the Angels. *Homer* there gives us a Scene of Men, Heroes, and Gods, mix'd together in Battel. *Mars* animates the contending Armies, and lifts up his Voice in such a manner, that it is heard distinctly amidst all the Shouts and Confusion of the Fight. *Jupiter* at the same time Thunders over their Heads ; while *Neptune* raises such a Tempest, that the whole Field of Battel and all the Tops of the Mountains shake about them. The Poet tells us, that *Pluto* himself, whose Habitation was in the very Center of the Earth, was so affrighted at the Shock, that he leapt from his Throne. *Homer* afterwards describes *Vulcan* as pouring down a Storm of Fire upon the River *Xanthus*, and *Minerva* as throwing a Rock at *Mars;* who, he tells us, cover'd seven Acres in his Fall.

As *Homer* has introduced into his Battel of the Gods every thing that is great and terrible in Nature, *Milton* has filled his Fight of good and bad Angels with all the like Circumstances of Horrour. The Shout of Armies, the Rattling of Brazen Chariots, the Hurling of Rocks and Mountains, the Earthquake, the Fire, the Thunder, are all of them employ'd to lift up the Reader's Imagination, and give him a suitable Idea of so great an Action. With what Art has the Poet represented the whole Body of the Earth trembling, even before it was created.

> *All Heaven resounded, and had Earth been then,*
> *All Earth had to its Center shook——*

In how sublime and just a manner does he afterwards describe the whole Heaven shaking under the Wheels of the Messiah's Chariot, with that Exception to the Throne of God?

> *——Under his burning Wheels*
> *The stedfast* Empyrean *shook throughout,*
> *All but the Throne it self of God——*

Notwithstanding the Messiah appears clothed with so much Terrour and Majesty, the Poet has still found means to make his Readers conceive an Idea of him, beyond what he himself was able to describe.

> *Yet half his Strength he put not forth, but checkt*
> *His Thunder in mid Volley; for he meant*
> *Not to destroy, but root them out of Heaven.*

In a Word, *Milton's* Genius, which was so great in it self, and so strengthened by all the helps of Learning, appears in

this Book every way equal to his Subject, which was the most
Sublime that could enter into the Thoughts of a Poet.   As he
knew all the Arts of affecting the Mind, he knew it was necessary to give it certain Resting-places and Opportunities of recovering it self from time to time : He has therefore with great
Address interspersed several Speeches, Reflections, Similitudes,
and the like Reliefs to diversify his Narration, and ease the
Attention of the Reader, that he might come fresh to his great
Action, and by such a Contrast of Ideas, have a more lively
taste of the nobler Parts of his Description.

XIII.

——Ut his exordia primis
Omnia, et ipse tener Mundi concreverit orbis.
Tum durare solum et discludere Nerea ponto
Cœperit, et rerum pauliatim sumere formas.—Virg.

LONGINUS has observed that there may be a Loftiness in
Sentiments, where there is no Passion, and brings
Instances out of Ancient Authors to support this his Opinion.
The Pathetick, as that great Critick observes, may animate and
inflame the Sublime, but is not essential to it.   Accordingly, as
he further remarks, we very often find that those who excel
most in stirring up the Passions, very often want the Talent of
writing in the great and sublime manner, and so on the contrary. *Milton* has shewn himself a Master in both these ways
of Writing.   The Seventh Book, which we are now entring
upon, is an Instance of that Sublime which is not mixed and
worked up with Passion.   The Author appears in a kind of
composed and sedate Majesty ; and tho' the Sentiments do not
give so great an Emotion as those in the former Book, they
abound with as magnificent Ideas.   The Sixth Book, like a
troubled Ocean, represents Greatness in Confusion ; the
seventh Affects the Imagination like the Ocean in a Calm, and
fills the Mind of the Reader, without producing in it any thing
like Tumult or Agitation.

　　The Critick above mentioned, among the Rules which he lays
down for succeeding in the sublime way of writing, proposes to
his Reader, that he should imitate the most celebrated Authors
who have gone before him, and been engaged in Works of the

same nature ; as in particular, that if he writes on a poetical Subject, he should consider how *Homer* would have spoken on such an Occasion. By this means one great Genius often catches the Flame from another, and writes in his Spirit, without copying servilely after him. There are a thousand shining Passages in *Virgil*, which have been lighted up by *Homer*.

Milton, tho' his own natural Strength of Genius was capable of furnishing out a perfect Work, has doubtless very much raised and ennobled his Conceptions, by such an Imitation as that which *Longinus* has recommended.

In this Book, which gives us an Account of the six Days Works, the Poet received but very few Assistances from Heathen Writers, who were Strangers to the Wonders of Creation. But as there are many glorious strokes of Poetry upon this Subject in Holy Writ, the Author has numberless Allusions to them through the whole course of this Book. The great Critick I have before mentioned, though an Heathen, has taken notice of the sublime Manner in which the Law-giver of the *Jews* has describ'd the Creation in the first Chapter of *Genesis ;* and there are many other Passages in Scripture, which rise up to the same Majesty, where this Subject is touched upon. *Milton* has shewn his Judgment very remarkably, in making use of such of these as were proper for his Poem, and in duly qualifying those high Strains of *Eastern* Poetry, which were suited to Readers whose Imaginations were set to an higher pitch than those of colder Climates.

Adam's Speech to the Angel, wherein he desires an Account of what had passed within the Regions of Nature before the Creation, is very great and solemn. The following Lines, in which he tells him, that the Day is not too far spent for him to enter upon such a subject, are exquisite in their kind.

> *And the great Light of Day yet wants to run*
> *Much of his Race, though steep, suspense in Heav'n*
> *Held by thy Voice ; thy potent Voice he hears,*
> *And longer will delay, to hear thee tell*
> *His Generation,* &c.

The Angel's encouraging our first Parents in a modest pursuit after Knowledge, with the Causes which he assigns for the Creation of the World, are very just and beautiful. The Messiah, by whom, as we are told in Scripture, the Worlds were made, comes forth in the Power of his Father, surrounded with an Host of Angels, and cloathed with such a Majesty as becomes his entring upon a Work, which, according to our Conceptions, appears the utmost Exertion of Omnipotence. What a beautiful Description has our Author raised upon that Hint in one of the Prophets. *And behold there came four Chariots out from between two Mountains, and the Mountains were Mountains of Brass.*

> *About his Chariot numberless were pour'd*
> Cherub *and* Seraph, *Potentates and Thrones,*
> *And Virtues, winged Spirits, and Chariots wing'd,*
> *From th' Armoury of God, where stand of old*
> *Myriads between two brazen Mountains lodg'd*
> *Against a solemn Day, harness'd at hand;*
> *Celestial Equipage! and now came forth*
> *Spontaneous, for within them Spirit liv'd,*
> *Attendant on their Lord: Heav'n open'd wide*
> *Her ever-during Gates, Harmonious Sound!*
> *On golden Hinges moving————*

I have before taken notice of these Chariots of God, and of these Gates of Heaven; and shall here only add, that *Homer* gives us the same Idea of the latter, as opening of themselves; tho' he afterwards takes off from it, by telling us, that the *Hours* first of all removed those prodigious Heaps of Clouds which lay as a Barrier before them.

I do not know any thing in the whole Poem more sublime than the Description which follows, where the Messiah is represented at the head of his Angels, as looking down into the *Chaos,* calming its Confusion, riding into the midst of it, and drawing the first Out-Line of the Creation.

> *On Heavenly Ground they stood, and from the Shore*
> *They view'd the vast immeasurable Abyss,*
> *Outrageous as a Sea, dark, wasteful, wild;*
> *Up from the bottom turn'd by furious Winds*
> *And surging Waves, as Mountains to assault*
> *Heaven's height, and with the Center mix the Pole.*
> *Silence, ye troubled Waves, and thou Deep, Peace!*
> *Said then th' Omnific Word, your Discord end:*
> *Nor staid; but, on the Wings of Cherubim*
> *Up-lifted, in Paternal Glory rode*
> *Far into* Chaos, *and the World unborn;*
> *For* Chaos *heard his Voice. Him all His Train*

*Follow'd in bright Procession, to behold
Creation, and the Wonders of his Might.
Then staid the fervid Wheels, and in his Hand
He took the Golden Compasses, prepar'd
In God's eternal Store, to circumscribe
This Universe, and all created Things:
One Foot he center'd, and the other turn'd
Round, through the vast Profundity obscure;
And said, Thus far extend, thus far thy bounds,
This be thy just Circumference, O World!*

The thought of the Golden Compasses is conceived altogether in *Homer's* Spirit, and is a very noble Incident in this wonderful Description. *Homer*, when he speaks of the Gods, ascribes to them several Arms and Instruments with the same greatness of Imagination. Let the Reader only peruse the Description of *Minerva's Ægis*, or Buckler, in the Fifth Book, with her Spear, which would overturn whole Squadrons, and her Helmet, that was sufficient to cover an Army drawn out of an hundred Cities: The Golden Compasses in the above-mentioned Passage appear a very natural Instrument in the Hand of him, whom *Plato* somewhere calls the Divine Geometrician. As Poetry delights in cloathing abstracted Ideas in Allegories and sensible Images, we find a magnificent Description of the Creation form'd after the same manner in one of the Prophets, wherein he describes the Almighty Architect as measuring the Waters in the Hollow of his Hand, meting out the Heavens with his Span, comprehending the Dust of the Earth in a Measure, weighing the Mountains in Scales, and the Hills in a Balance. Another of them describing the Supreme Being in this great Work of Creation, represents him as laying the Foundations of the Earth, and stretching a Line upon it: And in another place as garnishing the Heavens, stretching out the North over the empty Place, and hanging the Earth upon nothing. This last noble Thought *Milton* has express'd in the following Verse:

And Earth self-balanc'd on her Center hung.

The Beauties of Description in this Book lie so very thick, that it is impossible to enumerate them in this Paper. The Poet has employ'd on them the whole Energy of our Tongue. The several great Scenes of the Creation rise up to view one after another, in such a manner, that the Reader seems present at this wonderful Work, and to assist among the Choirs of

Angels, who are the Spectators of it. How glorious is the Conclusion of the first Day.

> ———— *Thus was the first Day Ev'n and Morn :*
> *Nor past uncelebrated nor unsung*
> *By the Celestial Quires, when Orient Light*
> *Exhaling first from Darkness they beheld;*
> *Birth-day of Heav'n and Earth ! with Joy and Shout*
> *The hollow universal Orb they fill'd.*

We have the same elevation of Thought in the third Day, when the Mountains were brought forth, and the Deep was made.

> *Immediately the Mountains huge appear*
> *Emergent, and their broad bare Backs up-heave*
> *Into the Clouds, their Tops ascend the Sky :*
> *So high as heav'd the tumid Hills, so low*
> *Down sunk a hollow Bottom, broad and deep,*
> *Capacious Bed of Waters————*

We have also the rising of the whole vegetable World described in this Day's Work, which is filled with all the Graces that other Poets have lavish'd on their Descriptions of the Spring, and leads the Reader's Imagination into a Theatre equally surprising and beautiful.

The several Glories of the Heav'ns make their Appearance on the Fourth Day.

> *First in his East the glorious Lamp was seen,*
> *Regent of Day; and all th' Horizon round*
> *Invested with bright Rays, jocund to round*
> *His Longitude through Heav'n's high Road : the gray*
> *Dawn, and the* Pleiades *before him danced,*
> *Shedding sweet Influence. Less bright the Moon,*
> *But opposite in levell'd West was set,*
> *His Mirror, with full face borrowing her Light*
> *From him, for other Lights she needed none*
> *In that aspect, and still that distance keeps*
> *Till Night; then in the East her turn she shines,*
> *Revolv'd on Heav'n's great Axle, and her Reign*
> *With thousand lesser Lights dividual holds,*
> *With thousand thousand Stars ! that then appear'd*
> *Spangling the Hemisphere————*

One would wonder how the Poet could be so concise in his Description of the six Days Works, as to comprehend them within the bounds of an Episode, and at the same time so particular, as to give us a lively Idea of them. This is still more remarkable in his Account of the Fifth and Sixth Days, in which he has drawn out to our View the whole Animal Creation, from the Reptil to the Behemoth. As the Lion and the Leviathan are two of the noblest Productions in the World of living Creatures, the Reader will find a most exquisite Spirit of Poetry in the Account which our Author gives us of them. The Sixth Day concludes with the Formation of Man, upon which the Angel takes occasion, as he did after the Battel in Heaven, to remind *Adam* of his Obedience, which was the principal Design of this his Visit.

The Poet afterwards represents the Messiah returning into Heaven, and taking a Survey of his great Work. There is something inexpressibly Sublime in this part of the Poem, where the Author describes that great Period of Time, filled with so many Glorious Circumstances ; when the Heavens and Earth were finished ; when the Messiah ascended up in triumph thro' the Everlasting Gates ; when he looked down with pleasure upon his new Creation ; when every Part of Nature seem'd to rejoice in its Existence ; when the Morning-Stars sang together, and all the Sons of God shouted for joy.

> *So Ev'n and Morn accomplish'd the sixth Day :*
> *Yet not 'till the Creator from his Work*
> *Desisting, tho' unwearied, up return'd,*
> *Up to the Heav'n of Heav'ns, his high Abode ;*
> *Thence to behold this new created World,*
> *Th' Addition of his Empire, how it shew'd*
> *In prospect from his Throne, how good, how fair,*
> *Answering his great Idea : Up he rode,*
> *Follow'd with Acclamation, and the Sound*
> *Symphonious of ten thousand Harps, that tuned*
> *Angelick Harmonies ; the Earth, the Air*
> *Resounding (thou remember'st, for thou heard'st)*
> *The Heavens and all the Constellations rung ;*
> *The Planets in their Station listning stood,*
> *While the bright Pomp ascended jubilant.*
> *Open, ye everlasting Gates, they sung,*
> *Open, ye Heav'ns, your living Doors ; let in*
> *The great Creator from his Work return'd*
> *Magnificent, his six Days Work, a World !*

I cannot conclude this Book upon the Creation, without mentioning a Poem which has lately appeared under that Title.

The Work was undertaken with so good an Intention, and is executed with so great a Mastery, that it deserves to be looked upon as one of the most useful and noble Productions in our *English* Verse.   The Reader cannot but be pleased to find the Depths of Philosophy enlivened with all the Charms of Poetry, and to see so great a Strength of Reason, amidst so beautiful a Redundancy of the Imagination.   The Author has shewn us that Design in all the Works of Nature, which necessarily leads us to the Knowledge of its first Cause.   In short, he has illustrated, by numberless and incontestable Instances, that Divine Wisdom, which the Son of *Sirach* has so nobly ascribed to the Supreme Being in his Formation of the World, when he tells us, that *He created her, and saw her, and numbered her, and poured her out upon all his Works.*

XIV.

Sanctius his animal, mentisque capacius altæ
Deerat adhuc, et quod dominari in cætera posset,
Natus homo est———— Ov. Met.

THE Accounts which *Raphael* gives of the Battel of Angels, and the Creation of the World, have in them those Qualifications which the Criticks judge requisite to an Episode. They are nearly related to the principal Action, and have a just Connexion with the Fable.

The eighth Book opens with a beautiful Description of the Impression which this Discourse of the Archangel made on our first Parents.   *Adam* afterwards, by a very natural Curiosity, enquires concerning the Motions of those Celestial Bodies which make the most glorious Appearance among the six days Works.   The Poet here, with a great deal of Art, represents *Eve* as withdrawing from this part of their Conversation, to Amusements more suitable to her Sex.   He well knew, that the Episode in this Book, which is filled with *Adam's* Account of his Passion and Esteem for *Eve*, would have been improper for her hearing, and has therefore devised very just and beautiful Reasons for her Retiring.

So spake our Sire, and by his Count'nance seem'd
Entring on studious Thoughts abstruse : which Eve
Perceiving, where she sat retired in sight,
With lowliness majestick, from her Seat,

And Grace, that won who saw to wish her Stay,
Rose; and went forth among her Fruits and Flowers
To visit how they prosper'd, Bud and Bloom,
Her Nursery: they at her coming sprung,
And touch'd by her fair Tendance gladlier grew.
Yet went she not, as not with such Discourse
Delighted, or not capable her Ear
Of what was high: Such Pleasure she reserved,
Adam relating, she sole Auditress;
Her Husband the Relater she preferr'd
Before the Angel, and of him to ask
Chose rather: he, she knew, would intermix
Grateful Digressions, and solve high Dispute
With conjugal Caresses; from his Lip
Not Words alone pleas'd her. O when meet now
Such Pairs, in Love and mutual Honour join'd!

The Angel's returning a doubtful Answer to *Adam's* Enquiries, was not only proper for the Moral Reason which the Poet assigns, but because it would have been highly absurd to have given the Sanction of an Archangel to any particular System of Philosophy. The chief Points in the *Ptolemaick* and *Copernican* Hypothesis are described with great Conciseness and Perspicuity, and at the same time dressed in very pleasing and poetical Images.

Adam, to detain the Angel, enters afterwards upon his own History, and relates to him the Circumstances in which he found himself upon his Creation; as also his Conversation with his Maker, and his first meeting with *Eve.* There is no part of the Poem more apt to raise the Attention of the Reader, than this Discourse of our great Ancestor; as nothing can be more surprizing and delightful to us, than to hear the Sentiments that arose in the first Man while he was yet new and fresh from the Hands of his Creator. The Poet has interwoven every thing which is delivered upon this Subject in Holy Writ with so many beautiful Imaginations of his own, that nothing can be conceived more just and natural than this whole Episode. As our Author knew this Subject could not but be agreeable to his Reader, he would not throw it into the Relation of the six days Works, but reserved it for a distinct Episode, that he might have an opportunity of expatiating upon it more at large. Before I enter on this part of the Poem, I cannot but take notice of two shining Passages in the Dialogue between *Adam* and the Angel. The first is that wherein our Ancestor gives an

Account of the pleasure he took in conversing with him, which contains a very noble Moral.

> *For while I sit with thee, I seem in Heav'n,*
> *And sweeter thy Discourse is to my Ear*
> *Than Fruits of Palm-tree (pleasantest to Thirst*
> *And Hunger both from Labour) at the hour*
> *Of sweet Repast : they satiate, and soon fill,*
> *Tho' pleasant; but thy Words with Grace divine*
> *Imbu'd, bring to their Sweetness no Satiety.*

The other I shall mention, is that in which the Angel gives a Reason why he should be glad to hear the Story *Adam* was about to relate.

> *For I that day was absent, as befel,*
> *Bound on a Voyage uncouth and obscure;*
> *Far on Excursion towards the Gates of Hell,*
> *Squar'd in full Legion (such Command we had)*
> *To see that none thence issued forth a Spy,*
> *Or Enemy, while God was in his Work,*
> *Lest he, incens'd at such Eruption bold,*
> *Destruction with Creation might have mix'd.*

There is no question but our Poet drew the Image in what follows from that in *Virgil's* sixth Book, where *Æneas* and the Sibyl stand before the Adamantine Gates, which are there described as shut upon the Place of Torments, and listen to the Groans, the Clank of Chains, and the Noise of Iron Whips, that were heard in those Regions of Pain and Sorrow.

> *————Fast we found, fast shut*
> *The dismal Gates, and barricado'd strong;*
> *But long ere our Approaching heard within*
> *Noise, other than the Sound of Dance or Song,*
> *Torment, and loud Lament, and furious Rage.*

Adam then proceeds to give an account of his Condition and Sentiments immediately after his Creation. How agreeably does he represent the Posture in which he found himself, the beautiful Landskip that surrounded him, and the Gladness of Heart which grew up in him on that occasion?

> *————As new waked from soundest Sleep,*
> *Soft on the flow'ry Herb I found me laid*
> *In balmy Sweat, which with his Beams the Sun*
> *Soon dried, and on the reaking Moisture fed.*

> *Streight towards Heav'n my wond'ring Eyes I turn'd,*
> *And gazed awhile the ample Sky, till rais'd*
> *By quick instinctive Motion, up I sprang,*
> *As thitherward endeavouring, and upright*
> *Stood on my Feet: About me round I saw*
> *Hill, Dale, and shady Woods, and sunny Plains,*
> *And liquid lapse of murmuring Streams; by these*
> *Creatures that liv'd, and mov'd, and walk'd, or flew,*
> *Birds on the Branches warbling; all things smil'd:*
> *With Fragrance, and with Joy my Heart o'erflow'd.*

Adam is afterwards describ'd as surprized at his own Existence, and taking a Survey of himself, and of all the Works of Nature. He likewise is represented as discovering by the Light of Reason, that he and every thing about him must have been the Effect of some Being infinitely good and powerful, and that this Being had a right to his Worship and Adoration. His first Address to the Sun, and to those Parts of the Creation which made the most distinguished Figure, is very natural and amusing to the Imagination.

> ——— *Thou Sun, said I, fair Light,*
> *And thou enlighten'd Earth, so fresh and gay,*
> *Ye hills and Dales, ye Rivers, Woods, and Plains,*
> *And ye that live and move, fair Creatures tell,*
> *Tell if you saw, how came I thus, how here?*

His next Sentiment, when upon his first going to sleep he fancies himself losing his Existence, and falling away into nothing, can never be sufficiently admired. His Dream, in which he still preserves the Consciousness of his Existence, together with his removal into the Garden which was prepared for his Reception, are also Circumstances finely imagined, and grounded upon what is delivered in Sacred Story.

These and the like wonderful Incidents in this Part of the Work, have in them all the Beauties of Novelty, at the same time that they have all the Graces of Nature. They are such as none but a great Genius could have thought of, tho', upon the perusal of them, they seem to rise of themselves from the Subject of which he treats. In a word, tho' they are natural, they are not obvious, which is the true Character of all fine Writing.

The Impression which the Interdiction of the Tree of Life left in the Mind of our first Parent, is describ'd with great

Strength and Judgment ; as the Image of the several Beasts and Birds passing in review before him is very beautiful and lively.

> ————*Each Bird and Beast behold*
> *Approaching two and two, these cowring low*
> *With Blandishment ; each Bird stoop'd on his Wing :*
> *I nam'd them as they pass'd*————

Adam, in the next place, describes a Conference which he held with his Maker upon the Subject of Solitude. The Poet here represents the supreme Being, as making an Essay of his own Work, and putting to the tryal that reasoning Faculty, with which he had endued his Creature. *Adam* urges, in this Divine Colloquy, the Impossibility of his being happy, tho' he was the Inhabitant of *Paradise*, and Lord of the whole Creation, without the Conversation and Society of some rational Creature, who should partake those Blessings with him. This Dialogue, which is supported chiefly by the Beauty of the Thoughts, without other poetical Ornaments, is as fine a Part as any in the whole Poem : The more the Reader examines the Justness and Delicacy of its Sentiments, the more he will find himself pleased with it. The Poet has wonderfully preserved the Character of Majesty and Condescension in the Creator, and at the same time that of Humility and Adoration in the· Creature, as particularly in the following Lines :

> *Thus I presumptuous ; and the Vision bright,*
> *As with a Smile more brightned, thus reply'd,* &c.
> ————*I, with leave of Speech implor'd*
> *And humble Deprecation, thus reply'd :*
> *Let not my Words offend thee, Heav'nly Power,*
> *My Maker, be propitious while I speak,* &c.

Adam then proceeds to give an account of his second Sleep, and of the Dream in which he beheld the Formation of *Eve.* The new Passion that was awaken'd in him at the sight of her, is touch'd very finely.

> *Under his forming Hands a Creature grew,*
> *Manlike, but different Sex : so lovely fair,*
> *That what seem'd fair in all the World, seem'd now*
> *Mean, or in her summ'd up, in her contain'd,*
> *And in her Looks ; which from that time infus'd*
> *Sweetness into my Heart, unfelt before :*

> *And into all things from her Air inspir'd*
> *The Spirit of Love and amorous Delight.*

Adam's Distress upon losing sight of this beautiful Phantom, with his Exclamations of Joy and Gratitude at the discovery of a real Creature, who resembled the Apparition which had been presented to him in his Dream ; the Approaches he makes to her, and his Manner of Courtship ; are all laid together in a most exquisite Propriety of Sentiments.

Tho' this Part of the Poem is work'd up with great Warmth and Spirit, the Love which is described in it is every way suitable to a State of Innocence. If the Reader compares the Description which *Adam* here gives of his leading *Eve* to the Nuptial Bower, with that which Mr. *Dryden* has made on the same occasion in a Scene of his *Fall of Man,* he will be sensible of the great care which *Milton* took to avoid all Thoughts on so delicate a Subject, that might be offensive to Religion or Good-Manners. The Sentiments are chaste, but not cold ; and convey to the Mind Ideas of the most transporting Passion, and of the greatest Purity. What a noble Mixture of Rapture and Innocence has the Author join'd together, in the Reflection which *Adam* makes on the Pleasures of Love, compared to those of Sense.

> *Thus have I told thee all my State, and brought*
> *My Story to the sum of earthly Bliss,*
> *Which I enjoy; and must confess to find*
> *In all things else Delight indeed, but such*
> *As us'd or not, works in the Mind no Change*
> *Nor vehement Desire; these Delicacies*
> *I mean of Taste, Sight, Smell, Herbs, Fruits and Flowers,*
> *Walks, and the Melody of Birds : but here*
> *Far otherwise, transported I behold,*
> *Transported touch; here Passion first I felt,*
> *Commotion strange ! in all Enjoyments else*
> *Superiour and unmov'd, here only weak*
> *Against the Charms of Beauty's powerful Glance.*
> *Or Nature fail'd in me, and left some Part*
> *Not Proof enough such Object to sustain;*
> *Or from my Side subducting, took perhaps*
> *More than enough; at least on her bestow'd*
> *Too much of Ornament in outward shew*
> *Elaborate, of inward less exact.*
> *————When I approach*
> *Her Loveliness, so absolute she seems*

And in herself compleat, so well to know
Her own, that what she wills to do or say
Seems wisest, vertuousest, discreetest, best:
All higher Knowledge in her Presence falls
Degraded: Wisdom in discourse with her
Loses discountenanc'd, and like Folly shews;
Authority and Reason on her wait,
As one intended first, not after made
Occasionally: and to consummate all,
Greatness of Mind, and Nobleness their Seat
Build in her loveliest, and create an Awe
About her, as a Guard angelick plac'd.

These Sentiments of Love, in our first Parent, gave the Angel such an Insight into Humane Nature, that he seems apprehensive of the Evils which might befall the Species in general, as well as *Adam* in particular, from the Excess of this Passion. He therefore fortifies him against it by timely Admonitions; which very artfully prepare the Mind of the Reader for the Occurrences of the next Book, where the Weakness of which *Adam* here gives such distant Discoveries, brings about that fatal Event which is the Subject of the Poem. His Discourse, which follows the gentle Rebuke he received from the Angel, shews that his Love, however violent it might appear, was still founded in Reason, and consequently not improper for *Paradise.*

Neither her outside Form so fair, nor aught
In Procreation common to all kinds,
(Tho' higher of the genial Bed by far,
And with mysterious Reverence I deem)
So much delights me, as those graceful Acts,
Those thousand Decencies that daily flow
From all her Words and Actions, mixt with Love
And sweet Compliance, which declare unfeign'd
Union of Mind, or in us both one Soul;
Harmony to behold in wedded Pair!

Adam's Speech, at parting with the Angel, has in it a Deference and Gratitude agreeable to an inferior Nature, and at the same time a certain Dignity and Greatness suitable to the Father of Mankind in his State of Innocence.

XV.

In te omnis domus inclinata recumbit.—Virg.

IF we look into the three great Heroick Poems which have appeared in the World, we may observe that they are built upon very slight Foundations. *Homer* lived near 300 Years after the *Trojan* War ; and, as the writing of History was not then in use among the *Greeks*, we may very well suppose, that the Tradition of *Achilles* and *Ulysses* had brought down but very few particulars to his Knowledge ; tho' there is no question but he has wrought into his two Poems such of their remarkable Adventures, as were still talked of among his Contemporaries.

The Story of *Æneas*, on which *Virgil* founded his Poem, was likewise very bare of Circumstances, and by that means afforded him an Opportunity of embellishing it with Fiction, and giving a full range to his own Invention. We find, however, that he has interwoven, in the course of his Fable, the principal Particulars, which were generally believed among the *Romans*, of *Æneas* his Voyage and Settlement in *Italy*.

The Reader may find an Abridgment of the whole Story as collected out of the ancient Historians, and as it was received among the *Romans*, in *Dionysius Halicarnasseus.*

Since none of the Criticks have consider'd *Virgil's* Fable, with relation to this History of *Æneas*, it may not, perhaps, be amiss to examine it in this Light, so far as regards my present Purpose. Whoever looks into the Abridgment above mentioned, will find that the Character of *Æneas* is filled with Piety to the Gods, and a superstitious Observation of Prodigies, Oracles, and Predictions. *Virgil* has not only preserved this Character in the Person of *Æneas*, but has given a place in his Poem to those particular Prophecies which he found recorded of him in History and Tradition. The Poet took the matters of Fact as they came down to him, and circumstanced them after his own manner, to make them appear the more natural, agreeable, or surprizing. I believe very many Readers have been shocked at that ludicrous Prophecy, which one of the *Harpyes* pronounces to the *Trojans* in the third Book, namely, that before they had built their intended City, they should be reduced by Hunger to eat their very Tables. But, when they hear that this was one of the Circumstances that had been transmitted to the *Romans* in the History of *Æneas*, they will think the Poet did very well in taking notice of it. The Historian above mentioned acquaints us, a Prophetess had foretold *Æneas*, that he should take his Voyage Westward, till his Companions should eat their Tables ; and that accordingly, upon his landing in *Italy*, as they were eating their Flesh upon Cakes of Bread, for want of other Conveniences, they afterwards fed on the Cakes themselves ; upon which one of the Company said merrily, *We are eating our Tables.* They immediately took the Hint, says the Historian, and concluded the Prophecy to be fulfilled. As *Virgil* did not think it proper to omit so material a particular in the History of *Æneas*, it may be worth while to consider with how much Judgment he has qualified it, and taken off every thing that might have appeared improper for a Passage in an Heroick Poem. The Prophetess who foretells it, is an Hungry *Harpy*, as the Person who discovers it is young *Ascanius.*

Heus etiam mensas consumimus, inquit Iulus !

Such an observation, which is beautiful in the Mouth of a Boy, would have been ridiculous from any other of the Company. I am apt to think that the changing of the *Trojan* Fleet into Water-Nymphs, which is the most violent Machine in the whole *Æneid,* and has given offence to several Criticks, may be accounted for the same way. *Virgil* himself, before he begins that Relation, premises, that what he was going to tell appeared incredible, but that it was justified by Tradition. What further confirms me that this Change of the Fleet was a celebrated Circumstance in the History of *Æneas*, is, that *Ovid* has given place to the same *Metamorphosis* in his Account of the heathen Mythology.

None of the Criticks I have met with having considered the Fable of the *Æneid* in this Light, and taken notice how the Tradition, on which it was founded, authorizes those Parts in it which appear the most exceptionable ; I hope the length of this Reflection will not make it unacceptable to the curious Part of my Readers.

The History, which was the Basis of *Milton's* Poem, is still shorter than either that of the *Iliad* or *Æneid.* The Poet has likewise taken care to insert every Circumstance of it in the Body of his Fable. The ninth Book, which we are here to consider, is raised upon that brief Account in Scripture, wherein we are told that the Serpent was more subtle than any Beast of the Field, that he tempted the Woman to eat of the forbidden Fruit, that she was overcome by this Temptation, and that *Adam* followed her Example. From these few Particulars, *Milton* has formed one of the most Entertaining Fables that Invention ever produced. He has disposed of these several Circumstances among so many beautiful and natural Fictions of his own, that his whole Story looks only. like a Comment upon sacred Writ, or rather seems to be a full and compleat Relation of what the other is only an Epitome. I have insisted the longer on this Consideration, as I look upon the Disposition and Contrivance of the Fable to be the principal Beauty of the ninth Book, which has more *Story* in it, and is fuller of Incidents, than any other in the whole Poem. *Satan's* traversing the Globe, and still keeping within the Shadow of the Night, as fearing to be discovered by the Angel of the Sun, who had before detected him, is one of those beautiful Imaginations with which he introduces this his second Series of Adventures. Having examined the Nature of every Creature, and found out one which was the most proper for his Purpose, he again returns to Paradise ; and, to avoid Discovery, sinks by Night with a River that ran under the Garden, and rises up again through a Fountain that issued from it by the Tree of Life. The Poet, who, as we have before taken notice, speaks as little as possible in his own Person, and, after the Example of *Homer*, fills every Part of his Work with Manners and Characters, introduces a Soliloquy of this infernal Agent, who was thus restless in the Destruction of Man. He is then describ'd as gliding through the Garden, under the resemblance of a Mist, in order to find out that Creature in which he design'd to tempt our first Parents. This Description has something in it very Poetical and Surprizing.

> *So saying, through each Thicket Dank or Dry,*
> *Like a black Mist, low creeping, he held on*
> *His Midnight Search, where soonest he might find*
> *The Serpent : him fast sleeping soon he found*
> *In Labyrinth of many a Round self-roll'd,*
> *His Head the midst, well stor'd with subtle Wiles.*

The Author afterwards gives us a Description of the Morning, which is wonderfully suitable to a Divine Poem, and peculiar to that first Season of Nature : He represents the Earth, before it was curst, as a great Altar, breathing out its Incense from all Parts, and sending up a pleasant Savour to

the Nostrils of its Creator ; to which he adds a noble Idea (
Adam and *Eve*, as offering their Morning Worship, and fillin
up the Universal Consort of Praise and Adoration.

> *Now when as sacred Light began to dawn*
> *In* Eden *on the humid Flowers, that breathed*
> *Their Morning Incense, when all things that breathe*
> *From th' Earth's great Altar send up silent Praise*
> *To the Creator, and his Nostrils fill*
> *With grateful Smell; forth came the human Pair,*
> *And join'd their vocal Worship to the Choir*
> *Of Creatures wanting Voice————*

The Dispute which follows between our two first Parents, i
represented with great Art : It proceeds from a Difference (
Judgment, not of Passion, and is managed with Reason, nc
with Heat : It is such a Dispute as we may suppose migl
have happened in *Paradise*, had Man continued Happy an
Innocent.   There is a great Delicacy in the Moralities whic
are interspersed in *Adam's* Discourse, and which the mos
ordinary Reader cannot but take notice of.   That Force c
Love which the Father of Mankind so finely describes in th
eighth Book, and which is inserted in my last *Saturday*
Paper, shews it self here in many fine Instances : As in thos
fond Regards he cast towards *Eve* at her parting from him.

> *Her long with ardent Look his Eye pursued*
> *Delighted, but desiring more her stay :*
> *Oft he to her his Charge of quick return*
> *Repeated; she to him as oft engaged*
> *To be return'd by noon amid the Bower.*

In his Impatience and Amusement during her Absence

> *————Adam the while,*
> *Waiting desirous her return, had wove*
> *Of choicest Flowers a Garland, to adorn*
> *Her Tresses, and her rural Labours crown :*
> *As Reapers oft are wont their Harvest Queen.*
> *Great Joy he promised to his thoughts, and new*
> *Solace in her return, so long delay'd.*

But particularly in that Passionate Speech, where seeing hei
irrecoverably lost, he resolves to perish with her rather than tc
live without her.

> ———*Some cursed Fraud*
> *Or Enemy hath beguil'd thee, yet unknown,*
> *And me with thee hath ruin'd; for with thee*
> *Certain my Resolution is to die!*
> *How can I live without thee; how forego*
> *Thy sweet Converse and Love so dearly join'd,*
> *To live again in these wild Woods forlorn?*
> *Should God create another* Eve, *and I*
> *Another Rib afford, yet loss of thee*
> *Would never from my Heart! no, no! I feel*
> *The Link of Nature draw me: Flesh of Flesh,*
> *Bone of my Bone thou art, and from thy State*
> *Mine never shall be parted, Bliss or Woe!*

The Beginning of this Speech, and the Preparation to it, are animated with the same Spirit as the Conclusion, which I have here quoted.

The several Wiles which are put in practice by the Tempter, when he found *Eve* separated from her Husband, the many pleasing Images of Nature which are intermix'd in this part of the Story, with its gradual and regular Progress to the fatal Catastrophe, are so very remarkable that it would be superfluous to point out their respective Beauties.

I have avoided mentioning any particular Similitudes in my Remarks on this great Work, because I have given a general Account of them in my Paper on the first Book. There is one, however, in this part of the Poem, which I shall here quote as it is not only very beautiful, but the closest of any in the whole Poem. I mean that where the Serpent is describ'd as rolling forward in all his Pride, animated by the evil Spirit, and conducting *Eve* to her Destruction, while *Adam* was at too great a distance from her to give her his Assistance. These several Particulars are all of them wrought into the following Similitude.

> ————*Hope elevates, and Joy*
> *Brightens his Crest; as when a wand'ring Fire,*
> *Compact of unctuous Vapour, which the Night*
> *Condenses, and the Cold environs round,*
> *Kindled through Agitation to a Flame,*
> *(Which oft, they say, some evil Spirit attends)*
> *Hovering and blazing with delusive Light,*
> *Misleads th' amaz'd Night-wanderer from his Way*
> *To Bogs and Mires, and oft through Pond or Pool,*
> *There swallow'd up and lost, from succour far.*

That secret Intoxication of Pleasure, with all those transient flushings of Guilt and Joy, which the Poet represents in our first Parents upon their eating the forbidden Fruit, to those flaggings of Spirits, damps of Sorrow, and mutual Accusations which succeed it, are conceiv'd with a wonderful Imagination, and described in very natural Sentiments.

When *Dido* in the fourth *Æneid* yielded to that fatal Temptation which ruined her, *Virgil* tells us the Earth trembled, the Heavens were filled with Flashes of Lightning, and the Nymphs howled upon the Mountain-Tops. *Milton*, in the same poetical Spirit, has described all Nature as disturbed upon *Eve's* eating the forbidden Fruit.

> *So saying, her rash Hand in evil hour*
> *Forth reaching to the Fruit, she pluckt, she eat:*
> *Earth felt the wound, and Nature from her Seat*
> *Sighing, through all her Works gave signs of Woe*
> *That all was lost————*

Upon *Adam's* falling into the same Guilt, the whole Creation appears a second time in Convulsions.

> *————————He scrupled not to eat*
> *Against his better knowledge; not deceiv'd,*
> *But fondly overcome with female Charm.*
> *Earth trembled from her Entrails, as again*
> *In Pangs, and Nature gave a second Groan,*
> *Sky lowred, and muttering Thunder, some sad drops*
> *Wept at compleating of the mortal Sin————*

As all Nature suffer'd by the Guilt of our first Parents, these Symptoms of Trouble and Consternation are wonderfully imagined, not only as Prodigies, but as Marks of her Sympathizing in the Fall of Man.

Adam's Converse with *Eve*, after having eaten the forbidden Fruit, is an exact Copy of that between *Jupiter* and *Juno* in the fourteenth *Iliad*. *Juno* there approaches *Jupiter* with the Girdle which she had received from *Venus;* upon which he tells her, that she appeared more charming and desirable than she had ever done before, even when their Loves were at the highest. The Poet afterwards describes them as reposing on a Summet of Mount *Ida*, which produced under them a Bed of Flowers, the *Lotos*, the *Crocus*, and the *Hyacinth;* and concludes his Description with their falling asleep.

Let the Reader compare this with the following Passage in *Milton*, which begins with *Adam's* Speech to *Eve*.

> *For never did thy Beauty, since the Day*
> *I saw thee first and wedded thee, adorn'd*
> *With all Perfections, so enflame my Sense*
> *With ardor to enjoy thee, fairer now*
> *Than ever, Bounty of this virtuous Tree.*
> *So said he, and forbore not Glance or Toy*
> *Of amorous Intent, well understood*
> *Of* Eve, *whose Eye darted contagious Fire.*
> *Her hand he seiz'd, and to a shady Bank*
> *Thick over-head with verdant Roof embower'd,*
> *He led her nothing loth : Flowr's were the Couch,*
> *Pansies, and Violets, and Asphodel,*
> *And Hyacinth, Earth's freshest softest Lap.*
> *There they their fill of Love, and Love's disport,*
> *Took largely, of their mutual Guilt the Seal,*
> *The Solace of their Sin, till dewy Sleep*
> *Oppress'd them* ————————

As no Poet seems ever to have studied *Homer* more, or to have more resembled him in the Greatness of Genius than *Milton*, I think I should have given but a very imperfect Account of his Beauties, if I had not observed the most remarkable Passages which look like Parallels in these two great Authors. I might, in the course of these criticisms, have taken notice of many particular Lines and Expressions which are translated from the *Greek* Poet ; but as I thought this would have appeared too minute and over-curious, I have purposely omitted them. The greater Incidents, however, are not only set off by being shewn in the same Light with several of the same nature in *Homer*, but by that means may be also guarded against the Cavils of the Tasteless or Ignorant.

XVI.

> ————*Quis talia fando*
> *Temperet à lachrymis ?*— —— Virg.

THE Tenth Book of *Paradise Lost* has a greater variety of Persons in it than any other in the whole Poem. The Author upon the winding up of his Action introduces all those who had any Concern in it, and shews with great Beauty the Influence which it had upon each of them. It is like the last Act of a well-written Tragedy, in which all who had a part in it are generally drawn up before the Audience, and represented under those Circumstances in which the Determination of the Action places them.

I shall therefore consider this Book under four Heads, in relation to the Celestial, the Infernal, the Human, and the Imaginary Persons, who have their respective Parts allotted in it.

To begin with the Celestial Persons: The Guardian Angels of *Paradise* are described as returning to Heaven upon the Fall of Man, in order to approve their Vigilance; their Arrival, their Manner of Reception, with the Sorrow which appear'd in themselves, and in those Spirits who are said to Rejoice at the Conversion of a Sinner, are very finely laid together in the following Lines.

> *Up into Heav'n from Paradise in haste*
> *Th' Angelick Guards ascended, mute and sad*
> *For Man; for of his State by this they knew:*
> *Much wond'ring how the subtle Fiend had stol'n*
> *Entrance unseen. Soon as th' unwelcome News*
> *From Earth arriv'd at Heaven-Gate, displeas'd*
> *All were who heard: dim Sadness did not spare*
> *That time Celestial Visages; yet mixt*
> *With Pity, violated not their Bliss.*
> *About the new-arriv'd, in multitudes*
> *Th' Ethereal People ran, to hear and know*
> *How all befel: They tow'rds the Throne supreme*
> *Accountable made haste to make appear*
> *With righteous Plea, their utmost vigilance,*
> *And easily approv'd; when the Most High*
> *Eternal Father, from his secret cloud,*
> *Amidst in thunder utter'd thus his voice.*

The same Divine Person, who in the foregoing Parts of this Poem interceded for our first Parents before their Fall, overthrew the Rebel Angels, and created the World, is now represented as descending to *Paradise*, and pronouncing Sentence upon the three Offenders. The Cool of the Evening, being a Circumstance with which Holy Writ introduces this great Scene, it is poetically described by our Author, who has also kept religiously to the Form of Words, in which the three several Sentences were passed upon *Adam*, *Eve*, and the Serpent. He has rather chosen to neglect the Numerousness of his Verse, than to deviate from those Speeches which are recorded on this great occasion. The Guilt and Confusion of our first Parents standing naked before their Judge, is touched with great Beauty. Upon the Arrival of *Sin* and *Death* into the Works of the Creation, the Almighty is again introduced as speaking to his Angels that surrounded him.

> *See! with what heat these Dogs of Hell advance,*
> *To waste and havock yonder World, which I*
> *So fair and good created; &c.*

The following Passage is formed upon that glorious Image in Holy Writ, which compares the Voice of an innumerable Host of Angels, uttering Hallelujahs, to the Voice of mighty Thunderings, or of many Waters.

> *He ended, and the Heavenly Audience loud*
> *Sung Hallelujah, as the sound of Seas,*
> *Through Multitude that sung: Just are thy Ways,*
> *Righteous are thy Decrees in all thy Works,*
> *Who can extenuate thee?——*

Tho' the Author in the whole Course of his Poem, and particularly in the Book we are now examining, has infinite Allusions to Places of Scripture, I have only taken notice in my Remarks of such as are of a Poetical Nature, and which are woven with great Beauty into the Body of this Fable. Of this kind is that Passage in the present Book, where describing *Sin* and *Death* as marching thro' the Works of Nature, he adds,

> *——Behind her Death*
> *Close following pace for pace, not mounted yet*
> *On his pale Horse——*

Which alludes to that Passage in Scripture, so wonderfully poetical, and terrifying to the Imagination. *And I look'd, and behold a pale Horse, and his Name that sat on him was* Death, *and* Hell *followed with him: and Power was given unto them over the fourth Part of the Earth, to kill with Sword, and with Hunger, and with Sickness, and with the Beasts of the Earth.* Under this first Head of Celestial Persons we must likewise take notice of the Command which the Angels receiv'd, to produce the several Changes in Nature, and sully the Beauty of the Creation. Accordingly they are represented as infecting the Stars and Planets with malignant Influences, weakning the Light of the Sun, bringing down the Winter into the milder Regions of Nature, planting Winds and Storms in several

Quarters of the Sky, storing the Clouds with Thunder, and in short, perverting the whole Frame of the Universe to the Condition of its criminal Inhabitants.   As this is a noble Incident in the Poem, the following Lines, in which we see the Angels heaving up the Earth, and placing it in a different Posture to the Sun from what it had before the Fall of Man, is conceived with that sublime Imagination which was so peculiar to this great Author.

> *Some say he bid his Angels turn ascanse*
> *The Poles of Earth twice ten Degrees and more*
> *From the Sun's Axle; they with Labour push'd*
> *Oblique the Centrick Globe———*

We are in the second place to consider the Infernal Agents under the view which *Milton* has given us of them in this Book. It is observed by those who would set forth the Greatness of *Virgil's* Plan, that he conducts his Reader thro' all the Parts of the Earth which were discover'd in his time. *Asia, Africk*, and *Europe* are the several Scenes of his Fable.   The Plan of *Milton's* Poem is of an infinitely greater Extent, and fills the Mind with many more astonishing Circumstances.   *Satan*, having surrounded the Earth seven times, departs at length from *Paradise*.   We then see him steering his Course among the Constellations, and after having traversed the whole Creation, pursuing his Voyage thro' the *Chaos*, and entring into his own Infernal Dominions.

His first appearance in the Assembly of fallen Angels, is work'd up with Circumstances which give a delightful Surprize to the Reader; but there is no Incident in the whole Poem which does this more than the Transformation of the whole Audience, that follows the Account their Leader gives them of his Expedition.   The gradual Change of *Satan* himself is describ'd after *Ovid's* manner, and may vie with any of those celebrated Transformations which are look'd upon as the most beautiful Parts in that Poet's Works.   *Milton* never fails of improving his own Hints, and bestowing the last finishing Touches to every Incident which is admitted into his Poem. The unexpected Hiss which rises in this Episode, the Dimensions and Bulk of *Satan* so much superior to those of the Infernal Spirits who lay under the same Transformation, with the annual Change which they are supposed to suffer, are Instances of this kind.   The Beauty of the Diction is very remarkable in this whole Episode, as I have observed in the sixth Paper of these Remarks the great Judgment with which it was contriv'd.

The Parts of *Adam* and *Eve*, or the human Persons, come next under our Consideration. *Milton's* Art is no where more shewn than in his conducting the Parts of these our first Parents. The Representation he gives of them, without falsifying the Story, is wonderfully contriv'd to influence the Reader with Pity and Compassion towards them. Tho' *Adam* involves the whole Species in Misery, his Crime proceeds from a Weakness which every Man is inclined to pardon and commiserate, as it seems rather the Frailty of Human Nature, than of the Person who offended. Every one is apt to excuse a Fault which he himself might have fallen into. It was the Excess of Love for *Eve*, that ruin'd *Adam*, and his Posterity. I need not add, that the Author is justify'd in this Particular by many of the Fathers, and the most orthodox Writers. *Milton* has by this means filled a great part of his Poem with that kind of Writing which the *French* Criticks call the *Tender*, and which is in a particular manner engaging to all sorts of Readers.

Adam and *Eve*, in the Book we are now considering, are likewise drawn with such Sentiments as do not only interest the Reader in their Afflictions, but raise in him the most melting Passions of Humanity and Commiseration. When *Adam* sees the several Changes in Nature produced about him, he appears in a Disorder of Mind suitable to one who had forfeited both his Innocence and his Happiness; he is filled with Horrour, Remorse, Despair; in the Anguish of his Heart he expostulates with his Creator for having given him an unasked Existence.

> *Did I request thee, Maker, from my Clay*
> *To mould me Man? did I sollicite thee*
> *From Darkness to promote me? or here place*
> *In this delicious Garden? As my Will*
> *Concurr'd not to my Being, 'twere but right*
> *And equal to reduce me to my Dust,*
> *Desirous to resign, and render back*
> *All I receiv'd——*

He immediately after recovers from his Presumption, owns his Doom to be just, and begs that the Death which is threatned him may be inflicted on him.

> *————Why delays*
> *His Hand to execute, what his Decree*
> *Fix'd on this day? Why do I overlive?*

> *Why am I mock'd with Death, and lengthen'd out*
> *To deathless Pain? how gladly would I meet*
> *Mortality my Sentence, and be Earth*
> *Insensible! how glad would lay me down,*
> *As in my Mother's Lap? there should I rest*
> *And sleep secure; his dreadful Voice no more*
> *Would thunder in my Ears: no fear of worse*
> *To me and to my Offspring, would torment me*
> *With cruel Expectation——*

This whole Speech is full of the like Emotion, and varied with all those Sentiments which we may suppose natural to a Mind so broken and disturb'd. I must not omit that generous Concern which our first Father shews in it for his Posterity, and which is so proper to affect the Reader.

> *————————Hide me from the Face*
> *Of God, whom to behold was then my heighth*
> *Of Happiness! yet well, if here would end*
> *The Misery, I deserv'd it, and would bear*
> *My own Deservings; but this will not serve;*
> *All that I eat, or drink, or shall beget*
> *Is propagated Curse. O Voice once heard*
> *Delightfully,* Increase *and* Multiply *;*
> *Now Death to hear!————*
> *————————In me all*
> *Posterity stands curst!   Fair Patrimony,*
> *That I must leave ye, Sons!   O were I able*
> *To waste it all my self, and leave you none!*
> *So disinherited, how would you bless*
> *Me, now your Curse!   Ah, why should all Mankind,*
> *For one Man's Fault, thus guiltless be condemn'd,*
> *If guiltless?   But from me what can proceed*
> *But all corrupt————*

Who can afterwards behold the Father of Mankind extended upon the Earth, uttering his midnight Complaints, bewailing his Existence, and wishing for Death, without sympathizing with him in his Distress?

> *Thus* Adam *to himself lamented loud*
> *Thro' the still Night; not now, (as ere Man fell)*
> *Wholesome, and cool, and mild, but with black Air*
> *Accompanied, with Damps and dreadful Gloom;*
> *Which to his evil Conscience represented*

> *All things with double Terror.   On the Ground*
> *Outstretch'd he lay ; on the cold Ground! and oft*
> *Curs'd his Creation ; Death as oft accus'd*
> *Of tardy Execution——*

The Part of *Eve* in this Book is no less passionate, and apt to sway the Reader in her Favour. She is represented with great Tenderness as approaching *Adam*, but is spurn'd from him with a Spirit of Upbraiding and Indignation, conformable to the Nature of Man, whose Passions had now gained the Dominion over him. The following Passage, wherein she is described as renewing her Addresses to him, with the whole Speech that follows it, have something in them exquisitely moving and pathetick.

> *He added not, and from her turn'd : But* Eve
> *Not so repulst, with Tears that ceas'd not flowing,*
> *And Tresses all disorder'd, at his feet*
> *Fell humble ; and embracing them, besought*
> *His Peace, and thus proceeding in her Plaint.*
> *Forsake me not thus,* Adam ! *Witness Heav'n*
> *What Love sincere, and Reverence in my Heart*
> *I bear thee, and unweeting have offended,*
> *Unhappily deceiv'd !   Thy Suppliant*
> *I beg, and clasp thy Knees ; bereave me not*
> *(Whereon I live !) thy gentle Looks, thy Aid,*
> *Thy Counsel, in this uttermost Distress,*
> *My only Strength, and Stay !   Forlorn of thee,*
> *Whither shall I betake me, where subsist ?*
> *While yet we live, (scarce one short Hour perhaps)*
> *Between us two let there be Peace,* &c.

Adam's Reconcilement to her is work'd up in the same Spirit of Tenderness. *Eve* afterwards proposes to her Husband, in the Blindness of her Despair, that to prevent their Guilt from descending upon Posterity they should resolve to live Childless ; or, if that could not be done, they should seek their own Deaths by violent Methods. As those Sentiments naturally engage the Reader to regard the Mother of Mankind with more than ordinary Commiseration, they likewise contain a very fine Moral. The Resolution of dying to end our Miseries, does not shew such a degree of Magnanimity as a Resolution to bear them, and submit to the Dispensations of Providence. Our Author has therefore, with great Delicacy, represented *Eve* as entertaining this Thought, and *Adam* as disapproving it.

We are, in the last place, to consider the Imaginary Persons, or *Death* and *Sin*, who act a large Part in this Book. Such beautiful extended Allegories are certainly some of the finest Compositions of Genius : but, as I have before observed, are not agreeable to the Nature of an Heroick Poem. This of *Sin* and *Death* is very exquisite in its Kind, if not considered as a Part of such a Work. The Truths contained in it are so clear and open, that I shall not lose time in explaining them ; but shall only observe, that a Reader who knows the Strength of the *English* Tongue, will be amazed to think how the Poet could find such apt Words and Phrases to describe the Actions of those two imaginary Persons, and particularly in that Part where *Death* is exhibited as forming a Bridge over the *Chaos;* a Work suitable to the Genius of *Milton.*

Since the Subject I am upon, gives me an Opportunity of speaking more at large of such Shadowy and Imaginary Persons as may be introduced into Heroick Poems, I shall beg leave to explain my self in a Matter which is curious in its Kind, and which none of the Criticks have treated of. It is certain *Homer* and *Virgil* are full of imaginary Persons, who are very beautiful in Poetry when they are just shewn, without being engaged in any Series of Action. *Homer* indeed represents *Sleep* as a Person, and ascribes a short Part to him in his *Iliad,* but we must consider that tho' we now regard such a Person as entirely shadowy and unsubstantial, the Heathens made Statues of him, placed him in their Temples, and looked upon him as a real Deity. When *Homer* makes use of other such Allegorical Persons, it is only in short Expressions, which convey an ordinary Thought to the Mind in the most pleasing manner, and may rather be looked upon as Poetical Phrases than Allegorical Descriptions. Instead of telling us, that Men naturally fly when they are terrified, he introduces the Persons of *Flight* and *Fear*, who, he tells us, are inseparable Companions. Instead of saying that the time was come when *Apollo* ought to have received his Recompence, he tells us, that the *Hours* brought him his Reward. Instead of describing the Effects which *Minerva's Ægis* produced in Battel, he tells us, that the Brims of it were encompassed by *Terror, Rout, Discord, Fury, Pursuit, Massacre,* and *Death.* In the same Figure of speaking, he represents *Victory* as following *Diomedes; Discord* as the Mother of Funerals and Mourning ; *Venus* as dressed by the *Graces; Bellona* as wearing *Terror* and *Consternation* like a Garment. I might give several other Instances out of *Homer*, as well as a great many out of *Virgil*. *Milton* has likewise very often made use of the same way of Speaking, as where he tells us, that *Victory* sat on the right Hand of the Messiah when he marched forth against the Rebel Angels ; that at the rising of the Sun the *Hours* unbarr'd the Gates of Light ; that *Discord* was the Daughter of *Sin*. Of the same nature are those Expressions, where describing the singing of the Nightingale, he adds, *Silence was pleased;* and upon the Messiah's bidding Peace to the *Chaos, Confusion heard his Voice*. I might add innumerable Instances of our Poet's writing in this beautiful Figure. It is plain that these I have mentioned, in which Persons of an imaginary Nature are introduced, are such short Allegories as are not designed to be taken in the literal Sense, but only to convey particular Circumstances to the Reader after an unusual and entertaining Manner. But when such Persons are introduced as principal Actors, and engaged in a Series of Adventures, they take too much upon them, and are by no means proper for an Heroick Poem, which ought to appear credible in its principal Parts. I cannot forbear therefore thinking that *Sin* and *Death* are as improper Agents in a Work of this nature, as *Strength* and *Necessity* in one of the Tragedies of *Eschylus*, who represented those two Persons nailing down *Prometheus* to a Rock, for which he has been justly censured by the greatest Criticks. I do not know any imaginary Person made use of in a more sublime manner of thinking than that in one of the Prophets, who describing God as descending from Heaven, and visiting the Sins of Mankind, adds that dreadful Circumstance, *Before him went the Pestilence*. It is certain this imaginary Person might have been described in all her purple Spots. The *Fever* might have marched before her, *Pain* might have stood at her right Hand, *Phrenzy* on her Left, and *Death* in her Rear. She might have been introduced as gliding down from the Tail of a Comet, or darted upon the Earth in a Flash of Lightning : She might have tainted the Atmosphere with her Breath ; the very glaring of her Eyes might have scattered Infection. But I believe every Reader will think, that in such sublime Writings the mentioning of her as it is done in Scripture, has something in it more just, as well as great, than all that the most fanciful Poet could have bestowed upon her in the Richness of his Imagination.

XVII.

————Crudelis ubique
Luctus, ubique favor, et plurima Mortis Imago.—Virg.

MILTON has shewn a wonderful Art in describing that variety of Passions which arise in our first Parents upon the Breach of the Commandment that had been given them. We see them gradually passing from the Triumph of their Guilt thro' Remorse, Shame, Despair, Contrition, Prayer, and Hope, to a perfect and compleat Repentance. At the end of the tenth Book they are represented as prostrating themselves upon the Ground, and watering the Earth with their Tears : To which the Poet joins this beautiful Circumstance, that they offer'd up their penitential Prayers, on the very Place where their Judge appeared to them when he pronounced their Sentence.

> *————They forthwith to the place*
> *Repairing where he judg'd them, prostrate fell*
> *Before him Reverent, and both confess'd*
> *Humbly their Faults, and Pardon begg'd, with Tears,*
> *Watering the Ground————*

There is a Beauty of the same kind in a Tragedy of *Sophocles,* where *Oedipus,* after having put out his own Eyes, instead of breaking his Neck from the Palace-Battlements (which furnishes so elegant an Entertainment for our *English* Audience) desires that he may be conducted to Mount *Cithæron,* in order to end his Life in that very Place where he was exposed in his Infancy, and where he should then have died, had the Will of his Parents been executed.

As the Author never fails to give a poetical Turn to his Sentiments, he describes in the Beginning of this Book the Acceptance which these their Prayers met with, in a short Allegory, form'd upon that beautiful Passage in holy Writ : *And another Angel came and stood at the Altar, having a golden Censer; and there was given unto him much Incense, that he should offer it with the Prayers of all Saints upon the Golden Altar, which was before the Throne: And the Smoak of the Incense which came with the Prayers of the Saints, ascended up before God.*

> ————*To Heav'n their Prayers*
> *Flew up, nor miss'd the Way, by envious Winds*
> *Blown vagabond or frustrate: in they pass'd*
> *Dimensionless through heav'nly Doors, then clad*
> *With Incense, where the Golden Altar fumed,*
> *By their great Intercessor, came in sight*
> *Before the Father's Throne————*

We have the same Thought expressed a second time in the Intercession of the Messiah, which is conceived in very Emphatick Sentiments and Expressions.

Among the Poetical Parts of Scripture, which *Milton* has so finely wrought into this Part of his Narration, I must not omit that wherein *Ezekiel* speaking of the Angels who appeared to him in a Vision, adds, that *every one had four Faces*, and that *their whole Bodies, and their Backs, and their Hands, and their Wings, were full of Eyes round about.*

> ————*The Cohort bright*
> *Of watchful Cherubims, four Faces each*
> *Had like a double* Janus, *all their Shape*
> *Spangled with Eyes————*

The Assembling of all the Angels of Heaven to hear the solemn Decree passed upon Man, is represented in very lively Ideas. The Almighty is here describ'd as remembring Mercy in the midst of Judgment, and commanding *Michael* to deliver his Message in the mildest Terms, lest the Spirit of Man, which was already broken with the Sense of his Guilt and Misery, should fail before him.

> ————*Yet lest they faint*
> *At the sad Sentence rigorously urg'd,*
> *For I behold them softned, and with Tears*
> *Bewailing their Excess, all Terror hide.*

The Conference of *Adam* and *Eve* is full of moving Sentiments. Upon their going abroad after the melancholy Night which they had passed together, they discover the Lion and the Eagle pursuing each of them their Prey towards the Eastern Gates of *Paradise*. There is a double Beauty in this Incident, not only as it presents great and just Omens, which are always agreeable in Poetry, but as it expresses that Enmity which was now produced in the Animal Creation.   The Poet to shew the like Changes in Nature, as well as to grace his Fable with a noble Prodigy, represents the Sun in an Eclipse.   This particular Incident has likewise a fine Effect upon the Imagination of the Reader, in regard to what follows ; for at the same time that the Sun is under an Eclipse, a bright Cloud descends in the Western Quarter of the Heavens, filled with an Host of Angels, and more luminous than the Sun it self.   The whole Theatre of Nature is darkned, that this glorious Machine may appear in all its Lustre and Magnificence.

> ———*Why in the East*
> *Darkness ere Day's mid-course, and morning Light*
> *More orient in that Western Cloud that draws*
> *O'er the blue Firmament a radiant White,*
> *And slow descends, with something Heav'nly fraught?*
>   *He err'd not, for by this the heav'nly Bands*
> *Down from a Sky of Jasper lighted now*
> *In Paradise, and on a Hill made halt ;*
> *A glorious Apparition*———

I need not observe how properly this Author, who always suits his Parts to the Actors whom he introduces, has employed *Michael* in the Expulsion of our first Parents from *Paradise*. The Archangel on this Occasion neither appears in his proper Shape, nor in that familiar Manner with which *Raphael* the sociable Spirit entertained the Father of Mankind before the Fall.   His Person, his Port, and Behaviour, are suitable to a Spirit of the highest Rank, and exquisitely describ'd in the following Passage.

> ———*Th' Archangel soon drew nigh,*
> *Not in his Shape Celestial; but as Man*
> *Clad to meet Man: over his lucid Arms*
> *A Military Vest of Purple flow'd,*
> *Livelier than* Melibœan, *or the Grain*
> *Of* Sarra, *worn by Kings and Heroes old,*
> *In time of Truce:* Iris *had dipt the Woof:*
> *His starry Helm, unbuckled, shew'd him prime*
> *In Manhood where Youth ended; by his side,*
> *As in a glistring Zodiack, hung the Sword,*
> Satan's *dire dread, and in his Hand the Spear.*
> Adam *bow'd low, he Kingly from his State*
> *Inclined not, but his coming thus declared,*

Eve's Complaint upon hearing that she was to be removed from the Garden of *Paradise*, is wonderfully beautiful :   The Sentiments are not only proper to the Subject, but have something in them particularly soft and womanish.

> *Must I then leave thee, Paradise?   Thus leave*
> *Thee, native Soil, these happy Walks and Shades,*
> *Fit haunt of Gods?   Where I had hope to spend*
> *Quiet, though sad, the respite of that Day*
> *That must be mortal to us both.   O Flow'rs,*
> *That never will in other Climate grow,*
> *My early Visitation, and my last*
> *At Even, which I bred up with tender Hand*
> *From the first opening Bud, and gave you Names;*
> *Who now shall rear you to the Sun, or rank*
> *Your Tribes, and water from th' ambrosial Fount?*
> *Thee, lastly, nuptial Bower, by me adorn'd*
> *With what to Sight or Smell was sweet; from thee*
> *How shall I part, and whither wander down*
> *Into a lower World, to this obscure*
> *And wild? how shall we breathe in other Air*
> *Less pure, accustom'd to immortal Fruits?*

Adam's Speech abounds with Thoughts which are equally moving, but of a more masculine and elevated Turn.   Nothing can be conceived more Sublime and Poetical than the following Passage in it.

> *This most afflicts me, that departing hence*
> *As from his Face I shall be hid, deprived*
> *His blessed Count'nance; here I could frequent,*
> *With Worship, place to place where he vouchsaf'd*
> *Presence Divine; and to my Sons relate,*
> *On this Mount he appear'd, under this Tree*
> *Stood visible, among these Pines his Voice*
> *I heard, here with him at this Fountain talk'd;*
> *So many grateful Altars I would rear*
> *Of grassy Turf, and pile up every Stone*
> *Of lustre from the Brook, in memory*
> *Or monument to Ages, and thereon*
> *Offer sweet-smelling Gums and Fruits and Flowers.*
> *In yonder nether World where shall I seek*
> *His bright Appearances, or Footsteps trace?*
> *For though I fled him angry, yet recall'd*
> *To Life prolong'd and promised Race, I now*

> *Gladly behold though but his utmost Skirts*
> *Of Glory, and far off his Steps adore.*

The Angel afterwards leads *Adam* to the highest Mount of *Paradise*, and lays before him a whole Hemisphere, as a proper Stage for those Visions which were to be represented on it. I have before observed how the Plan of *Milton's* Poem is in many Particulars greater than that of the *Iliad* or *Æneid. Virgil's* Hero, in the last of these Poems, is entertained with a Sight of all those who are to descend from him ; but though that Episode is justly admired as one of the noblest Designs in the whole *Æneid,* every one must allow that this of *Milton* is of a much higher Nature. *Adam's* Vision is not confined to any particular Tribe of Mankind, but extends to the whole Species.

In this great Review which *Adam* takes of all his Sons and Daughters, the first Objects he is presented with exhibit to him the Story of *Cain* and *Abel,* which is drawn together with much Closeness and Propriety of Expression. That Curiosity and natural Horror which arises in *Adam* at the Sight of the first dying Man, is touched with great Beauty.

> *But have I now seen Death ? is this the way*
> *I must return to native Dust ? O Sight*
> *Of Terror foul, and ugly to behold,*
> *Horrid to think, how horrible to feel !*

The second Vision sets before him the Image of Death in a great Variety of Appearances. The Angel, to give him a general Idea of those Effects which his Guilt had brought upon his Posterity, places before him a large Hospital or Lazar-House, fill'd with Persons lying under all kinds of mortal Diseases. How finely has the Poet told us that the sick Persons languished under lingering and incurable Distempers, by an apt and judicious use of such Imaginary Beings as those I mentioned in my last *Saturday's* Paper.

> *Dire was the tossing, deep the Groans.* Despair
> *Tended the Sick, busy from Couch to Couch ;*
> *And over them triumphant* Death *his Dart*
> *Shook, but delay'd to strike, though oft invoked*
> *With Vows, as their chief Good and final Hope.*

The Passion which likewise rises in *Adam* on this Occasion, is very natural.

> *Sight so deform, what Heart of Rock could long*
> *Dry-eyed behold? Adam could not, but wept,*
> *Tho' not of Woman born; Compassion quell'd*
> *His best of Man, and gave him up to Tears.*

The Discourse between the Angel and *Adam*, which follows, abounds with noble Morals.

As there is nothing more delightful in Poetry than a Contrast and Opposition of Incidents, the Author, after this melancholy Prospect of Death and Sickness, raises up a Scene of Mirth, Love, and Jollity. The secret Pleasure that steals into *Adam's* Heart as he is intent upon this Vision, is imagined with great Delicacy. I must not omit the Description of the loose female Troop, who seduced the Sons of God, as they are called in Scripture.

> *For that fair female Troop thou saw'st, that seem'd*
> *Of Goddesses, so Blithe, so Smooth, so Gay,*
> *Yet empty of all Good wherein consists*
> *Woman's domestick Honour and chief Praise;*
> *Bred only and compleated to the taste*
> *Of lustful Appetence, to sing, to dance,*
> *To dress, and troule the Tongue, and roll the Eye:*
> *To these that sober Race of Men, whose Lives*
> *Religious titled them the Sons of God,*
> *Shall yield up all their Virtue, all their Fame*
> *Ignobly, to the Trains and to the Smiles*
> *Of those fair Atheists——*

The next Vision is of a quite contrary Nature, and filled with the Horrors of War. *Adam* at the Sight of it melts into Tears, and breaks out in that passionate Speech,

> *————————O what are these!*
> *Death's Ministers, not Men, who thus deal Death*
> *Inhumanly to Men, and multiply*
> *Ten Thousandfold the Sin of him who slew*
> *His Brother: for of whom such Massacre*
> *Make they but of their Brethren, Men of Men?*

Milton, to keep up an agreeable Variety in his Visions, after having raised in the Mind of his Reader the several Ideas of Terror which are conformable to the Description of War, passes on to those softer Images of Triumphs and Festivals, in that Vision of Lewdness and Luxury which ushers in the Flood.

As it is visible that the Poet had his Eye upon *Ovid's* Account of the universal Deluge, the Reader may observe with how much Judgment he has avoided every thing that is redundant or puerile in the *Latin* Poet. We do not here see the Wolf swimming among the Sheep, nor any of those wanton Imaginations, which *Seneca* found fault with, as unbecoming the great Catastrophe of Nature. If our Poet has imitated that Verse in which *Ovid* tells us there was nothing but Sea, and that this Sea had no Shore to it, he has not set the Thought in such a Light as to incur the Censure which Criticks have passed upon it. The latter part of that Verse in *Ovid* is idle and superfluous, but just and beautiful in *Milton.*

> *Jamque mare et tellus nullum discrimen habebant,*
> *Nil nisi pontus erat, deerant quoque littora ponto.*—Ovid.

> ————*Sea cover'd Sea,*
> *Sea without Shore*———— Milton.

In *Milton* the former Part of the Description does not forestall the latter. How much 'more great and solemn on this Occasion is that which follows in our *English* Poet,

> ————*And in their Palaces*
> *Where Luxury late reign'd, Sea-Monsters whelp'd*
> *And stabled*————

than that in *Ovid,* where we are told that the Sea-Calfs lay in those Places where the Goats were used to browze? The Reader may find several other parallel Passages in the *Latin* and *English* Description of the Deluge, wherein our Poet has visibly the Advantage. The Sky's being overcharged with Clouds, the descending of the Rains, the rising of the Seas, and the Appearance of the Rainbow, are such Descriptions as every one must take notice of. The Circumstance relating to *Paradise* is so finely imagined, and suitable to the Opinions of many learned Authors, that I cannot forbear giving it a Place in this Paper.

> ————*Then shall this Mount*
> *Of Paradise by might of Waves be mov'd*
> *Out of his Place, push'd by the horned Flood*
> *With all his Verdure spoil'd, and Trees adrift*
> *Down the great River to the op'ning Gulf,*
> *And there take root, an Island salt and bare,*
> *The haunt of Seals and Orcs and Sea-Mews clang.*

The Transition which the Poet makes from the Vision of the Deluge, to the Concern it occasioned in. *Adam*, is exquisitely graceful, and copied after *Virgil*, though the first Thought it introduces is rather in the Spirit of *Ovid*.

> *How didst thou grieve then*, Adam, *to behold*
> *The End of all thy Offspring, End so sad,*
> *Depopulation ! thee another Flood*
> *Of Tears and Sorrow, a Flood thee also drown'd,*
> *And sunk thee as thy Sons; till gently rea'd*
> *By th' Angel, on thy Feet thou stood'st at last,*
> *Tho' comfortless, as when a Father mourns*
> *His Children, all in view destroy'd at once.*

I have been the more particular in my Quotations out of the eleventh Book of *Paradise Lost*, because it is not generally reckoned among the most shining Books of this Poem ; for which Reason the Reader might be apt to overlook those many Passages in it which deserve our Admiration.   The eleventh and twelfth are indeed built upon that single Circumstance of the Removal of our first Parents from *Paradise;* but tho' this is not in it self so great a Subject as that in most of the foregoing Books, it is extended and diversified with so many surprising Incidents and pleasing Episodes, that these two last Books can by no means be looked upon as unequal Parts of this Divine Poem.   I must further add, that had not *Milton* represented our first Parents as driven out of *Paradise*, his Fall of Man would not have been compleat, and consequently his Action would have been imperfect.

XVIII.

Segnius irritant animos demissa per aures
Quam quæ sunt oculis subjecta fidelibus—— Hor.

MILTON, after having represented in Vision the History of Mankind to the first great Period of Nature, dispatches the remaining part of it in Narration.   He has devised a very handsome Reason for the Angel's proceeding with *Adam* after this manner ; though doubtless the true Reason was the Difficulty which the Poet would have found to have shadowed out so mixed and complicated a Story in visible Objects. I could wish, however, that the Author had done it, whatever Pains it might have cost him. To give my Opinion freely, I think that the exhibiting part of the History of Mankind in Vision, and part in Narrative, is as if an History-Painter should put in Colours one half of his Subject, and write down the remaining part of it. If *Milton's* Poem flags any where, it is in this Narration, where in some places the Author has been so attentive to his Divinity, that he has neglected his Poetry. The Narration, however, rises very happily on several Occasions, where the Subject is capable of Poetical Ornaments, as particularly in the Confusion which he describes among the Builders of *Babel*, and in his short Sketch of the Plagues of *Egypt*. The Storm of Hail and Fire, with the Darkness that overspread the Land for three Days, are described with great Strength. The beautiful Passage which follows, is raised upon noble Hints in Scripture :

> ——————————*Thus with ten Wounds*
> *The River-Dragon tamed at length submits*
> *To let his Sojourners depart, and oft*
> *Humbles his stubborn Heart ; but still as Ice*
> *More harden'd after Thaw, till in his Rage*
> *Pursuing whom he late dismiss'd, the Sea*
> *Swallows him with his Host, but them lets pass*
> *As on dry Land between two Chrystal Walls,*
> *Aw'd by the Rod of* Moses *so to stand*
> *Divided*——————

The *River-Dragon* is an Allusion to the Crocodile, which inhabits the *Nile*, from whence *Egypt* derives her Plenty. This Allusion is taken from that Sublime Passage in *Ezekiel*, *Thus saith the Lord God, behold I am against thee*, Pharaoh King of Egypt, *the great Dragon that lieth in the midst of his Rivers, which hath said, my River is mine own, and I have made it for my self.* *Milton* has given us another very noble and poetical Image in the same Description, which is copied almost Word for Word out of the History of *Moses*.

> *All Night he will pursue, but his Approach*
> *Darkness defends between till morning Watch;*
> Then through the fiery Pillar and the Cloud
> God looking forth, will trouble all his Host,
> And craze their Chariot Wheels: *when by command*

> Moses *once more his potent Rod extends*
> *Over the Sea: the Sea his Rod obeys:*
> *On their embattell'd Ranks the Waves return*
> *And overwhelm their War*————

As the principal Design of this *Episode* was to give *Adam* an Idea of the Holy Person, who was to reinstate human Nature in that Happiness and Perfection from which it had fallen, the Poet confines himself to the Line of *Abraham*, from whence the *Messiah* was to Descend. The Angel is described as seeing the Patriarch actually travelling towards the *Land of Promise*, which gives a particular Liveliness to this part of the Narration.

> *I see him, but thou canst not, with what Faith,*
> *He leaves his Gods, his Friends, his Native Soil,*
> Ur *of* Chaldæa, *passing now the Ford*
> *To* Haran, *after him a cumbrous Train*
> *Of Herds and Flocks, and numerous Servitude;*
> *Not wand'ring poor, but trusting all his Wealth*
> *With God, who call'd him, in a Land unknown.*
> Canaan *he now attains, I see his Tents*
> *Pitch'd about* Sechem, *and the neighbouring Plain*
> *Of* Moreh, *there by Promise he receives*
> *Gifts to his Progeny of all that Land,*
> *From* Hamath *Northward to the Desart South.*
> (*Things by their Names I call, though yet unnamed.*)

As *Virgil's* Vision in the sixth *Æneid* probably gave *Milton* the Hint of this whole *Episode*, the last Line is a Translation of that Verse, where *Anchises* mentions the Names of Places, which they were to bear hereafter.

> *Hæc tum nomina erunt, nunc sunt sine nomine terræ.*

The Poet has very finely represented the Joy and Gladness of Heart which rises in *Adam* upon his discovery of the Messiah. As he sees his Day at a distance through Types and Shadows, he rejoices in it : but when he finds the Redemption of Man compleated, and *Paradise* again renewed, he breaks forth in Rapture and Transport ;

> *O Goodness infinite, Goodness immense !*
> *That all this Good of Evil shall produce,* &c.

416

I have hinted in my sixth Paper on *Milton*, that an Heroick Poem, according to the Opinion of the best Criticks, ought to end happily, and leave the Mind of the Reader, after having conducted it through many Doubts and Fears, Sorrows and Disquietudes, in a State of Tranquility and Satisfaction. *Milton's* Fable, which had so many other Qualifications to recommend it, was deficient in this Particular. It is here therefore, that the Poet has shewn a most exquisite Judgment, as well as the finest Invention, by finding out a Method to supply this natural Defect in his Subject. Accordingly he leaves the Adversary of Mankind, in the last View which he gives us of him, under the lowest State of Mortification and Disappointment. We see him chewing Ashes, grovelling in the Dust, and loaden with supernumerary Pains and Torments. On the contrary, our two first Parents are comforted by Dreams and Visions, cheared with Promises of Salvation, and, in a manner, raised to a greater Happiness than that which they had forfeited : In short, *Satan* is represented miserable in the height of his Triumphs, and *Adam* triumphant in the height of Misery.

Milton's Poem ends very nobly. The last Speeches of *Adam* and the Arch-Angel are full of Moral and Instructive Sentiments. The Sleep that fell upon *Eve*, and the Effects it had in quieting the Disorders of her Mind, produces the same kind of Consolation in the Reader, who cannot peruse the last beautiful Speech which is ascribed to the Mother of Mankind, without a secret Pleasure and Satisfaction.

> *Whence thou return'st, and whither went'st, I know ;*
> *For God is also in Sleep, and Dreams advise,*
> *Which he hath sent propitious, some great Good*
> *Presaging, since with Sorrow and Heart's Distress*
> *Wearied I fell asleep : but now lead on ;*
> *In me is no delay : with thee to go,*
> *Is to stay here ; without thee here to stay,*
> *Is to go hence unwilling : thou to me*
> *Art all things under Heav'n, all Places thou,*
> *Who for my wilful Crime art banish'd hence.*
> *This farther Consolation yet secure*
> *I carry hence ; though all by me is lost,*
> *Such Favour, I unworthy, am vouchsafed,*
> *By me the promised Seed shall all restore.*

The following Lines, which conclude the Poem, rise in a most glorious Blaze of Poetical Images and Expressions.

Heliodorus in his *Æthiopicks* acquaints us, that the Motion of the Gods differs from that of Mortals, as the former do not stir their Feet, nor proceed Step by Step, but slide o'er the Surface of the Earth by an uniform Swimming of the whole Body. The Reader may observe with how Poetical a Description *Milton* has attributed the same kind of Motion to the Angels who were to take Possession of *Paradise*.

> *So spake our Mother* Eve, *and* Adam *heard*
> *Well pleas'd, but answer'd not; for now too nigh*
> *Th' Archangel stood, and from the other Hill*
> *To their fix'd Station, all in bright Array*
> *The Cherubim descended; on the Ground*
> *Gliding meteorous, as evening Mist*
> *Ris'n from a River, o'er the Marish glides,*
> *And gathers ground fast at the Lab'rer's Heel*
> *Homeward returning. High in Front advanc'd,*
> *The brandish'd Sword of God before them blaz'd*
> *Fierce as a Comet——*

The Author helped his Invention in the following Passage, by reflecting on the Behaviour of the Angel, who, in Holy Writ, has the Conduct of *Lot* and his Family. The Circumstances drawn from that Relation are very gracefully made use of on this Occasion.

> *In either Hand the hastning Angel caught*
> *Our lingring Parents, and to th' Eastern Gate*
> *Led them direct; and down the Cliff as fast*
> *To the subjected Plain; then disappear'd.*
> *They looking back, &c.*

The Scene which our first Parents are surprized with, upon their looking back on *Paradise,* wonderfully strikes the Reader's Imagination, as nothing can be more natural than the Tears they shed on that Occasion.

> *They looking back, all th' Eastern side beheld*
> *Of* Paradise, *so late their happy Seat,*
> *Wav'd over by that flaming Brand, the Gate*
> *With dreadful Faces throng'd and fiery Arms:*
> *Some natural Tears they dropp'd, but wiped them soon;*
> *The World was all before them, whereto chuse*
> *Their Place of Rest, and Providence their Guide.*

If I might presume to offer at the smallest Alteration in this divine Work, I should think the Poem would end better with the Passage here quoted, than with the two Verses which follow :

They hand in hand, with wandering Steps and slow,
Through Eden *took their solitary Way.*

These two Verses, though they have their Beauty, fall very much below the foregoing Passage, and renew in the Mind of the Reader that Anguish which was pretty well laid by that Consideration,

The world was all before them, where to chuse
Their Place of Rest, and Providence their Guide.

The Number of Books in *Paradise Lost* is equal to those of the *Æneid.* Our Author in his first Edition had divided his Poem into ten Books, but afterwards broke the seventh and the eleventh each of them into two different Books, by the help of some small Additions. This second Division was made with great Judgment, as any one may see who will be at the pains of examining it. It was not done for the sake of such a Chimerical Beauty as that of resembling *Virgil* in this particular, but for the more just and regular Disposition of this great Work.

Those who have read *Bossu,* and many of the Criticks who have written since his Time, will not pardon me if I do not find out the particular Moral which is inculcated in *Paradise Lost.* Though I can by no means think, with the last mentioned *French* Author, that an Epick Writer first of all pitches upon a certain Moral, as the Ground-Work and Foundation of his Poem, and afterwards finds out a Story to it : I am, however, of opinion, that no just Heroick Poem ever was or can be made, from whence one great Moral may not be deduced. That which reigns in *Milton*, is the most universal and most useful that can be imagined ; it is in short this, *That Obedience to the Will of God makes Men happy, and that Disobedience makes them miserable.* This is visibly the Moral of the principal Fable, which turns upon *Adam* and *Eve*, who continued in *Paradise*, while they kept the command that was given them, and were driven out of it as soon as they had transgressed. This is likewise the Moral of the principal Episode, which shews us how an innumerable Multitude of Angels fell from their State of Bliss, and were cast into Hell upon their Disobedience. Besides this great Moral, which may be looked upon as the

Soul of the Fable, there are an Infinity of Under-Morals which are to be drawn from the several parts of the Poem, and which makes this Work more useful and instructive than any other Poem in any Language.

Those who have criticized on the *Odyssey*, the *Iliad*, and *Æneid*, have taken a great deal of Pains to fix the Number of Months and Days contained in the Action of each of those Poems. If any one thinks it worth his while to examine this Particular in *Milton*, he will find that from *Adam's* first Appearance in the fourth Book, to his Expulsion from *Paradise* in the twelfth, the Author reckons ten Days. As for that part of the Action which is described in the three first Books, as it does not pass within the Regions of Nature, I have before observed that it is not subject to any Calculations of Time.

I have now finished my Observations on a Work which does an Honour to the *English* Nation. I have taken a general View of it under these four Heads, the Fable, the Characters, the Sentiments, and the Language, and made each of them the Subject of a particular Paper. I have in the next Place spoken of the Censures which our Author may incur under each of these Heads, which I have confined to two Papers, though I might have enlarged the Number, if I had been disposed to dwell on so ungrateful a Subject. I believe, however, that the severest Reader will not find any little fault in Heroick Poetry, which this Author has fallen into, that does not come under one of those Heads among which I have distributed his several Blemishes. After having thus treated at large of *Paradise Lost*, I could not think it sufficient to have celebrated this Poem in the whole, without descending to Particulars. I have therefore bestowed a Paper upon each Book, and endeavoured not only to prove that the Poem is beautiful in general, but to point out its Particular Beauties, and to determine wherein they consist. I have endeavoured to shew how some Passages are beautiful by being Sublime, others by being Soft, others by being Natural; which of them are recommended by the Passion, which by the Moral, which by the Sentiment, and which by the Expression. I have likewise endeavoured to shew how the Genius of the Poet shines by a happy Invention, a distant Allusion, or a judicious Imitation; how he has copied or improved *Homer* or *Virgil*, and raised his own Imaginations by the Use which he has made of several Poetical Passages in Scripture. I might have inserted also several Passages of *Tasso*, which our Author has imitated; but as I do not look upon *Tasso* to be a sufficient Voucher, I would not perplex my

Reader with such Quotations, as might do more Honour to the *Italian* than the *English* Poet. In short, I have endeavoured to particularize those innumerable kinds of Beauty, which it would be tedious to recapitulate, but which are essential to Poetry, and which may be met with in the Works of this great Author. Had I thought, at my first engaging in this design, that it would have led me to so great a length, I believe I should never have entered upon it ; but the kind Reception which it has met with among those whose Judgments I have a value for, as well as the uncommon Demands which my Bookseller tells me have been made for these particular Discourses, give me no reason to repent of the Pains I have been at in composing them.

Miscellaneous Papers.

MISCELLANEOUS PAPERS.

Sir Roger de Coverley's Household.

(*Spectator*, *No.* 106.)

HAVING often received an Invitation from my Friend Sir ROGER DE COVERLEY to pass away a Month with him in the Country, I last Week accompanied him thither, and am settled with him for some time at his Country-house, where I intend to form several of my ensuing Speculations. Sir ROGER, who is very well acquainted with my Humour, lets me rise and go to Bed when I please, dine at his own Table or in my Chamber as I think fit, sit still and say nothing without bidding me be merry. When the Gentlemen of the Country come to see him, he only shews me at a Distance : As I have been walking in his Fields I have observed them stealing a Sight of me over an Hedge, and have heard the Knight desiring them not to let me see them, for that I hated to be stared at.

I am the more at Ease in Sir ROGER'S Family, because it consists of sober and staid Persons ; for as the Knight is the best Master in the World, he seldom changes his Servants ; and as he is beloved by all about him, his Servants never care for leaving him ; by this means his Domesticks are all in Years, and grown old with their Master. You would take his Valet de Chambre for his Brother, his Butler is grey-headed, his Groom is one of the gravest Men that I have ever seen, and his Coachman has the Looks of a Privy-Counsellor. You see the Goodness of the Master even in the old House-dog, and in a grey Pad that is kept in the Stable with great Care and Tenderness out of Regard to his past Services, tho' he has been useless for several Years.

I could not but observe with a great deal of Pleasure the Joy that appeared in the Countenances of these ancient Domesticks upon my Friend's Arrival at his Country-Seat. Some of them could not refrain from Tears at the Sight of their old Master ; every one of them press'd forward to do something for him, and seemed discouraged if they were not employed. At the same time the good old Knight, with a Mixture of the Father and the Master of the Family, tempered the Enquiries after his own Affairs with several kind Questions relating to themselves. This Humanity and good Nature engages every Body to him, so that when he is pleasant upon any of them, all his Family are in good Humour, and none so much as the Person whom he diverts himself with : On the contrary, if he coughs, or betrays any Infirmity of old Age, it is easy for a Stander-by to observe a secret Concern in the Looks of all his Servants.

My worthy Friend has put me under the particular Care of his Butler, who is a very prudent Man, and, as well as the rest of his Fellow-Servants, wonderfully desirous of pleasing me, because they have often heard their Master talk of me as of his particular Friend.

My chief Companion, when Sir ROGER is diverting himself in the Woods or the Fields, is a very venerable Man who is ever with Sir ROGER, and has lived at his House in the Nature of a Chaplain above thirty Years. This Gentleman is a Person of good Sense and some Learning, of a very regular Life and obliging Conversation : He heartily loves Sir ROGER, and knows that he is very much in the old Knight's Esteem, so that he lives in the Family rather as a Relation than a Dependant.

I have observed in several of my Papers, that my Friend Sir ROGER, amidst all his good Qualities, is something of an Humourist ; and that his Virtues, as well as Imperfections, are as it were tinged by a certain Extravagance, which makes them particularly *his*, and distinguishes them from those of other Men. This Cast of Mind, as it is generally very innocent in it self, so it renders his Conversation highly agreeable, and more delightful than the same Degree of Sense and Virtue would appear in their common and ordinary Colours. As I was walking with him last Night, he asked me how I liked the good Man whom I have just now mentioned? and without staying for my Answer told me, That he was afraid of being insulted with Latin and Greek at his own Table ; for which Reason he desired a particular Friend of his at the University to find him out a Clergyman rather of plain Sense than much Learning, of a good Aspect, a clear Voice, a sociable Temper, and, if possible, a Man that understood a little of Back-Gammon. My Friend, says Sir ROGER, found me out this Gentleman, who, besides the Endowments required of him, is, they tell me, a good Scholar, tho' he does not shew it. I have given him the Parsonage of the Parish ; and because I know his Value have settled upon him a good Annuity for Life. If he outlives me, he shall find that he was higher in my Esteem than perhaps he thinks he is. He has now been with me thirty Years ; and tho' he does not know I have taken Notice of it, has never in all that time asked anything of me for himself, tho' he is every Day solliciting me for something in behalf of one or other of my Tenants his Parishioners. There has not been a Law-suit in the Parish since he has liv'd among them : If any Dispute arises they apply themselves to him for the Decision ; if they do not acquiesce in his Judgment, which I think never happened above once or twice at most, they appeal to me. At his first settling with me, I made him a Present of all the good Sermons which have been printed in *English,* and only begg'd of him that every *Sunday* he would pronounce one of them in the Pulpit. Accordingly, he has digested them into such a Series, that they follow one another naturally, and make a continued System of practical Divinity.

As Sir ROGER was going on in his Story, the Gentleman we were talking of came up to us ; and upon the Knight's asking him who preached to morrow (for it was *Saturday* Night) told us, the Bishop of St. *Asaph* in the Morning, and Dr. *South* in the Afternoon. He then shewed us his List of Preachers for the whole Year, where I saw with a great deal of Pleasure Archbishop *Tillotson,* Bishop *Saunderson,* Doctor *Barrow,* Doctor *Calamy,* with several living Authors who have published Discourses of Practical Divinity. I no sooner saw this venerable Man in the Pulpit, but I very much approved of my Friend's insisting upon the Qualifications of a good Aspect and a clear Voice ; for I was so charmed with the Gracefulness of his Figure and Delivery, as well as with the Discourses he pronounced, that I think I never passed any Time more to my Satisfaction. A Sermon repeated after this Manner, is like the Composition of a Poet in the Mouth of a graceful Actor.

I could heartily wish that more of our Country Clergy would follow this Example ; and instead of wasting their Spirits in laborious Compositions of their own, would endeavour after a handsome Elocution, and all those other Talents that are proper to enforce what has been penned by greater Masters. This would not only be more easy to themselves, but more edifying to the People.—*Addison.*

Will. Wimble.

(*Spectator, No.* 108.)

AS I was Yesterday Morning walking with Sir ROGER before
his House, a Country-Fellow brought him a huge Fish,
which, he told him, Mr. *William Wimble* had caught that very
Morning ; and that he presented it, with his Service to him,
and intended to come and dine with him.   At the same Time
he delivered a Letter, which my Friend read to me as soon as
the Messenger left him.

  Sir ROGER,
 'I Desire you to accept of a Jack, which is the best I have
'caught this Season.   I intend to come and stay with you a
'Week, and see how the Perch bite in the *Black River*.   I
'observed with some Concern, the last time I saw you upon
'the Bowling-Green, that your Whip wanted a Lash to it ; I
'will bring half a dozen with me that I twisted last Week,
'which I hope will serve you all the Time you are in the
'Country.   I have not been out of the Saddle for six Days last
'past, having been at *Eaton* with Sir *John's* eldest Son.   He
'takes to his Learning hugely.   I am,
     SIR, Your Humble Servant,
        Will Wimble.

This extraordinary Letter, and Message that accompanied it,
made me very curious to know the Character and Quality of the
Gentleman who sent them ; which I found to be as follows.
Will. Wimble is younger Brother to a Baronet, and descended
of the ancient Family of the *Wimbles*.   He is now between
Forty and Fifty ; but being bred to no Business and born to no
Estate, he generally lives with his elder Brother as Superin-
tendant of his Game.   He hunts a Pack of Dogs better than
any Man in the Country, and is very famous for finding out a
Hare.   He is extreamly well versed in all the little Handicrafts
of an idle Man : He makes a *May-fly* to a miracle ; and
furnishes the whole Country with Angle-Rods.   As he is a
good-natur'd officious Fellow, and very much esteem'd upon
account of his Family, he is a welcome Guest at every House,
and keeps up a good Correspondence among all the Gentlemen
about him.   He carries a Tulip-root in his Pocket from one to
another, or exchanges a Puppy between a Couple of Friends

that live perhaps in the opposite Sides of the County. *Will.* is a particular Favourite of all the young Heirs, whom he frequently obliges with a Net that he has weaved, or a Setting-dog that he has *made* himself: He now and then presents a Pair of Garters of his own knitting to their Mothers or Sisters ; and raises a great deal of Mirth among them, by enquiring as often as he meets them *how they wear?* These Gentleman-like Manufactures and obliging little Humours, make *Will.* the darling of the Country.

Sir ROGER was proceeding in the Character of him, when we saw him make up to us with two or three Hazle-Twigs in his Hand that he had cut in Sir ROGER'S Woods, as he came through them, in his Way to the House. I was very much pleased to observe on one Side the hearty and sincere Welcome with which Sir ROGER received him, and on the other, the secret Joy which his Guest discover'd at Sight of the good old Knight. After the first Salutes were over, *Will.* desired Sir ROGER to lend him one of his Servants to carry a Set of Shuttlecocks he had with him in a little Box to a Lady that lived about a Mile off, to whom it seems he had promis'd such a Present for above this half Year. Sir ROGER'S Back was no sooner turned but honest *Will.* began to tell me of a large Cock-Pheasant that he had sprung in one of the neighbouring Woods, with two or three other Adventures of the same Nature. Odd and uncommon Characters are the Game that I look for, and most delight in ; for which Reason I was as much pleased with the Novelty of the Person that talked to me, as he could be for his Life with the springing of a Pheasant, and therefore listned to him with more than ordinary Attention.

In the midst of his Discourse the Bell rung to Dinner, where the Gentleman I have been speaking of had the Pleasure of seeing the huge Jack, he had caught, served up for the first Dish in a most sumptuous Manner. Upon our sitting down to it he gave us a long Account how he had hooked it, played with it, foiled it, and at length drew it out upon the Bank, with several other Particulars that lasted all the first Course. A Dish of Wild-fowl that came afterwards furnished Conversation for the rest of the Dinner, which concluded with a late Invention of *Will's* for improving the Quail-Pipe.

Upon withdrawing into my Room after Dinner, I was secretly touched with Compassion towards the honest Gentleman that had dined with us ; and could not but consider with a great deal of Concern, how so good an Heart and such busy Hands were wholly employed in Trifles ; that so much Humanity should be so little beneficial to others, and so much Industry so little advantageous to himself. The same Temper of Mind and Application to Affairs might have recommended him to the publick Esteem, and have raised his Fortune in another Station of Life. What Good to his Country or himself might not a Trader or Merchant have done with such useful tho' ordinary Qualifications?

Will. Wimble's is the Case of many a younger Brother of a great <u>Family</u>, who had rather see their Children starve like Gentlemen, than thrive in a Trade or Profession that is beneath their Quality. This Humour fills several Parts of *Europe* with Pride and Beggary. It is the Happiness of a Trading Nation, like ours, that the younger Sons, tho' uncapable of any liberal Art or Profession, may be placed in such a Way of Life, as may perhaps enable them to vie with the best of their Family: Accordingly we find several Citizens that were launched into the World with narrow Fortunes, rising by an honest Industry to greater Estates than those of their elder Brothers. It is not improbable but *Will.* was formerly tried at Divinity, Law, or Physick; and that finding his Genius did not lie that Way, his Parents gave him up at length to his own Inventions. But certainly, however improper he might have been for Studies of a higher Nature, he was perfectly well turned for the Occupations of Trade and Commerce. As I think this is a Point which cannot be too much inculated, I shall desire my Reader to compare what I have here written with what I have said in my Twenty first Speculation.—*Addison.*

Sir Roger de Coverley in his Portrait Gallery.

(Spectator, No. 109.)

I WAS this Morning walking in the Gallery, when Sir ROGER entered at the End opposite to me, and advancing towards me, said, he was glad to meet me among his Relations the DE COVERLEYS, and hoped I liked the Conversation of so much good Company, who were as silent as myself. I knew he alluded to the Pictures, and as he is a Gentleman who does not a little value himself upon his ancient Descent, I expected he would give me some Account of them. We were now arrived at the upper End of the Gallery, when the Knight faced towards one of the Pictures, and as we stood before it, he

entered into the Matter, after his blunt way of saying Things,
as they occur to his Imagination, without regular Introduction,
or Care to preserve the Appearance of Chain of Thought.

' It is, said he, worth while to consider the Force of Dress ;
' and how the Persons of one Age differ from those of another,
' merely by that only.   One may observe also, that the general
' Fashion of one Age has been followed by one particular Set of
' People in another, and by them preserved from one Genera-
' tion to another.   Thus the vast jetting Coat and small Bonnet,
' which was the Habit in *Harry* the Seventh's Time, is kept on
' in the Yeomen of the Guard ; not without a good and politick
' View, because they look a Foot taller, and a Foot and an half
' broader : Besides that the Cap leaves the Face expanded, and
' consequently more terrible, and fitter to stand at the Entrance
' of Palaces.

' This Predecessor of ours, you see, is dressed after this
' manner, and his Cheeks would be no larger than mine, were
' he in a Hat as I am.   He was the last Man that won a Prize
' in the Tilt-Yard (which is now a Common Street before
' *Whitehall.*)   You see the broken Lance that lies there by his
' right Foot : He shivered that Lance of his Adversary all to
' Pieces ; and bearing himself, look you, Sir, in this manner, at
' the same time he came within the Target of the Gentleman
' who rode against him, and taking him with incredible Force
' before him on the Pommel of his Saddle, he in that manner
' rid the Turnament over, with an Air that shewed he did it
' rather to perform the Rule of the Lists, than expose his
' Enemy ; however, it appeared he knew how to make use of a
' Victory, and with a gentle Trot he marched up to a Gallery
' where their Mistress sat (for they were Rivals) and let him
' down with laudable Courtesy and pardonable Insolence.   I
' don't know but it might be exactly where the Coffee-house
' is now.

' You are to know this my Ancestor was not only of a military
' Genius, but fit also for the Arts of Peace, for he played on the
' Base-Viol as well as any Gentlemen at Court ; you see where
' his Viol hangs by his Basket-hilt Sword.   The Action at the
' Tilt-yard you may be sure won the fair Lady, who was a Maid
' of Honour, and the greatest Beauty of her Time ; here she
' stands, the next Picture.   You see, Sir, my Great Great Great
' Grandmother has on the new-fashioned Petticoat, except that
' the Modern is gather'd at the Waste ; my Grandmother
' appears as if she stood in a large Drum, whereas the Ladies
' now walk as if they were in a Go-Cart.   For all this Lady was

' bred at Court, she became an Excellent Country-Wife, she
' brought ten Children, and when I shew you the Library, you
' shall see in her own Hand (allowing for the Difference of the
' Language) the best Receipt now in *England* both for an
' Hasty-pudding and a White-pot.

    ' If you please to fall back a little, because 'tis necessary to
' look at the three next Pictures at one View ; these are three
' Sisters. She on the right Hand, who is so very beautiful, died
' a Maid ; the next to her, still handsomer, had the same Fate,
' against her Will ; this homely thing in the middle had both
' their Portions added to her own, and was stolen by a neigh-
' bouring Gentleman, a Man of Stratagem and Resolution, for
' he poisoned three Mastiffs to come at her, and knocked down
' two Deer-stealers in carrying her off. Misfortunes happen in
' all Families : The Theft of this Romp and so much Mony,
' was no great matter to our Estate. But the next Heir that
' possessed it was this soft Gentleman, whom you see there :
' Observe the small Buttons, the little Boots, the Laces, the
' Slashes about his Cloaths, and above all the Posture he is
' drawn in, (which to be sure was his own choosing ;) you see
' he sits with one Hand on a Desk writing, and looking as it
' were another way, like an easy Writer, or a Sonneteer : He
' was one of those that had too much Wit to know how to live
' in the World ; he was a Man of no Justice, but great good
' Manners ; he ruined every Body that had any thing to do
' with him, but never said a rude thing in his Life ; the most
' indolent Person in the World, he would sign a Deed that
' passed away half his Estate with his Gloves on, but would not
' put on his Hat before a Lady if it were to save his Country.
' He is said to be the first that made Love by squeezing the
' Hand. He left the Estate with ten thousand Pounds Debt
' upon it, but however by all Hands I have been informed that
' he was every way the finest Gentleman in the World. That
' Debt ·lay heavy on our House for one Generation, but it was
' retrieved by a Gift from that honest Man you see there, a
' Citizen of our Name, but nothing at all a-kin to us. I know
' Sir ANDREW FREEPORT has said behind my Back, that this
' Man was descended from one of the ten Children of the Maid
' of Honour I shewed you above ; but it was never made out.
' We winked at the thing indeed, because Mony was wanting at
' that time.

    Here I saw my Friend a little embarrassed, and turned my
Face to the next Portraiture.

    Sir ROGER went on with his Account of the Gallery in the

following Manner. ' This Man (pointing to him I looked at) I
' take to be the Honour of our House. Sir HUMPHREY DE
' COVERLEY; he was in his Dealings as punctual as a Trades-
' man, and as generous as a Gentleman. He would have
' thought himself as much undone by breaking his Word, as if
' it were to be followed by Bankruptcy. He served his Country
' as Knight of this Shire to his dying Day. He found it no
' easy matter to maintain an Integrity in his Words and
' Actions, even in things that regarded the Offices which were
' incumbent upon him, in the Care of his own Affairs and
' Relations of Life, and therefore dreaded (tho' he had great
' Talents) to go into Employments of State, where he must be
' exposed to the Snares of Ambition. Innocence of Life and
' great Ability were the distinguishing Parts of his Character ;
' the latter, he had often observed, had led to the Destruction
' of the former, and used frequently to lament that Great and
' Good had not the same Signification. He was an excellent
' Husbandman, but had resolved not to exceed such a Degree
' of Wealth ; all above it he bestowed in secret Bounties many
' Years after the Sum he aimed at for his own Use was attained.
' Yet he did not slacken his Industry, but to a decent old Age
' spent the Life and Fortune which was superfluous to himself,
' in the Service of his Friends and Neighbours.

Here we were called to Dinner, and Sir ROGER ended the
Discourse of this Gentleman, by telling me, as we followed the
Servant, that this his Ancestor was a brave Man, and narrowly
escaped being killed in the Civil Wars ; ' For,' said he, ' he was
' sent out of the Field upon a private Message, the Day before
' the Battel of *Worcester.*' The Whim of narrowly escaping by
having been within a Day of Danger, with other Matters above-
mentioned, mixed with good Sense, left me at a Loss whether I
was more delighted with my Friend's Wisdom or Simplicity.—
Steele.

Apparitions.

(*Spectator, No.* 110.)

AT a little distance from Sir ROGER'S House, among the
Ruins of an old Abby, there is a long Walk of aged
Elms ; which are shot up so very high, that when one passes
under them, the Rooks and Crows that rest upon the Tops of

them seem to be cawing in another Region.   I am very much delighted with this sort of Noise, which I consider as a kind of natural Prayer to that Being who supplies the Wants of his whole Creation, and who, in the beautiful Language of the *Psalms*, feedeth the young Ravens that call upon him.   I like this Retirement the better, because of an ill Report it lies under of being *haunted;* for which Reason (as I have been told in the Family) no living Creature ever walks in it besides the Chaplain. My good Friend the Butler desired me with a very grave Face not to venture my self in it after Sun-set, for that one of the Footmen had been almost frighted out of his Wits by a Spirit that appear'd to him in the Shape of a black Horse without an Head ; to which he added, that about a Month ago one of the Maids coming home late that way with a Pail of Milk upon her Head, heard such a Rustling among the Bushes that she let it fall.

I was taking a Walk in this Place last Night between the Hours of Nine and Ten, and could not but fancy it one of the most proper Scenes in the World for a Ghost to appear in. The Ruins of the Abby are scattered up and down on every Side, and half covered with Ivy and Elder-Bushes, the Harbours of several solitary Birds which seldom make their Appearance till the Dusk of the Evening.   The Place was formerly a Church-yard, and has still several Marks in it of Graves and Burying-Places.   There is such an Eccho among the old Ruins and Vaults, that if you stamp but a little louder than ordinary, you hear the Sound repeated.   At the same time the Walk of Elms, with the Croaking of the Ravens which from time to time are heard from the Tops of them, looks exceeding solemn and venerable.   These Objects naturally raise Seriousness and Attention ; and when Night heightens the Awfulness of the Place, and pours out her supernumerary Horrors upon every thing in it, I do not at all wonder that weak Minds fill it with Spectres and Apparitions.

Mr. Locke, in his Chapter of the Association of Ideas, has very curious Remarks to shew how by the Prejudice of Education one Idea often introduces into the Mind a whole Set that bear no Resemblance to one another in the Nature of things. Among several Examples of this Kind, he produces the following Instance.   *The Ideas of Goblins and Sprights have really no more to do with Darkness than Light: Yet let but a foolish Maid inculcate these often on the Mind of a Child, and raise them there together, possibly he shall never be able to separate them again so long as he lives : but Darkness shall ever after-*

*wards bring with it those frightful Ideas, and they shall be so
joined, that he can no more bear the one than the other.*

As I was walking in this Solitude, where the Dusk of the
Evening conspired with so many other Occasions of Terrour, I
observed a Cow grazing not far from me, which an Imagination
that is apt to *startle* might easily have construed into a black
Horse without an Head : And I dare say the poor Footman
lost his Wits upon some such trivial Occasion.

My Friend Sir ROGER has often told me with a great deal of
Mirth, that at his first coming to his Estate he found three
Parts of his House altogether useless ; that the best Room in it
had the Reputation of being haunted, and by that means was
locked up ; that Noises had been heard in his long Gallery, so
that he could not get a Servant to enter it after eight a Clock
at Night ; that the Door of one of his Chambers was nailed up,
because there went a Story in the Family that a Butler had
formerly hang'd himself in it ; and that his Mother, who lived
to a great Age, had shut up half the Rooms in the House, in
which either her Husband, a Son, or Daughter had died. The
Knight seeing his Habitation reduced to so small a Compass,
and himself in a manner shut out of his own House, upon the
Death of his Mother ordered all the Apartments to be flung
open, and *exorcised* by his Chaplain, who lay in every Room
one after another, and by that Means dissipated the Fears
which had so long reigned in the Family.

I should not have been thus particular upon these ridiculous
Horrours, did I not find them so very much prevail in all Parts
of the Country. At the same time I think a Person who is thus
terrify'd with the Imagination of Ghosts and Spectres much
more reasonable than one who, contrary to the Reports of all
Historians sacred and prophane, ancient and modern, and to
the Traditions of all Nations, thinks the Appearance of Spirits
fabulous and groundless : Could not I give myself up to this
general Testimony of Mankind, I should to the Relations of
particular Persons who are now living, and whom I cannot distrust in other Matters of Fact. I might here add, that not only
the Historians, to whom we may join the Poets, but likewise the
Philosophers of Antiquity have favoured this Opinion. *Lucretius* himself, though by the Course of his Philosophy he was
obliged to maintain that the Soul did not exist separate from
the Body, makes no Doubt of the Reality of Apparitions, and
that Men have often appeared after their Death. This I think
very remarkable ; he was so pressed with the Matter of Fact
which he could not have the Confidence to deny, that he was

forced to account for it by one of the most absurd unphilo-sophical Notions that was ever started. He tells us, That the Surface of all Bodies are perpetually flying off from their re-spective Bodies, one after another ; and that these Surfaces or thin Cases that included each other whilst they were joined in the Body like the Coats of an Onion, are sometimes seen entire when they are separated from it ; by which means we often be-hold the Shapes and Shadows of Persons who are either dead or absent.

I shall dismiss this Paper with a Story out of *Josephus*, not so much for the sake of the Story it self as for the moral Reflec-tions with which the Author concludes it, and which I shall here set down in his own Words. ' *Glaphyra* the Daughter of ' King *Archelaus*, after the Death of her two first Husbands ' (being married to a third, who was Brother to her first Hus-' band, and so passionately in love with her that he turned off ' his former Wife to make room for this Marriage) had a very ' odd kind of Dream. She fancied that she saw her first Hus-' band coming towards her, and that she embraced him with ' great Tenderness ; when in the midst of the Pleasure which ' she expressed at the Sight of him, he reproached her after the ' following manner : *Glaphyra*, says he, thou hast made good ' the old Saying, That Women are not to be trusted. Was not ' I the Husband of thy Virginity? Have I not Children by ' thee ? How couldst thou forget our Loves so far as to enter ' into a second Marriage, and after that into a third, nay to take ' for thy Husband a Man who has so shamelessly crept into the ' Bed of his Brother? However, for the sake of our passed ' Loves, I shall free thee from thy present Reproach, and make ' thee mine for ever. *Glaphyra* told this Dream to several ' Women of her Acquaintance, and died soon after. I thought ' this Story might not be impertinent in this Place, wherein I ' speak of those Kings : Besides that, the Example deserves to ' be taken notice of as it contains a most certain Proof of the ' Immortality of the Soul, and of Divine Providence. If any ' Man thinks these Facts incredible, let him enjoy his own ' Opinion to himself, but let him not endeavour to disturb the ' Belief of others, who by Instances of this Nature are excited ' to the Study of Virtue.'—*Addison.*

Witchcraft.

(*Spectator*, No. 117.)

THERE are some Opinions in which a Man should stand Neuter, without engaging his Assent to one side or the other. Such a hovering Faith as this, which refuses to settle upon any Determination, is absolutely necessary to a Mind that is careful to avoid Errors and Prepossessions. When the Arguments press equally on both sides in Matters that are indifferent to us, the safest Method is to give up our selves to neither.

It is with this Temper of Mind that I consider the Subject of Witchcraft. When I hear the Relations that are made from all Parts of the World, not only from *Norway* and *Lapland*, from the *East* and *West Indies*, but from every particular Nation in *Europe*, I cannot forbear thinking that there is such an Intercourse and Commerce with Evil Spirits, as that which we express by the Name of Witch-craft. But when I consider that the ignorant and credulous Parts of the World abound most in these Relations, and that the Persons among us, who are supposed to engage in such an Infernal Commerce, are People of a weak Understanding and a crazed Imagination, and at the same time reflect upon the many Impostures and Delusions of this Nature that have been detected in all Ages, I endeavour to suspend my Belief till I hear more certain Accounts than any which have yet come to my Knowledge. In short, when I consider the Question, whether there are such Persons in the World as those we call Witches? my Mind is divided between the two opposite Opinions ; or rather (to speak my Thoughts freely) I believe in general that there is, and has been such a thing as Witch-craft ; but at the same time can give no Credit to any particular Instance of it.

I am engaged in this Speculation, by some Occurrences that I met with Yesterday, which I shall give my Reader an Account of at large. As I was walking with my Friend Sir ROGER by the side of one of his Woods, an old Woman applied herself to me for my Charity. Her Dress and Figure put me in mind of the following Description in *Otway*.

> *In a close Lane as I pursu'd my Journey,*
> *I spy'd a wrinkled* Hag, *with Age grown double,*
> *Picking dry Sticks, and mumbling to her self.*
> *Her Eyes with scalding Rheum were gall'd and red,*

Cold Palsy shook her Head; her Hands seem'd wither'd;
And on her crooked Shoulders had she wrap'd
The tatter'd Remnants of an old striped Hanging,
Which served to keep her Carcase from the Cold:
So there was nothing of a Piece about her.
Her lower Weeds were all o'er coarsely patch'd
With diff'rent-colour'd Rags, black, red, white, yellow,
And seem'd to speak Variety of Wretchedness.

As I was musing on this Description, and comparing it with the Object before me, the Knight told me, that this very old Woman had the Reputation of a Witch all over the Country, that her Lips were observed to be always in Motion, and that there was not a Switch about her House which her Neighbours did not believe had carried her several hundreds of Miles. If she chanced to stumble, they always found Sticks or Straws that lay in the Figure of a Cross before her. If she made any Mistake at Church, and cryed *Amen* in a wrong Place, they never failed to conclude that she was saying her Prayers backwards. There was not a Maid in the Parish that would take a Pin of her, though she would offer a Bag of Mony with it. She goes by the Name of *Moll White*, and has made the Country ring with several imaginary Exploits which are palmed upon her. If the Dairy Maid does not make her Butter come so soon as she should have it, *Moll White* is at the Bottom of the Churn. If a Horse sweats in the Stable, *Moll White* has been upon his Back. If a Hare makes an unexpected escape from the Hounds, the Huntsman curses *Moll White*. Nay, (says Sir ROGER) I have known the Master of the Pack, upon such an Occasion, send one of his Servants to see if *Moll White* had been out that Morning.

This Account raised my Curiosity so far, that I begged my Friend Sir ROGER to go with me into her Hovel, which stood in a solitary Corner under the side of the Wood. Upon our first entering Sir ROGER winked to me, and pointed at something that stood behind the Door, which, upon looking that Way, I found to be an old Broomstaff. At the same time he whispered me in the Ear to take notice of a Tabby Cat that sat in the Chimney-Corner, which, as the old Knight told me, lay under as bad a Report as *Moll White* her self; for besides that *Moll* is said often to accompany her in the same Shape, the Cat is reported to have spoken twice or thrice in her Life, and to have played several Pranks above the Capacity of an ordinary Cat.

I was secretly concerned to see Human Nature in so much Wretchedness and Disgrace, but at the same time could not forbear smiling to hear Sir ROGER, who is a little puzzled about the old Woman, advising her as a Justice of Peace to avoid all Communication with the Devil, and never to hurt any of her Neighbours' Cattle. We concluded our Visit with a Bounty, which was very acceptable.

In our Return home, Sir ROGER told me, that old *Moll* had been often brought before him for making Children spit Pins, and giving Maids the Night-Mare ; and that the Country People would be tossing her into a Pond and trying Experiments with her every Day, if it was not for him and his Chaplain.

I have since found upon Enquiry, that Sir ROGER was several times staggered with the Reports that had been brought him concerning this old Woman, and would frequently have bound her over to the County Sessions, had not his Chaplain with much ado perswaded him to the contrary.

I have been the more particular in this Account, because I hear there is scarce a Village in *England* that has not a *Moll White* in it. When an old Woman begins to doat, and grow chargeable to a Parish, she is generally turned into a Witch, and fills the whole Country with extravagant Fancies, imaginary Distempers and terrifying Dreams. In the mean time, the poor Wretch that is the innocent Occasion of so many Evils begins to be frightened at her self, and sometimes confesses secret Commerce and Familiarities that her Imagination forms in a delirious old Age. This frequently cuts off Charity from the greatest Objects of Compassion, and inspires People with a Malevolence towards those poor decrepid Parts of our Species, in whom Human Nature is defaced by Infirmity and Dotage.— *Addison.*

Sunday at Sir Roger de Coverley's.

(*Spectator, No.* 112.)

I AM always very well pleased with a Country *Sunday ;* and think, if keeping holy the Seventh Day were only a human Institution, it would be the best Method that could have been thought of for the polishing and civilizing of Mankind. It is certain the Country-People would soon degenerate into a kind of Savages and Barbarians, were there not such frequent Returns of a stated Time, in which the whole Village meet together with their best Faces, and in their cleanliest Habits, to converse with one another upon indifferent Subjects, hear their Duties explained to them, and join together in Adoration of the Supreme Being. *Sunday* clears away the Rust of the whole Week, not only as it refreshes in their Minds the Notions of Religion, but as it puts both the Sexes upon appearing in their most agreeable Forms, and exerting all such Qualities as are apt to give them a Figure in the Eye of the Village. A Country-Fellow distinguishes himself as much in the *Church-yard,* as a Citizen does upon the *Change,* the whole Parish-Politicks being generally discussed in that Place either after Sermon or before the Bell rings.

My Friend Sir ROGER, being a good Churchman, has beautified the Inside of his Church with several Texts of his own chusing: He has likewise given a handsome Pulpit-Cloth, and railed in the Communion-Table at his own Expence. He has often told me, that at his coming to his Estate he found his Parishioners very irregular; and that in order to make them kneel and join in the Responses, he gave every one of them a Hassock and a Common-prayer Book: and at the same time employed an itinerant Singing-Master, who goes about the Country for that Purpose, to instruct them rightly in the Tunes of the Psalms; upon which they now very much value themselves, and indeed out-do most of the Country Churches that I have ever heard.

As Sir ROGER is Landlord to the whole Congregation, he keeps them in very good Order, and will suffer no Body to sleep in it besides himself; for if by chance he has been surprized into a short Nap at Sermon, upon recovering out of it he stands up and looks about him, and if he sees any Body else nodding, either wakes them himself, or sends his Servant to them. Several other of the old Knight's Particularities break out upon these Occasions: Sometimes he will be lengthening out a Verse in the Singing-Psalms, half a Minute after the rest of the Congregation have done with it; sometimes, when he is pleased with the Matter of his Devotion, he pronounces *Amen* three or four times to the same Prayer; and sometimes stands up when every Body else is upon their Knees, to count the Congregation, or see if any of his Tenants are missing.

I was Yesterday very much surprised to hear my old Friend, in the Midst of the Service, calling out to one *John Matthews* to mind what he was about, and not disturb the Congregation. This *John Matthews* it seems is remarkable for being an idle

Fellow, and at that Time was kicking his Heels for his Diversion. This Authority of the Knight, though exerted in that odd Manner which accompanies him in all Circumstances of Life, has a very good Effect upon the Parish, who are not polite enough to see any thing ridiculous in his Behaviour ; besides that the general good Sense and Worthiness of his Character makes his Friends observe these little Singularities as Foils that rather set off than blemish his good Qualities.

As soon as the Sermon is finished, no Body presumes to stir till Sir ROGER is gone out of the Church. The Knight walks down from his Seat in the Chancel between a double row of his Tenants, that stand bowing to him on each Side ; and every now and then enquires how such an one's Wife, or Mother, or Son, or Father do, whom he does not see at Church ; which is understood as a secret Reprimand to the Person that is absent.

The Chaplain has often told me, that upon a Catechising-day, when Sir ROGER has been pleased with a Boy that answers well, he has ordered a Bible to be given him next Day for his Encouragement ; and sometimes accompanies it with a Flitch of Bacon to his Mother. Sir ROGER has likewise added five Pounds a Year to the Clerk's Place ; and that he may encourage the young Fellows to make themselves perfect in the Church-Service, has promised upon the Death of the present Incumbent, who is very old, to bestow it according to Merit.

The fair Understanding between Sir ROGER and his Chaplain, and their mutual Concurrence in doing Good, is the more remarkable, because the very next Village is famous for the Differences and Contentions that rise between the Parson and the 'Squire, who live in a perpetual State of War. The Parson is alway preaching at the 'Squire, and the 'Squire to be revenged on the Parson never comes to Church. The 'Squire has made all his Tenants Atheists and Tithe-Stealers ; while the Parson instructs them every *Sunday* in the Dignity of his Order, and insinuates to them in almost every Sermon, that he is a better Man than his Patron. In short, Matters are come to such an Extremity, that the 'Squire has not said his Prayers either in publick or private this half Year ; and that the Parson threatens him, if he does not mend his Manners, to pray for him in the Face of the whole Congregation.

Feuds of this Nature, though too frequent in the Country, are very fatal to the ordinary People ; who are so used to be dazled with Riches, that they pay as much Deference to the Understanding of a Man of an Estate, as of a Man of Learning ; and are very hardly brought to regard any Truth, how important soever it may be, that is preached to them, when they know there are several Men of five hundred a Year who do not believe it.—*Addison.*

Sir Roger de Coverley at the Assizes.

(*Spectator, No.* 122.)

A MAN'S first Care should be to avoid the Reproaches of his own Heart ; his next, to escape the Censures of the World : If the last interferes with the former, it ought to be entirely neglected ; but otherwise, there cannot be a greater Satisfaction to an honest Mind, than to see those Approbations which it gives it self seconded by the Applauses of the Publick : A Man is more sure of his Conduct, when the Verdict which he passes upon his own Behaviour is thus warranted and confirmed by the Opinion of all that know him.

My worthy Friend Sir ROGER is one of those who is not only at Peace within himself, but beloved and esteemed by all about him.   He receives a suitable Tribute for his universal Benevolence to Mankind, in the Returns of Affection and Good-will, which are paid him by every one that lives within his Neighbourhood.   I lately met with two or three odd Instances of that general Respect which is shown to the good old Knight.   He would needs carry *Will. Wimble* and myself with him to the County-Assizes : As we were upon the Road *Will. Wimble* joined a couple of plain Men who rid before us, and conversed with them for some Time ; during which my Friend Sir ROGER acquainted me with their Characters.

The first of them, says he, that has a Spaniel by his Side, is a Yeoman of about an hundred Pounds a Year, an honest Man : He is just within the Game-Act, and qualified to kill an Hare or a Pheasant : He knocks down a Dinner with his Gun twice or thrice a Week ; and by that means lives much cheaper than those who have not so good an Estate as himself.   He would be a good Neighbour if he did not destroy so many Partridges ; in short, he is a very sensible Man ; shoots flying ; and has been several times Foreman of the Petty-Jury.

The other that rides along with him is *Tom Touchy*, a Fellow famous for *taking the Law* of every Body.   There is not one in the Town where he lives that he has not sued at a Quarter-Sessions.   The Rogue had once the Impudence to go to Law with the *Widow*.   His Head is full of Costs, Damages, and Ejectments : He plagued a couple of honest Gentlemen so long for a Trespass in breaking one of his Hedges, till he was forced to sell the Ground it enclosed to defray the Charges of the Prosecution : His Father left him fourscore Pounds a Year ; but he has *cast* and been cast so often, that he is not now worth thirty. I suppose he is going upon the old Business of the Willow-Tree.

As Sir ROGER was giving me this Account of *Tom Touchy*, *Will. Wimble* and his two Companions stopped short till we came up to them. After having paid their Respects to Sir ROGER, *Will.* told him that Mr. *Touchy* and he must appeal to him upon a Dispute that arose between them. *Will.* it seems had been giving his Fellow-Traveller an Account of his Angling one Day in such a Hole ; when *Tom Touchy*, instead of hearing out his Story, told him that Mr. such an One, if he pleased, might *take the Law of him* for fishing in that Part of the River. My Friend Sir ROGER heard them both, upon a round Trot ; and after having paused some time told them, with the Air of a Man who would not give his Judgment rashly, that *much might be said on both Sides.* They were neither of them dissatisfied with the Knight's Determination, because neither of them found himself in the Wrong by it : Upon which we made the best of our Way to the Assizes.

The Court was sat before Sir ROGER came ; but notwithstanding all the Justices had taken their Places upon the Bench, they made room for the old Knight at the Head of them ; who for his Reputation in the Country took occasion to whisper in the Judge's Ear, *That he was glad his Lordship had met with so much good Weather in his Circuit.* I was listening to the Proceeding of the Court with much Attention, and infinitely pleased with that great Appearance and Solemnity which so properly accompanies such a Publick Administration of our Laws ; when, after about an Hour's Sitting, I observed to my great Surprize, in the Midst of a Trial, that my Friend Sir ROGER was getting up to speak. I was in some Pain for him, till I found he had acquitted himself of two or three Sentences, with a Look of much Business and great Intrepidity.

Upon his first Rising the Court was hushed, and a general Whisper ran among the Country People that Sir ROGER *was up.* The Speech he made was so little to the Purpose, that I shall not trouble my Readers with an Account of it ; and I believe was not so much designed by the Knight himself to inform the Court, as to give him a Figure in my Eye, and keep up his Credit in the Country.

I was highly delighted, when the Court rose, to see the Gentlemen of the Country gathering about my old Friend, and striving who should compliment him most ; at the same time that the ordinary People gazed upon him at a distance, not a little admiring his Courage, that was not afraid to speak to the Judge.

In our Return home we met with a very odd Accident ; which I cannot forbear relating, because it shews how desirous all who know Sir ROGER are of giving him Marks of their Esteem.   When we were arrived upon the Verge of his Estate, we stopped at a little Inn to rest our selves and our Horses. The Man of the House had it seems been formerly a Servant in the Knight's Family ; and to do Honour to his old Master, had some time since, unknown to Sir ROGER, put him up in a Sign-post before the Door ; so that *the Knight's Head* had hung out upon the Road about a Week before he himself knew any thing of the Matter.   As soon as Sir ROGER was acquainted with it, finding that his Servant's Indiscretion proceeded wholly from Affection and Good-will, he only told him that he had made him too high a Compliment ; and when the Fellow seemed to think that could hardly be, added with a more decisive Look, That it was too great an Honour for any Man under a Duke ; but told him at the same time, that it might be altered with a very few Touches, and that he himself would be at the Charge of it.   Accordingly they got a Painter by the Knight's Directions to add a pair of Whiskers to the Face, and by a little Aggravation to the Features to change it into the *Saracen's Head.*   I should not have known this Story had not the Inn-keeper, upon Sir ROGER'S alighting, told him in my Hearing, That his Honour's Head was brought back last Night with the Alterations that he had ordered to be made in it.   Upon this my Friend with his usual Chearfulness related the Particulars above-mentioned, and ordered the Head to be brought into the Room.   I could not forbear discovering greater Expressions of Mirth than ordinary upon the Appearance of this monstrous Face, under which, notwithstanding it was made to frown and stare in a most extraordinary manner, I could still discover a distant Resemblance of my old Friend. Sir ROGER, upon seeing me laugh, desired me to tell him truly if I thought it possible for People to know him in that Disguise. I at first kept my usual Silence ; but upon the Knight's conjuring me to tell him whether it was not still more like himself than a *Saracen*, I composed my Countenance in the best manner I could, and replied, *That much might be said on both Sides.*

These several Adventures, with the Knight's Behaviour in them, gave me as pleasant a Day as ever I met with in any of my Travels.—*Addison.*

Gypsies.

(*Spectator, No.* 130.)

AS I was Yesterday riding out in the Fields with my Friend Sir ROGER, we saw at a little Distance from us a Troop of Gypsies. Upon the first Discovery of them, my Friend was in some doubt whether he should not exert the Justice of the Peace upon such a Band of Lawless Vagrants ; but not having his Clerk with him, who is a necessary Counsellor on these Occasions, and fearing that his Poultry might fare the worse for it, he let the Thought drop : But at the same time gave me a particular Account of the Mischiefs they do in the Country, in stealing People's Goods and spoiling their Servants. If a stray Piece of Linnen hangs upon an Hedge, says Sir ROGER, they are sure to have it ; if the Hog loses his Way in the Fields, it is ten to one but he becomes their Prey ; our Geese cannot live in Peace for them ; if a Man prosecutes them with Severity, his Hen-roost is sure to pay for it : They generally straggle into these Parts about this Time of the Year ; and set the Heads of our Servant-Maids so agog for Husbands, that we do not expect to have any Business done as it should be whilst they are in the Country. I have an honest Dairy-maid who crosses their Hands with a Piece of Silver every Summer, and never fails being promised the handsomest young Fellow in the Parish for her pains. Your Friend the Butler has been Fool enough to be seduced by them ; and, though he is sure to lose a Knife, a Fork, or a Spoon every time his Fortune is told him, generally shuts himself up in the Pantry with an old Gypsie for above half an Hour once in a Twelvemonth. Sweet-hearts are the things they live upon, which they bestow very plentifully upon all those that apply themselves to them. You see now and then some handsome young Jades among them : The Sluts have very often white Teeth and black Eyes.

Sir ROGER observing that I listned with great Attention to his Account of a People who were so entirely new to me, told me, That if I would they should tell us our Fortunes. As I was very well pleased with the Knight's Proposal, we rid up and communicated our Hands to them. A *Cassandra* of the Crew, after having examined my Lines very diligently, told me,

That I loved a pretty Maid in a Corner, that I was a good Woman's Man, with some other Particulars which I do not think proper to relate. My Friend Sir ROGER alighted from his Horse, and exposing his Palm to two or three that stood by him, they crumpled it into all Shapes, and diligently scanned every Wrinkle that could be made in it; when one of them, who was older and more Sun-burnt than the rest, told him, That he had a Widow in his Line of Life: Upon which the Knight cried, Go, go, you are an idle Baggage; and at the same time smiled upon me. The Gypsie finding he was not displeased in his Heart, told him, after a farther Enquiry into his Hand, that his True-love was constant, and that she should dream of him to-night: My old Friend cried Pish, and bid her go on. The Gypsie told him that he was a Batchelour, but would not be so long; and that he was dearer to some Body than he thought: The Knight still repeated, She was an idle Baggage, and bid her go on. Ah Master, says the Gypsie, that roguish Leer of yours makes a pretty Woman's Heart ake; you ha'nt that Simper about the Mouth for Nothing—The uncouth Gibberish with which all this was uttered like the Darkness of an Oracle, made us the more attentive to it. To be short, the Knight left the Money with her that he had crossed her Hand with, and got up again on his Horse.

As we were riding away, Sir ROGER told me, that he knew several sensible People who believed these Gypsies now and then foretold very strange things; and for half an Hour together appeared more jocund than ordinary. In the Height of his good-Humour, meeting a common Beggar upon the Road who was no Conjurer, as he went to relieve him he found his Pocket was picked: That being a Kind of Palmistry at which this Race of Vermin are very dextrous.

I might here entertain my Reader with Historical Remarks on this idle profligate People, who infest all the Countries of *Europe*, and live in the midst of Governments in a kind of Commonwealth by themselves. But instead of entering into Observations of this Nature, I shall fill the remaining Part of my Paper with a Story which is still fresh in *Holland*, and was printed in one of our Monthly Accounts about twenty Years ago. 'As the *Trekschuyt*, or Hackney-boat, which carries 'Passengers from *Leyden* to *Amsterdam*, was putting off, a Boy 'running along the Side of the Canal desired to be taken in; 'which the Master of the Boat refused, because the Lad had 'not quite Money enough to pay the usual Fare. An eminent 'Merchant being pleased with the Looks of the Boy, and

' secretly touched with Compassion towards him, paid the
' Money for him, and ordered him to be taken on board. Upon
' talking with him afterwards, he found that he could speak
' readily in three or four Languages, and learned upon farther
' Examination that he had been stoln away when he was a
' Child by a Gypsie, and had rambled ever since with a Gang
' of those Strollers up and down several Parts of *Europe*. It
' happened that the Merchant, whose Heart seems to have
' inclined towards the Boy by a secret kind of Instinct, had
' himself lost a Child some Years before. The Parents, after a
' long Search for him, gave him for drowned in one of the
' Canals with which that Country abounds ; and the Mother
' was so afflicted at the Loss of a fine Boy, who was her only
' Son, that she died for Grief of it. Upon laying together all
' Particulars, and examining the several Moles and Marks by
' which the Mother used to describe the Child when he was first
' missing, the Boy proved to be the Son of the Merchant whose
' Heart had so unaccountably melted at the Sight of him. The
' Lad was very well pleased to find a Father who was so rich,
' and likely to leave him a good Estate ; the Father on the
' other hand was not a little delighted to see a Son return to
' him, whom he had given for lost, with such a Strength of
' Constitution, Sharpness of Understanding, and Skill in
' Languages.' Here the printed Story leaves off ; but if I may
give credit to Reports, our Linguist having received such
extraordinary Rudiments towards a good Education, was afterwards trained up in every thing that becomes a Gentleman ;
wearing off by little and little all the vicious Habits and
Practises that he had been used to in the Course of his
Peregrinations : Nay, it is said, that he has since been
employed in foreign Courts upon National Business, with great
Reputation to himself and Honour to those who sent him, and
that he has visited several Countries as a publick Minister, in
which he formerly wander'd as a Gypsie.—*Addison.*

The Merchant.

(*Spectator, No.* 174.)

THERE is scarce any thing more common than Animosities
between Parties that cannot subsist but by their Agreement : this was well represented in the Sedition of the Members
of the humane Body in the old *Roman* Fable. Is is often the

Case of lesser confederate States against a superior Power, which are hardly held together, though their Unanimity is necessary for their common Safety: and this is always the Case of the landed and trading Interest of *Great Britain :* the Trader is fed by the Product of the Land, and the landed Man cannot be clothed but by the Skill of the Trader ; and yet those Interests are ever jarring.

We had last Winter an Instance of this at our Club, in Sir ROGER DE COVERLEY and Sir ANDREW FREEPORT, between whom there is generally a constant, though friendly, Opposition of Opinions.   It happened that one of the Company, in an Historical Discourse, was observing, that *Carthaginian* Faith was a proverbial Phrase to intimate Breach of Leagues.   Sir ROGER said it could hardly be otherwise : That the *Carthaginians* were the greatest Traders in the World ; and as Gain is the chief End of such a People, they never pursue any other : The Means to it are never regarded ; they will, if it comes easily, get Money honestly ; but if not, they will not scruple to attain it by Fraud or Cozenage : And indeed, what is the whole Business of the Trader's Account, but to over-reach him who trusts to his Memory ?   But were that not so, what can there great and noble be expected from him whose Attention is for ever fixed upon ballancing his Books, and watching over his Expences ?   And at best, let Frugality and Parsimony be the Virtues of the Merchant, how much is his punctual Dealing below a Gentleman's Charity to the Poor, or Hospitality among his Neighbours ?

CAPTAIN SENTRY observed Sir ANDREW very diligent in hearing Sir ROGER, and had a mind to turn the Discourse, by taking notice in general, from the highest to the lowest Parts of human Society, there was a secret, tho' unjust, Way among Men, of indulging the Seeds of ill Nature and Envy, by comparing their own State of Life to that of another, and grudging the Approach of their Neighbour to their own Happiness ; and on the other Side, he who is the less at his Ease, repines at the other who, he thinks, has unjustly the Advantage over him. Thus the Civil and Military Lists look upon each other with much ill Nature ; the Soldier repines at the Courtier's Power, and the Courtier rallies the Soldier's Honour ; or, to come to lower Instances, the private Men in the Horse and Foot of an Army, the Carmen and Coachmen in the City Streets, mutually look upon each other with ill Will, when they are in Competition for Quarters or the Way, in their respective Motions.

It is very well, good Captain, interrupted Sir ANDREW :

You may attempt to turn the Discourse if you think fit ; but I must however have a Word or two with Sir ROGER, who, I see, thinks he has paid me off, and been very severe upon the Merchant. I shall not, continued he, at this time remind Sir ROGER of the great and noble Monuments of Charity and Publick Spirit, which have been erected by Merchants since the Reformation, but at present content my self with what he allows us, Parsimony and Frugality. If it were consistent with the Quality of so antient a Baronet as Sir ROGER, to keep an Account, or measure Things by the most infallible Way, that of Numbers, he would prefer our Parsimony to his Hospitality. If to drink so many Hogsheads is to be Hospitable, we do not contend for the Fame of that Virtue ; but it would be worth while to consider, whether so many <u>Artificers</u> at work ten Days together by my Appointment, or so many Peasants made merry on Sir ROGER'S Charge, are the Men more obliged ? I believe the Families of the Artificers will thank me, more than the Households of the Peasants shall Sir ROGER. Sir ROGER gives to his Men, but I place mine above the Necessity or Obligation of my Bounty. I am in very little Pain for the *Roman* Proverb upon the *Carthaginian* Traders ; the *Romans* were their professed Enemies: I am only sorry no *Carthaginain* Histories have come to our Hands ; we might have been taught perhaps by them some Proverbs against the *Roman* Generosity, in fighting for and bestowing other People's Goods. But since Sir ROGER has taken Occasion from an old Proverb to be out of Humour with Merchants, it should be no Offence to offer one not quite so old in their Defence. When a Man happens to break in *Holland,* they say of him that *he has not kept true Accounts.* This Phrase, perhaps, among us, would appear a soft or humorous way of speaking, but with that exact Nation it bears the highest Reproach ; for a Man to be Mistaken in the Calculation of his Expence, in his Ability to answer future Demands, or to be impertinently sanguine in putting his Credit to too great Adventure, are all Instances of as much Infamy as with gayer Nations to be failing in Courage or common Honesty.

Numbers are so much the Measure of every thing that is valuable, that it is not possible to demonstrate the Success of any Action, or the Prudence of any Undertaking, without them. I say this in Answer to what Sir ROGER is pleased to say, That little that is truly noble can be expected from one who is ever poring on his Cash-book, or ballancing his Accounts. When I have my Returns from abroad, I can tell to a Shilling, by the

Help of Numbers, the Profit or Loss by my Adventure ; but I ought also to be able to shew that I had Reason for making it, either from my own Experience or that of other People, or from a reasonable Presumption that my Returns will be sufficient to answer my Expence and Hazard ; and this is never to be done without the Skill of Numbers. For Instance, if I am to trade to *Turkey*, I ought beforehand to know the Demand of our Manufactures there, as well as of their Silks in *England*, and the customary Prices that are given for both in each Country. I ought to have a clear Knowledge of these Matters beforehand, that I may presume upon sufficient Returns to answer the Charge of the Cargo I have fitted out, the Freight and Assurance out and home, the Custom to the Queen, and the Interest of my own Money, and besides all these Expences a reasonable Profit to my self. Now what is there of Scandal in this Skill ? What has the Merchant done, that he should be so little in the good Graces of Sir ROGER ? He throws down no Man's Enclosures, and tramples upon no Man's Corn ; he takes nothing from the industrious Labourer ; he pays the poor Man for his Work ; he communicates his Profit with Mankind ; by the Preparation of his Cargo and the Manufacture of his Returns, he furnishes Employment and Subsistence to greater Numbers than the richest Nobleman ; and even the Nobleman is obliged to him for finding out foreign Markets for the Produce of his Estate, and for making a great Addition to his Rents ; and yet 'tis certain, that none of all these Things could be done by him without the Exercise of his Skill in Numbers.

This is the Oeconomy of the Merchant ; and the Conduct of the Gentleman must be the same, unless by scorning to be the Steward, he resolves the Steward shall be the Gentleman. The Gentleman, no more than the Merchant, is able, without the Help of Numbers, to account for the Success of any Action, or the Prudence of any Adventure. If, for Instance, the Chace is his whole Adventure, his only Returns must be the Stag's Horns in the great Hall, and the Fox's Nose upon the Stable Door. Without Doubt Sir ROGER knows the full Value of these Returns ; and if beforehand he had computed the Charges of the Chace, a Gentleman of his Discretion would certainly have hanged up all his Dogs, he would never have brought back so many fine Horses to the Kennel, he would never have gone so often, like a Blast, over Fields of Corn. If such too had been the Conduct of all his Ancestors, he might truly have boasted at this Day, that the Antiquity of his Family had never been sullied by a Trade ; a Merchant had never been permitted with his whole Estate to purchase a Room for his Picture in the Gallery of the COVERLEYS, or to claim his Descent from the Maid of Honour. But 'tis very happy for Sir ROGER that the Merchant paid so dear for his Ambition. 'Tis the Misfortune of many other Gentlemen to turn out of the Seats of their Ancestors, to make way for such new Masters as have been more exact in their Accounts than themselves ; and certainly he deserves the Estate a great deal better, who has got it by his Industry, than he who has lost it by his Negligence.—*Steele.*

Sir Roger de Coverley in Town.

(*Spectator, No.* 269.)

I WAS this Morning surprised with a great knocking at the Door, when my Landlady's Daughter came up to me, and told me, that there was a Man below desired to speak with me. Upon my asking her who it was, she told me it was a very grave elderly Person, but that she did not know his Name. I immediately went down to him, and found him to be the Coachman of my worthy Friend Sir ROGER DE COVERLEY. He told me that his Master came to Town last Night, and would be glad to take a Turn with me in *Gray's-Inn* Walks. As I was wondring in my self what had brought Sir ROGER to Town, not having lately received any Letter from him, he told me that his Master was come up to get a Sight of Prince *Eugene*, and that he desired I would immediately meet him.

I was not a little pleased with the Curiosity of the old Knight, though I did not much wonder at it, having heard him say more than once in private Discourse, that he looked upon Prince *Eugenio* (for so the Knight always calls him) to be a greater Man than *Scanderbeg*.

I was no sooner come into *Grays-Inn* Walks, but I heard my Friend upon the Terrace hemming twice or thrice to himself with great Vigour, for he loves to clear his Pipes in good Air (to make use of his own Phrase) and is not a little pleased with any one who takes notice of the Strength which he still exerts in his Morning Hems.

I was touched with a secret Joy at the Sight of the good old Man, who before he saw me was engaged in Conversation with a Beggar-Man that had asked an Alms of him. I could hear my Friend chide him for not finding out some Work ; but at the same time saw him put his Hand in his Pocket and give him Six-pence.

Our Salutations were very hearty on both Sides, consisting of many kind Shakes of the Hand, and several affectionate Looks which we cast upon one another. After which the Knight told me my good Friend his Chaplain was very well, and much at my Service, and that the *Sunday* before he had made a most incomparable Sermon out of Dr. *Barrow*. I have left, says he, all my Affairs in his Hands, and being willing to lay an Obligation upon him, have deposited with him thirty Marks, to be distributed among his poor Parishioners.

He then proceeded to acquaint me with the Welfare of *Will Wimble*. Upon which he put his Hand into his Fob and presented me in his Name with a Tobacco-Stopper, telling me that *Will* had been busy all the Beginning of the Winter in turning great Quantities of them ; and that he made a Present of one to every Gentleman in the Country who has good Principles, and smoaks. He added, that poor *Will* was at present under great Tribulation, for that *Tom Touchy* had taken the Law of him for cutting some Hazel Sticks out of one of his Hedges.

Among other Pieces of News which the Knight brought from his Country-Seat, he informed me that *Moll White* was dead ; and that about a Month after her Death the Wind was so very high, that it blew down the End of one of his Barns. But for my own part, says Sir ROGER, I do not think that the old Woman had any hand in it.

He afterwards fell into an Account of the Diversions which had passed in his House during the Holidays ; for Sir ROGER, after the laudable Custom of his Ancestors, always keeps open House at *Christmas*. I learned from him that he had killed eight fat Hogs for the Season, that he had dealt about his Chines very liberally amongst his Neighbours, and that in particular he had sent a string of Hogs-puddings with a pack of Cards to every poor Family in the Parish. I have often thought, says Sir ROGER, it happens very well that *Christmas* should fall out in the Middle of the Winter. It is the most dead uncomfortable Time of the year, when the poor People would suffer very much from their Poverty and Cold, if they had not good Cheer, warm Fires, and *Christmas* Gambols to support them. I love to rejoice their poor Hearts at this season, and to see the whole Village merry in my great Hall. I allow a double Quantity of Malt to my small Beer, and set it a running for twelve Days to every one that calls for it. I have always a

Piece of cold Beef and a Mince-Pye upon the Table, and am wonderfully pleased to see my Tenants pass away a whole Evening in playing their innocent Tricks, and smutting one another. Our Friend *Will Wimble* is as merry as any of them, and shews a thousand roguish Tricks upon these Occasions.

I was very much delighted with the Reflection of my old Friend, which carried so much Goodness in it. He then launched out into the Praise of the late Act of Parliament for securing the Church of *England*, and told me, with great Satisfaction, that he believed it already began to take Effect, for that a rigid Dissenter, who chanced to dine at his House on *Christmas* Day, had been observed to eat very plentifully of his Plumb-porridge.

After having dispatched all our Country Matters, Sir ROGER made several Inquiries concerning the Club, and particularly of his old Antagonist Sir ANDREW FREEPORT. He asked me with a kind of Smile, whether Sir ANDREW had not taken Advantage of his Absence, to vent among them some of his Republican Doctrines ; but soon after gathering up his Countenance into a more than ordinary Seriousness, Tell me truly, says he, don't you think Sir ANDREW had a Hand in the Pope's Procession————but without giving me time to answer him, Well, well, says he, I know you are a wary Man, and do not care to talk of publick Matters.

The Knight then asked me, if I had seen Prince *Eugenio*, and made me promise to get him a Stand in some convenient Place where he might have a full Sight of that extraordinary Man, whose Presence does so much Honour to the *British* Nation. He dwelt very long on the Praises of this Great General, and I found that, since I was with him in the Country, he had drawn many Observations together out of his reading in *Baker's* Chronicle, and other Authors, who always lie in his Hall Window, which very much redound to the Honour of this Prince.

Having passed away the greatest Part of the Morning in hearing the Knight's Reflections, which were partly private, and partly political, he asked me if I would smoak a Pipe with him over a Dish of Coffee at *Squire's*. As I love the old Man, I take Delight in complying with every thing that is agreeable to him, and accordingly waited on him to the Coffee-house, where his venerable Figure drew upon us the Eyes of the whole Room. He had no sooner seated himself at the upper End of the high Table, but he called for a clean Pipe, a Paper of Tobacco, a Dish of Coffee, a Wax-Candle, and the *Supplement* with such an Air of Cheerfulness and Good-humour, that all the Boys in the Coffee-room (who seemed to take pleasure in serving him) were at once employed on his several Errands, insomuch that no Body else could come at a Dish of Tea, till the Knight had got all his Conveniencies about him.—-*Addison.*

Sir Roger de Coverley at Westminster Abbey.

(*Spectator*, No. 329.)

MY Friend Sir ROGER DE COVERLEY told me t'other Night, that he had been reading my Paper upon *Westminster Abby*, in which, says he, there are a great many ingenious Fancies. He told me at the same time, that he observed I had promised another Paper upon *the Tombs*, and that he should be glad to go and see them with me, not having visited them since he had read History. I could not at first imagine how this came into the Knight's Head, till I recollected that he had been very busy all last Summer upon *Baker's* Chronicle, which he has quoted several times in his Disputes with Sir ANDREW FREEPORT since his last coming to Town. Accordingly I promised to call upon him the next Morning, that we might go together to the *Abby*.

I found the Knight under his Butler's Hands, who always shaves him. He was no sooner Dressed, than he called for a Glass of the Widow *Trueby's* Water, which he told me he always drank before he went abroad. He recommended me to a Dram of it at the same time, with so much Heartiness, that I could not forbear drinking it. As soon as I had got it down, I found it very unpalatable; upon which the Knight observing that I had made several wry Faces, told me that he knew I should not like it at first, but that it was the best thing in the World against the Stone or Gravel.

I could have wished indeed that he had acquainted me with the Virtues of it sooner; but it was too late to complain, and I knew what he had done was out of Good-will. Sir ROGER told me further, that he looked upon it to be very good for a Man whilst he staid in Town, to keep off Infection, and that he got together a Quantity of it upon the first News of the Sickness being at *Dantzick:* When of a sudden turning short to one of his Servants, who stood behind him, he bid him call a Hackney-Coach, and take care it was an elderly Man that drove it.

He then resumed his Discourse upon Mrs. *Trueby's* Water, telling me that the Widow *Trueby* was one who did more good than all the Doctors and Apothecaries in the County : That she distilled every Poppy that grew within five Miles of her ; that she distributed her Water *gratis* among all Sorts of People ; to which the Knight added, that she had a very great Jointure, and that the whole Country would fain have it a Match between him and her ; and truly, says Sir ROGER, if I had not been engaged, perhaps I could not have done better.

His Discourse was broken off by his Man's telling him he had called a Coach. Upon our going to it, after having cast his Eye upon the Wheels, he asked the Coachman if his Axel-tree was good ; upon the Fellow's telling him he would warrant it, the Knight turned to me, told me he looked like an honest Man, and went in without further Ceremony.

We had not gone far, when Sir ROGER popping out his Head, called the Coach-man down from his Box, and upon his presenting himself at the Window, asked him if he smoaked ; as I was considering what this would end in, he bid him stop by the way at any good Tobacconist's, and take in a Roll of their best *Virginia.* Nothing material happen'd in the remaining part of our Journey, till we were set down at the West-end of the *Abby.*

As we went up the Body of the Church, the Knight pointed at the Trophies upon one of the new Monuments, and cry'd out, A brave Man, I warrant him ! Passing afterwards by Sir *Cloudsly Shovel,* he flung his Hand that way, and cry'd Sir *Clously Shovel !* a very gallant Man ! As we stood before *Busby's* Tomb, the Knight utter'd himself again after the same Manner, Dr. *Busby,* a great Man ! he whipp'd my Grandfather ; a very great Man ! I should have gone to him myself, if I had not been a Blockhead : a very great Man !

We were immediately conducted into the little Chappel on the right hand. Sir ROGER planting himself at our Historian's Elbow, was very attentive to every thing he said, particularly to the Account he gave us of the Lord who had cut off the King of *Morocco's* Head. Among several other Figures, he was very well pleased to see the Statesman *Cecil* upon his Knees ; and, concluding them all to be great Men, was conducted to the Figure which represents that Martyr to good Housewifry, who died by the prick of a Needle. Upon our Interpreter's telling us, that she was a Maid of Honour to Queen *Elizabeth,* the Knight was very inquisitive into her Name and Family ; and after having regarded her Finger for some time, I wonder, says he, that Sir *Richard Baker* has said nothing of her in his Chronicle.

We were then convey'd to the two Coronation-Chairs, where my old Friend, after having heard that the Stone underneath the most ancient of them, which was brought from *Scotland*, was called *Jacob's Pillar*, sat himself down in the Chair ; and looking like the Figure of an old *Gothick* King, asked our Interpreter, What Authority they had to say, that *Jacob* had ever been in *Scotland?* The Fellow, instead of returning him an Answer, told him, that he hoped his Honour would pay his Forfeit. I could observe Sir ROGER a little ruffled upon being thus trepanned ; but our Guide not insisting upon his Demand, the Knight soon recovered his good Humour, and whispered in my Ear, that if WILL. WIMBLE were with us, and saw those two Chairs, it would go hard but he would get a Tobacco-Stopper out of one or t'other of them.

Sir ROGER, in the next Place, laid his Hand upon *Edward* the Third's Sword, and leaning upon the Pummel of it, gave us the whole History of the *Black Prince;* concluding, that in Sir *Richard Baker's* Opinion, *Edward* the Third was one of the greatest Princes that ever sate upon the *English* Throne.

We were then shewn *Edward* the Confessor's Tomb ; upon which Sir ROGER acquainted us, that he was the first who touched for the Evil ; and afterwards *Henry* the Fourth's, upon which he shook his Head, and told us there was fine Reading in the Casualties in that Reign.

Our Conductor then pointed to that Monument where there is the Figure of one of our *English* Kings without an Head ; and upon giving us to know, that the Head, which was of beaten Silver, had been stolen away several Years since : Some Whig, I'll warrant you, says Sir ROGER ; you ought to lock up your Kings better; they will carry off the Body too, if you don't take care.

THE glorious Names of *Henry* the Fifth and Queen *Elizabeth* gave the Knight great Opportunities of shining, and of doing Justice to Sir *Richard Baker*, who, as our Knight observed with some Surprize, had a great many Kings in him, whose Monuments he had not seen in the Abby.

For my own part, I could not but be pleased to see the Knight shew such an honest Passion for the Glory of his Country, and such a respectful Gratitude to the Memory of its Princes.

I must not omit, that the Benevolence of my good old Friend, which flows out towards every one he converses with, made him

very kind to our Interpreter, whom he looked upon as an
extraordinary Man ; for which reason he shook him by the
Hand at parting, telling him, that he should be very glad to see
him at his Lodgings in *Norfolk-Buildings*, and talk over these
Matters with him more at leisure.—*Addison.*

Sir Roger de Coverley at the Play.

(*Spectator, No.* 335.)

MY Friend Sir ROGER DE COVERLEY, when we last met
together at the Club, told me, that he had a great mind
to see the new Tragedy with me, assuring me at the same
time, that he had not been at a Play these twenty Years.
The last I saw, said Sir ROGER, was the *Committee*, which
I should not have gone to neither, had not I been told beforehand that it was a good Church-of-*England* Comedy. He then
proceeded to enquire of me who this Distrest Mother was ;
and upon hearing that she was *Hector's* Widow, he told me
that her Husband was a brave Man, and that when he was a
School-boy he had read his Life at the end of the Dictionary.
My Friend asked me, in the next place, if there would not be
some danger in coming home late, in case the *Mohocks* should
be Abroad. I assure you, says he, I thought I had fallen into
their Hands last Night; for I observed two or three lusty black
Men that follow'd me half way up *Fleet-street*, and mended
their pace behind me, in proportion as I put on to get away
from them. You must know, continu'd the Knight with a
Smile, I fancied they had a mind to *hunt* me ; for I remember
an honest Gentleman in my Neighbourhood, who was served
such a trick in King *Charles* the Second's time ; for which
reason he has not ventured himself in Town ever since. I
might have shown them very good Sport, had this been their
Design ; for as I am an old Fox-hunter, I should have turned
and dodg'd, and have play'd them a thousand tricks they had
never seen in their Lives before. Sir ROGER added, that if
these Gentleman had any such Intention, they did not succeed
very well in it : for I threw them out, says he, at the End of
Norfolk street, where I doubled the Corner, and got shelter in
my Lodgings before they could imagine what was become of
me. However, says the Knight, if Captain SENTRY will make
one with us to-morrow night, and if you will both of you call
upon me about four a-Clock, that we may be at the House

before it is full, I will have my own Coach in readiness to attend you, for *John* tells me he has got the Fore-Wheels mended.

The Captain, who did not fail to meet me there at the appointed Hour, bid Sir ROGER fear nothing, for that he had put on the same Sword which he made use of at the Battel of *Steenkirk*. Sir ROGER'S Servants, and among the rest my old Friend the Butler, had, I found, provided themselves with good Oaken Plants, to attend their Master upon this occasion. When he had placed him in his Coach, with my self at his Left-Hand, the Captain before him, and his Butler at the Head of his Footmen in the Rear, we convoy'd him in safety to the Play-house, where, after having marched up the Entry in good order, the Captain and I went in with him, and seated him betwixt us in the Pit. As soon as the House was full, and the Candles lighted, my old Friend stood up and looked about him with that Pleasure, which a Mind seasoned with Humanity naturally feels in its self, at the sight of a Multitude of People who seem pleased with one another, and partake of the same common Entertainment. I could not but fancy to myself, as the old Man stood up in the middle of the Pit, that he made a very proper Center to a Tragick Audience. Upon the entring of *Pyrrhus*, the Knight told me, that he did not believe the King of *France* himself had a better Strut. I was indeed very attentive to my old Friend's Remarks, because I looked upon them as a Piece of natural Criticism, and was well pleased to hear him at the Conclusion of almost every Scene, telling me that he could not imagine how the Play would end. One while he appeared much concerned for *Andromache;* and a little while after as much for *Hermione:* and was extremely puzzled to think what would become of *Pyrrhus*.

When Sir ROGER saw *Andromache's* obstinate Refusal to her Lover's Importunities, he whisper'd me in the Ear, that he was sure she would never have him; to which he added, with a more than ordinary Vehemence, you can't imagine, Sir, what 'tis to have to do with a Widow. Upon *Pyrrhus* his threatning afterwards to leave her, the Knight shook his Head, and muttered to himself, Ay, do if you can. This Part dwelt so much upon my Friend's Imagination, that at the close of the Third Act, as I was thinking of something else, he whispered in my Ear, These Widows, Sir, are the most perverse Creatures in the World. But pray, says he, you that are a Critick, is this Play according to your Dramatick Rules, as you call them? Should your People in Tragedy always talk to be understood?

Why, there is not a single Sentence in this Play that I do not know the Meaning of.

The Fourth Act very luckily begun before I had time to give the old Gentleman an Answer: Well, says the Knight, sitting down with great Satisfaction, I suppose We are now to see *Hector's* Ghost. He then renewed his Attention, and, from time to time, fell a praising the Widow. He made, indeed, a little Mistake as to one of her Pages, whom at his first entering, he took for *Astyanax;* but he quickly set himself right in that Particular, though, at the same time, he owned he should have been very glad to have seen the little Boy, who, says he, must needs be a very fine Child by the Account that is given of him. Upon *Hermione's* going off with a Menace to *Pyrrhus*, the Audience gave a loud Clap ; to which Sir ROGER added, On my Word, a notable young Baggage !

As there was a very remarkable Silence and Stillness in the Audience during the whole Action, it was natural for them to take the Opportunity of these Intervals between the Acts, to express their Opinion of the Players, and of their respective Parts. Sir ROGER hearing a Cluster of them praise *Orestes*, struck in with them, and told them, that he thought his Friend *Pylades* was a very sensible Man ; as they were afterwards applauding *Pyrrhus*, Sir ROGER put in a second time ; And let me tell you, says he, though he speaks but little, I like the old Fellow in Whiskers as well as any of them. Captain SENTRY seeing two or three Waggs who sat near us, lean with an attentive Ear towards Sir ROGER, and fearing lest they should Smoke the Knight, pluck'd him by the Elbow, and whisper'd something in his Ear, that lasted till the Opening of the Fifth Act. The Knight was wonderfully attentive to the Account which *Orestes* gives of *Pyrrhus* his Death, and at the Conclusion of it, told me it was such a bloody Piece of Work, that he was glad it was not done upon the Stage. Seeing afterwards *Orestes* in his raving Fit, he grew more than ordinary serious, and took occasion to moralize (in his way) upon an Evil Conscience, adding, that *Orestes, in his Madness, looked as if he saw something.*

As we were the first that came into the House, so we were the last that went out of it ; being resolved to have a clear Passage for our old Friend, whom we did not care to venture among the justling of the Crowd. Sir ROGER went out fully satisfied with his Entertainment, and we guarded him to his Lodgings in the same manner that we brought him to the Playhouse ; being highly pleased, for my own part, not only with

the Performance of the excellent Piece which had been presented, but with the Satisfaction which it had given to the good
old Man.—*Addison.*

Sir Roger de Coverley's Visit to Spring-Garden.

(*Spectator, No.* 383.)

AS I was sitting in my Chamber, and thinking on a Subject
for my next *Spectator*, I heard two or three irregular
Bounces at my Landlady's Door, and upon the opening of it, a
loud chearful Voice enquiring whether the Philosopher was at
Home.   The Child who went to the Door answered very
Innocently, that he did not Lodge there.   I immediately recollected that it was my good Friend Sir ROGER'S Voice ; and
that I had promised to go with him on the Water to *Spring-
Garden,* in case it proved a good Evening.   The Knight put
me in mind of my Promise from the Bottom of the Stair-Case,
but told me that if I was Speculating he would stay below till I
had done.   Upon my coming down, I found all the Children of
the Family got about my old Friend, and my Landlady herself,
who is a notable prating Gossip, engaged in a Conference with
him ; being mightily pleased with his stroaking her little Boy
upon the Head, and bidding him be a good Child and mind his
Book.
   We were no sooner come to the *Temple* Stairs, but we were
surrounded with a Crowd of Watermen, offering us their respective Services.   Sir ROGER, after having looked about him very
attentively, spied one with a Wooden-Leg, and immediately
gave him Orders to get his Boat ready.   As we were walking
towards it, *You must know,* says Sir ROGER, *I never make
use of any body to row me, that has not either lost a Leg or an
Arm.   I would rather bate him a few Strokes of his Oar, than
not employ an honest Man that has been wounded in the Queen's
Service.   If I was a Lord or a Bishop, and kept a Barge, I
would not put a Fellow in my Livery that had not a
Wooden-Leg.*
   My old Friend, after having seated himself, and trimmed the
Boat with his Coachman (who, being a very sober Man, always
serves for Ballast on these Occasions) we made the best of our
way for *Fox-Hall.*   Sir ROGER obliged the Waterman to give
us the History of his Right Leg, and hearing that he had left it
at *La Hogue,* with many Particulars which passed in that

glorious Action, the Knight in the Triumph of his Heart made several Reflections on the Greatness of the *British* Nation ; as, that one *Englishman* could beat three *Frenchmen;* that we could never be in danger of Popery so long as we took care of our Fleet ; that the *Thames* was the noblest River in *Europe;* that *London Bridge* was a greater piece of Work, than any of the seven Wonders of the World ; with many other honest Prejudices which naturally cleave to the Heart of a true *Englishman.*

After some short Pause, the old Knight turning about his Head twice or thrice, to take a Survey of this great Metropolis, bid me observe how thick the City was set with Churches, and that there was scarce a single Steeple on this side *Temple-Bar.* *A most Heathenish Sight!* says Sir ROGER : *There is no Religion at this End of the Town.* *The fifty new Churches will very much mend the Prospect ; but Church-work is slow, Church-work is slow !*

I do not remember I have any where mentioned, in Sir ROGER'S Character, his Custom of saluting every Body that passes by him with a Good-morrow or a Good-night. This the old Man does out of the overflowings of his Humanity, though at the same time it renders him so popular among all his Country Neighbours, that it is thought to have gone a good way in making him once or twice Knight of the Shire. He cannot forbear this Exercise of Benevolence even in Town, when he meets with any one in his Morning or Evening Walk. It broke from him to several Boats that passed by us upon the Water ; but to the Knight's great Surprize, as he gave the Good-night to two or three young Fellows a little before our Landing, one of them, instead of returning the Civility, asked us what queer old Put we had in the Boat, and whether he was not ashamed to go a Wenching at his Years? with a great deal of the like *Thames*-Ribaldry. Sir ROGER seem'd a little shocked at first, but at length assuming a Face of Magistracy, told us, *That if he were a* Middlesex *Justice, he would make such Vagrants know that Her Majesty's Subjects were no more to be abused by Water than by Land.*

We were now arrived at *Spring-Garden*, which is exquisitely pleasant at this time of Year. When I considered the Fragrancy of the Walks and Bowers, with the Choirs of Birds that sung upon the Trees, and the loose Tribe of People that walked under their Shades, I could not but look upon the Place as a kind of *Mahometan* Paradise. Sir ROGER told me it put him in mind of a little Coppice by his House in the Country, which his Chaplain used to call an Aviary of Nightingales. *You must understand*, says the Knight, *there is nothing in the World that pleases a Man in Love so much as your Nightingale. Ah, Mr.* SPECTATOR ! *the many Moon-light Nights that I have walked by my self, and thought on the Widow by the Musick of the Nightingales !* He here fetched a deep Sigh, and was falling into a Fit of musing, when a Masque, who came behind him, gave him a gentle Tap upon the Shoulder, and asked him if he would drink a Bottle of Mead with her? But the Knight, being startled at so unexpected a Familiarity, and displeased to be interrupted in his Thoughts of the Widow, told her, *She was a wanton Baggage*, and bid her go about her Business.

We concluded our Walk with a Glass of *Burton*-Ale, and a Slice of Hung-Beef. When we had done eating our selves, the Knight called a Waiter to him, and bid him carry the remainder to the Waterman that had but one Leg. I perceived the Fellow stared upon him at the oddness of the Message, and was going to be saucy ; upon which I ratified the Knight's Commands with a Peremptory Look.

As we were going out of the Garden, my old Friend, thinking himself obliged, as a Member of the *Quorum*, to animadvert upon the Morals of the Place, told the Mistress of the House, who sat at the Bar, That he should be a better Customer to her Garden, if there were more Nightingales, and fewer Strumpets. —*Addison.*

Death of Sir Roger de Coverley.

(*Spectator*, No. 517.)

WE last night received a Piece of ill News at our Club, which very sensibly afflicted every one of us. I question not but my Readers themselves will be troubled at the hearing of it. To keep them no longer in Suspence, Sir ROGER DE COVERLY *is dead.* He departed this Life at his House in the Country, after a few Weeks Sickness. Sir ANDREW FREEPORT has a Letter from one of his Correspondents in those Parts, that informs him the old Man caught a Cold at the County-Sessions, as he was very warmly promoting an Address of his own penning, in which he succeeded according to his Wishes. But this Particular comes from a Whig-Justice of Peace, who was always Sir ROGER'S Enemy and Antagonist. I have Letters both from the Chaplain and Captain *Sentry*

which mention nothing of it, but are filled with many
Particulars to the Honour of the good old Man. I have like-
wise a Letter from the Butler, who took so much care of me
last Summer when I was at the Knight's House. As my
Friend the Butler mentions, in the Simplicity of his Heart,
several Circumstances the others have passed over in Silence,
I shall give my Reader a Copy of his Letter, without any
Alteration or Diminution.

Honoured Sir,

'Knowing that you was my old Master's good Friend, I
'could not forbear sending you the melancholy News of his
'Death, which has afflicted the whole Country, as well as his
'poor Servants, who loved him, I may say, better than we did
'our Lives. I am afraid he caught his Death the last County
'Sessions, where he would go to see Justice done to a poor
'Widow Woman, and her Fatherless Children, that had been
'wronged by a neighbouring Gentleman; for you know, Sir,
'my good Master was always the poor Man's Friend. Upon
'his coming home, the first Complaint he made was, that he
'had lost his Roast-Beef Stomach, not being able to touch
'a <u>Sirloin,</u> which was served up according to Custom; and
'you know he used to take great Delight in it. From that
'time forward he grew worse and worse, but still kept a good
'Heart to the last. Indeed we were once in great Hope of his
'Recovery, upon a kind Message that was sent him from the
'Widow Lady whom he had made love to the Forty last Years
'of his Life; but this only proved a Light'ning before Death.
'He has bequeathed to this Lady, as a token of his Love, a
'great Pearl Necklace, and a Couple of Silver Bracelets set with
'Jewels, which belonged to my good old Lady his Mother: He
'has bequeathed the fine white Gelding, that he used to ride
'a hunting upon, to his Chaplain, because he thought he would
'be kind to him, and has left you all his Books. He has, more-
'over, bequeathed to the Chaplain a very pretty Tenement with
'good Lands about it. It being a very cold Day when he made
'his Will, he left for Mourning, to every man in the Parish, a
'great Frize-Coat, and to every Woman a black Riding-hood.
'It was a most moving Sight to see him take leave of his poor
'Servants, commending us all for our Fidelity, whilst we were
'not able to speak a Word for weeping. As we most of us are
'grown Gray-headed in our Dear Master's Service, he has left
'us Pensions and Legacies, which we may live very comfort-
'ably upon, the remaining part of our Days. He has be-

' queath'd a great deal more in Charity, which is not yet come
' to my Knowledge, and it is peremptorily said in the Parish,
' that he has left Mony to build a Steeple to the Church ; for
' he was heard to say some time ago, that if he lived two Years
' longer, *Coverly* Church should have a Steeple to it. The
' Chaplain tells every body that he made a very good End, and
' never speaks of him without Tears. He was buried according
' to his own Directions, among the Family of the *Coverly's,* on
' the Left Hand of his Father Sir *Arthur.* The Coffin was
' carried by Six of his Tenants, and the Pall held up by Six of
' the *Quorum:* The whole Parish follow'd the Corps with heavy
' Hearts, and in their Mourning Suits, the Men in Frize, and
' the Women in Riding-Hoods. Captain SENTRY, my Master's
' Nephew, has taken Possession of the Hall-House, and the
' whole Estate. When my old Master saw him a little before
' his Death, he shook him by the Hand, and wished him Joy
' of the Estate which was falling to him, desiring him only to
' make good Use of it, and to pay the several Legacies, and the
' Gifts of Charity which he told him he had left as Quit-rents
' upon the Estate. The Captain truly seems a courteous Man,
' though he says but little. He makes much of those whom my
' Master loved, and shews great Kindness to the old House-
' dog, that you know my poor Master was so fond of. It would
' have gone to your Heart to have heard the Moans the dumb
' Creature made on the Day of my Master's Death. He has
' ne'er joyed himself since ; no more has any of us. 'Twas the
' melancholiest Day for the poor People that ever happened in
' *Worcestershire.* This being all from,

Honoured Sir,
Your most Sorrowful Servant
Edward Biscuit.

' *P.S.* ' My Master desired, some Weeks before he died, that
' a Book which comes up to you by the Carrier should be given
' to Sir *Andrew Freeport,* in his Name.

This Letter, notwithstanding the poor Butler's Manner of
writing it, gave us such an Idea of our good old Friend, that
upon the reading of it there was not a dry Eye in the Club.
Sir *Andrew* opening the Book, found it to be a Collection of
Acts of Parliament. There was in particular the Act of Uni-
formity, with some Passages in it marked by Sir *Roger's* own
Hand. Sir *Andrew* found that they related to two or three
Points, which he had disputed with Sir *Roger* the last time he

appeared at the Club. Sir *Andrew*, who would have been merry at such an Incident on another Occasion, at the sight of the old Man's Hand-writing burst into Tears, and put the Book into his Pocket. Captain *Sentry* informs me, that the Knight has left Rings and Mourning for every one in the Club.—*Addison.*

Alexander Selkirk.

(*The Englishman*, No. 26.)

UNDER the Title of this Paper, I do not think it foreign to my Design, to speak of a Man born in Her Majesty's Dominions, and relate an Adventure in his Life so uncommon, that it's doubtful whether the like has happen'd to any other of human Race. The Person I speak of, is *Alexander Selkirk*, whose Name is familiar to Men of Curiosity, from the Fame of his having lived four Years and four Months alone in the Island of *Juan Fernandez*. I had the pleasure frequently to converse with the Man soon after his Arrival in *England*, in the Year 1711. It was matter of great Curiosity to hear him, as he is a Man of good Sense, give an Account of the different Revolutions in his own Mind in that long Solitude. When we consider how painful Absence from Company, for the space of but one Evening, is to the generality of Mankind, we may have a Sense how painful this necessary and constant Solitude was to a Man bred a Sailor, and ever accustomed to enjoy, and suffer, eat, drink, and sleep, and perform all Offices of Life in Fellowship and Company. He was put ashore from a leaky Vessel, with the Captain of which he had had an irreconcilable Difference; and he chose rather to take his Fate in this Place, than in a crazy Vessel, under a disagreeable Commander. His Portion were a Sea-Chest, his wearing Clothes and Bedding, a Fire-lock, a Pound of Gun-powder, a large quantity of Bullets, a Flint and Steel, a few Pounds of Tobacco, an Hatchet, a Knife, a Kettle, a Bible, and other Books of Devotion; together with Pieces that concern'd Navigation, and his Mathematical Instruments. Resentment against his Officer, who had ill used him, made him look forward on this Change of Life, as the more eligible one, till the instant in which he saw the Vessel put off; at which moment, his Heart yearned within him, and melted at the parting with his Comrades and all human Society at once. He had in Provisions for the Sustenance of Life, but the quantity of two Meals, the Island abounding only with wild Goats, Cats and Rats. He judged it most probable, that he should find more immediate and easy Relief, by finding Shell-fish on the Shore, than seeking Game with his Gun. He accordingly found great quantities of Turtles, whose Flesh is extreamly delicious, and of which he frequently eat very plentifully on his first Arrival, till it grew disagreeable to his Stomach, except in Jellies. The Necessities of Hunger and Thirst, were his greatest Diversions from the Reflection on his lonely Condition. When those Appetites were satisfied, the Desire of Society was as strong a Call upon him, and he appeared to himself least necessitous when he wanted every thing ; for the Supports of his Body were easily attained, but the eager Longings for seeing again the Face of Man, during the Interval of craving bodily Appetites, were hardly supportable. He grew dejected, languid, and melancholy, scarce able to restrain from doing himself Violence, till by degrees, by the Force of Reason, and frequent reading of the Scriptures, and turning his Thoughts upon the Study of Navigation, after the space of eighteen Months, he grew thoroughly reconciled to his Condition. When he had made this Conquest, the Vigour of his Health, Disengagement from the World, a constant, chearful, serene Sky, and a temperate Air, made his Life one continual Feast, and his Being much more joyful than it had before been irksome. He now taking Delight in every thing, made the Hutt, in which he lay, by Ornaments which he cut down from a spacious Wood, on the side of which it was situated, the most delicious Bower, fann'd with continual Breezes and gentle Aspirations of Wind, that made his Repose after the Chase equal to the most sensual Pleasures.

I FORGET to observe, that during the Time of his Dissatisfaction, Monsters of the Deep, which frequently lay on the Shore, added to the Terrors of his Solitude, the dreadful Howlings and Voices seemed too terrible to be made for human Ears : But upon the Recovery of his Temper, he could with Pleasure not only hear their Voices, but approach the Monsters themselves with great Intrepidity. He speaks of Sea-Lions, whose Jaws and Tails were capable of seizing or breaking the Limbs of a Man, if he approach'd them : But at that time his Spirits and Life were so high, that he could act so regularly and unconcerned, that merely from being unruffled in himself, he killed them with the greatest Ease imaginable : For observing, that tho their Jaws and Tails were so terrible, yet the Animals being mighty slow in working themselves round, he had nothing to do but place himself exactly opposite to their Middle, and as close to them as possible, and he dispatched them with his Hatchet at Will.

THE Precautions which he took against Want, in case of Sickness, was to lame Kids when very young, so as that they might recover their Health, but never be capable of Speed. These he had in great Numbers about his Hutt ; and when he was himself in full Vigour, he could take at full Speed the swiftest Goat running up a Promontory, and never failed of catching them, but on a Descent.

HIS Habitation was extremely pester'd with Rats, which gnaw'd his Clothes and Feet when sleeping. To defend him against them, he fed and tamed Numbers of young Kitlings, who lay about his Bed, and preserved him from the Enemy. When his Clothes were quite worn out, he dried and tacked together the Skins of Goats, with which he clothed himself, and was enured to pass through Woods, Bushes, and Brambles with as much Carelessness and Precipitance as any other Animal. It happened once to him, that running on the Summit of a Hill, he made a Stretch to seize a Goat ; with which under him, he fell down a Precipice, and lay sensless for the space of three Days, the Length of which time he measured by the Moon's Growth since his last Observation. This manner of Life grew so exquisitely pleasant, that he never had a moment heavy upon his hands ; his Nights were untroubled, and his Days joyous, from the Practice of Temperance and Exercise. It was his manner to use stated Hours and Places for Exercises of Devotion, which he performed aloud, in order to keep up the Faculties of Speech, and to utter himself with greater Energy.

WHEN I first saw him, I thought, if I had not been let into his Character and Story, I could have discerned that he had been much separated from Company, from his Aspect and Gesture ; there was a strong but chearful Seriousness in his Look, and a certain disregard to the ordinary things about him, as if he had been sunk in Thought. When the Ship, which brought him off the Island, came in, he received them with the greatest Indifference, with relation to the Prospect of going off with them, but with great satisfaction in an Opportunity to refresh and help them ; the Man frequently bewail'd his return to the World, which could not, he said, with all its Enjoyments, restore him to the Tranquillity of his Solitude. Tho I had frequently conversed with him, after a few Months Absence, he met me in the Street ; and though he spoke to me, I could not recollect that I had seen him : familiar Converse in this Town had taken off the Loneliness of his Aspect, and quite altered the Air of his Face.

This plain Man's Story is a memorable Example, that he is happiest, who confines his Wants to natural Necessities ; and he that goes further in his Desires, increases his Wants in proportion to his Acquisitions ; or to use his own Expression, *I am now worth eight hundred Pounds, but shall never be so happy, as when I was not worth a Farthing.*

A Domestic Picture.

(*Tatler, No.* 95.)

THERE are several Persons who have many Pleasures and Entertainments in their Possession which they do not enjoy. It is therefore a kind and good Office to acquaint them with their own Happiness, and turn their Attention to such Instances of their good Fortune which they are apt to overlook. Persons in the married State often want such a Monitor, and pine away their Days, by looking upon the same Condition in Anguish and Murmur, which carries with it in the Opinion of others a Complication of all the Pleasures of Life, and a Retreat from its Inquietudes.

I am led into this Thought by a Visit I made an old Friend, who was formerly my Schoolfellow. He came to Town last Week with his Family for the Winter, and yesterday Morning sent me Word his Wife expected me to Dinner. I am as it were at Home at that House, and every Member of it knows me for their Well-wisher. I cannot indeed express the Pleasure it is, to be met by the Children with so much Joy as I am when I go thither : The Boys and Girls strive who shall come first, when they think it is I that am knocking at the Door ; and that Child which loses the Race to me, runs back again to tell the Father it is Mr. *Bickerstaff.* This Day I was led in by a pretty Girl, that we all thought must have forgot me ; for the Family has been out of Town these Two Years. Her knowing me again was a mighty Subject with us, and took up our Discourse at the first Entrance. After which they began to rally me upon a Thousand little Stories they heard in the Country, about my Marriage to one of my Neighbour's Daughters : Upon which the Gentleman my Friend said, Nay, if Mr. *Bickerstaff* marries a Child of any of his old Companions, I hope mine shall have the Preference; there's Mrs. *Mary* is now Sixteen, and would make him as fine a Widow as the best of them : But I know him too well; he is so enamoured with the very Memory of those who flourished in our Youth, that he will not so much as look upon the modern Beauties. I remember, old Gentleman, how often you went Home in a Day to refresh your Countenance and Dress, when *Teraminta* reigned in your Heart. As we came up in the Coach, I repeated to my Wife some of your Verses on her. With such Reflections on little Passages which happened long ago, we passed our Time during a chearful and elegant Meal. After Dinner, his Lady left the Room, as did also the Children. As soon as we were alone, he took me by the Hand ; Well, my good Friend, says he, I am heartily glad to see thee ; I was afraid you would never have seen all the Company that dined with you to-Day again. Do not you think the good Woman of the House a little altered, since you followed her from the Playhouse, to find out who she was, for me ? I perceived a Tear fall down his Cheek as he spoke, which moved me not a little. But to turn the Discourse, said I, She is not indeed quite that Creature she was when she returned me the Letter I carried from you ; and told me, She hoped, as I was a Gentleman, I would be employ'd no more to trouble her who had never offended me, but would be so much the Gentleman's Friend as to disswade him from a Pursuit which he could never succeed in. You may remember, I thought her in earnest, and you were forced to employ your Cousin *Will*, who made his Sister get acquainted with her for you. You cannot expect her to be for ever Fifteen. Fifteen? replied my good Friend : Ah ! You little understand, you that have lived a Bachelor, how great, how exquisite, a Pleasure there is in being really beloved ! It is impossible that the most beauteous Face in Nature should raise in me such pleasing Ideas, as when I look upon that excellent Woman. That Fading in her Countenance is chiefly caused by her watching me in my Fever. This was followed by a Fit of Sickness, which had like to have carried her off last Winter. I tell you sincerely, I have so many Obligations to her, that I cannot with any sort of Moderation think of her present State of Health. But as to what you say of Fifteen, she gives me every Day Pleasures beyond what I ever knew in the Possession of her Beauty, when I was in the Vigour of Youth. Every Moment of her Life brings me fresh Instances of her Complacency to my Inclinations, and her Prudence in Regard to my Fortune. Her Face is to me much more beautiful than when I first saw it ; there is no Decay in any Feature which I cannot trace from the very Instant it was occasioned, by some anxious Concern for my Welfare and Interests. Thus at the same Time, methinks, the Love I conceived towards her for what she was, is heightened by my Gratitude for what she is. The Love of a Wife is as much above the idle Passion commonly called by that Name, as the loud Laughter of Buffoons is inferior to the elegant Mirth of Gentlemen. Oh ! she is an inestimable Jewel. In her Examination of her Household Affairs, she shows a certain Fearfulness to find a Fault, which makes her Servants obey her like Children ; and the meanest we have, has an ingenuous Shame for an Offence, not always to be seen in Children in other Families. I speak freely to you, my old Friend, ever since her Sickness, Things that gave me the quickest Joy before, turn now to a certain Anxiety. As the Children play in the next Room, I know the poor Things by their Steps, and am considering what they must do, should they lose their Mother in their tender Years. The Pleasure I used to take in telling my Boy Stories of Battles, and asking my Girl Questions about the Disposal of her Baby, and the Gossiping of it, is turned into inward Reflection and Melancholy.

He would have gone on in this tender Way, when the good Lady entered, and, with an inexpressible Sweetness in her Countenance told us, she had been searching her Closet for something very good, to treat such an old Friend as I was. Her Husband's Eyes sparkled with Pleasure at the Chearfulness of her Countenance ; and I saw all his Fears vanish in an Instant. The Lady observing something in our Looks which showed we had been more serious than ordinary, and seeing her Husband receive her with great Concern under a forced Chearfulness, immediately guessed at what we had been talking of ; and, applying her self to me, said, with a Smile, Mr. *Bickerstaff*, do not believe a Word of what he tells you, I shall still live to have you for my Second, as I have often promised you, unless he takes more Care of himself than he has done since his coming to Town. You must know, he tells me, That he finds *London* is a much more healthy Place than the Country ; for he sees several of his old Acquaintance and School-fellows are here, young Fellows with full-bottomed Periwigs. I could scarce keep him this Morning from going out open-breasted. My Friend, who is always extremely delighted with her agreeable Humour, made her sit down with us. She did it with that Easiness which is peculiar to Women of Sense ; and to keep up the good Humour she had brought in with her, turned her

Raillery upon me. Mr. *Bickerstaff*, you remember you followed me one Night from the Play-house ; supposing you should carry me thither tomorrow Night, and lead me into the Front-Box. This put us into a long Field of Discourse about the Beauties, who were Mothers to the present, and shined in the Boxes Twenty Years ago. I told her, I was glad she had transferred so many of her Charms, and I did not question but her eldest Daughter was within half a Year of being a Toast.

We were pleasing ourselves with this fantastical Preferment of the young Lady, when on a sudden we were alarm'd with the Noise of a Drum, and immediately entered my little Godson to give me a Point of War. His Mother, between Laughing and Chiding, would have put him out of the Room ; but I would not part with him so. I found, upon Conversation with him, tho' he was a little noisy in his Mirth, that the Child had excellent Parts, and was a great Master of all the Learning on t'other Side Eight Years old. I perceived him a very great Historian in *Æsop's* Fables ; but he frankly declared to me his Mind, That he did not delight in that Learning, because he did not believe they were true ; for which Reason, I found he had very much turned his Studies for about a Twelvemonth past, into the Lives and Adventures of Don *Bellianis* of *Greece*, *Guy* of *Warwick*, the *Seven Champions*, and other Historians of that Age. I could not but observe the Satisfaction the Father took in the Forwardness of his Son ; and that these Diversions might turn to some Profit, I found the Boy had made Remarks, which might be of Service to him during the Course of his whole Life. He would tell you the Mismanagements of *John Hickathrift*, find Fault with the passionate Temper in *Bevis* of *Southampton*, and love St. *George* for being the Champion of *England* ; and by this Means, had his Thoughts insensibly moulded into the Notions of Discretion, Virtue, and Honour. I was extolling his Accomplishments, when the Mother told me, That the little Girl who led me in this Morning, was in her Way a better Scholar than he. Betty (says she) deals chiefly in Fairies and Sprights ; and sometimes in a Winter Night, will terrify the Maids with her Accounts, till they are afraid to go up to Bed.

I sat with them till it was very late, sometimes in merry, sometimes in serious Discourse, with this particular Pleasure, which gives the only true Relish to all Conversation, a Sense that every one of us liked each other. I went Home, considering the different Conditions of a married Life and that of a Bachelor ; and I must confess, it struck me with a secret

Concern, to reflect, that whenever I go off, I shall leave no Traces behind me. In this pensive Mood I returned to my Family ; that is to say, to my Maid, my Dog and my Cat, who only can be the better or worse for what happens to me.— *Steele.*

Printed by WALTER SCOTT, *Felling, Newcastle-upon-Tyne.*

THE SCOTT LIBRARY.

Cloth, Uncut Edges, Gilt Top.   Price 1s. 6d. per Volume.

VOLUMES ALREADY ISSUED—

1 MALORY'S ROMANCE OF KING ARTHUR AND THE
Quest of the Holy Grail.   Edited by Ernest Rhys.

2 THOREAU'S WALDEN.   WITH INTRODUCTORY NOTE
by Will H. Dircks.

3 THOREAU'S "WEEK."   WITH PREFATORY NOTE BY
Will H. Dircks.

4 THOREAU'S ESSAYS.   EDITED, WITH AN INTRO-
duction, by Will H. Dircks.

5 CONFESSIONS OF AN ENGLISH OPIUM-EATER, ETC.
By Thomas De Quincey.   With Introductory Note by William Sharp.

6 LANDOR'S IMAGINARY CONVERSATIONS.   SELECTED,
with Introduction, by Havelock Ellis.

7 PLUTARCH'S LIVES (LANGHORNE).   WITH INTRO-
ductory Note by B. J. Snell, M.A.

8 BROWNE'S RELIGIO MEDICI, ETC.   WITH INTRO-
duction by J. Addington Symonds.

9 SHELLEY'S ESSAYS AND LETTERS.   EDITED, WITH
Introductory Note, by Ernest Rhys.

10 SWIFT'S PROSE WRITINGS.   CHOSEN AND ARRANGED,
with Introduction, by Walter Lewin.

11 MY STUDY WINDOWS.   BY JAMES RUSSELL LOWELL.
With Introduction by R. Garnett, LL.D.

12 LOWELL'S ESSAYS ON THE ENGLISH POETS.   WITH
a new Introduction by Mr. Lowell.

13 THE BIGLOW PAPERS.   BY JAMES RUSSELL LOWELL.
With a Prefatory Note by Ernest Rhys.

London: WALTER SCOTT, LIMITED, 24 Warwick Lane.

THE SCOTT LIBRARY—continued.

14 GREAT ENGLISH PAINTERS. SELECTED FROM Cunningham's *Lives*. Edited by William Sharp.

15 BYRON'S LETTERS AND JOURNALS. SELECTED, with Introduction, by Mathilde Blind.

16 LEIGH HUNT'S ESSAYS. WITH INTRODUCTION AND Notes by Arthur Symons.

17 LONGFELLOW'S "HYPERION," "KAVANAH," AND "The Trouveres." With Introduction by W. Tirebuck.

18 GREAT MUSICAL COMPOSERS. BY G. F. FERRIS. Edited, with Introduction, by Mrs. William Sharp.

19 THE MEDITATIONS OF MARCUS AURELIUS. EDITED by Alice Zimmern.

20 THE TEACHING OF EPICTETUS. TRANSLATED FROM the Greek, with Introduction and Notes, by T. W. Rolleston.

21 SELECTIONS FROM SENECA. WITH INTRODUCTION by Walter Clode.

22 SPECIMEN DAYS IN AMERICA. BY WALT WHITMAN. Revised by the Author, with fresh Preface.

23 DEMOCRATIC VISTAS, AND OTHER PAPERS. BY Walt Whitman. (Published by arrangement with the Author.)

24 WHITE'S NATURAL HISTORY OF SELBORNE. WITH a Preface by Richard Jefferies.

25 DEFOE'S CAPTAIN SINGLETON. EDITED, WITH Introduction, by H. Halliday Sparling.

26 MAZZINI'S ESSAYS: LITERARY, POLITICAL, AND Religious. With Introduction by William Clarke.

7 PROSE WRITINGS OF HEINE. WITH INTRODUCTION by Havelock Ellis.

28 REYNOLDS'S DISCOURSES. WITH INTRODUCTION by Helen Zimmern.

29 PAPERS OF STEELE AND ADDISON. EDITED BY Walter Lewin.

30 BURNS'S LETTERS. SELECTED AND ARRANGED, with Introduction, by J. Logie Robertson, M.A.

London: WALTER SCOTT, LIMITED, 24 Warwick Lane.

THE SCOTT LIBRARY—continued.

31 VOLSUNGA SAGA. WILLIAM MORRIS. WITH INTRO-
duction by H. H. Sparling.

32 SARTOR RESARTUS. BY THOMAS CARLYLE. WITH
Introduction by Ernest Rhys.

33 SELECT WRITINGS OF EMERSON. WITH INTRO-
duction by Percival Chubb.

34 AUTOBIOGRAPHY OF LORD HERBERT. EDITED,
with an Introduction, by Will H. Dircks.

35 ENGLISH PROSE, FROM MAUNDEVILLE TO
Thackeray. Chosen and Edited by Arthur Galton.

36 THE PILLARS OF SOCIETY, AND OTHER PLAYS. BY
Henrik Ibsen. Edited, with an Introduction, by Havelock Ellis.

37 IRISH FAIRY AND FOLK TALES. EDITED AND
Selected by W. B. Yeats.

38 ESSAYS OF DR. JOHNSON, WITH BIOGRAPHICAL
Introduction and Notes by Stuart J. Reid.

39 ESSAYS OF WILLIAM HAZLITT. SELECTED AND
Edited, with Introduction and Notes, by Frank Carr.

40 LANDOR'S PENTAMERON, AND OTHER IMAGINARY
Conversations. Edited, with a Preface, by H. Ellis.

41 POE'S TALES AND ESSAYS. EDITED, WITH INTRO-
duction, by Ernest Rhys.

42 VICAR OF WAKEFIELD. BY OLIVER GOLDSMITH.
Edited, with Preface, by Ernest Rhys.

43 POLITICAL ORATIONS, FROM WENTWORTH TO
Macaulay. Edited, with Introduction, by William Clarke.

44 THE AUTOCRAT OF THE BREAKFAST-TABLE. BY
Oliver Wendell Holmes.

45 THE POET AT THE BREAKFAST-TABLE. BY OLIVER
Wendell Holmes.

46 THE PROFESSOR AT THE BREAKFAST-TABLE. BY
Oliver Wendell Holmes.

47 LORD CHESTERFIELD'S LETTERS TO HIS SON.
Selected, with Introduction, by Charles Sayle.

THE SCOTT LIBRARY—continued.

48 STORIES FROM CARLETON. SELECTED, WITH INTROduction, by W. Yeats.

49 JANE EYRE. BY CHARLOTTE BRONTË. EDITED BY Clement K. Shorter.

50 ELIZABETHAN ENGLAND. EDITED BY LOTHROP Withington, with a Preface by Dr. Furnivall.

51 THE PROSE WRITINGS OF THOMAS DAVIS. EDITED by T. W. Rolleston.

52 SPENCE'S ANECDOTES. A SELECTION. EDITED, with an Introduction and Notes, by John Underhill.

53 MORE'S UTOPIA, AND LIFE OF EDWARD V. EDITED, with an Introduction, by Maurice Adams.

54 SADI'S GULISTAN, OR FLOWER GARDEN. TRANSlated, with an Essay, by James Ross.

55 ENGLISH FAIRY AND FOLK TALES. EDITED BY E. Sidney Hartland.

56 NORTHERN STUDIES. BY EDMUND GOSSE. WITH a Note by Ernest Rhys.

57 EARLY REVIEWS OF GREAT WRITERS. EDITED BY E. Stevenson.

58 ARISTOTLE'S ETHICS. WITH GEORGE HENRY Lewes's Essay on Aristotle prefixed.

59 LANDOR'S PERICLES AND ASPASIA. EDITED, WITH an Introduction, by Havelock Ellis.

60 ANNALS OF TACITUS. THOMAS GORDON'S TRANSlation. Edited, with an Introduction, by Arthur Galton.

61 ESSAYS OF ELIA. BY CHARLES LAMB. EDITED, with an Introduction, by Ernest Rhys.

62 BALZAC'S SHORTER STORIES. TRANSLATED BY William Wilson and the Count Stenbock.

63 COMEDIES OF DE MUSSET. EDITED, WITH AN Introductory Note, by S. L. Gwynn.

64 CORAL REEFS. BY CHARLES DARWIN. EDITED, with an Introduction, by Dr. J. W. Williams.

London: WALTER SCOTT, LIMITED, 24 Warwick Lane.

THE SCOTT LIBRARY—continued.

65 SHERIDAN'S PLAYS. EDITED, WITH AN INTRO-
duction, by Rudolf Dircks.

66 OUR VILLAGE. BY MISS MITFORD. EDITED, WITH
an Introduction, by Ernest Rhys.

67 MASTER HUMPHREY'S CLOCK, AND OTHER STORIES.
By Charles Dickens. With Introduction by Frank T. Marzials.

68 TALES FROM WONDERLAND. BY RUDOLPH
Baumbach. Translated by Helen B. Dole.

69 ESSAYS AND PAPERS BY DOUGLAS JERROLD. EDITED
by Walter Jerrold.

70 VINDICATION OF THE RIGHTS OF WOMAN. BY
Mary Wollstonecraft. Introduction by Mrs. E. Robins Pennell.

71 "THE ATHENIAN ORACLE." A SELECTION. EDITED
by John Underhill, with Prefatory Note by Walter Besant.

72 ESSAYS OF SAINTE-BEUVE. TRANSLATED AND
Edited, with an Introduction, by Elizabeth Lee.

73 SELECTIONS FROM PLATO. FROM THE TRANS-
lation of Sydenham and Taylor. Edited by T. W. Rolleston.

74 HEINE'S ITALIAN TRAVEL SKETCHES, ETC. TRANS-
lated by Elizabeth A. Sharp. With an Introduction from the French of
Theophile Gautier.

75 SCHILLER'S MAID OF ORLEANS. TRANSLATED,
with an Introduction, by Major-General Patrick Maxwell.

76 SELECTIONS FROM SYDNEY SMITH. EDITED, WITH
an Introduction, by Ernest Rhys.

THE SCOTT LIBRARY may be had in the following Bindings:—
Cloth, uncut edges, gilt top, 1s. 6d. ; Half-Morocco, gilt top, antique ;
Red Roan, gilt edges, etc.

London: WALTER SCOTT, LIMITED, 24 Warwick Lane.

GREAT WRITERS.

A NEW SERIES OF CRITICAL BIOGRAPHIES.

Edited by Prof. E. S. ROBERTSON and FRANK T. MARZIALS.

A Complete Bibliography to each Volume, by J. P. ANDERSON, British Museum, London.

Cloth, Uncut Edges, Gilt Top.   Price 1/6.

VOLUMES ALREADY ISSUED—

LIFE OF LONGFELLOW.   By PROF. ERIC S. ROBERTSON.
"A most readable little work."—*Liverpool Mercury.*

LIFE OF COLERIDGE.   By HALL CAINE.
"Brief and vigorous, written throughout with spirit and great literary skill."—*Scotsman.*

LIFE OF DICKENS.   By FRANK T. MARZIALS.
"Notwithstanding the mass of matter that has been printed relating to Dickens and his works . . . we should, until we came across this volume, have been at a loss to recommend any popular life of England's most popular novelist as being really satisfactory.   The difficulty is removed by Mr. Marzials's little book."—*Athenæum.*

LIFE OF DANTE GABRIEL ROSSETTI.   By J. KNIGHT.
"Mr. Knight's picture of the great poet and painter is the fullest and best yet presented to the public."—*The Graphic.*

LIFE OF SAMUEL JOHNSON.   By COLONEL F. GRANT.
"Colonel Grant has performed his task with diligence, sound judgment, good taste, and accuracy."—*Illustrated London News.*

LIFE OF DARWIN.   By G. T. BETTANY.
"Mr. G. T. Bettany's *Life of Darwin* is a sound and conscientious work."—*Saturday Review.*

LIFE OF CHARLOTTE BRONTË.   By A. BIRRELL.
"Those who know much of Charlotte Brontë will learn more, and those who know nothing about her will find all that is best worth learning in Mr. Birrell's pleasant book."—*St. James' Gazette.*

LIFE OF THOMAS CARLYLE.   By R. GARNETT, LL.D.
"This is an admirable book.   Nothing could be more felicitous and fairer than the way in which he takes us through Carlyle's life and works."—*Pall Mall Gazette.*

London : WALTER SCOTT, LIMITED, 24 Warwick Lane.

SELECTED THREE-VOL. SETS

IN NEW BROCADE BINDING.

6s. per Set, in Shell Case to match.

O. W. HOLMES SERIES—

Autocrat of the Breakfast-Table.

The Professor at the Breakfast-Table.

The Poet at the Breakfast Table.

LANDOR SERIES—

Landor's Imaginary Conversations.

Pentameron.

Pericles and Aspasia.

THREE ENGLISH ESSAYISTS—

Essays of Elia.

Essays of Leigh Hunt.

Essays of William Hazlitt.

THREE CLASSICAL MORALISTS—

Meditations of Marcus Aurelius.
Teaching of Epictetus.
Morals of Seneca.

WALDEN SERIES—

Thoreau's Walden.
Thoreau's Week.
Thoreau's Essays.

FAMOUS LETTERS—

Letters of Burns.
Letters of Byron.
Letters of Shelley.

LOWELL SERIES—

My Study Windows.
The English Poets.
The Biglow Papers.

IBSEN'S FAMOUS PROSE DRAMAS.

Edited by WILLIAM ARCHER.

Complete in Five Vols. Crown 8vo, Cloth, Price 3/6 each.
Set of Five Vols., in Case, 17/6; in Half Morocco, in Case, 32/6.

"We seem at last to be shown men and women as they are; and at first it is more than we can endure. . . All Ibsen's characters speak and act as if they were hypnotised, and under their creator's imperious demand to reveal themselves. There never was such a mirror held up to nature before: it is too terrible. . . . Yet we must return to Ibsen, with his remorseless surgery, his remorseless electric-light, until we, too, have grown strong and learned to face the naked—if necessary, the flayed and bleeding—reality."—SPEAKER (London).

VOL. I. "A DOLL'S HOUSE," "THE LEAGUE OF YOUTH," and "THE PILLARS OF SOCIETY." With Portrait of the Author, and Biographical Introduction by WILLIAMARCHER.

VOL. II. "GHOSTS," "AN ENEMY OF THE PEOPLE," and "THE WILD DUCK." With an Introductory Note.

VOL. III. "LADY INGER OF ÖSTRÅT," "THE VIKINGS AT HELGELAND," "THE PRETENDERS." With an Introductory Note and Portrait of Ibsen.

VOL. IV. "EMPEROR AND GALILEAN." With an Introductory Note by WILLIAM ARCHER.

VOL. V. "ROSMERSHOLM," "THE LADY FROM THE SEA," "HEDDA GABLER." Translated by WILLIAM ARCHER. With an Introductory Note.

The sequence of the plays *in each volume* is chronological; the complete set of volumes comprising the dramas thus presents them in chronological order.

"The art of prose translation does not perhaps enjoy a very high literary status in England, but we have no hesitation in numbering the present version of Ibsen, so far as it has gone (Vols. I. and II.), among the very best achievements, in that kind, of our generation."—*Academy.*

"We have seldom, if ever, met with a translation so absolutely idiomatic."—*Glasgow Herald.*

LONDON: WALTER SCOTT, LIMITED, 24 WARWICK LANE.

THE CANTERBURY POETS.

THE CANTERBURY POETS—continued.

DAYS OF THE YEAR ....With Introduction by William Sharp.
POPE ....Edited by John Hogben.
HEINE ....Edited by Mrs. Kroeker.
BEAUMONT AND FLETCHER ....Edited by John S. Fletcher.
BOWLES, LAMB, &c. ....Edited by William Tirebuck.
EARLY ENGLISH POETRY.........Edited by H. Macaulay Fitzgibbon.
SEA MUSIC ....Edited by Mrs Sharp.
HERRICK..Edited by Ernest Rhys.
BALLADES AND RONDEAUS...............Edited by J. Gleeson White.
IRISH MINSTRELSY ....Edited by H. Halliday Sparling.
MILTON'S PARADISE LOST ......Edited by J. Bradshaw, M.A., LL.D.
JACOBITE BALLADS ....Edited by G. S. Macquoid.
AUSTRALIAN BALLADS ....Edited by D. B. W. Sladen, B.A.
MOORE ....Edited by John Dorrian.
BORDER BALLADS ....Edited by Graham R. Tomson.
SONG-TIDE ....By Philip Bourke Marston.
ODES OF HORACE.............Translations by Sir Stephen de Vere, Bt.
OSSIAN ....Edited by George Eyre-Todd.
ELFIN MUSIC ....Edited by Arthur Edward Waite.
SOUTHEY.............................Edited by Sidney R. Thompson.
CHAUCER ....Edited by Frederick Noël Paton.
POEMS OF WILD LIFE.........Edited by Charles G. D. Roberts, M.A.
PARADISE REGAINED............Edited by J. Bradshaw, M.A., LL.D.
CRABBE ....Edited by E. Lamplough.
DORA GREENWELL ....Edited by William Dorling.
FAUST ....Edited by Elizabeth Craigmyle.
AMERICAN SONNETS ....Edited by William Sharp.
LANDOR'S POEMS ....Edited by Ernest Radford.
GREEK ANTHOLOGY ....Edited by Graham R. Tomson.
HUNT AND HOOD ....Edited by J. Harwood Panting.
HUMOROUS POEMS ....Edited by Ralph H. Caine.
LYTTON'S PLAYS ....Edited by R. Farquharson Sharp.
GREAT ODES........................Edited by William Sharp.
MEREDITH'S POEMS...................Edited by M. Betham-Edwards.
PAINTER-POETS ....Edited by Kineton Parkes.
WOMEN POETS ....Edited by Mrs. Sharp.
LOVE LYRICS ....Edited by Percy Hulburd.
AMERICAN HUMOROUS VERSE ....Edited by James Barr.
MINOR SCOTCH LYRICS ....Edited by Sir George Douglas.
CAVALIER LYRISTS.....................Edited by Will H. Dircks.
GERMAN BALLADS.................Edited by Elizabeth Craigmyle.
SONGS OF BERANGER ....Translated by William Toynbee.

London: WALTER SCOTT, LIMITED, 24 Warwick Lane.